DARK PROMISE

APOCALYPTIC URBAN FANTASY

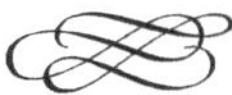

ANN GIMPEL

Edited by

K. R. SHIELDS

Illustrated by

FIONA JAYDE

CONTENTS

DARK PROMISE

SOUL STORM, BOOK THREE

Apocalyptic Urban Fantasy
By
Ann Gimpel

Some choices tear your heart out, but they can't ever be undone

COPYRIGHT PAGE

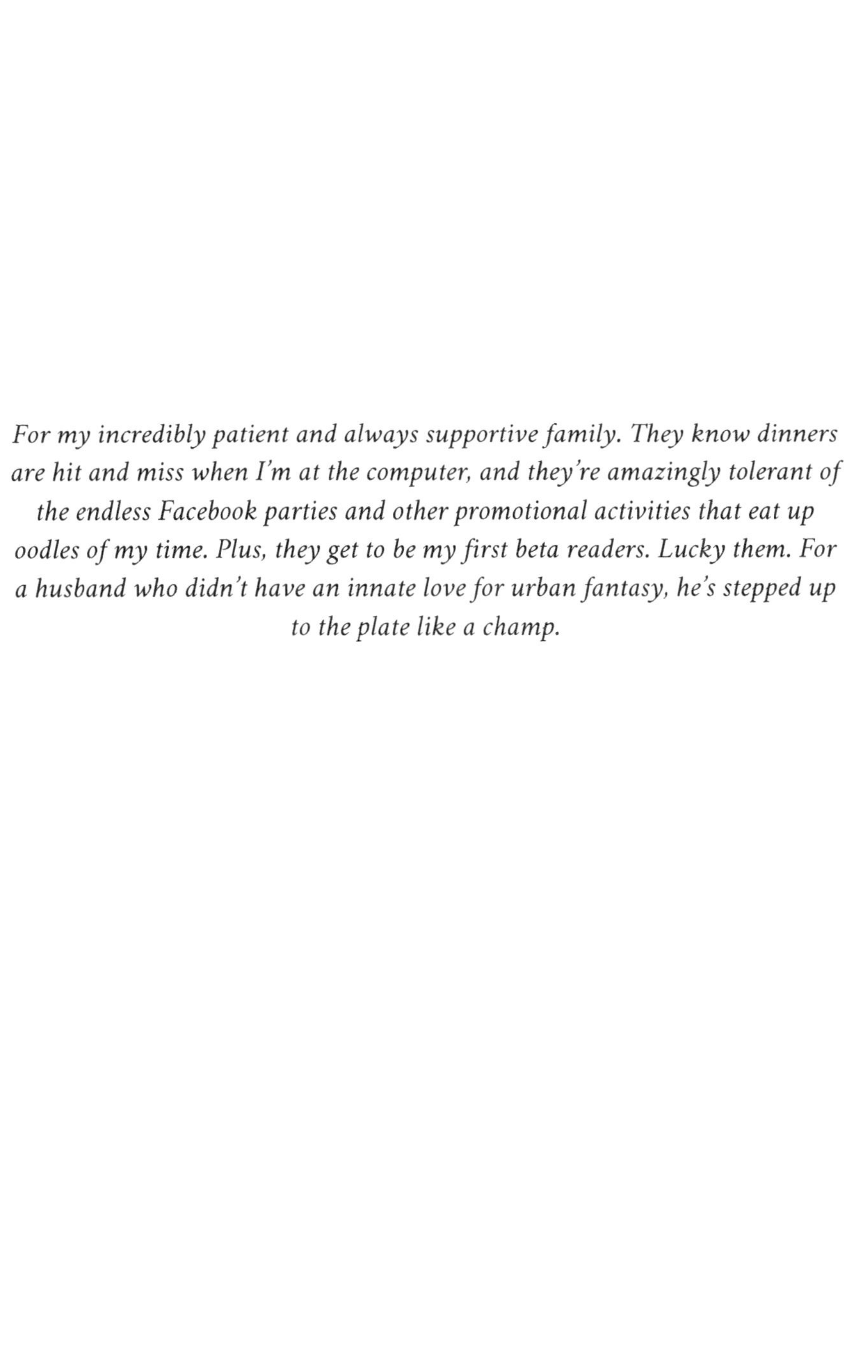

For my incredibly patient and always supportive family. They know dinners are hit and miss when I'm at the computer, and they're amazingly tolerant of the endless Facebook parties and other promotional activities that eat up oodles of my time. Plus, they get to be my first beta readers. Lucky them. For a husband who didn't have an innate love for urban fantasy, he's stepped up to the plate like a champ.

ACKNOWLEDGMENTS

I'd like to send warm hugs and thanks to the wonderful women who beta read this book for me. Karen Mikhael, Bridgette Thoroughman, Cherri-Anne Boitson, Heather Stanley, Shelly Small, and Holli Greer. Warm thoughts to Fiona Jayde too. She's the best cover artist ever. And then there are my author friends who helped with editing. It truly takes a village and I'm so grateful for every single person who's jumped in to support my writing career.

BOOK DESCRIPTION: DARK PROMISE

ara and Trevor flee Seattle in the wake of rising chaos. Demons converge on what's left of civilization, urging it to implode even faster.

Constantly hungry, besieged by dark forces, Lara and Trevor need every resource they've developed as a couple to keep from ripping each other apart. Neither of them trust Lara's half-baked magic, but it's all that stands between survival and certain death for them and their unborn child.

The remote location that was supposed to solve all their problems actually made them worse. Rash choices throw Trevor into a confrontation with his deepest fears, but he doesn't back down. Lara's life hangs in the balance, and he'll do anything to get her back. Anything.

PROLOGUE

Gradoxst slipped away from the festivities. His Goblin commanders were so drunk they could barely stand; they'd never notice his absence. Once he'd put some distance between himself and the revelry, he allowed his lips to draw back in a sneer. He needed his Goblin cohorts, at least right now, but their coarse ways disgusted him. They reeked of dead meat, and the dirtier they were, the more they liked it.

He knew better than to let them know how he truly felt. Gradoxst wasn't under any illusions. The Goblins would turn on him in a trice if they could see into his mind. A muted laugh bubbled past his lips. Not much danger on that front. Mind reading was a Sidhe skill. As far as he knew, he was the only Sidhe who'd embraced darkness in millennia.

As he walked toward the castle in the *Dreaming*, Gradoxst recalled the day long ago when the gods picked Raven over him. Even now, thousands of years later, anger ate at his guts like acid at the memory. To be sure, he'd waited his turn, but the gods had passed him over many times. Finally, sick of waiting for the recognition he deserved, Gradoxst had taken matters in hand. The gods weren't the only ones who could augment his power.

He walked beneath an impressive stone archway that curved fifteen feet above his head. The castle was made of flat gray stones so cunningly arranged it was hard to see where one block ended and the next began. A sense of pride in Sidhe workmanship filled him, but he pushed it aside.

Gradoxst needed to hurry. The stones would recognize his Sidhe blood and allow him entrance. But they'd sense soon enough he'd parlayed with Demons. By then he needed to be well ensconced in the lowest level of the castle for his plan to succeed. He grinned, pleased with himself. To be sure, he and the Goblins were gradually wresting the *Dreaming* from the Sidhe. If he was successful, today would hasten things dramatically.

He trotted down curving stone staircases ever deeper into the earth. His mage light bobbed along beside him, adding a crimson tinge to things. A shudder ran through the rock. He knew he'd been discovered and broke into a run, sucking air like a bellows. He cursed his ancient bones. Every step made something ache.

What he wouldn't give to be young again. Truly young, before he'd traded sidestepping the aging process to enhance his magic. He still remembered the lascivious grin on the Demon lord's face as he'd asked if Gradoxst was quite sure he was willing to relinquish the *appearance of youth.* The second he'd nodded, his body had felt as if it were on fire. When he'd staggered to a mirror, he'd been shocked to see a seamed face and rheumy eyes staring back at him.

He breathed a calming spell as he ran, aiming it at the rocks. They were always slow to react. He might still make it in time—but only if he gave it everything he had.

Pushing open a heavy door, he raced into a subterranean chamber and immediately placed his hands on two adjacent walls. The incantation he'd readied spilled out almost before his hands were in the proper juxtaposition. He sent his will into the stones, along with a curse that would separate the full-blooded Sidhe fighting him from the roots of their power. Careful to maintain his own link, he concentrated on the Sidhe he'd met in battle over the past month. One by one, he clipped the strands.

The stones trembled. A high, wild sound filled the air. It took a second before Gradoxst realized he was laughing. "Yesssss," he squealed. "It's working. Once I have control of the castle, it's only a matter of time before the rest of the *Dreaming* belongs to me."

He hadn't quite figured out how he'd manage to send the Goblins packing after he no longer needed them, but he was certain he'd think of something. Furthermore, he thought it likely the stones themselves would undo his handiwork. He just hoped they couldn't work fast enough to sabotage his plans.

"You do not belong here!" echoed through the chamber.

"You're absolutely correct," Gradoxst answered the sentient rocks. "And there's not a damned thing you can do about it now."

CHAPTER 1

$\mathcal{L}$ara McInnis sat at an old-fashioned foot treadle sewing machine, working her way through a stack of ripped and worn clothing. As she pulled another pair of Trevor's work pants from under the presser foot, she shook her head and shoved a few long strands of coppery hair out of her eyes with an absentminded gesture.

"I don't see why it's so hard to keep things decent out here," she muttered, pulling thread through the built-in cutter behind the needle holder. Sitting straighter, she rotated her shoulder blades. As soon as she moved, Gunter, a seven-month-old German Shepherd, rose from where he'd been lying in a corner of the room and came to her, shoving his nose against her leg. His rough outer coat was still damp from an earlier romp outdoors.

"You're right," she announced to the dog. "I've been sitting here way too long. Bet you'd like to go outside and stretch those legs." The dog whined, tossed his head, and trotted to the door, looking over his shoulder as if to say, *aren't you coming?* He shook himself from stem to stern, black fur flying. Lara eyed the dust bunnies in the corners of the room and started to laugh. Cleaning was a pretty low priority when you had to hunt down your food before you could cook it—with no friendly neighborhood store to bail you out.

It hadn't seemed safe to venture as far as Skykomish, let alone a larger city, to replenish their supplies. Her thoughts turned to the riots and food shortages that had driven them out of Seattle and she shivered.

She wondered what time it was. She'd stopped glancing at her wrist for the watch that wasn't there a couple months before. Getting to her feet, she strode briskly to the window and craned her neck to see if she could determine the juxtaposition of the sun in the sky.

Aw crap! It can't be that late.

Apparently, she'd been sitting at the sewing machine for hours, since it was closing on late afternoon.

A sudden chill ran through her. Maybe she'd imagined it, but it felt as is if someone just walked over her grave. Lara shook her head to clear the uneasiness. Her pregnancy made her hypersensitive. That was probably it.

"Come on." She clucked to Gunter as she clattered down the stairs of the rustic, turn-of-the-century lodge that had become her home four months before. Pushing the front door open so the dog could go outside, she scanned the empty yard. Trevor and Brad had left that morning to go hunting. She didn't understand why they hadn't returned yet.

"Brrr." She shivered, pulling the door shut. Lara wasn't worried about the dog. He never ranged far from home. As she paced through the one large room that comprised the bottom floor of the house to the kitchen end of things—passing assorted soft furniture and overflowing bookshelves along the way—she was more than a little worried about her menfolk, though.

She'd joined her life to Trevor's well over twenty years before. Brad was a much newer addition to their household. He'd become part of their family after she'd helped rescue his daughter from Goblins that had kidnapped her. Her usual sadness whenever she thought about Adriana surfaced, and Lara offered a silent prayer to the goddess for the lovely, blonde seventeen-year-old buried behind their barn.

Brad had been a cop. A detective actually. She and Trevor first met him when he'd apprehended the violent husband of one of her patients, who'd been intent on murdering her. Fortune had tossed them together, and he'd been a part of their lives—in one way or another—ever since.

Lara lifted the lid on the cast iron soup pot she'd begun mixing ingredients into hours before. A fetching smell rose to greet her. Snapping up a spoon, she first stirred, then tasted, the bean and canned vegetable mélange, flavored with the last of a chicken they'd killed two days before. "Not bad," she murmured, wishing for more salt. They'd run out of that last week.

The dog scratched at the back door, and she went to let him in. He ran to her and shook himself, water droplets going every which way. "Okay, okay," she laughed. "I get that it's still raining out there." *February. Or is it March by now? Has it done anything but rain this entire winter?*

She shrugged a wool cloak over her shoulders, pushed her long braids under its hood, and looked at the dog, eyebrows raised. "Do you want to come?" she asked. "I have to milk the goats and look for eggs."

She'd just walked out onto the wide porch that wrapped all around the house, dog prancing before her, when she felt something curious. Laying a hand on her gently swelling stomach, she stopped, heart filling with wonder as she willed the sensation to return. Yes, there it was again. Like the gentlest of fish tails, brushing against her insides. Sudden tears pricked behind her lids, threatening to overflow.

"Elizabeth," she breathed. "You really are in there." And then she felt foolish. Lara was old to be having a child, and a first child at that. But joy at the life quickening within her brimmed over, and she hummed a tuneless song as she picked up the milking pail and trudged across the muddy yard to the barn. Her boots squished in the ever-present muck. It had rained so much—and snowed when it wasn't raining—nothing ever had a chance to dry out. She shook back her hood and bent to the first goat. The animal stared accusingly at her out of its rectangular eyes.

"I know I'm late," she told it. "The way today has gone, you're lucky I got here at all." But the goat just made goat noises, and Lara stopped talking to it. Eggs in the basket and milk in the pail, she started for the house, noticing light was fading from the day. Her thoughts turned to Trevor and Brad again.

Where the hell were they?

She poured half the milk into a bowl to sour and split the rest between two bottles. As she worked, she thought about Trevor with his blond good looks and his devastating past. She'd been a psychologist before fate had plunked her down at this remote farm. And he'd been a flight attendant. They'd led a pretty posh life. Especially compared with the way things were now.

The dog whined. Her head came up sharply, wondering if it was the men coming back. She rushed to the window, peering out into the gloom-shrouded yard, but it was tough to make out much of anything through the wavy, fin-de-siècle glass.

Reaching for her cloak, she realized she'd never taken it off, and she ran out the back door shouting, "Trevor? Trev, that you?" The slightest of echoes rolled off nearby canyon walls, muted by evergreens growing thickly around the clearing that held the three-story log house. Gunter rubbed up next to her, wet fur against wet wool. He whined again.

"What is it, boy?" she asked anxiously as she scanned the darkening yard. Just as she was about to go back inside, her moonstone amulet began what she'd come to recognize as its warning dirge. It was a magic moonstone, and its assessment of danger was never wrong. Lara laid a hand over her heart; suddenly it was beating far too fast.

"Trevor," she gasped. "Something's happened. It must have, or else he'd be back by now." Kicking herself for not being more vigilant about the time, Lara knew she had to look for him. That was what the amulet was trying to tell her. It was only half an hour from full dark, and she didn't have any idea what direction he and Brad had taken.

She stood there for half a minute, flummoxed, trying to figure out what to do. It would've been helpful to confer with Lillian, Raven, or Elidora, but they'd left yesterday. In contrast to previous leave-takings, Raven wasn't sure just when they'd be back.

"Yeah, I could really use their magic right about now," she muttered as she thought about the three Sidhe—well, Raven was actually more of a mage and a god—who'd taught her everything she knew about how to summon and control her own magical abilities. She'd been late learning about them too, just like she was late becoming a mother.

Lillian's voice filled her mind. *I have been many things in my lifetime.* It was a wee bit early for psychology, but I did spend years as a local wise-woman, handing out advice.

Wishing for some of that advice now, Lara trooped back into the house for warm gloves, a flashlight, and a few bandages. Stuffing things into a backpack, she poured some mead into a flask, tucking that in as well. The dog milled about as she ran this way and that, gathering things.

By the time she was finally as prepared as she could be, it was almost totally dark. She considered taking one of the two horses, but decided it would be too risky. She didn't ride well as it was, and a journey in the dark, where she couldn't see to guide the animal, seemed particularly unwise. If the horse threw her, she might lose the baby. Besides, she'd never tried mixing her magic with horseback riding before, and this didn't seem like a good time to start.

"Damn!" She realized she hadn't eaten since breakfast. Before letting herself and Gunter out the door, she damped the fire under her soup and grabbed some leftover cornbread. Out in the yard, she stuffed crumbs into her mouth, chewing hastily. Then she stood still, quieted her mind like Lillian had taught her, and grasped the moonstone. Nothing happened. It took her a minute or two to understand and, fuming with irritation at the delay, she tugged off one of her gloves, placing her hand on the magical gem, flesh to stone.

The familiar jolt of power rocked her. Four paths opened: one leading up, one down, one to a grassy glade, and another to a babbling brook. "Tell me," she spoke harshly. "Which should I take?" The moonstone just thrummed in her hand.

Her mind was in too much turmoil to sense anything. Lara forced herself to breathe as she stood in the bone-chilling rain. After what felt like ages, the timbre of the amulet changed, and she understood she was to tread the road going down into the earth.

"All right," she said evenly, turned to Gunter, and sent him back onto the porch. She couldn't take the time to escort him. Once the magic took her, she didn't dare deviate from the path it set. She wasn't proficient enough yet, even with the boost from her pregnancy.

Lara started walking. She'd taken each of the paths at least a time or two, but this route was by far the hardest for her. The sensation of earth closing about her was claustrophobic. She fought terror as every step led her farther and farther from the familiar. Some of the spirit paths were kind, but not this one. Lara trusted the amulet, though. She gripped it so hard the edges of the gold setting cut into her hand. As her blood dribbled out, the amulet's song intensified. Lillian's voice rang in her mind. *Blood consecrates all.*

She worried about Gunter, but even a minor shift in her concentration caused the dirt walls about her to waver, moving even closer. She wrenched her attention back to the moonstone and her missing love.

Lara's breath was ragged. Her steps felt leaden—each one a struggle—when the earth beneath her feet shifted, leading upward. For the briefest of moments she was afraid she'd collapse and die in this magical realm, with millions of tons of dirt as her crypt, but the amulet pricked her hand, and she pulled herself together.

Just keep walking. Yes, that's right. One step in front of the other. If I think about this, I'll be lost. Her body ached. The hand glued to the amulet was cramping. As the slope under her boots steepened, she wondered how much longer she could keep going before her legs refused to obey.

Suddenly, as it always was when she trod the magic-imbued ways, the dirt fell away like a curtain pulled open by an unseen puppeteer. She was back in the forest, and it was completely dark. Disoriented, she had no idea how far she'd traveled or where home might be. Cupping her hands around her mouth, she cried out for Trevor, understanding this was where the goddess had led her. Her voice, barely there after her minutes—or had it been hours?—underground cracked, so she dropped her pack to retrieve a water bottle took a slug, and tried again.

"Trevor? Trevor?"

"Lara!" His oh-so-welcome voice reverberated off to her left.

"Yes, it's me. I'm coming." Heart hammering in her chest like a frightened bird, she sent hasty prayers to Brigid and Artemis for keeping him safe. At least she thought he was safe. He could still talk. Why hadn't he come home? Had he gotten lost? She shook her head. *Not possible. He's always had the bearings of an Indian scout.*

"This way. Hurry, Lara!" His voice spurred her into action. Pulling out the flashlight she'd carefully conserved for emergencies, she shouldered her pack and moved toward the sound, using her light to avoid tripping over the thick, wet undergrowth. *Good thing I didn't bring one of the horses. They'd have caught a hoof in that mess and gone down for sure. Besides, then I wouldn't have had magic to help me, and I'd probably still be wandering about in the forest screaming my brains out.*

The two men came into sight quickly. Trevor knelt on the ground next to Brad, who was propped against a tree. Scrambling to his feet as soon as he saw her, Trevor opened his arms and drew her close when she ran into his arms.

"Blimey, love, but you're a sight for sore eyes." His British accent, pronounced as ever, cheered her, and she hugged him hard.

"What happened?" she asked, inhaling Trevor's enticing scent that mingled with the wet wool he wore.

"Someone else has been out here," Trevor said, a hard edge in his voice. "Must've been, because Brad stepped into a trap. Lucky it was just for mountain lions or coyotes. If it'd been a bear trap, he would've lost his foot. As it is, he's lost a lot of blood. We tried walking a few times, but he always started bleeding so badly, I worried he'd pass out. And I can't carry him."

Lifting her head from Trevor's shoulder, Lara looked about nervously. What if someone was watching them? Her hand snaked to the amulet in search of clues, but it lay passively in her grasp.

"Nicked an artery. Or maybe a vein." Brad's weary voice rose from his bed on the ground. "Kept thinking if we just rested it a bit and bandaged it tight, it'd let up. But it never did. Maybe because we didn't have much in the way of bandages." He hesitated, then added, "Trap was rusty, so it might've been here for a long time."

"How far are we from home?" Worries about the trap's owner lurking somewhere in the darkness nagged at Lara.

"But you just found us," Trevor said and then shook his head. "Sorry. Wasn't thinking. Guess you couldn't have tracked us. It's dark. Must've used your magic." He was still hanging onto her for all he was worth.

She pushed back to look at him. Wet, blond curls clung to his skull, but his ever-so-blue eyes shone with happiness that she'd found them. She hunkered down, playing her light over Brad. His normally pale complexion was even whiter than usual. A wool cap covered his shaggy, white-blond hair, and his bearded face was pinched with pain. She patted his hand and then rocked back on her heels and pushed to her feet.

"By the time I knew you weren't coming back," she explained to both of them, "it was well toward twilight. I asked the goddess for help, which is why I have no idea where the farmhouse is." She shucked her pack and pulled out the flask. "Here." She handed it to Brad. "Drink some of this. It should help. I'll take a look at your leg and try to get it better wrapped. I brought bandages."

Brad extended a hand for the flask, uncapped it, and took a deep draught. And then one more. She dragged her pack over next to him and twisted around, handing Trevor her flashlight. "Don't know what the hell we're going to do when we run out of batteries. Maybe by then I'll have mastered that mage light thing Lillian keeps trying to teach me.

"Anyway, hold the light steady."

Branches made squelching sounds as Trevor repositioned himself. When she got a good look at the lower part of Brad's pant leg, she gasped and then clapped a hand over her mouth. "Sorry," she mumbled.

"Yeah, I know. It's pretty bad." Brad's voice was weak. "Remember, I was an Army medic before I was a cop."

"Okay." She drew in a breath. "I hadn't actually forgotten that, but it wasn't front and center, either. Since you've had that training, what would you do with a wound like this?"

"Cut the pant leg away, clean it, stitch it, and put a tourniquet higher up if it wouldn't stop bleeding."

She rummaged through her pack for what she'd brought. "With all this water," she waved a hand at the falling rain, "you'd think there'd be a brook somewhere nearby. Is there?"

"Yes. About fifty feet to the north," Trevor replied. "If I go for water, I can't hold the light."

"I'll manage," she said tersely, already using a multi-faceted pocketknife with a small pair of scissors to cut through the blood-soaked denim of Brad's jeans. "Rain'll help some. But it would be good to sluice a decent stream of water over what's under here. How long ago did this happen?"

"A few hours," Trevor said sheepishly. "Kept trying to tell him we needed to stop and tend to it, but he wanted to keep going. And then he got so weak we had to stop."

She turned her attention back to Brad's leg. "There. Just a little more."

Trevor handed her the light and she balanced it in her lap. "Back directly," he said.

Lara snipped at the thick fabric. It didn't help that the scissor blades were only an inch long. At least they were sharp. When the fabric finally fell away, her eyes widened. "Jesus Christ," she breathed. "It's down to the bone in one spot here. No wonder it wouldn't stop bleeding."

He's going to get an infection unless we can get this clean and keep it that way.

"Need antibiotics." He spoke in a remarkably matter-of-fact tone. Almost as if he were discussing someone else's injury.

"Uh-huh. When was your last tetanus shot?"

"Not sure. But it's up-to-date. Had to be for the police force."

Thank God. One less thing to worry about.

She heard Trevor's boots trampling through wet vegetation. For a moment, she thought maybe they should boil the water, then she stifled a sour laugh. Odds of getting a fire going out here were practically nil.

Trevor bent over her and a long, low whistle escaped him.

"Never mind that," she said tersely. "Just pour." Once he finished, she added, "Sorry. Haven't had nearly enough to eat today. So I'm grumpy."

"I noticed," he replied with a touch of understated humor.

She dredged bandage material out of her pack. Working quickly, she wound layers of gauze from Brad's ankle halfway to his knee, following it up with a good-sized Ace wrap.

"That should do it," she said. "It really didn't bleed much while I was dressing it." The corners of her mouth turned downward. "Should've gone to medical school. Too bad I wasn't a shade more prescient about the future."

She picked up her flashlight, moving it to illuminate Brad Archer's gaunt face. "If both of us help you," she asked, "do you think you could walk?"

"I have to," he said, reaching both hands toward Trevor. "Come on," he urged. "Don't worry about hurting me. Just help me up." A muted yelp escaped the normally taciturn detective, as Trevor pulled him to his feet.

Lara threw everything into her pack and hoisted it onto her back. "You never did tell me. How far are we from home?" She walked to Brad's side and looped an arm around his waist to help support him. Trevor took the other side, placing his arm just below Lara's.

"About an hour, I think," Trevor replied. "There's a game trail just over there." He pointed with his free hand. "But they're only helpful if you're traveling single file. We'll put Brad in the middle. That way he'll have an easier time walking."

They made slow progress since the ground on either side of the trail was uneven and choked with plants and vines. Lara's flashlight got dimmer and dimmer. "Damn!" she swore. "It's about to die. Not that it'll be much worse than what we've had for the past while. The light's been so weak, it hasn't been any good at all. How much farther do you think?"

"Not sure," Trevor murmured. "Part of me thinks we should've been there by now."

A chill ran down Lara's spine. The Goblins and Demons were far from gone. Gradoxst, sort of a Demon who'd started out as a Sidhe, had it in for her. He'd been hounding her for months. Eyes widening in horror, she wondered if he'd laid the trap. Things rusted quickly in the ever-damp Pacific Northwest. It could've been set last month—or last week—for all she knew. Lara shifted her gaze from side to side, trying to see.

Was Gradoxst lurking in the darkness, watching them?

"Hang on," she said, slowing so she could reach for the amulet with her free hand. It had been strangely silent since leading her to Brad. Usually it maintained a soothing hum.

Closing her Earth eyes, she reached for the place where she could see things through her third eye. Brad's fading energy and Trevor's warm concern pulsed against her, but she didn't sense Goblins anywhere near. Breath whooshed out of her, and she knew how tense she'd been.

Lara was fairly certain the amulet could lead them home, except she'd never used it as a dowsing rod before. She was just contemplating what to do next and how to bend the amulet to her will, when a gibbous moon slid from behind a cloud, shedding a greenish glow on the damp landscape.

"Artemis and her moon," Trevor cried and blew an enthusiastic kiss skyward. "Things are looking better, love."

Startled out of a half trance, Lara thought about the goddess who'd saved Trevor from certain death at the hands of a Goblin and smiled to herself. *Who knows? Perhaps things are getting better.* "Hush, dear. I'm trying to concentrate."

He shook his head. "I know where we are now. I can see some landmarks. I got a bit off course is all. We're only about a quarter mile from home. It's just off to our left."

She stared at the thick, evergreen forest. *Landmarks? Shit, it all looks the same to me.* "Are you sure?"

He nodded then asked, "How you doing, Brad? Can you make it another ten minutes or so?"

An almost imperceptible moan was followed by, "Yes. Lara did a good job. I don't think I'm bleeding anymore."

True to Trevor's uncanny sense of direction, even Lara knew they were close to home after five more minutes of walking. They came to the brook bubbling down from Troublesome Mountain. Tonight it was more like a raging torrent, so they followed the bank until they reached the bridge. Water lapped over its rough log planks. Gunter's excited barks rang out, and the young Shepherd raced out of the shadows of the yard to dance around them, nipping and yapping shamelessly.

"Enough." Trevor reached down to calm the over-excited dog. "Yes, we're home. We wouldn't leave you here by yourself, silly."

The porch steps weren't as difficult as Lara feared they might be. Brad had obviously spent time on crutches, and he leaned on both of them in lieu of putting weight on his injured leg. As they passed through the door and into the farmhouse, Trevor said, "I'll get the fire going."

"And I'll heat some water to do a better job cleaning your leg," Lara told Brad once they'd settled him on one of the sofas in the living room. She dropped her pack and hustled toward her soup pot, stumbling with weariness as she shucked her sodden wool cloak and draped it over a peg in the kitchen.

Wonder if I can coax a fire with magic or if I'm too done in. Peering into the woodstove's firebox, she was pleasantly surprised to see coals. She tossed in more wood, scooped a mug of lukewarm soup out of her pot, and slurped it down greedily. She'd just started on a second mug, when both soup and water seemed warm enough for Brad.

"Trev?"

He was by her side in an instant. "I'll take some for Brad and me." He ladled soup into two more mugs.

"Great, I'll run upstairs for clean linen and get a basin of hot water."

"You sure?" He put down the mugs and spun her to face him, hands on her shoulders. "You look knackered, love. Sure you don't want me to get those towels?"

"I'd say we're about equal in the knackered department." She laughed, trying to copy his accent and failing miserably.

"I'm not pregnant," he pointed out, lowering one hand to place it protectively over her midsection.

"It's not a disease," she countered. "Just go give Brad his soup. He needs liquids since he lost so much blood. There's some leftover cornbread too, if he feels like it."

"Well, even if he doesn't, I do. I'm so hungry the nosh could be boiled Goblins, and I'd suck it down anyway."

When Lara came into the living room, towels draped over one arm, balancing a basin of steaming water, she was heartened to see the men eating and finishing off the mead from the flask in her pack. Brad's color looked a smidge better too.

"Nurse Nancy, at your service," she quipped, settling herself at the end of the sofa. Brad's boots were already off, and Trevor had removed the detective's soaking wet socks. The fire had warmed the room nicely, and the socks were steaming on the ornamental grate in front of the open fireplace.

"If your feet are as wet as his," she looked hard at Trevor, "maybe you should get your boots off too."

She unwound the Ace wrap. Brad had been correct that his wound had finally quit bleeding. When she got all the bandages off, she surveyed the damage in light from a kerosene lamp. "There's only this one place that looks really bad to me," she said. "The rest of it is just a series of puncture wounds from the jaws of the trap."

"Those are the worst kind," Brad noted as he craned his neck to assess his injuries. "Because they're deep, they're really prone to infection."

"I brought iodine with me from upstairs." She drew a bottle of Betadine from a pocket. "That should help."

"Maybe." Brad sounded dubious. "Antibiotics would be better. Do we have any?"

"I don't think so." Trevor scratched at his wet curls.

"We left in such a hurry," Lara added, "we weren't as thorough as we should have been." She rolled her eyes. "Raven predicted gloom and doom if we didn't drop everything and skedaddle. Does it hurt?" She tucked towels under Brad's leg, pouring hot water over the wound to finish cleaning dirt and debris out of it.

"Some. But it's not bad. Let me help." He took the cloth from her and scrubbed his leg far more vigorously than she'd been doing. "I know what I can tolerate," he explained, wincing. "Give me another one." He held out his hand for a fresh towel.

Once the wound was as clean as Lara thought it was going to get, she furled her brows at Brad and asked, "What do you think? Do we saturate it with iodine and leave it open?" The detective nodded. She dribbled disinfectant over each place the skin was torn.

Straightening, she picked up the mead flask. "Is there any left?" Without waiting for an answer, she upended it, licking droplets off the neck of the bottle when she was done swallowing. "Why don't you sack out here?" she suggested to Brad.

Despite all the empty bedrooms on the second and third floors, Brad had settled in one of the outbuildings. The arrangement offered all of them privacy. If things got worse, though, she thought it would be easier if they didn't have to drag him back into the house.

He didn't answer. When she looked at him, his eyes were already closed.

Trevor touched her arm. Placing a finger over his lips, he gathered the blood-soaked towels and cooling basin of water, gesturing for her to follow him. "Water still hot?" he asked as they reached the kitchen.

"Should be," she replied wearily. Falling into a chair, she supported her head on an upraised hand.

"Great. I'll just brew us up a nice cuppa. Do you want any more to eat?" At her nod, he ladled soup into a mug and cut her a generous slice of cornbread before selecting tealeaves and pouring water over them. Gunter, who'd been asleep, lurched muzzily to Lara's side, probably hoping she'd drop something.

"Feel like talking?" she asked between bites.

"Sure." Trevor ate like a starving person, chewing and swallowing as fast as he could manage.

"If that wound gets infected…" Her voice trailed off.

"I've already thought about that," he broke in. "We did have antibiotics back at home. Lots of them. We were twits not to bring any. They wouldn't have taken up any space at all."

"So?" She blew out a tired breath. "They may as well be on Mars for all the good they'll do Brad. Tomorrow I'll hunt for wild onions and garlic and try to make a poultice. Maybe Elidora and Lillian will be back by then. I'm sure they know how to treat infections."

"Do you know where they went?"

Lara shook her head. "They were even more close-mouthed about their plans than usual this time."

"Humph." Trevor sipped his tea. He looked across at Lara, a touch of defiance in his expression. "Hear me out before you say anything."

Cocking her head to one side, she gestured with the hand not holding her fork. "Whatever it is, Trev, out with it. I'm so tired I'm starting to wonder if I'll be able to climb the stairs to our bed."

"If Brad gets worse, and Raven and them don't come back in time, I'll take one of the cars and go find him some medicine. I probably won't have to go all the way to Seattle—"

"What?" she screeched, incredulous. Her eyes flew open in spite of her exhaustion. "You can't do that. Raven said we can't leave. That it's too dangerous. They've left here these last four months, so they know what it's like out there. We haven't. They said—"

"I don't care what they said." Trevor's voice had the mulish tone it got whenever he was determined to do something. "I'm not going to stand by and let Brad die." He hesitated. "Look, Lara. It's late and we're both shattered beyond measure. Let's let this percolate, and we can talk about it more in the morning."

She drained her tea, stood, and clumped toward the stairs too stunned by his pronouncement—and far too worn out—to attempt anything further in the way of conversation.

CHAPTER 2

The next day was rolling toward afternoon, and the Sidhe still hadn't returned. Rotating one shoulder blade, followed by the other, Trevor worked at loosening tension that made his back ache. He'd tried to reason with Lara that morning while they were still in bed, but she'd become practically hysterical at the idea of him leaving.

"Yesterday I was afraid I'd never be able to find you," she moaned, "and now you're bound and determined to do exactly what Raven and the Sidhe told us not to."

When she'd gotten around to saying she wasn't about to raise their baby all by herself, he gave up and pulled her close. While she'd let him fold her into his arms, she'd been uncharacteristically stiff, which meant she was angry—or scared. Maybe both.

Out in the shop, Trevor sorted seeds so they could get a start indoors before being transplanted into the yet-to-be designed garden area. After several mistakes, he slammed his fist down on his makeshift workbench. Tomato seeds from an open packet flew everywhere. "Bloody fucking hell," he swore as he bent to gather the tiny particles, stuffing each one into mounds of dirt he'd placed in old

23

egg cartons. They'd been an unexpected find, stored behind stacks of garbage.

He exhaled sharply. Simply getting the outbuildings into sufficient order to use them for anything but storage had occupied close to two months. Without Brad's help, it would've taken far longer. There'd been useful things, like the egg cartons, but far more in the way of junk that ended up in the rubbish bin.

Still plucking seeds from other debris littering the floor, Trevor's thoughts returned to the previous evening. Once Lara realized he and Brad should've been home, she'd worried herself half sick about them. Raven and Lillian had done a hell of a job brainwashing her about the perils of travel outside the warded safety of the house and grounds. The wards extended to the yard and outbuildings. At least he thought they did. Elidora had expressed doubts in that regard.

"Face it," he muttered half aloud as he teased out his motives for wanting to take one of the cars and leave—at least for a while. "I'm curious about what's out there." The small towns along the Highway Two corridor had been pretty much intact the night he and Lara fled from Seattle. Fuel had been outrageous, but at least there'd been open gas stations that had some. And the small markets were still stocked with staple foods.

He chewed on his lower lip and reminded himself their canned goods were all but gone. Despite Raven and the Sidhes' promises to bring whatever was needed, something happened that had captured most of their attention for the last month. Raven, far from chatty on a good day, had become downright taciturn, refusing to reply to even the most ordinary conversation. Forget about asking him questions. He just looked at you with those inscrutable, gray eyes, tossed his black hair back out of the way, and stomped out of the room.

Lillian had mostly focused on teaching Lara magic. As Trevor thought about it, he realized the red-haired Sidhe with the clear, green eyes had been gone far more than she'd been present. And Elidora, the local witch-woman from the village in northern England where he was born, hadn't spent any too much time with them either.

Ever since Gren, her longtime companion, had sacrificed himself closing a corridor between the worlds that Goblins were pouring through, the Sidhe with the long, black hair and bottomless dark eyes had been a shadow of her former self. She *was* interested in Brad, though. Trevor was sure of it. She spent long hours sitting close to the detective, murmuring in her soft brogue. Though reticent at first, Brad gradually warmed to her.

Humph! After the wasteland his marriage was, no wonder he finds attention—any attention—pleasing.

Trevor stared at the floor and workbench, hunting for stray seeds. Until they could plant and harvest, there'd be no more. None of them knew shit about farming. He hoped that wouldn't turn around to bite them in the butt. They'd be buggered if a goodly percentage of what they planted didn't turn into something they could eat.

Once his thoughts turned to food, an image of Lara rose, troubling him. She wasn't eating nearly enough, particularly given her pregnancy was nearly half gone. And she was working far harder than she ever had in their other life—demanding, physical labor that burned up lots of calories. He considered a foray into Skykomish again. It wouldn't take long to determine if the local market still had food, and if he could wrangle some antibiotics out of a drugstore.

Trevor smiled crookedly. Despite not having a doctor's prescription, he was close to certain he could get a pharmacist to turn loose of a few pills. Particularly after he told him what the problem was. And offered to pay generously. Likely the bloke would even know which antibiotic would be best for Brad's type of wound.

"Lara was spot on," he mumbled. "Too bad none of us know much about medicine." While he understood something about antibiotics being specific for different types of infections, he didn't have even the slightest clue which one would be good for the deep puncture-type wounds in Brad's leg.

No Internet to look it up on, either.

Speaking of Brad, I probably ought to check on him.

In an attempt to tidy things, Trevor swept the loose dirt from the workbench into one of his hands. He sprinkled it over the egg carton segments in case he'd missed a seed or two. Light was another problem. It was fairly dark in the shop unless he left the door open. But if he did, rain blew in.

"Bloody hell, I miss living on Queen Anne Hill. Never would have guessed how much I'd long for electricity," he groused, pulling the shop door open. He had to pull hard since the wood had swollen from all the rain, and the bottom of the door dragged against the concrete floor, making a sound like a squalling kitten.

He stared out into the muddy yard. It didn't seem possible, but it had finally stopped raining. Patches of blue were peppered among the clouds. The break in the previous night's storm had only lasted a couple hours. By the time he and Lara dragged themselves into bed, the thrum of rain on their windows had re-established a steady rhythm.

"Oh, there you are." Lara picked her way across the mud-slick yard, her boots making little squelching noises.

"Told you where I'd be," he said, hoping her earlier fit of temper had subsided.

She folded her arms around him. "Yes. I know. Guess I was so upset I wasn't being rational. Or listening very well." She moved back far enough to look at him. "I'm sorry. I know you were trying to plan ahead to help Brad if things get worse for him." Lara rushed on, barely stopping to draw another breath. "I don't talk much about it, but the magic really does have a price. It drains me, especially now that we don't have enough to eat."

He pulled her close, feeling relieved she was thinking again and not just reacting. *So I was right about her being exhausted and half-starved.* "You need to take better care of yourself," he said against her hair, the swell of her belly against him a reminder of just how high the stakes were. "How's Brad doing?"

"About the same as last night, I think," she replied, voice muted since her head pressed close to his shoulder. "But I'm not sure it means all that much. It takes time for infections to set in."

He nodded. "Yes, love. And when they do, they're all that much harder to treat, as I recall."

She turned her face up for a kiss, then unwound her arms and stepped back. "You're right about that." Lara hesitated. "I hoped we'd see *someone* today, but…"

He knew she meant Raven or the Sidhe. "I hoped we would too," he concurred and waited to find out what was on her mind. Something was. They'd spent too many years together for him not to recognize when she had something to say.

She cleared her throat and looked at him, her dark eyes uneasy. "I know I made an unholy fuss last night. Maybe it's because I'm pregnant. God knows I was close to the end of my reserves what with all the magic I'd expended, but if Brad's not any better by tomorrow—and the Sidhe aren't back—maybe you could go as far as Skykomish." She dropped her gaze looking sheepish. "While you're there, maybe you could try to pick up more food."

He started to laugh. It was just a chuckle or two at first, but in no time at all, he threw his head back, and tears streamed down the stubble on his cheeks. "So you're as sick of rice and oatmeal as I am?" he managed to choke out.

"Guess so." She giggled. "And I find that even I have lost my taste for canned food. Not that there's enough of it left to worry about, mind you."

"Come on." He'd just grabbed her arm when Gunter trotted around the corner with a small, mangled rodent firmly clamped in his jaws. The dog dropped the still-twitching vole at Trevor's feet, his tail thumping excitedly.

"Hey, you got one," Trevor exclaimed, petting the dog's damp fur. "Nice work."

"Good boy," Lara cooed, removing a glove to pet him too. "You're doing better than we are at this point."

Trevor snorted. "I suppose he's sick of rice too."

Apparently having soaked up enough in the way of praise, the gangly adolescent dog snatched up his kill. He bounded across the yard and onto the front porch where he settled in.

"Speaking of hunting—" Lara began, but Trevor shook his head.

"Didn't scare up any game at all yesterday. Of course, we weren't out there very long before Brad stumbled into that trap."

Lara looked askance at him. "Since you mentioned it, how'd he manage to do that?"

Well, how did he?

"You know, love, it's the damnedest thing, but I just don't know. One minute we were trying to be quiet in case anything worth shooting was nearby, and the next Brad shrieked like Banshees were after him. Thank Christ it wasn't dark. I had a bloody hard time as it was finding the release catch. We used traps and snares when I was a boy, but I'd never seen one quite like that before."

Silence hovered between them. He figured she was trying to make sense of what he'd just told her. Lara had a fine, analytical mind. If something odder than bad luck was afoot, she might be able to untangle it. Ever since yesterday's accident he'd had an uncomfortable feeling he was missing something.

"Interesting," she murmured at last. "There's no one else out here that I know of. We've lived here for over four months, and I haven't seen or heard anything that might suggest other people anywhere nearby. So where did that trap come from?"

Even though she'd asked a question, he knew it was rhetorical, and held his peace, waiting.

She shook her head, the corners of her mouth twisted into a frown. "I just don't know," she said at length. "Brad thinks the damned thing might have been there for years. He said that again over breakfast, but my intuition suggests otherwise."

"The amulet?"

"It began pricking me yesterday about the time I realized you two weren't coming back. At least not under your own steam. And it's been somewhat on the chatty side today too. It tolls a mild warning vibration when things are slipping, but not yet entirely out of hand."

"Do you think Gradoxst, or one of his ilk, has come back?" As he thought about the rogue Sidhe turned Demon who'd sucked energy out of the Jung Institute in Zurich for years, a chill marched down Trevor's spine like a renegade icicle.

"Maybe," she agreed reluctantly. Some of the color drained out of her face, and she reached for the amulet.

Watching her, Trevor thought, Christ. Those bloody Sidhe just dumped us out here. We're no better than lame ducks ripe for the plucking.

"Let's go check on Brad," Lara suggested, apparently unwilling to tackle discussing Gradoxst. "I haven't looked in on him since I left him with some tea and the last of the cornbread a couple hours ago."

"Where were you?"

"Upstairs, sewing. I'm still trying to get through all the mending, so I can finish the blanket that's on the loom."

When they came into the front room, Brad was sitting up. "What are you doing?" Lara asked, concern radiating from her.

"Thought I'd take my dishes back to the kitchen." He quirked an eyebrow her way.

"I can do that," Trevor said. "How about if we take a look at your leg?" He peered meaningfully at Brad's ankle, covered by a pair of clean sweat pants.

"I already looked at it," Brad snapped.

Something about the detective's tone soured Trevor's stomach. "And?" He walked over and sat next to Brad on the couch.

"Not great. That one place where it's so deep is generating a lot of pus."

"Maybe we need to put more iodine on it," Lara offered.

Brad shook his head. "We could, but it's a perfect place for anaerobic bacteria to grow. I need penicillin and Flagyl—or maybe Clindamycin—so I don't end up with a bone infection. They're hell to get rid of. Saw a lot of that in the field hospitals in the Middle East."

Okay, so now I know what to ask the pharmacist for. "How about if we douse it with hot water again?" Trevor asked, trying to infuse confidence into his voice.

Brad pushed heavily to his feet. When he weighted his leg, a sharp grunt escaped him. Trevor leaped up, extending a hand, but Brad brushed it aside. Slightly taller, Brad looked down at Trevor. "We can do all that," he said through gritted teeth. "Hot water, iodine, but I suspect it won't make a helluva lot of difference. What I need to do is get in my car while I can still drive and see if there's a drugstore in Skykomish that's still operating. If there's not one there, I'll check Monroe."

He made his way slowly toward the kitchen. Looking back over his shoulder, he stopped walking and said, "Your magical friends have been pretty secretive here of late. Do you know where they are?" When no one said anything, he muttered something incomprehensible before heading for the sink, dishes rattling slightly in his outstretched hand.

Trevor looked at Lara, who shrugged. "Why look at me?" she asked. "I already told you I have no idea where they went. Although I suppose I could try to raise Lillian through the amulet."

"Why don't you do that?" Trevor moved close to her, speaking quietly near her ear. "If you find her, tell her we need help."

Lara walked thoughtfully up the stairs. Her hand sought the amulet of its own accord. Though the Sidhe weren't exactly human, they had enough in the way of traits she recognized from long years as a psychotherapist for her to understand how worried they'd been the past few weeks. She'd tried to draw Lillian out, since she felt closer to her than the others, but the Sidhe just looked at her, sadness brimming from her green eyes, and shook her head.

What's gone wrong? Lara asked herself. Raven and the Sidhe had been so helpful at the beginning; she'd just assumed their help would continue. The way things were turning out, Lara was starting to wish they'd taken their chances and remained in riot-torn Seattle.

"That's stupid," she growled, irritated. "We couldn't have stayed there. But it's getting harder to live here too. We should have brought way more food, since we moved in November when winter was just getting going." She passed the top riser and plodded heavily down the hall, deep in thought.

Gunter started barking from the front porch, and it didn't sound as if Trevor was playing with him.

What the fuck?

Her head snapped up. She moved briskly into her sewing room and stared out the windows, grateful only the ground floor had thick glass that was hard to see through. The yard on that side of the house was empty, so she raced for the second floor library where windows looked out over the front porch, but she couldn't see anything amiss. The dog was still barking and growling like mad. Trevor—or maybe Brad— must have let him inside since his yammering grew much louder.

Tabling trying to raise Lillian, she flew back down the stairs. Trevor and Brad stood in the corner of the great room next to the guns. Trevor slapped a magazine into Brad's automatic rifle.

"What—?" she began, but Brad waved her to silence.

She marched across the room. When she was right next to the men, she whispered. "Did you see anyone out there? Because I sure didn't, and I looked from the upstairs windows."

"Maybe." Brad spoke softly. "Glass in these damned windows on the main floor is a pain in the ass. I thought I saw something flash past when I went to bring the dog in, though. And the goats are making a hell of a racket."

Who could be out there?

Lara's mouth was suddenly dry, and her heart rate escalated, hammering against her ribs. "W—what did you see?" It was hard to talk, since her mouth felt as if it was stuffed with sawdust.

"Not sure."

Trevor slipped into his coat. "Go upstairs," he told her in a gruff tone that betrayed his nervousness. "Probably safer." He turned to Brad. "So I just disengage the safety," he pointed at a lever on the barrel, "aim, and shoot?"

Nodding, Brad said. "Yup, pretty easy all in all. It'll mow through fucking near anything."

"It didn't kill that Goblin who was here the night I found you in our yard," Trevor muttered under his breath. Glancing at him, Brad just snorted and shrugged.

The terror ratcheting through Lara ramped up another notch or two. "You're going to go outside?" she asked in a strangled-sounding voice.

"Well," Trevor said brusquely, "one of us has to. Brad can't. So that leaves me. I have to go see what has the dog and goats riled up."

"Oh." *Not much point in telling him not to. He's right. We do need to know.*

"Okay." she said, struggling to keep her voice even and not collapse in a shrieking heap, which was what she wanted to do. "What do you need from me?"

The look of gratitude Trevor flashed her warmed her heart. *He's got enough troubles. He doesn't need a hysterical wife on top of everything else.*

"Just stay in here and keep down."

"We'll both go upstairs," Brad said. "We'll be safer up there. 'Sides, at least one of us has to be well enough to drive out of here if it comes to that."

Lara trailed after Brad as he hobbled up the risers. She extended a hand in case he needed help and mulled over what he'd said. *It's like a theme,* she thought. *Both he and Trevor are fixated on leaving here. Is it just an odd coincidence, or is something magical playing us like marionettes?*

She sought the amulet, curving her fingers around the enchanted moonstone. Its gloom-and-doom dirge was escalating. Was it the same refrain from when she and the Sidhe had rescued Adriana from an otherworldly beach between the worlds? The one that meant Goblins were near? She focused all her attention, but wasn't sure.

Goddammit, Lillian. Where the fuck are you?

Because she couldn't think of anything else to do once she got Brad settled on one of the beds scattered throughout the rambling old guesthouse, she plucked one of Raven's books from its perch in the library, settled into a chair, and searched for answers to their dilemma. She couldn't risk entering a trance state to raise Lillian, not if something hideous happened and the men needed her to react quickly.

Her heart rattled against her ribcage, beating so hard that breathing became a struggle. Trevor, her Trevor, was out there all alone. He'd been gone for at least fifteen minutes. She forced her attention back to the page in front of her, but the lines swam and merged. Lara rubbed her eyes.

Gunter, who'd followed her up the stairs, sat by her side, his ears pricked forward straining to hear something. A worried-sounding whine escaped the young dog, followed by another.

"That does it." She slammed the book shut startling the dog, who whimpered again nervously. "It's not like this thing has an index where I can look up Goblin marauders and what to do about them."

Wanting someone to talk with, she went to find Brad, but he'd fallen asleep. When she looked closely at him, her heart sank. Deep circles etched under his eyes, and the normally taut skin on his face sagged. She laid a gentle hand on his forehead. He stirred and she pulled it back, but not before she determined he felt decidedly warm.

The men are right. We will have to leave here. At least one of us and maybe all of us. The staccato report of automatic weapon fire broke the silence of the afternoon. Instinctively, she threw herself on the floor.

Brad rolled on top of her. "It's okay, Lara," he grunted, obviously in pain. "That was my gun."

"Shouldn't we go out to try to help him?" A shrill, panicked note underscored her words.

"No. We stay here until it's over."

She wanted to move. Run down the stairs and outside to convince herself Trevor was still alive, but Brad's weight pinned her to the floor. He'd never let her do something he considered foolish. Fuming, she muttered, "You don't have to lay on me. I won't leave until—"

"Until we hear one of the downstairs doors open," Brad finished for her. "Then we go down together. Damn it. Should've brought the shotgun up here with us." He moved and sent an appraising glance her way. "If there's some method you have of raising the Sidhe with that thing," he pointed at the amulet, "I say go for it."

She shook her head. "I can't. Not until this plays itself out."

CHAPTER 3

Trevor let himself out the kitchen door, Brad's Heckler and Koch tucked under his arm. In a distant corner of his brain, he thought he must be mad to march off to face Christ-only-knew-what with a weapon he'd never fired before. *Feels like it did the night I snuck out into the dark to see who had the night vision lamp. This gun didn't do shit when Brad fired it that night. Not against Goblins.* With memories swamping him, Trevor felt ill. He tightened his grip on the gun's stock, and his breath came way too fast as he scanned the yard for movement.

The only reason he'd survived that other night was because a goddess had intervened. He didn't figure he'd be that lucky twice. Besides, the supernatural creatures seemed to have other things on their minds. He'd cornered Elidora a couple days before to ask what was wrong. The Carlisle witch-woman mumbled something cryptic in Celtic Gaelic. Trying to decipher it after she left, he wondered if the *Dreaming* might not be under Demon attack.

Standing on the bottom step, with the comforting bulk of the house behind him, Trevor tried reaching out with all his senses. At first, the frantic beat of his heart drumming in his ears overwhelmed everything else. He forced himself to take some steadying breaths.

Somewhere between them, he caught a sense of something not quite right, and the fine hairs on the nape of his neck quivered. He peered anxiously around the familiar yard, illuminated by strands of sunlight peeking through fluffy clouds. Nothing moved. In an effort to be methodical, he shifted his gaze from left to right, then back again.

Still nothing.

Is something hiding in the trees? That's what they did last time. A vision of the Goblin that had jumped Brad rose unbidden, and Trevor bit hard on his lower lip. "No Goblins," he mumbled. "They haven't been here since that night. No reason they should come back."

Bolstered somewhat by the sound of his own voice, he straightened his back, seeking courage to move away from the house. None of the animals were making any unusual noises like they would if they were frightened. Whatever had stirred up the goats before must have left. He checked the safety—clicking it off with fingers that weren't as steady as he might have liked—and patted his pocket for the spare magazines Brad had shoved into his hand, the last of the ammunition for the automatic rifle.

"Best get moving," he muttered, striding purposefully across the yard. He glanced from side to side to reassure himself no one else was there. Deciding to check the barn first, since it was closest to the house, he altered course. When he got there, he unlatched the door and pushed it open.

"Mary, mother of God," he gasped and fell back a step, as he took in a scene out of the nine levels of *Dante's Inferno*. Something—or someone—had slaughtered the goats. Blood was everywhere. The floor was slick with it, and it blotched the walls. Nausea roiled through him. Trevor struggled not to vomit. A muted bleat came from somewhere. As he sought its source, a kid crept from under one of the corpses mewling piteously.

"Poor thing." Trevor reached down to stroke the small creature. It shook as it nuzzled his hand. He wondered how it had escaped, then realized its mother must have thrown herself atop her child. The reality of what the carnage meant hit home. He tasted fear, bitter and acrid. A metallic taste filled his mouth, burning its way deep into his soul.

Goblins. There are Goblins here. There must be. No animal could have done this and latched the door behind him.

Trevor's head snapped up. He felt sure he heard something, its feet slogging through the mud. Lurching to the still-open barn door, he opened fire, swinging the weapon in a broad swath, while trying to avoid firing directly at the house. He still didn't see anything, but he knew in his guts he wasn't alone. Hadn't been since he set foot in the yard. That was why he felt so odd. He fired another burst, hoping against hope to hit something.

A shriek, and then another, assailed him. It sounded like someone was being murdered five feet away. He twisted wildly from side to side, but didn't see a thing. His mind rebelled at the contradiction. He lunged to pick up the kid and make a run for the house, but something closed about him from behind. Panting hot and fast, he swung the gun barrel sideways to hit whatever was there, but didn't have enough reach.

Laughter brayed. The same damned, maniacal laughter he'd heard the last time Goblins showed up. A cloying miasma, reminiscent of road kill lying in the sun too long, clogged his nostrils.

Even though he still couldn't see what had him, steel bands wrapped around his chest. Breathing became difficult. He considered yelling for Brad, but didn't want either the crippled detective or, God forbid, Lara, anywhere near what was happening to him. Fear clawed at his belly. The edges of his vision grayed as his oxygen supply diminished.

"For bloody fuck's sake, I'm going to die here," he growled, just before the darkness swirling ever closer dragged him downward.

When Trevor hadn't come back into the house for far too long after they heard the last rifle volley, Lara said, "We need to go down there."

Staring resolutely at the detective, she silently dared him to contradict her statement.

"You're right," he said, nodding resignedly. "We do. Something's wrong."

The dog had stopped whining shortly after the gunfire stopped, but he still looked worried, sticking close to Lara as she ran down the stairs.

Brad's, "Wait for me," followed her.

I suppose he'll want to load the shotgun, she thought, her jaw clenched with worry. Limping up behind her, Brad indeed headed for the shotgun, dropping shells into the barrel with practiced ease.

"Stay behind me," he said, staggering slightly as his bad leg balked at the rapid movement. "Make the dog stay inside. One less thing to worry about."

Lara nodded. Good thing he knows how to do this. Because I sure don't.

The detective moved with a knowledge born from long years of police work. At the bottom of the porch stairs, he pointed out Trevor's boot prints leading toward the barn.

"How do you know they're his?" she whispered.

"Because they're deeper than the others," he replied in a normal voice. "Something bad happened. I feel it. But whoever—or whatever —was here, they're gone now. Don't ask how I know. I just do."

She stared at the impressions Brad had labeled as Trevor's. Try as she might, she couldn't see a damned bit of difference between them and all the other footprints littering the yard. Lara tried reaching out with her psychic side, but the amulet was disconcertingly silent. Cupping her hands around her mouth, she shouted, "Trevor? Trev?"

"Humph," Brad muttered after a few seconds of silence. "Not good. Means he can't answer, or he's beyond the reach of your voice which isn't very likely." Brad limped across the yard, his lips drawn together into a hard line. When he got to the barn, he called over his shoulder. "Door's open. Did you leave it like that?"

"No. We always shut it. There's that baby goat." She hurried across the yard toward him.

His muffled grunt brought her up short. He spun to face her, holding out a hand. "Uh-uh. Not for you."

"What do you mean not for me?" She tried to shoulder past him, but even with his leg wound he held her at bay easily. Anxiety ate at her like a rabid animal, and her mouth flooded with saliva. She wondered if she was going to be sick. "What's in there, Brad?"

"Dead goats," he said succinctly. "And my rifle."

Wrenching out of his grasp with a strength she didn't know she possessed, she raced through the open door. A scream ripped out of her as she stood immobilized, staring at the bloodbath. Even though she raised shaky hands to her mouth to stifle the next scream, it came anyway. And another after it.

Brad turned her away from the blood and guts strewn about the barn floor. "Better if you don't look," he said brusquely.

A tiny bleat tore at her heart and she said, "The kid's not dead. We need to get him out of there."

"I'll do it." Letting go of her shoulders, Brad went deeper inside the barn. When he emerged, the month old goat was tucked under one arm.

"If Trev's not in there." She pointed with a trembling hand. "Where is he?"

Brad shook his head. "My cop senses tell me he's not here. Whoever left that mess in the barn isn't either."

"But we didn't hear any engine noise," she pleaded, desperate for a return of rational thought. "How could someone have kidnapped him if we didn't hear them leave?" All of a sudden, she knew the answer. Her mind filled with visions of a deadly vortex Gradoxst had set up, leading from her office to another world. One inhabited by Demons. Almost as if it wanted her to feel even worse, the damned amulet pricked her with its warning vibrations, sending wave after wave of ice into her blood.

As memories threatened to tear her apart, standing still talking was more than she could bear. Lara sprinted for the other outbuildings, checking each methodically. Every few minutes, she cried Trevor's name, but all the buildings were empty. Their three cars were still lined up next to Raven's ancient Ford back behind the shop. When she came to the enclosed paddock and saw the other goats and their two horses contentedly munching grass, she blew out a tense breath. At least the orphaned kid would have milk to drink.

The truth sank in. The unspeakable had happened and Gradoxst—or his henchmen—had taken Trevor. She sank into the mud next to the paddock. Shrieks tore out of her. She cursed Lillian, Raven, and every god and goddess she could think of. If it hadn't been for them, she and Trevor would still be in Seattle.

"Lara." Brad's voice was very close. "Get up. You won't do any good getting soaked to the skin." He paused. "If you'd stayed in Seattle, both of you would probably be dead by now."

Calmed by the flat, straightforward tone in his voice, she looked up and brushed impatiently at tears pouring down her face. "We have to look for him," she said, snuffling noisily.

"Do you know how to do that?" he asked.

"Not without Raven and the Sidhe," she admitted grimly. "At least not yet. Maybe what I need to know is buried in one of those fucking books."

"Maybe it is," he said gently. "Why don't you grab a book or two and the dog? We're going into town. I need drugs. You can read while I drive."

She tried to meet his eyes as another sob rose from the broken place inside her.

"Lara." Brad's tone sharpened. "Trevor didn't walk out of here. While you were looking through the buildings, I tracked him. He walked from the house to the barn. Period. End of story. I'll see what I can salvage in the way of meat from those goats while you're getting yourself together."

A pall settled over her like a shroud. Even though she'd come to the same conclusion about Trevor, hearing Brad say it out loud was like nailing a coffin shut with someone still alive inside. Because Trevor *was* alive. She knew he was. She could still feel the connection they had. "He's not dead," she said, reaching out a hand so Brad could help her up.

"If you say so," he replied, his voice carefully neutral.

It didn't take her years of training as a psychotherapist to tell he had other opinions about that.

"Change into something dry while you're in the house scaring up those books. No point in catching your death." He looked pointedly at her soaked clothing. "If I'm not done with the goats by the time you come back out here, you'll have to help. We can't leave that mess. It'll draw every predator within a fifty mile radius. And we can't waste all that meat."

Lara plodded dully toward the house. Her heart ached. *Whatever will I do without him?* Shivering, she remembered Elidora saying almost the exact same words when Gren disappeared. Feeling as if her insides were made of broken glass, jabbing every time she moved, she muttered, "I have to figure out how to get him back. There's got to be a way." The amulet tolled a gloomy dirge as she grasped a handrail.

It didn't take long to shuck her wet things. For once, she remembered to hang her discarded garments over something. Moving in a daze, she found herself back out in the yard, Gunter dancing next to her. He obviously didn't understand his daddy was missing.

Brad had brought Trevor's old Ford pickup around to the front yard, but he wasn't in it. She pulled open the passenger door and tossed her handbag and the books onto the seat. Thinking it would probably be easier if Gunter wasn't mucking about in the gore in the barn, she shooed him into the truck and closed the door.

She found Brad in the barn. He'd donned an old rubber apron Trevor found in the shop, and he had a saw in his hand. He half turned at the sound of her muted, "How can I help?"

"Get that hose we rigged up that brings water from the creek. I'm nearly done here and we'll need to sluice the place down."

"What are we going to do the preserve the meat?"

He turned to face her. "It won't be all that good since there's blood in it. Salvaged what I could, though. We need all the food we can get. Rinsed it in the rain barrel."

A flash of pain crossed his face, and Lara assumed he put too much weight on his bad leg. "Don't let me forget to empty the barrel. Won't be good for anything now. Anyway," he pointed to a pile of bloody goat flesh lying on a tarp in the wheelbarrow, "I got the smoker going out in the shop. We can toss the meat in before we leave."

Nodding numbly, she went to retrieve the hose.

A long time later, she and Brad clambered into the truck, stumbling over the dog, who greeted them effusively. The burn barrel —where they'd incinerated the inedible parts—was still smoldering, but Brad had deemed it didn't pose any danger to leave it that way with everything as wet as it was.

"Okay," she breathed wearily. "Let's see what's out there."

Brad just grunted, slipped the truck into gear, and for the first time since they'd arrived the previous November, they drove away from the house.

"Aw shit." Lara reached out a hand. "Go back. We need more money. There's not much in my purse."

"I got some before I started in with the goats. Two thousand bucks. Hope it'll be enough." After an awkward hesitation he added. "Uh, Trevor showed me where you guys keep your cash and stuff."

"It's okay, Brad. You don't need to apologize." She glanced at him. "We're in this together."

They drove in silence. Lara opened one of the books, searching for something, anything, she could do to get Trevor back from wherever the Goblins—assuming it was Goblins—had taken him. After reading a few pages, she turned to Brad. "No matter who took Trevor, Gradoxst is behind this. I just know he is."

"Seems logical," Brad grunted.

Lara set her mouth in a hard line. "He could be a poster child for delusions of grandeur. It's why he spent all those years at the Jung

Institute masquerading as an analyst. He may have sold his soul to the Demons, but in his secret places, he probably misses being a Sidhe."

"You're conjecturing."

"Yes, I am," she agreed. "But it fits."

"What does your theory have to do with him kidnapping Trevor?"

She shrugged. "I think it's a way to get back at me. I'm who he really wants, but I don't have a clue why that is." Brad didn't say anything further, so she went back to reading.

She was puzzling through a chapter she hadn't looked at before when the truck lurched off onto a side road. "What are you doing? We're not in town yet."

"We're close. Thought I'd run ahead and take a peek. No point driving into an ambush."

"Maybe I should go—" she began, but he shook his head.

"Nope. I'm taking the automatic rifle. You keep the shotgun. If you see anyone, shoot first and ask questions later." He slipped out of the car, yelping when he weighted his leg. "Goddamn it," he spat as he reached into the back for his gun and told Gunter to stay put.

Watching him limp away, Lara's jaw clenched. *Shoot first, huh? Jesus Christ, this is America. Since when did it become okay to shoot someone I've never even met before?* She remembered all Trevor's efforts to get her out of the city as oil supplies dwindled, power outages escalated, and food became scarce. There'd been two riots before they'd escaped that had left thousands dead, including Arabel, her well-loved friend and receptionist. Just as she was settling into a funk, Brad's lanky form came into view. He hauled himself into the cab and started the engine.

"Well?" she asked.

"Martial law. It'll be okay, I can flash my cop ID. If anyone asks— and they likely will—we're just passing through. Came from a little farm outside Monroe. We're driving you to your mother's in Idaho, since you're pregnant."

It never occurred to her that they'd need an alibi. Swallowing, she said, "Yeah, sure. Whatever you think will get us through this. Are we just going to keep driving east? If lots of law enforcement are out, won't they be watching us?"

"You're smart, Doctor." He gave her an appraising glance. "That's one of the things I've always liked about you. Yes, that's exactly what we're going to do. There's a spur road about a mile down that links back to this one. Found it when I was following you and Trevor after you first left Seattle. We will have to be careful, though. If anyone tries to tail us, we'll have to do something about it."

Yeah. Shoot first. Lara bit back her distaste for violence.

They crossed the bridge over the Skykomish River and parked. Lara eyed a posted, hand-painted sign with letters several inches high: *Only those with business in this town may stop. All others continue straight on through. Next fuel forty-five miles. THIS MEANS YOU.*

She was just getting out when a sheriff's car pulled up next to them. A short, squat, bald man, with a uniform that strained across his substantial abdomen, struggled out of his squad car. "Hold it right there, ma'am," he said.

Brad shoved his shield across the seat. "Show that to him, honey, will you?" Turning to a barking Gunter, he added, "Ssht. Be a good boy. You have to stay."

In the time it took Brad to work his way around the truck, the sheriff—Smoley according to his badge—had taken the detective shield from Lara and examined it. "You have photo ID to match this?" he asked brusquely.

"Of course." Smiling, Brad flashed his driver's license and another piece of police ID.

"Thanks, Detective." The sheriff shook Brad's hand. "What brings you to Skykomish?"

"Couple things. My wife's pregnant. It's just too unsettled in Seattle, so I thought I'd leave her with her family in Idaho, at least until the baby's born. And I, uh, had a bit of an accident. Need antibiotics."

"So you're just passing through?"

Brad nodded. "Took a week's leave from the force. Would've taken her," he jerked a thumb toward Lara, "a while back, but they couldn't spare me."

Sheriff Smoley inclined his head sympathetically. "Yeah, things are rough to the west. Where the two of you been living?"

"Outside Monroe," Lara offered. "We used to be in Seattle, but we had to leave."

Apparently deciding the two of them wouldn't threaten his little town, the sheriff holstered the gun he'd been holding. "Go ahead." He waved expansively. "Not much here, but the drug store probably has penicillin, and the market's still got a few things."

"Thanks." Brad shook Smoley's hand before limping toward the pharmacy half a block away. "Come on, honey," he called over one shoulder. "Be sure to lock the truck."

She caught up with him while he was talking animatedly with the pharmacist, an Asian with tired-looking eyes and a shock of straight, black hair. Brad had his pant leg rolled up, one foot balanced on a handy chair. "...couldn't find an MD," he told the pharmacist. "And I don't want to end up with osteomyelitis."

Clucking, the pharmacist poured pills into bottles. "Take this one four times a day." He handed Brad a bottle. "And this one twice. No alcohol—if you could even find the stuff, which I doubt." Turning, he consulted a well-thumbed notebook. "Let's see, that will be five hundred forty dollars."

Lara's eyes widened. "What?" she gasped. "Surely—"

Brad shot her a silencing look while counting out bills. "Say, you wouldn't happen to have any prenatal vitamins." He smiled winningly at the other man. "My wife's expecting."

The druggist brightened for the first time since they came into his store. "Certainly," he said. "Just a minute." Riffling through an open box, he pulled out a bottle. "There's a hundred pills, so three-and-a-half months' worth. How many?"

"How much?" Lara asked, still flabbergasted by what the antibiotics cost.

"I'll throw the first one in with the antibiotics. The second one will be forty bucks."

"We'll take two then," Brad announced, adding to the stack of bills next to the register. "How about some water so I can get a couple of these on board?"

Once they were out on the sidewalk, Lara said. "That was outrageous. Penicillin costs nothing. And if—"

"Quiet," he murmured. "If you say too much, anyone listening will figure we've been out of commission for a long time. Come on. Let's see what's in the store. Seems to me, we've got another fifteen hundred to spend."

They left the small store half an hour later. It turned out they had more than enough money, since the amounts people could buy were limited. Once they figured out the rationing system, they piled the maximum allowed into their cart. Despite her grief, Lara was practically salivating by the time they dropped just over a thousand dollars on the counter and left the store with eight bags of groceries. Pawing frantically through one the minute they got back to the truck, she pulled out an orange and tore the peeling off.

"Need to take the dog out," she said around a mouthful of fruit.

Brad shook his head. "No. What we need is to get out of town. Sheriff Smoley doesn't seem to be anywhere in sight. Neither is the other guy. I saw him when I did that reconnaissance at the front end of this. It's a good time to leave. We'll stop soon for Gunter."

They'd been driving for a while when she said, "Trevor predicted there'd be martial law—and rationing." She sighed, saddened beyond words by what had happened. "Wish I would've listened to him. Maybe if we'd left before I got tangled up with Gradoxst..."

Stop playing the what ifs. Her inner voice sounded sharp—and despondent. The amulet jabbed her. She felt like ripping it off her neck. What damned good did it do if it couldn't protect those she loved?

Brad cleared his throat. "I looked for a newspaper in the pharmacy and the store, but didn't see one."

"Funny," she mumbled, "so did I. Shelves in the pharmacy were all empty too. Everything he had was piled behind the counter. And did you notice? Both the pharmacy and the store had old-fashioned cash registers. No computers in sight."

"Guess that means no more Internet. At least not out here," he said thoughtfully. "Hmm. That looks like a good spot. I'm going to stop in that clearing." He pulled onto a side road and killed the engine.

The dog, who'd been uncharacteristically subdued for most of their trip, regained a bit of his exuberance as he ran from tree to tree sniffing. They herded him back into the truck after a short while and headed for home.

"You wanted to make sure no one followed us," she said shrewdly.

He glanced at her, his craggy features solemn. "Yes. That's the main reason I stopped. We've got enough in the way of troubles, Lara. No need to court new ones. I'm wondering just what we'll find when we get home. I spent most of the time you were reading trying to figure out why the hell Gradoxst snagged Trevor." He hesitated. "I don't totally buy your idea that he did it as a backhanded way to get to you. Why not just lay a trap for you and be done with it?"

"Because Trevor was the one who left the house," she said bitterly. "If it had been you or me, we'd be the ones in Gradoxst's personal hell right now."

"Did you try to raise the Sidhe?"

She shook her head. "That's not as easy as it seems. After we get back and I've eaten, I'll work on it."

"You've been eating ever since we got into the car," he pointed out.

She shot him a measured glance. "So have you. That's what happens to people who are half-starved when they finally get around food again."

"Touché, Doctor."

"You know," she murmured, "we were the only people in that town, other than the cop and shopkeepers."

"I noticed," he said dryly. "Struck me as passing strange. Guess they enforce that sign they have tacked up. I saw one every fifty feet or so

—on both sides of the street. And in the store, it said you could only shop once a month."

"Welcome to America." She grimaced. "Now go home."

Upstairs in her room, Lara rubbed the mounded lump of her growing belly. It wasn't really very big yet, but her body *was* different. No more waist and heavier breasts. For a moment she worried about the delivery if Elidora and Lillian couldn't be there, then she forced her mind away from that slippery slope. It wouldn't take much to slide back into the puddle of despair that had enveloped her earlier. The baby moved inside her, and she clasped both hands over her belly. "We'll get Daddy back, Elizabeth," she murmured. "We will. I promise."

Her thoughts turned to their evening's pig-out in the kitchen. She'd eaten oranges and crackers and cheese. Brad, who was almost as good a cook as Trevor, had prepared some tough little pork chops and fried up a skillet full of potatoes and onions. He'd taken two more of the antibiotics and they'd worked together to clean his wound, which looked a little better. After that, he'd headed outside to see how close to done the smoked goat meat was and check on the other animals.

It was cold in the room, but she tossed off her clothes anyway, perched on the bed, grasped the amulet, and called for Lillian. Skin pebbling into gooseflesh, she wished she knew how to raise Raven or the Sidhe without undressing. For a long while nothing happened. She was just about to give up and pull the warmth of the covers over herself, when Raven appeared, shimmering and insubstantial. Too preoccupied and heartsick to feel even marginally modest about her nakedness, she spat out what had happened to Trevor. Next she told him about Brad's ankle and that they'd gone into town. By the time she was done, she was weeping.

"Hold." Raven's voice was the barest of whispers. "I'm sorry we haven't been more help, daughter, but we are losing the *Dreaming*. Lillian, Elidora, and I are here, as are others. With all that, there are barely a hundred of us against, perhaps, a thousand Goblins led by Gradoxst. The civil unrest has strengthened them beyond what any of us expected. All that's left to us is the sacred cave where you met Brigid. We know they have Trevor. He's imprisoned here in one of their enclaves."

"He's alive," Lara broke in, gasping for air between sobs. "I knew it. I knew he wasn't dead."

"He will be if we can't turn the tide." Raven's form wavered.

"Wait." She extended her hands, pleading. "Don't go yet. How can I help him?"

"Be strong." She heard his voice in her head. "If we all but believe, the goddess will help us find a way. And Lara…"

But he was gone. If there were any last exhortations, she didn't hear them.

CHAPTER 4

$\mathcal{L}$ara reached through a sticky, opaque barrier. Just on the other side, Trevor thrust a hand toward her too. "Just a little more, dear," she urged. "We can get you out."

"It's a dream, Lara." Trevor's voice was gentle. "He told me he'd lure you here in your dreams. You have to wake up, love. You must leave. If you spend too much time with me, he'll have you as well."

"No," she protested, fighting panic. "I found you. Psyche led me here. Just reach for me." Her voice broke. Try as she might, she couldn't touch him. She gritted her teeth and pushed for all she was worth against the spider-webby strands. Her hands bled, leaving crimson streaks on the barrier.

"Lara." Trevor's voice was harsher this time. "You have to wake up. You can't stay here. If you do all will be lost. He wants you and Elizabeth. All I am is bait."

That got her attention. Lara pulled her hands to her sides, blood running warm down her fingers. "Gradoxst?"

"Yes. Him and others."

"I love you. I'll figure out a way to get you out of there."

"I love you too, Lara. Now do whatever you do in your visions to get back to where you started." He turned away from her. Chains looped around both his ankles, and he was shackled to metal hoops embedded in a rock wall.

Reluctantly, she envisioned their bedroom. At first nothing happened. She still stood outside Trevor's prison looking in. Nerves jangling, she tried again. Harder this time. Finally, mist rose about her, and she felt as if she were falling.

Lara came back into herself curled in a tangle of sheets and the comforter, shaking with cold. Gunter, who always slept in their room, jumped on her, licking frantically at her face.

Was I dreaming? Did my body go along for the dream ride? Is that why the dog's so upset?

"It's okay," she crooned to Gunter. "I sure wish you could talk." As she unsnarled herself from the welter of bedcovers, she examined the backs of her hands in moonlight streaming through the second story windows. Long, red welts ran down them extending halfway to her elbows. Blood dripped slowly onto the sheets.

"Guess that answers one question," she muttered, shaken. "My body went with me." She stared at the pool of moonlight. "Artemis," she called, feeling foolish but plowing ahead anyway, "Trevor's been captured by Goblins. You have to help me get him back." The moonlight shimmered oddly, and hope speared through her.

She heard me. She must have.

Or else a cloud floated past, in front of the moon, her cynical side noted.

Stumbling from the bed, confused and not knowing what to think, she threw on a robe, went into the nearby bathroom, and ran cold water into the basin. Sometimes the gravity feed system froze, but not tonight. Using the amulet for assistance, she warmed the water and washed her abraded arms with soap.

A gentle tap rattled the door. "You okay, Lara?" Brad's deep voice was actually welcome.

"Yeah. Be out in a minute."

When she opened the door, he was leaning against the wall,

favoring his bad leg. "Did I wake you?" she asked, tugging her robe more firmly around her.

"Dog did. At first he was whining and barking. I got up and knocked, but you didn't answer. I took a chance and pushed your door open, but you, uh weren't here." He shrugged, but his forehead was creased with concern. "Haven't slept at all since then. Not that it's any of my business, but where were you?"

Lara walked back into her bedroom and glanced out the window. The moonlight had faded and the sky was beginning to lighten. "It's nearly dawn. Want to talk about this over a cup of coffee?"

He nodded. "I'm already dressed. I'll go down and get it going."

By the time breakfast was over, she'd told him about her talk with Raven and her dream voyage to Trevor's prison. Setting down her coffee cup, she said, "That's about all. But there's got to be *something* we can do. I even asked Artemis for help when moonlight filtered into the room." She laughed uncomfortably.

"Humph." Brad snorted, making almost exactly the same sound Trevor often did. "That's quite a tale there, Doctor. You must be exhausted."

"Now that you pointed it out," she said sourly, "I am. Thanks. Not that it matters, there're things to be done. Just like every day. At least it's not raining." Realization dawned that he'd been worried about her and she softened her tone. "How's your leg?"

"Better, I think. Doesn't hurt quite as much when I walk on it."

"Did he give you enough pills? I meant to ask yesterday, but why'd he turn loose of them without a prescription?"

"I think he gave me a full course of both antibiotics. Before you got there, he told me the town's only doc had been killed by vandals who thought he had drugs in his clinic. That's when they put up all those signs, and law enforcement began patrolling so rigorously."

"Mmph." She narrowed her eyes. "Too bad they know who we are. If we'd known they still had food, we could've concocted a different story. Like we were planning on settling on the outskirts of town or something."

"Wouldn't have mattered."

"Why not?" She got up to get the coffee pot. Bringing it back to the table, she shook the pot in his direction, and he raised his cup for a refill.

"Shopping is only allowed once a month."

"Oh yeah, I'd forgotten that part. It's still better than nothing," she pointed out. "It'll take another couple months before we can even start to grow anything. Much less have something we could harvest."

He cleared his throat. "I did some thinking last night. You need time—uninterrupted time—to work on your magic." She opened her mouth to protest, but he waved her to silence. "No, Lara, let me finish. I can milk goats and gather eggs and do all the cooking. I can also finish up with the seed project Trevor had going out in the shop and take care of the animals. The most important thing is developing a plan to get him back. We need your magic to do that. I can't help you directly, but I can clear the decks to give you time."

She felt the burning prick of tears behind her eyelids. When she looked at him, her eyes welled over. "Thanks, Brad," she said softly. "I'll start right now if it's all right with you." The amulet's excited hum told her it approved.

"Of course," he said gruffly. "That's why I offered. No time to waste, really. Looks like you'll also have to figure out something so you don't get sucked into the *Dreaming* every night. That's where Raven said Trevor was, didn't he?"

"Yes." She ground out the word. "Clever of Gradoxst. He must know the moonstone in my amulet was mined in the *Dreaming*. It wants to go back there. Makes it pretty easy for him to draw me through the dream portal, body and soul."

"Yeah, I thought about that too, though not in exactly the same light." He hesitated. "Uh, don't take this wrong, but I think it would be better if I slept near you. That way I can keep hold of you with a length of rope or something." He blushed and stammered slightly. "At least we can make sure your body stays here."

She drew back, staring at him. "If that's some sort of ill-timed proposition," she began angrily and then shook her head. "Ach, Brad, don't mind me. I know you're just trying to protect me. We can talk more about it tonight. Right now I'm going to take advantage of the time you've offered to see if I can't learn something."

She pushed herself up from the table. Gunter, who was used to her morning ritual, got up too, heading for the kitchen door, tail wagging happily.

"I'll take him out," Brad said, looking at her with worried eyes. "You run along."

~

As MUCH AS a week might have passed. She wasn't sure. Brad brought her food. He found a long piece of rope in one of the outbuildings and fashioned a tether he tied around her wrist at night. The first night, he'd slept on the floor with the other end wrapped around his waist. After that, she told him to drag one of the other beds into the room so he could be comfortable. Anyway, the rope was working. There'd been dreams, but no more corporeal trips to the *Dreaming*.

Her dreams were frightening, though. They took her to Trevor almost every night. But since she wasn't really *there*, he thought the sound of her voice was a hallucination and refused to talk to her. The most painful part was watching him fade. Every night he looked a little more worn, his dear face pale and sunken-in, his shoulders slumped in defeat. One night, there were fresh bruises on one cheek, and she wondered what he'd done to raise Gradoxst's ire. She tried to ask, tried to tell him she loved him, but he began to cry, and it broke her heart.

After teaching herself some basic defensive moves, which drew heat from the Earth to chuck at adversaries, Lara found a part in one of Raven's books that taught acolytes how to project either their minds or their bodies—or both—over long distances. Since she'd need to master that skill to have any hope of getting Trevor back, she'd worked on it for the past several days, but hadn't made much progress.

"Goddammit!" Reaching for the closest thing she could find, she lobbed it at the wall. The crystal pitcher shattered on impact. Lara winced, her anger at the universe replaced by disgust with herself. As she tromped to the hearth to get a dustbin and brush to sweep up her mess, she forced herself to take a few deep breaths.

Trying to learn magic without the Sidhe as mentors was hard. Not impossible, but deucedly difficult, as Trevor would have said. She smiled sadly at the thought of him and vowed to try harder. The amulet had developed a different note throughout her efforts—almost as if it were urging her on. It wasn't happy about her fall from grace with the pitcher, though. And its current tone dripped censure.

She laid down the dustbin and gripped the amulet. *If you know how to help me with this, for Christ's sake do something other than hum.*

But the amulet was silent, and an image of Trevor's wasted face rose before her. "I have to figure out how to do this," she muttered. Blowing out a frustrated breath, she picked up the book once again, trying to discover what she was doing wrong.

Three more failed attempts later, Lara forced herself to stop and think about the words on the page in front of her, reading through the instructions for what felt like the hundredth time. They hadn't changed. And she was doing exactly what they said. What the hell was wrong? Why wasn't the spell working for her?

Is it because I'm a blend of human and Sidhe? This was written by the Sidhe. Maybe it only works for them.

She lurched to her feet, pacing up and down the well-appointed library. As she glanced at the spines of Raven's books, she got an idea and hunkered down to read their titles. She'd just settled in with a couple she thought might help when Brad knocked softly on the library door. "You may as well come on in," she called out. "I'm not much closer than I was a week ago."

The second he pushed the door open, Gunter raced in, propelling himself into her lap. Trevor had been gone for long enough that the dog was clearly worried about the whereabouts of his human pack members. He licked her chin and whined while she buried her hands in his fur, trying to soothe him.

"Yes, little one, Momma's here. Sorry I haven't been better company, but I'm trying to get Daddy back—for all of us."

"Any luck?" Brad looked at her, his blue eyes sad.

She shook her head. "No, but I'm trying something different. There're some other books that might give me a new angle on getting to the *Dreaming*."

"Do you suppose I could come too?"

The question was so unexpected, she didn't know what to say. After an awkward pause, she murmured, "Uh, I'm not sure. The Sidhe took me there, but I'm part of whatever they are. I have no idea if you could come."

"Trevor's there."

"Uh-huh, and he looks worse every time I see him."

"Yes," Brad agreed. "But we wouldn't be staying. We'd only be there long enough to extricate him."

Watching Brad, it was apparent he'd spent quite a bit of time thinking about his proposal. His shoulders held a stubborn set she'd come to recognize. It had been there when he'd argued with Trevor about taking the time to insert silver into all their ammunition. After one particularly heated exchange, Brad ignored Trevor's protests and moved forward to design a primitive kiln so he could melt some badly tarnished, antique silver pieces they'd discovered hidden away in one of the outbuildings. He'd made silver pellets, painstakingly inserting them into each shell. Lara wasn't quite sure how he sealed off the hole so it wouldn't disgorge the pellet before the bullet hit its target, but he'd been satisfied with the end product.

She'd asked Raven about the silver in the house, particularly since she'd thought iron should be their undoing. He'd looked at her as if she were a rather dim-witted child, while explaining, "We can coexist with silver in the same room so long as we're not deranged enough to actually *touch* it."

Lara drew her brows together into a thin, troubled line. She missed Raven and wished he was with them, not fighting Demons a million psychic miles away.

When she looked at Brad again, her expression grew serious. "I'm not even sure I can get *myself* there, and then Trevor and me back," she said quietly. "My magic's not all that strong. You'd be taking a chance."

"I'll risk it," he said gruffly.

Lara stroked the dog who'd curled up on her lap. He'd grown so fast he didn't exactly fit, but it was obviously important to him to be as close to her as he could. "What about him?" She pointed at Gunter.

"He can hunt. He'd be fine for a while."

"Yes, but what if we, uh, couldn't come back?"

"He'll either find himself another family or try to hook up with the wolves I've seen nosing around from time to time."

"They'd eat him."

Brad shook his head in exasperation. "We can't cover every eventuality. If we don't come back here, your child will probably lose her chance at life too."

She winced. What he said was true, but it was excruciating to hear. For a moment, she wondered if she should risk Elizabeth's life trying to rescue Trevor. She thought about the realities of trying to deliver her child without the Sidhe there to help. Focusing her gaze on Brad, she asked, "Have you ever delivered a baby?"

A ghost of a smile crossed his austere features. "Now that you mention it, yes. Five to be precise. But they were straightforward births. If you're asking because you're worried Elidora won't be able to get back here for you, the answer's more complicated." He coughed and cleared his throat. "So long as nothing goes wrong, I think I can handle things. But if the baby isn't turned properly, or doesn't drop into the birth canal… I'm far from a trained midwife, and we don't have even rudimentary medical instruments."

"I could die."

"Yes," he said simply. "You could."

She glanced at her hands, wound in the dog's thick, winter coat. "That makes this easier. I have to figure out a way to get Trev back. If you want to come along to help, well, that's fine by me."

"What made you change your mind about me coming?" His husky voice held an undercurrent of curiosity.

"Life." She let go of the dog and spread her hands in front of her. "There aren't any guarantees. I could play it safe, settle in with you…" She eyed him. "Don't say anything. You and I both know that's likely what would happen if Trevor never came back. Oh, it would be gradual, but we'd eventually find comfort in one another. That's how these things tend to work."

A sad sigh escaped before she went on. "But that's the easy path. And I'm not going to do that. I love Trevor. He's the only man I've ever loved and, if what Raven and the Sidhe say is true, we're bound to one another at some karmic level. So I'm going to chance it and do my damnedest to go after him. Even if it means my life—and the life of our child. That's my path, and I see it clearly before me. It's not necessarily yours, though."

"I know that," he interrupted. "But you and Trevor—" His voice cracked with barely suppressed emotion. "You're the closest thing I have to family, especially now that Adriana's gone. I wouldn't feel right sending you off alone to whatever you'll find in that hellish Goblin stronghold. I know it means leaving Gunter to an uncertain fate." Hearing his name, the dog looked up and woofed softly at Brad. "But I've made my decision." The detective folded his arms across his chest. "Besides, Elidora's there. Maybe I can help her too."

Lara's lips curved into a soft smile. "Thanks, Brad."

"No thanks necessary. I owe you. Remember, I sold you out to Gradoxst."

"Yes, but you didn't truly know what you were doing."

"Well, I should have. Case closed." He stood to leave. "I'll give you some time with those new books. While you're at it, try to pick up some of those defensive maneuvers where the Sidhe gather power and lob it with their hands."

She furled her brows. "Been there. Done that. That part, at least, was easy. Figured I ought to do that first, in case I fell into the *Dreaming* by mistake as I worked on how to get myself there."

"Smart cookie." He grinned approvingly, then headed out the door, clucking for the dog. Gunter just looked at him.

"It's okay," she said. "All I'm doing is reading. He can stay with me."

Almost as if the Shepherd understood, he thumped his tail against her leg.

"I'll bring your supper in a couple hours."

"No need," she said. "I'll come down. And Brad?"

He turned to face her. "Uh-huh?"

"How's your leg? Don't think I've asked about it in days."

"It's healing. Still quite stiff, but the wound doesn't look infected anymore."

"Any clues about who set that trap?"

"Nope. But then I've stayed pretty close to home. Got to work on dinner." He pulled the door closed behind him.

As it snicked shut, she pried one of Raven's books out from under Gunter and scanned the table of contents. Finding something that looked promising, she turned to the indicated page. As she read, her breath caught in her throat.

Yes. That's probably what's missing. If I mingle this incantation with the one in the other book, I should have it!

CHAPTER 5

*T*revor wrapped his arms around himself to fend off the chill in his cell. Uneven gray stones lined the walls. The floor was made of stones too, but accumulated filth covered them to a depth of several inches. Water tricked down the walls, lending a dankness to the stale air. If he was going to die, Trevor wished heartily it had happened in his barn, surrounded by familiar things.

He used his pocketknife to saw at his shackles. For some unknown reason, the Goblins hadn't bothered to search him. Lazy, manky blighters. His cracked lips split into a bitter smile. He'd figured out he was in the Dreaming from eavesdropping on the guards. Their language was a perversion of Celtic Gaelic and, after an initial period of confusion, he found he could interpret it. He thought the Sidhe might be close by from what Elidora had told him before she left that last time. If he could just free himself, maybe there'd be some hope of throwing in his lot with them.

Assuming he could find them before the Goblins hunted him down.

For about the thousandth time, his mind replayed how he'd waltzed into Gradoxst's trap like a brain-damaged sheep. He was grateful Lara hadn't been the one ensnared, but he felt foolish just the same. "Should've known better," he muttered, as he continued to hack at whatever alloy held him to the wall. Fortunately it was soft. Weak as he was, he was making reasonable progress. One leg was all but free and the other halfway there.

The downside was most of the silver had chipped off the stainless steel blade of his knife. He'd been careful to gather up the chips and shards, wrapping them diligently in his handkerchief. It was possible he could figure out a way to use them against his captors. He had so little at his disposal, the idea of overlooking even the slightest advantage was unthinkable. Even though he'd given Brad a raft of shit about his silver project, he felt grateful now. If he ever escaped from this hellhole, he'd make a point of thanking the detective.

His thoughts turned to Lara. After that first night where she'd visited his prison in corporeal form, he hadn't encouraged further contact. Gradoxst had been quite clear Lara was the one he wanted. Somehow, the ancient Sidhe-turned-Demon knew she was pregnant and, for some perverted reason, it thrilled him. Trevor shuddered, chills cascading down his wasted frame. He bit his lower lip in frustration, tasting blood.

Still fixated on Lara, his heart ached. She needed him. And he needed her. He was frantic she'd try to use her half-baked magic and end up getting caught herself. *I'll just have to get myself out of here before she puts herself at risk.* Another inner voice piped up challenging him, telling him he needed some bloody *ideas*, goddammit, before he could do much of anything.

Heavy footsteps pounded his way, making his head snap up as he listened intently.

"Bloody fuck!" He pulled his blade back. The expletive was muted, but he quickly shoved his knife into the pocket where he kept it hidden, scanning the floor for silver chips, while listening for the guards. He picked up three gleaming silver shards, his senses on high alert. Sticking his leg out to one side, he saw blood running down his ankle. He swiped at it with filthy fingers, then wiped them on his grimy pants. Trevor began to breathe again when the footsteps passed his cell, and he heard the guards still chattering away to one another. His jaw clenched at how cheerful they sounded.

Like the seven fucking dwarfs in Snow White.

He blew out an irritated breath, flexed his ankle to ease the pain, and carefully added the silver to a respectable pile in his handkerchief. Bending to inspect the shackle he'd been working on, a wide grin split his face. His chapped lips hurt, but he couldn't stop smiling. When he licked them he tasted blood. It didn't dilute his joy one whit.

"Got it," he breathed. Both ankles could be freed with a quick twist. Lurching carefully to his feet, he shuffled to the bucket they'd left for him and pissed into it. He was trying to drink enough to pee at least a couple times a day. But he also wanted to test the shackles to make sure they didn't fall off his legs when he moved. He wished they hadn't taken his boots. The floor was cold. Disgusting feeling debris slithered around his feet whenever he walked and squished between his toes. He'd stopped thinking about what might be in it early on.

Satisfied he could maintain the illusion of still being chained to the wall, he went back to the bench—that doubled as a cot—and tried to hatch up a plan while he examined his feet, picking crudlets from his trip to the pee bucket out of them. His inner voice was right. He needed something more cohesive than the incoherent thoughts of escape rambling about in his brain.

His guards were mostly drunk at night. They'd even offered him some of their disgusting swill when they got into their cups. That would be the time to escape—when their heads were muddled. *If I can get out of here, how will I find the Sidhe? What if I'm wrong and they're not nearby?* His empty stomach cramped. Sitting in the Goblins' prison rotting until he starved wasn't an option. He had to do something while he still had some strength left.

Once he'd figured out their language, eavesdropping on his guards had yielded unexpected amounts of information. He'd found out Goblins were but one type of Demon. Imps, Djinns, Wiricows, Shape Shifters, and a host of others with unpronounceable names rounded out the group.

Not surprisingly, Demon species mostly hated one another. Apparently, the Goblins and some of the Shape Shifters had formed an uneasy alliance, lured by the promise of rich mining opportunities in the *Dreaming*. Gradoxst had told his allies it would be an easy victory. As the Sidhe hadn't proven especially cooperative in that regard, dissention was rippling through the Demon ranks. The guards outside his cell even talked about letting him go to show Gradoxst what they thought of his empty promises. Trevor racked his brain trying to figure out how he might spin that knowledge to his advantage. It was hard to think. He felt dizzy and nauseous.

He glanced at the cracked and broken bowl that held the last meal they'd brought him. It didn't smell quite as bad cold as it did warm. And it was the same fare the guards ate, since the odor permeated everything, including them when they got close enough for him to smell them, which was at about fifty paces. He snorted. Goblins stank. The whole place reeked of them. It was sort of a decomposing garbage smell reminiscent of urban rot in large cities in third world countries: excrement mixed with putrid sweat from long-unwashed bodies, with overtones of decaying vegetation.

Understanding he needed nourishment to come up with a plan, Trevor picked up the bowl, not examining its contents too closely. He fished out a chunk of something, popped it into his mouth and chewed minimally—just enough to get it into shape to swallow. Then he followed it with another. He made the mistake of looking at the next piece. It was a rat's tail.

Aw Jesus, I'm eating rat.

For a moment, he thought he was going to puke. He forced himself to breathe through his mouth—shallow, panting breaths.

"Keep it down," he muttered, "else this will have been for naught." It took a few minutes, but his nausea passed. He put the tail back in the bowl, opting for something less recognizable. *It's just protein,* he reminded himself. *Something I need.*

At first, he'd wondered why Gradoxst hadn't killed him outright. The fallen Sidhe clarified that before dumping him in his cell. "You are an enticement," he'd said in a patronizing tone. "Your lovely wife and that delectable child-to-be are who I want. *They* have power I can use."

Trevor wasn't under any illusions. Once the Demon had Lara, his own lifespan would likely be measured in seconds. Anger, born of helplessness, churned through him. He forced himself to keep eating

The bowl was empty except for the rat tail. Trevor reached for the water jug and swallowed. "There," he croaked. "Not so bad as all that." His stomach hurt, but he tried to convince his brain it was because he hadn't eaten in the days since his capture, not because he'd just consumed poison. He'd find out soon enough which it was.

When a span of time had passed, he breathed a sigh of relief. His stomach had subsided. If the food was tainted, at least it was a slow-acting substance. He didn't actually think the Goblins were smart enough as a group to concoct something as subtle as arsenic. Gradoxst was, but insofar as Trevor had seen, his captor had his hands full masterminding the current campaign to corrupt the *Dreaming* and wrest it from the Sidhe.

Gradoxst was enough of a bully, he'd have returned to Trevor's cell to taunt him if the wily old bastard could've freed up the time.

So they have limits too, he thought to himself. There's got to be a way I can capitalize on that.

His eyelids were heavy, so he took a chance and let them fall. He'd been worried at first that the Goblins would do unspeakable things to him in his sleep, but they seemed less interested in him than they would have been in, well, in practically anything. Their conversation was rarely about him, except for the brief exchange about letting him go. Mostly they talked about the too-slow-for-their-liking progress ousting the Sidhe. From what Trevor could tell, his friends were holed up in some sort of sacred cave.

Must be the heart of the Dreaming that Lara told me about, he decided just before sleep took him.

"*Son.*" Raven's voice sounded in Trevor's mind.

Thinking it was part of a jumbled dream, Trevor clung

tenaciously to badly needed rest. He lay on his side, shackled feet drawn up so his knees curled against his chest. During the little sleep he'd gotten, this felt like by far the most defensible position. One hand rested atop his knife hilt. The other one was stuffed into the jacket pocket where the silver chips were, in case he needed to chuck them at a Goblin's face.

"Trevor!" Raven's voice held a stern note.

Remembering that tone, Trevor let go of the wisps of his dream and blearily said, "What?"

"No. Do not answer me aloud. Simply thinking will do it."

Finally understanding Raven was actually talking to him, Trevor's eyes flew open. His heart rattled against his ribs. *"Okay,"* he agreed cautiously. *"Where are you?"*

"Not far. Is Lara all right?"

"Uh, yes. Far as I know, she's fine." Trevor struggled to clear his sleep-fuzzed brain. *"But she's going to try to get me out of here."*

"Yes, we know that," the mage interrupted with a return of the high-handed manner Trevor recalled all too well.

"So go to her and tell her not to." As he thought about it, that seemed by far the simplest solution. That way he could take his time figuring out how to escape.

"Would that it were so straightforward." The mage hesitated. *"I cannot leave here until there is some conclusion. Depending on the outcome, I may not be able to leave at all."*

"Can't you go to her in a vision or something?"

"I can if she summons me. So far, she's only done that once, right after your capture. While I knew you were here, I've been too busy fighting those infernal Goblins and Shape Shifters to reassure you that we were close." Raven made a sound somewhere between a growl and a snort. *"Sorry I wasn't a bit quicker."*

"I figured out where I was from listening to the Goblins." Trevor hesitated, then persisted doggedly, still worried sick about Lara. *"You're in my mind. I don't understand why you can't be in hers."*

"Because you're very close and she's not." Raven's voice held an

undercurrent of irritation. The mage wasn't overly fond of answering questions, so Trevor switched to a more neutral topic.

"The others?" Trevor asked. *"Lillian and Elidora?"*

"Here with me. As are others you have not yet met. As usual, you're wasting time asking questions that aren't important."

Trevor waited. Raven had contacted him. That must mean he wanted something or had some purpose. Trevor had never known the mage to do anything that wasn't well thought out.

"How are you bound?" Raven asked after a lengthy pause.

"Uh, I'm not. At least not by what I couldn't break easily."

Raven inhaled sharply. *"That is good news, human. It simplifies things greatly."*

No more words were forthcoming. Trevor waited. He tried calling for Raven in his mind. He even called softly for him aloud to no avail. "Was it a hallucination?" he muttered. "Did I imagine all that because I want out of here so badly?"

As he mulled the conversation over and over in his mind, Trevor decided it couldn't have been anything but real. *What should I do? Should I wait until he contacts me again, or should I figure out how to get myself out of here? Maybe if I can get out of this building, or cave or wherever it is they're holding me, he'll be able to help me.*

Though he was exhausted, Trevor wasn't the least bit sleepy. Repositioning himself so he was sitting up, he continued to work on the conundrum of his escape.

"Human!" The rough tones of a Goblin trying to speak English, grated against his ears.

"What?" Trevor shrank back against the wall, trying to sound terrified. It wasn't difficult, since he was frightened of his captors, though not as much as he'd been initially.

"We been knocking. Bowl."

Was I so lost in thought I didn't hear?

"Sure. Here." Picking up his dish, Trevor got up, walked the few feet that spanned his cell and pushed the bowl through the hole near the bottom of the thick wooden door.

"You eat." Surprise was apparent even through the Goblin's thick accent.

"Is that a problem?" Trevor asked, but all he heard was the clomp of heavy boots moving away from his door. Footsteps returned soon enough with another steaming dish of the slop that passed for food. It smelled so bad, Trevor's eyes began to water, and he shuffled back to his bunk to get as far away from the door as possible.

He'd just drifted off again, hoping against hope for further contact from Raven when the door of his cell opened abruptly, hitting the food bowl. Its foul contents splattered all over the floor.

"Not a problem. We will get you more." The Swiss-German accent of Gradoxst's cultured voice raked across Trevor's nerves. Had the Demon somehow discovered Raven had contacted him? Trevor recoiled against the cold, damp wall behind his bunk, heart racing.

Gradoxst kicked the food dish out beyond the cell door, shouting in Goblin speech. Though he kept his face studiedly neutral, Trevor understood Gradoxst was calling for someone to mop up the spilled stew and get more.

A Goblin materialized within seconds and asked why they couldn't just scoop the shit off the floor, put it back in the bowl, and give it to Trevor. Gradoxst backhanded him. The Goblin muttered curses as he bent to retrieve the bowl.

Dressed in an old-fashioned black linen suit, Gradoxst looked like a tall, stoop-shouldered, nineteenth century European gentleman out for a stroll in the countryside. His white hair curled gently next to his face, and a cunning intelligence shone from shrewd, dark eyes.

"We shall have more for you in just a moment," he said in Celtic Gaelic.

Trevor tried to look bemused. "Ah, what?" he asked in English.

"Vielleicht möchten Sie lieber Deutsch sprechen?"

"Ja, Sie haben Recht. Ich kann Deutsch," Trevor replied, thinking it best to not totally underplay his facility with languages, since Gradoxst clearly knew he spoke more than just English.

"Enough of this little game." Gradoxst switched to his accented English. "Tell me, how are you liking your stay with us so far?"

He's got to be joking. "Um, fine," Trevor muttered, trying to figure out what Gradoxst was up to.

"Food is acceptable? Bed not too hard?"

Trevor felt the other man's eyes rake over him. *What the bloody blazes is he doing?* "You know perfectly well the food is crap," Trevor replied crisply. "Since when are wooden slats anything other than hard?" He rapped with one knuckle on the bench that also served as his bed.

"We have not managed to quell that spirit of yours. Good." Gradoxst produced a parody of a smile, displaying yellowed, uneven teeth.

Trevor waited. If ever there were a game of cat and mouse, this was it. Except he wasn't overly fond of playing the mouse. The rancid food from earlier congealed into a greasy mass in his stomach. His breath came faster. Sweat gathered in his armpits, and he smelled his own fear.

"I find," Gradoxst purred after several minutes had passed, "that I miss, shall we say, cultured company. I believe I would find it entertaining to move you into my quarters. You could serve me. As a former flight attendant, I suspect you would have a delightful savoir-faire. These military types," he rolled his eyes in a grotesque gesture, "simply do not understand the meaning of gracious living." He furled snow-white eyebrows at Trevor. "The view from my rooms is much better. And you might find the food more to your liking."

Trevor looked at his hands, laced together in his lap. This had to be some sort of trap. Did Gradoxst want him closer because he knew about Raven? Could he possibly know about the close-to-severed shackles?

Never mind all that. This could be my chance to make a break for it. Tell him yes.

Looking up, Trevor found the rogue Sidhe's gaze fixed on him. Were there any vestiges of Sidhe magic left that hadn't been perverted? He tried to look past the cunning gleam in Gradoxst's ancient eyes, but gave it up for wasted effort.

Since he hadn't managed to come up with a credible plan to escape from his cell, Trevor sucked in a desperate breath and nodded slowly. "Okay."

"Glorious, perfectly glorious." Gradoxst crossed the cell and clapped a hand on Trevor's shoulder. He wrinkled his patrician nose. "My, you are a bit on the odiferous side. But that's easily fixed. You can bathe in the stream outside my quarters."

Has he gone mad? "Even in my current condition," Trevor tried to maintain his dignity, "I smell far better than those odious creatures out there." He waved a hand toward the open cell door.

"Really?" Gradoxst's voice held an odd note. "I had not noticed." Removing his avuncular hand from Trevor's shoulder, he casually hauled back and slapped him across the face. "I prefer inferiors who do not have opinions."

Trevor laid a hand over his stinging cheek. "I'll do my best to remember that, *sir*," he said, his British accent very clipped. *Aw shit, what have I gotten myself into?* For the briefest of moments, he considered telling Gradoxst to take his offer and shove it up his arse— and then he stopped. There was no way out of his current prison. If there were, he'd have come up with it long since. Maybe there'd be more of an opportunity to escape in what the Demon was offering. There'd almost have to be, if he was going to serve, and serve effectively.

"Ich werde in Kürze nach Ihnen schicken lassen." Gradoxst turned abruptly on his heel and left Trevor's cell, pulling the door shut behind him with an unsettling thud.

"So you'll send someone for me presently, will you?" Trevor inquired sarcastically to the air in his cell. He remembered his leg irons and grimaced. What punishment lay in store once that transgression was discovered?

CHAPTER 6

"**O**kay, sweetie. You've got to get down."

Gunter craned his neck around and looked at her. Seemingly understanding, with the uncanny intuition common to his breed, the young Shepherd hopped down, stretching out his legs one at a time once he was back on the floor. He padded to the door, whining softly.

She quirked an eyebrow. "Hmm…now you're psychic too? Guess you know Momma's got more work to do." Unkinking her legs, she got up, opened the door, and smiled softly as the dog headed for the stairs. She took a measured breath. Light was fading from the day.

"I'll just try this once," she promised herself. "Then I'll go down to dinner."

Lara grasped the amulet, pleading for assistance. She was afraid if Trevor stayed with the Goblins much longer he'd pass beyond whatever assistance she could offer. The moonstone thrummed in her hand, apparently as keyed up as she was. Except she was apprehensive. No telling how the stone was feeling. Or if it had feelings at all.

She took a next-to-final look at the instructions in the new book. She'd walked through the original incantation so many times, she had that one memorized. It was just a matter of slotting in a few new steps, interspersed with those she knew so well. *Maybe I should go down and tell Brad what I'm doing.* She shook her head impatiently. "I'm scared," she muttered. "That's the main problem. I'm afraid it will work and I won't be able to control where I go or if I can come back."

Lara whispered some words as she flipped to another page in the book. At least according to this author's views of magic, those words should be enough to bring her back to where she'd begun.

"Okay," she said, her mouth drawn into a tight line. "Here we go." She began to chant. No one was more surprised than she when the familiar walls of the library wavered and started to fade. A fine mist rose about her. Despite an almost desperate exhortation from the amulet, Lara spoke the words to stop her spell, and the room solidified around her, mist fading into shadows.

"It worked," she gasped, falling into a nearby chair, weak-kneed. *Yes,* her inner voice agreed. *It did. And I managed to stop it too. But maybe that's because it had barely gotten started.*

"Never mind," she said. "This is the closest I've managed to come. I'll take it. I'm going downstairs to find Brad. This means we can go after Trev. Maybe even tonight." The amulet, which had begun chiding her the second she aborted her spell, subsided after her last comment. With a light heart, she glanced out the two big windows that looked over the front yard. Rays from the setting sun bounced off still-damp vegetation, iridescent and welcoming.

"Maybe this will work better than I think," she murmured, borrowing a phrase that was one of Trevor's favorites. Of the two of them, he'd been by far the most optimistic.

The dog greeted her at the bottom of the stairs. She stopped to pet him, then went hunting for Brad. Since the first floor was one large room, it was instantly apparent he wasn't inside. It was milking time. He could be with the goats or busy with a myriad of other things that always needed doing out of doors.

Passing through the kitchen, she lifted the lids on a couple pots to taste and stir. While lacking Trevor's gourmet flair, Brad did a more-than-credible job in the kitchen. He'd told her that his wife, Barbara, stopped cooking for him about the time she'd taken up with other men. Laughing wryly, he relayed that he'd taught himself to cook in self-defense, as well as to make sure his young daughter, Adriana, had enough to eat. After another spoonful of a hominy-esque stew, she snugged into her cloak and let herself out the back door, inviting Gunter to come along.

Lara cupped her hands around her mouth. "Brad," she called out. "Brad, where are you?" He didn't answer. Anxiety rose quickly. Suddenly tight muscles pulled her neck and shoulders painfully straight. Racing from one outbuilding to the next, she felt worse and worse when his familiar form didn't crawl out from under a piece of machinery. Too late, she realized she'd trampled over any boot prints she might've followed. When she stopped to catch her breath and think where he might have gone, the baby squirmed within her. After that first quickening, Elizabeth made her presence known on a regular basis.

This is just like looking for Trevor, an unpleasant inner voice intoned.

"Oh, no, it's not," she answered back tartly. "For one thing, there're no dead animals."

She eyed the westering sun, estimating that perhaps another hour of daylight remained. Lara considered going to look for Brad, but didn't think she'd be successful the way she'd been locating Trevor. She had a bond with him that didn't exist between her and the detective. Disconsolate and riding herd on burgeoning worry souring her stomach, Lara trudged back into the house. She damped the fire under Brad's dinner, telling herself he'd surely be back soon. He wouldn't have left all that food to boil away to nothing.

When she couldn't think of anything else to do, she sat heavily at the table. A note in Brad's neat script was balanced against an empty wine bottle.

Lara, There have been some odd things coming too close to the house for comfort. I've gone to investigate. Not sure, but there may be a link to that trap I stumbled into. Should be back before dark. Brad. P.S. Probably better if you lock up and keep the dog inside with you.

The note hadn't been too upsetting—until she read his postscript. Shoving to her feet, she went to where the men kept the guns. Sure enough, Brad's Hoch and Keckler was missing. Nervous energy thrummed through her. She forced herself back to the table and marshaled enough energy to light a kerosene lamp, focusing power from the amulet to help.

"Let's see," she muttered. "It can't have been much more than an hour since he left the library. The afternoon was on its way out then, and I told him I was just going to do a bit more and come down to supper. If he's only been gone for a short time, he can't be too far away."

Bullshit. She shook her head in annoyance. With those long legs he could've covered better than four miles. Maybe more. Even so, if it wasn't so close to dark, she'd risk leaving the spelled environs of the house to hunt for him.

Glumly, she rested her chin on steepled fingers. Dinner actually smelled good, but the last thing she felt like doing was eating. Then the baby moved again.

"All right. All right. You want dinner. I get it." Standing, she plucked a bowl from off the sideboard and ladled some stew into it. She added the vegetable mélange from the other pot, pumped some water into a glass and plopped down dispiritedly at the table.

As she picked listlessly at her food, she couldn't stand the direction her thoughts were going, so she got to her feet and went into the front room. Planting herself in front of one of the many bookshelves, she selected a volume at random and brought it back to the table where she propped it open against the wine bottle that had supported Brad's note.

"*Poems of John Donne, Volume One,*" she read off the spine, easily recognizing the well-worn volume as one of Trevor's. Doggedly, she opened it and began to read, hoping against hope that the next sound she heard would be the heavy tromp of Brad's boots on the porch stairs.

∼

BRAD CLATTERED DOWN THE STEPS, leaving Lara to her research in the library. He winced as he weighted his leg. Despite what he'd told Lara, it was far from healed. Something had been nagging at him for the past few days, but he hadn't wanted to bother her with it. Lord knew she had enough on her mind. He understood how much she missed Trevor. He could see it in the sad set of her shoulders and her wistful expression. Nights were the worst, though. She cried in her sleep, moaning Trevor's name over and over again. He'd wanted to comfort her, but she'd probably misinterpret his intentions. Instead, he lay awake while her heart-wrenching little animal sounds of despair tore his guts to shreds.

Pounding a fist into his open palm in frustration, he glanced at dinner simmering on the stove. *Not much more to do here. Should I?* Brad struggled with the wisdom of the plan forming in his mind. His years in law enforcement had taught him to follow his instincts—and make quick decisions.

"Yeah." Brad snorted. "He who hesitates is lost. Truer words were never spoken. Cops who hesitate end up dead."

But I'm not a cop anymore.

"Wanna bet?" he smirked, heading for his gun. He needed more ammunition, but he could tackle that problem tomorrow. Making sure the rifle had a full magazine, he started out the door. As an afterthought, he turned and scratched out a note, dropping it where Lara would be sure to see it, just in case this little reconnaissance took longer than he anticipated.

Brad whistled as he limped out of the yard. It felt good to be doing something about what he'd started thinking of as *the problem*. It had actually started a couple days after they returned from their foray into town. He'd been crossing the yard at dusk when something skittered away, just at the edges of his peripheral vision. He'd stilled instantly, looking after the flash of movement. Five long minutes passed, but nothing else stirred.

It happened again the next afternoon. He thought he heard something mucking through the thick, tangled undergrowth right outside the perimeter of the yard. When he went to check it out, he found broken branches and footprints. Those gave him pause. They were made by someone who wasn't wearing shoes, the imprint of a foot clear in the soft dirt.

He considered his strategy as he headed up the dirt road away from Skykomish. He hadn't spent much time looking in that direction and wanted to see if, perhaps, other houses existed that Raven hadn't told them about. *It doesn't have to be Goblins. Much more likely I'll find other people.* As he walked, favoring his wounded leg, he thought about Lara. And Elidora.

The witch-woman kindled something dark and gritty in him. A part he'd never known he possessed. The first time she reached for him, he'd drawn back, shocked. "B—but," he'd protested. "Your husband…"

"Och aye," she'd agreed sadly, her brogue silkily soft. "He were twin to me heart, and for aeons mind you, but he is gane where I canna follow. Yet the love o' life burns on. Will ye no' partake o' it wi' me?"

He'd thought he shouldn't, but Elidora had turned to him, raised soft lips, and twined her arms around his waist, pressing herself against him. Her scent was intoxicating, a heady mix of musk and flowers. The minute he kissed her, he fell into a lust so deep he finally understood the shattering strength of physical bonding.

Soon, he moved beyond thought. After a lifetime of keeping his emotions under firm control, he was embarrassed at the primitive heat surging through him. At the way he'd practically torn her clothing to get it out of the way as she laughed knowingly, urging him on with fingers and tongue. With the abandon of a randy teenager, his dick rose again and again, until the two of them lay in a grassy glade shaken and panting.

"Ye needed that, laddie," she sighed as she sat up, rearranging her skirts. "As did I. Thank you hartly." Taking his hand, she murmured, "I'm no' expectin' ye'll properly ken, but Gren… Well, he wouldna begrudge us this. Love is a gift, a grant. An' a dear ane, at that. If there were more lovin' and less warrin', well, t'would be a far better warld."

The only other woman Brad had ever been with was his wife—unless you counted his mother. Brad winced at the thought, a sour taste filling the back of his throat. That had come to an abrupt halt as soon as he'd gotten old enough to kick her in the shins and tell her if she ever touched him *there* again, he'd call in the law. He'd only been about nine or ten, but she'd left him alone after that, picking on his younger brother, who was far more amenable. He shook his head to clear one of the less pleasant images from the fucked up family he came from.

It was far easier to think about Elidora, who was all heat and curves and claws. He'd had welts for days where she'd dug her teeth and nails into him. Brad felt a stirring in his nether regions at the memory, and he reached down to rearrange himself. It was always the same with Elidora. An instantaneous burst of passion that obliterated everything else. She managed to spirit him off somewhere private each time she visited and, after a while, he stopped feeling like he was helping her cheat on the husband whose spirit was locked away in the *Dreaming* for all eternity.

Looking about him, Brad noted landmarks along the wide logging road. So far, there hadn't been any signs of human habitation. Not a tire track, not a footprint, not a hoof print. Belatedly, he thought he probably should have jumped on one of the horses. Or, better yet, taken a car. He could've covered far more ground. But he was used to patrolling on foot when looking for clues. And the simple joy of movement was enticing in and of itself. Though it would have been better without the pain that battered him if he stepped too hard on his injured leg.

Maybe tomorrow I can come back with the truck if I don't find anything tonight.

Thoughts turning inward again, he brought up an image of Lara with her slowly growing belly. *Just like a Madonna.* A bemused smile curved the corners of his mouth. He'd been stunned when she'd said so matter-of-factly that the two of them would probably take up with one another if Trevor never came back.

Stunned and pleased.

Brad knew all too well that, Elidora aside, he was half in love with Lara. Had been ever since he'd first laid eyes on her that afternoon in her house on Queen Anne Hill. She'd come barreling down a long, circular staircase clutching sheets soiled from Beauchamp masturbating on them. Furious and beautiful all at the same time, with her long, red hair churning around her and her dark eyes snapping dangerously.

Brad stopped walking while he tried to collect his thoughts. Once he'd gotten to know Trevor, he really, really liked the man. In fact, Trevor had quickly become the closest thing to a friend Brad had ever had. That made his feelings for Lara much more confusing—and disturbing. In a lot of ways, the sexual romps with Elidora were a perfect diversion.

Suddenly his senses pricked him. Something had changed. It was subtle enough, but the energy of the fading day was definitely different. With instincts born from long years on the police force, Brad melted into the nearby wood, choosing a large tree trunk for cover. Once he felt less exposed, he searched the gathering darkness to pinpoint what had attracted his attention. He'd tossed his night vision lamp into his pack just in case, but it wasn't quite dark enough to need it yet. The device was a real battery hog. Since they were running out of batteries, he didn't want to waste them unnecessarily.

There. Just across the road, the slightest movement flagged his eyes, drawing them. Brad thought about calling out, but stopped himself. *What the fuck am I going to say? Police. Come out with your hands up.* He bit back a laugh. That was his *other* life. Out here he had no partner, no backup car, no handcuffs, no pepper spray, no baton. Just him, his hands, his five senses, and his gun. He clicked off the safety, staring intently at where he'd just seen something move.

There it was again. He clamped his jaws together, waiting. *Should I shoot?*

That's what you told Lara to do, he told himself. Shoot first, ask questions later.

But now that it came down to it, he found he was more curious than scared.

"Hey," he called, infusing authority into his tone. "Come on out nice and slow. I know you're over there. If you come out with your hands where I can see them, I won't hurt you." Once the words were out, he wondered if they'd been a lie.

Probably not. If it's a Goblin, it won't do a thing except try to jump me. If it's a person, what happens is anyone's guess.

Brad waited, but nothing happened. No one came out of the undergrowth, and he didn't see any more flashes of anything. After ten minutes, he wondered if he'd been wrong about there being something alive across the road. "No time like the present to find out," he growled, knowing if he waited much longer, he wouldn't be able to see without the lamp.

Gun at the ready, he traipsed over to where he'd seen movement and searched through the undergrowth. Branches had been snapped off, but it was too dark to check for footprints. He sucked in a breath. "Yes," he breathed, gently pulling a jagged strip of rough, black cloth off one of the sticker bushes. "Someone—or something—was here after all." Pocketing the cloth, he stepped onto the road, thinking it was past time to be heading back. Lara had enough on her mind without worrying about him.

He stopped in the middle of the road, sending his well-honed senses outward, but he didn't detect a thing. Somehow, whoever was there had managed to slip through the thick undergrowth without making any noise. Brad wondered how the hell they'd managed to do that. He had a moment's apprehension, thinking about being jumped from behind as he strode rapidly toward home. Mentally shrugging, he figured the same gift that had always saved him would kick in if he were in danger.

The pain in his leg escalated. He bit back a yelp when his foot hit a hole in the dirt road. *Should've wrapped it with something.*

He was nearing the last of three road junctions when the skin on the back of his neck began to crawl. It was totally dark. Since he hadn't wanted to take the time to stop and put on his headlamp, he couldn't see much. Hesitating, he urged his ears to preternatural sharpness and was rewarded with a muted snap off to his right. Feinting left, he stepped off the road with the intention of circling round to trap whoever was tracking him. He cursed himself for not strapping on the red lens that would have parted the darkness, as he worked his way behind where he'd heard the noise.

A sudden chill unnerved him. He'd had the same thing happen more than once during his time as a detective. Without any conscious prodding from him, a constellation of pieces that seemingly had no relationship suddenly clunked into a cohesive whole.

Lara.

Whatever was engaging him out here—yet not coming too close—was doing it to keep him away from the house. He wasn't sure how he knew, but he did. The second the insight flooded his mind, he recognized it as truth.

Brad ran for all he was worth toward home. If the thing pacing him had meant to hurt him, it would have long since. Liquid fire speared up and down his leg. He pushed it aside. Speed was all that mattered. He considered trying to navigate Troublesome Creek, so he could use the forest as cover. No telling what he'd find back at the house. But the creek was deep and so fast he wasn't sure he'd be able to find a spot to cross it if he didn't use the bridge. He checked the safety on his gun again, reassured by the solid feel of the familiar stock in his hand.

Chugging across the bridge into the generous clearing that held Raven's farmhouse, Brad's breath came fast. Shock pinned him in place. The whole damned house was glowing. And pulsating. His blood congealed in his veins as he realized what a fool he'd been. Bodies lay in the dirt. Others stood in random order, scattered about the yard.

Guess they don't know about military formation. Wonder what else they don't know?

The house cast just enough light for him to see that the abominations were grotesque parodies of humans. Mottled skin, hanks of hair, half dressed—they looked like ragtag leftovers from a genetically modified, rebel army. Just like the thing that had jumped him—and damn near killed him—the night he'd crept into this same yard intent on finding Lara, his only link to his missing daughter.

Thank Christ, Lara had followed his instructions and stayed inside. Or had she? He stared hard at the house, willing her to be within the safety of its walls. Trevor had told him the house was spelled to repel evil. Damn if it didn't look as if it was doing just that.

Brad assessed what was in the yard. Only a dozen or so of the Goblin spawn were still standing. They milled about as if waiting for something. *Orders from Goblin headquarters delivered telepathically?* Face screwed into a grimace, Brad opened fire, spraying the figures with his silver-infused shells.

As soon as the last Goblin fell, screeching out his pain and cursing *silverrrr*, a word Brad recognized even in Gaelic, he charged up the steps facing outward. He swung his rifle from side to side, prepared to shoot anything that moved.

He didn't have to knock. The wide front door swung open with a white-faced Lara and a barking Gunter on the other side. She slammed it behind him, turning the old-fashioned key in its lock. "Where the fuck did you go?" she screamed, anger blazing from her dark eyes. "You said you'd be home before dark."

"I—it was all a set-up," he panted, still out of breath. His leg hurt so bad, it was nearly all he could think about. "They wanted me away from here—"

"No shit," she interrupted bitterly. "I killed a bunch of them, but it's too fucking dark to see how many more are out there."

"Not many, and I killed them."

She just stared at him, not saying anything.

When he looked at her, her hands were balled into fists. She quivered with rage. *Not that I don't deserve it. Leaving here was really stupid. What the hell was I thinking?*

"Uh, look. Lara. I am sorry. You're right. I never should've left you alone. They tried to lure me away from here. And they succeeded. I should've taken one of the cars to go look for clues. Or I shouldn't have left at all." As the truth washed over him, he was shaken by its implications. "They played me like a goddamned fiddle. Jesus. What's wrong with me? I know better. All those handy little suggestions that my mind conveniently came up with. And every damned one of them pushing me to leave."

Light flashed outside the windows. Lara turned the key and threw open the door. Power erupted from her hands. "Take that, you bastards," she cried. "Rot in hell."

Christ. Wish I could do that.

Turning to him, she snarled. "I thought you said they were all dead."

He shook his head, needing to think, and said, "They were when I came inside." He gritted his teeth to block out pain from his leg. *Where were fresh troops coming from? Was there a passageway to a Demon world nearby?*

Lara retreated into the house and slammed the door, her hair loose and belly heaving. He thought he'd never seen anything quite so beautiful. The moonstone, suspended from its golden chain, glowed a deep pink against her woolen top.

"Don't look at me like that," she snapped, turning away from him.

"Sorry." Aware his emotions were far too close to the surface, Brad scrabbled to grasp the cool detachment that had served him throughout the wasteland of his marriage and his job as a cop. But it was a struggle, almost as if, once unleashed, the part of him that *could* feel wanted to be more than a bit player.

They stood like that for long minutes with Gunter prowling

between them, whining. Finally, the set of her spine softened infinitesimally, and she turned toward him. "How's that defensive perimeter?" she asked, eying him coolly.

"Huh?"

"You've been pretty emotionally insulated ever since I met you. Those barriers seem to have fallen."

"I'm sure I don't know what you're talking about," he stammered, feeling heat rise to his face.

She quirked an eyebrow. "That's bullshit, Detective. As you've said to me, you're a cop, so you know things. Well, let's not forget I'm a therapist. I recognize the sound of defense mechanisms when they crack wide open." She laughed hollowly and went to the front door again.

"What are you doing?"

"Checking to see if they've gone. The house has this…vibration when it's trying to defend itself. I haven't felt it in the past few minutes."

Once she mentioned it, he did notice that the energy field he'd sensed when he entered the house had shifted. Quieted somehow. She closed the door and walked back over to him.

"Want to come sit down?" she invited in an almost-normal voice. "We have things to tell one another." She blew out a tightly held breath. "Like why you got a wild hair up your ass and decided to leave. Jesus, Brad," her liquid, dark eyes filled with pain, "I finally figured out how we could go after Trev. I wanted to do that *tonight*."

"And I ruined it. I truly am sorry." He glanced away, feeling like an ass. "I was just so sure—"

"That's because they wanted you to think that," she explained, moving slowly toward the kitchen. "I have this." Half turning to face him, she pointed at the amulet. "It's sort of like a truth meter. I can figure out if something I'm feeling is real, or fabricated in some way by Demons or Goblins."

"Humph. It'd be helpful if I had one," he muttered, trailing after her. "By the way, that pyrotechnics display was quite impressive."

She perched awkwardly in one of the chairs, offering him a weak smile. "Thanks. That part was pretty easy. But I suppose it was good to have an opportunity to practice. Problem is, the magic drains me. I feel so weak, there's no way we could go after Trevor now. I don't think I'd even be able to move a pebble out of this house, much less the two of us." She hesitated. "What I suppose that means is, if I have to tap into the destructive side of things while we're trying to free Trev, I won't have enough in the way of power left to get all of us back here. Damn." She drew her brows together in consternation.

"All the more reason for me to come along. So I can take care of the fighting part." Guilt flooded him. If it hadn't been for his harebrained field trip earlier, Trevor might be back with them now, sitting at the familiar table and…

He scooped up her empty bowl from the table. "I'll get you something to eat," he mumbled, finding it hard to meet her direct gaze as he lumbered across the kitchen. "Maybe by tomorrow…"

"Feed yourself. I already ate. Your limp is way worse," she observed, frowning.

"I ran back here once I figured out I'd been played for a sucker. Leg didn't like it." He plonked the bowl in front of his seat at the table and sat heavily. "I'm sure it will be all right."

"We'll look at your wound after you eat." Lara pushed to her feet and walked to the stove. "Not really hungry," she said, "but maybe if I eat a little more, my energy will recover faster."

Feeling cowed and not very hungry either, Brad forced himself to eat.

CHAPTER 7

Trevor huddled on his bench. Hours passed, but no one came for him. Had Gradoxst's visit been part of a sly deception? Try as he might, Trevor couldn't figure out what advantage his captor might've gained from their conversation. He'd solved the problem of his mostly-severed shackles, though. Making a decision, he stepped out of them. The Goblin guards seemed fairly stupid. He planned to tell them Gradoxst had freed him in preparation for moving him to another location. If he got really lucky, the guards would accept his explanation and forget to ask Gradoxst whether it was true.

Dinner came and went with another bowl of the nauseating mixture that passed for food. He choked it down. It didn't seem quite so bad this time.

Heh. Maybe I'm getting used to this rotgut garbage.

More likely, I'm starving and desperate.

Trevor rubbed the side of his face. It was sore where Gradoxst had struck him, but it didn't seem as if the skin had broken. "Good thing," he muttered bleakly. "Manky cocksucker'd probably give me a hell of an infection."

He got to his feet and paced the length of his cell. It felt good to be able to stretch out his legs without dragging the metal chains behind him. He ignored the putrid slime on the floor. From time to time, he called Raven in his mind. If the mage could arrange some sort of rescue, there'd probably never be a better time. But Raven didn't answer.

No windows in his cell meant Trevor had no way to assess the passage of time. The door had two slits in it, one low and one high, allowing dim light to filter in from the passageway outside. Because he'd been semi-conscious when he was dumped here, he had no idea what sort of building he was in. Judging from water running down the dirt and stone walls, he assumed he was underground. He'd considered trying to dig his way out, but his waning strength coupled with the fact he didn't know how far he'd have to dig, dampened that plan.

He'd just settled back on his bench, girding himself for another chilly night, when a troubling thought struck him about Lara. She visited him nightly in her dreams. What would happen if she came to him when he was in closer proximity to Gradoxst?

Trevor assumed Psyche led Lara to him because the goddess thought the two of them belonged together. Maybe she'd be smart enough to protect Lara, but she hadn't done all that great a job so far.

He sucked in an uneasy breath. Maybe *that* was why Gradoxst really wanted to move him. To make it easier to get his filthy hands on Lara. *Sodding hell. Makes sense.* A sinking feeling twisted his stomach into an uncomfortable knot.

While he saw the rank and file Goblins as one step up from brain-damaged, Trevor wasn't under any illusions about Gradoxst. The Sidhe prince, who'd fallen from grace and embraced evil, was extremely bright, totally without scruples, and appallingly dangerous. Wrapping his arms around his torso, Trevor tried to think. He'd already agreed to Gradoxst's plan. What would happen if he casually said something like, "You know, old chap, I've rethought things here. And I've decided I'd just as soon remain in my current quarters."

The thought was so ludicrous he laughed aloud, then clapped a hand over his mouth. He did *not* want to alert the guards to come look in on him. Not with the shackle problem to be faced.

"Be still and listen."

Raven. It's Raven. Trevor's eyes flew open, searching the gloom of his prison. His heart beat faster, and he clutched at the worn fabric of his filthy jacket.

"The Dark One will move you to where he is. Go willingly. It will be far easier for us to help you from there."

Trevor wanted to ask a hundred questions. Like when this would happen and how to keep Lara out of his dreams, but Raven had told him to be still. Trevor swallowed his desperation, waiting for whatever the mage would tell him next.

"Good. You're following my directions. For once." Raven chuckled. *"Lara is safe. We'll try to keep her that way. We are making progress. I'm more hopeful than I was at this time yesterday. Gren found a way to help."*

"Raven—" Trevor couldn't help himself.

"Ssht. When the Demon comes for you, be humble. Do not talk back or give him any reason to doubt you. His downfall is his pride. If you can make him believe you admire him, albeit reluctantly, perhaps he'll extend you more latitude."

Silence stretched for so long, he was certain Raven had left, but the mage's deep voice sounded again in his mind. *"We will come for you just as soon as we can. Remember, no heroics."*

"Ah yes, that would be my downfall," Trevor mumbled. "Playing the hero." Unbidden, an image of himself as a fifteen-year-old bending over his dead sister's body painted itself behind his closed lids. He saw the unnatural bend in her neck where the rope had snapped it and the bulge of her pregnant belly. Fury at his father flamed hot, but he forced himself to put the vision aside. Nothing he could do about that now. It'd happened close to thirty-five years ago, for chrissakes.

A sudden racket sounded outside the door to his cell. Trevor cowered on his bunk, mouth dry as a month-long drought. The door swung open, hitting the far wall with an ominous thud.

Gradoxst stood there, grinning like a fool. "Perfect," he practically purred. "I was waiting for some *feelings* from you. Anger is one of my favorites." He sniggered, sounding deranged. "Come, come. What are you waiting for? I know you sawed through your leg irons. Where did you think you were going to go?"

Something dangled from one of Gradoxst's hands. Trevor realized it was his boots just about the time they flew through the air, narrowly missing his head.

Remembering Raven's instructions, Trevor plucked his boots out of the muck on the floor and slipped them on his feet, not bothering with the laces. He started toward the open cell door wondering if Gradoxst, who was looking crazier by the minute, would slam it in his face and caper off, laughing like a demented court jester.

Nothing like that happened. With his heart pounding like a trip hammer, Trevor walked through the arched doorway into a corridor with a stone floor. Off to one side, Goblins were playing a dice game. When Trevor eyed the pile of loot between them, he felt ill. Body parts served as poker chips: fingers, toes, an arm. Where had they come from?

"Good. Good. Fear is *almost* as nourishing as anger." Gradoxst chortled, sporting a feral grin that made him look like a gargoyle. "Come with me."

Trevor wrenched his gaze away from the macabre stakes in the dice game and asked mildly, "Which way might that be, then?"

"I would like it far better if you thought about patricide." The Demon suggested silkily, his voice rumbling low in the back of his throat.

Reining in disgust, Trevor obligingly culled up an image of his father.

"You are going to cooperate." Gradoxst sounded surprised. "Much better for you that way." He rubbed his hands together. "I just knew you would be a good choice. Take that staircase, just there."

They climbed for a long time. Not only had his prison been underground, but submerged by a good two hundred feet or better. In his weakened condition, Trevor wondered if he'd make it to the top long before he got there. He tripped over his untied bootlaces and nearly fell several times. The thought of sunlight on his face—or even moonlight—drove him on, though. No wonder his cell had felt so oppressive.

Yeah, good thing I didn't try to dig myself out. It would have taken years.

He smelled fresh air, and a bone-deep hunger surged through him. Raven's last message made far more sense. Now that he understood how deeply he'd been buried, Trevor recognized the difficulty inherent in any sort of rescue logistics. Daylight laved his face. He squinted against the brightness.

"I agree," Gradoxst said in a conversational tone. "Much too bright out here, but it is a necessary evil. Keep up now." He took off at a fast trot. Trevor shambled after him. After a time, his pupils constricted and he looked out on the *Dreaming*. Trevor rubbed his eyes with grimy knuckles. It looked just like the hill country of Scotland. Wild and beautiful. Lush and green with pink and purple heather blooming. If he hadn't been frightened of what might happen if he fell too far behind, he'd have thrown himself atop a heather bush and kissed it. The scent of life and growing things was exhilarating after the fetid dampness of his cell.

"Here we are." Gradoxst, who sounded positively gleeful, took a hard right turn and disappeared into a hillside through an opening Trevor hadn't seen until his captor turned sideways to slither through. "Much nicer. Do you not agree?"

Trevor blinked, astonishment sweeping through him. It *was* nice. Someone had created a homey little space inside a large hillock. Woven carpets and soft cushions filled the comfortable home. Light filtered in through cunningly crafted cutouts high in the walls. "Quite lovely," he murmured.

"If you are very, very good, you may stay." Gradoxst looked at him meaningfully. "That means you shall do exactly as I instruct without delay."

"Yes, I understand." *Not so different from being a flight attendant after all.* Trevor was tired, so weary he swayed on his feet. But he was determined not to anger the Demon. "How may I serve you?"

"My, someone trained you well. Make me a meal." Coming close, Gradoxst grabbed Trevor's wrist, long nails digging into his flesh. A rotten, half-decayed smell that he'd attempted to camouflage with flowery cologne wafted from him. "You cannot eat. Not even one bite of what you prepare for me. I will tell you what—and when—you may eat. Do we understand one another?"

"Quite well. Have you any meal preferences, then?"

"Surprise me."

Trevor glanced about, decided the kitchen alcove had to be behind a curtain, and let himself into the tidy space. His mouth began watering almost instantly. Fruits and bins brimming with grains sat on the counter. A cold box—chilled by a cleverly constructed sleeve that funneled cold water around it—yielded cheeses and chunks of meat. Spices hung in bunches from low rafters. A partially eaten loaf of bread sat on a board next to a tub of butter.

This home must have belonged to a Sidhe. Wonder if there's anything here I could use to poison the old bastard.

"Uh-uh. Naughty boy. I heard that. Lovely energy, though. We just need to redirect it."

"If you can hear my thoughts, I may as well say them out loud."

"So long as you do not bore me, that might be acceptable."

Trevor washed his hands, enjoying sluicing filth from them. He kept up a meaningless line of prattle as he built up the fire in the wood-burning stove from the well-filled wood box and proceeded to dump something that looked a lot like barley into a pot of water. Chopped vegetables and meat went into a skillet. Weighting one of many knives in his hand, Trevor put a lid on his inner dialogue, since it would have detailed rushing Gradoxst and running him through.

As Trevor spoke aloud, he experimented with modulating his thoughts and discovered to his amazement that, so long as he was talking with Gradoxst, the Demon couldn't read his mind. *Who would have thought this would be so easy?* he asked himself, just after he tossed out a mental wish the rogue Sidhe would choke on his own vomit.

Gradoxst apparently didn't notice. He was still answering a question Trevor had posed about John Keat's poetry without missing a beat. Interestingly, his captor was extraordinarily well-read, with a taste for the English Romantics.

"There we go." Trevor laid a plate on a table in front of Gradoxst. He linked his hands together behind his back and put a few paces between himself and the Demon. "Anything further, sir?"

"Yes. You may sit and talk with me while I eat. I find I am enjoying our discussion."

Trevor clamped his jaws together. He'd been hoping for the relative sanctity of the kitchen where he could curl up in a corner and try to sleep. Pushing back Raven's warning, he smiled winningly. "Certainly. But if you wish my company, I need food as well. I fear your hospitality whist I was in my cell was somewhat lacking."

Gradoxst, who'd picked up a fork, laid it back down menacingly. "You dare tell me what *you* need," he snarled, dark fire flashing from his eyes. Almost casually, he raised a hand. A lightning bolt hit Trevor's arm, and his ragged jacket caught fire. The smell of burning flesh and charred wool mingled with fresh-cooked food into a putrid mélange.

Trevor yelped, dropping to the floor as he batted at the flames. Pain lanced through his arm. He struggled to preserve what he could of his skin, but the fire burned with a mind of its own. He was just scrambling to his feet to head for the water pump in the kitchen when Gradoxst looked up from his meal and barked a word in the Goblins' tongue. The fire vanished as quickly as it had come.

"You cannot leave this room until I tell you." Gradoxst laughed nastily. "I believe you have just seen what happens when you do something that displeases me."

Trevor moaned. His arm was lobster red from hand to elbow and it throbbed like hell. Grabbing onto a table, he pulled himself to his feet and bowed in Gradoxst's general direction. *Got to keep it together here.* "Sorry, sir. I am merely human. Not a god like yourself. But if I do not eat for protracted periods, I become weak and less able to…serve." He hesitated, then decided to lay it on even thicker. "I too, was quite enjoying our discussion. We could extend it to Shelley and Lord Byron, but I do need sustenance. And a cold cloth for my arm."

The Demon just stared at him. Trevor stammered on. "A—and Jung. I've read practically his entire works, since Lara has the series. If you'd like to discuss him, well…"

"You have read Jung?" Gradoxst hunkered forward. He stopped ladling food into his mouth.

Trevor struggled to maintain a pleasant demeanor. He knew just how perilous a game he was playing. The rogue Sidhe may be vain, but he was far from stupid.

"Yes, quite," Trevor agreed, smiling blandly. "Food? Cold water?"

"Go get yourself something. But be quick about it. I became fascinated with archetypes while at the Institute. We shall discuss them over our meal."

After Trevor got through muttering his *thank-yous* and backing out of the room, practically bowing and scraping, he made a concerted effort not to whoop with delight that his gambit paid off. Sweat dripped down his sides. He smelled the sour tang of his fear. Pulling at the pump handle, he stuck his arm under the stream of cold water, sucking in a grateful breath as the pain abated a bit. He soaked a dishcloth, wrapping it around his arm as he ate out of the pots—too hungry to wait until he could carry a plate into the front room. Cooking without sampling in his current half-starved state had been agonizing.

"You will return this instant."

"Coming, sir," Trevor replied, trying to sound as deferential as possible. He wasn't interested in being the brunt of any more displays of Gradoxst's temper. Hastily dishing up a plate for himself, he was cautious to keep his portions modest. No point in giving his captor any reason to overturn his food onto the floor.

He carried a bottle of spirits under one arm as he returned to the main room and settled on the floor across from the Demon. "Mead?"

"Bah. The Sidhe's drink is swill."

Raven was right about Gradoxst's monumental ego. Cloaking his thoughts by feeding the Demon questions about Jungian archetypes as he ate, Trevor wondered how well Raven had known Gradoxst before he'd defected.

"Do you mind?" Trevor quirked an eyebrow and lifted the mead bottle. Before Gradoxst could say no, Trevor followed that question with another one. "The Magician archetype. What can you tell me about that? I believe there's some relationship betwixt that one and the King…"

He let his voice trail off as he pried the wax seal off the top of the bottle. Trevor didn't think he'd ever tasted anything quite so welcome as the liquor that flowed down his throat. It reminded him of Gren. Sadness rose, but he covered it with another query.

All in all it was fairly easy to divert Gradoxst. Trevor didn't have to say all that much. The Demon loved to listen to himself pontificate. About the only thing Trevor needed to do was keep the questions coming.

He was wondering how he could get back to the kitchen to rewet his cold water bandage when Gradoxst held up a hand and snapped, "Be quiet."

A bit stunned, Trevor bit off the comment he'd been in the middle of and rose to his feet, waiting. "Take your plate, sir?" he inquired, back in full flight attendant mode.

"Yes. Stay in the kitchen. My men are coming. They must need something."

Trevor had no sooner disappeared behind the curtain, his and Gradoxst's plates in hand and the mead bottle tucked under one arm, when he felt different energies—oddities in the air currents that he'd come to associate with magic. Seconds later, a cacophony of rough voices speaking the Goblin tongue filled the small space.

Once he'd done more first aid on his arm, Trevor retreated to a corner of the kitchen, where he sat on the floor and proceeded to finish what was on his plate, while eavesdropping. Something was helping his pain, maybe the mead, maybe the cold water. He smiled grimly. It was a relief to not have his entire consciousness focused on his throbbing forearm.

To cloak his thoughts, he kept up a muted out loud dialogue between bites, consisting of, "Scared. I'm scared," while soaking in what the Goblin field marshals told Gradoxst about their failing campaign to wrest the *Dreaming* from the Sidhe. Reports of mounting losses filled Trevor with a joy he knew he had to totally annihilate. He couldn't let Gradoxst find out he understood the Goblin tongue, or he'd be tossed right back into his cell, pleasant conversation on a variety of erudite topics be damned. It might be an inconvenience, but Gradoxst would come up with another strategy to snatch Lara that didn't include Trevor's skills as a manservant.

He tipped the mead bottle back again. When he finished eating, he clambered to his feet and went to work cleaning up the mess he'd made in the kitchen. Raven was right to be optimistic. The Sidhe had reclaimed a significant portion of the *Dreaming* that had been in Goblin hands, apparently by gathering disembodied spirits like Gren and borrowing heavily from their magic. Since they no longer had bodies, there was nothing the Goblins could do against them. It had been a brilliant move on someone's part because it provided a deadly enemy that couldn't be disabled by either brute force or magic.

The Goblin horde was in partial retreat. Two of Gradoxst's visitors wanted to call off the entire operation, but three saw it differently. From the sound of things, they were slugging it out on the other side of the curtain.

After a time, Gradoxst's voice rose above the din of Goblins hurting one another. "Enough. Back to your posts. You must try harder. We are *not* leaving. This was part of my kingdom and I want it back." His voice rose to a near shriek on the last word. After a few seconds of silence, he added, "Is that clear?"

So that's it. Trevor whistled softly to cover his inner dialogue. The fallen prince in Paradise Lost wants his home back. Hmm, wonder if the old fart is game to talk about Milton?

Grunts and assorted snorts blatted from the front room.

"What are the lazy lot of you waiting for?" Gradoxst growled. "I shall be along presently to inspect the fortifications." The subtle shift of magic came, brushing against his senses. Once it settled, Trevor was fairly sure it was just him and Gradoxst again. He busied himself with drying a pot he'd just washed.

"Get out here."

Trevor sprang through the curtained opening with alacrity, pot still clutched in one hand. "Sir?"

"I must leave for a short time. I shall bind you."

"Oh, you really needn't bother—" Trevor began and then stopped at the look on Gradoxst's face.

"You must think me as stupid as my men are. Put that pot down and sit there." The Demon pointed to a corner.

"W—will it hurt?" Trevor tried to look terrified, hoping against hope Gradoxst might not bind him as efficiently if he saw Trevor as harmless and frightened. Gutsy prisoners attempted escapes. Those whose spirits were already broken stayed put.

The Demon rolled his eyes. "That little act does not become you. *Sit down.*"

Trevor slid into the indicated spot. Gradoxst began to chant in a guttural language Trevor truly didn't understand. Though he fought against the spell, he felt consciousness slipping away.

CHAPTER 8

*L*ara trudged wearily up the stairs. Brad would be along to tether her, but she'd asked him to give her at least half an hour to herself. They'd had a difficult conversation over their late dinner and tending his leg, mostly because she was still angry with him for being taken in by the Goblins' subliminal suggestions and inadvertently sabotaging her plans.

If only he'd told her what he was thinking of doing— *Well, even if he had, what then? Would I have recognized, truly recognized, what he was feeling was bogus?* Her jaw tightened as she understood that she'd also been convinced someone was stalking the perimeter of the house. If she hadn't been so preoccupied trying to force a crash course in magic, she'd likely have done pretty much the same thing. Gone on a wild goose chase to hunt for clues.

"Ought to tell him," she muttered, reaching for her hairbrush. "And apologize." Her hair had been unbound for most of the day; it took a long time to get all the snarls out. As she separated sections, smoothing them one at a time, she thought about Brad. His reserved demeanor, bordering on asceticism—that had been like a trademark— was all but gone. In its place was a more genuine person, but she'd seen what was in his eyes earlier in the evening. He thought he was in love with her, though the adoration radiating from him had to be more infatuation than love. You couldn't love someone you didn't know very well.

"Oh, stop trying to philosophize this to death," she grumbled. "Doesn't matter if it's love or infatuation or lust. It's going to create problems down the line."

If they did manage to get Trevor back, she wondered how the three of them would go back to coexisting. Hitting a snag in her hair, she yanked hard and bit back a cry when the tangle didn't give. As she worked her fingers into the knot, she chewed on her lower lip. *We're already here. It's not like there's anywhere else to go. We'll just have to make it work somehow.*

She'd moved on to cleaning her teeth when she heard Brad's heavy tread on the risers, followed by the click of dog claws. When she walked into the bedroom, carrying the candle she was using for light in its holder, the detective was perched awkwardly on his bed, twirling one end of the long rope in his big hands. Gunter, lying beside him, thumped his tail at her approach.

"I'm sorry, Brad." She put the candle down, then sat on the far side of his bed. Reaching over, she ruffled the dog's fur. "I was pretty hard on you downstairs. None of us has a crystal ball, and I probably would've gone out to look for the mysterious intruders too—if I hadn't been so busy."

He cocked his head to one side. "Really? You're not just saying that?"

"Really. And Brad…"

"Yeah?"

"Let's leave first thing tomorrow, assuming my magic's recovered by then." She hesitated. "Maybe I'll learn something more tonight while I'm sleeping that can help us."

"Okay. I'm game." He rubbed at his leg, stifling a grunt. "We'll discuss our strategy as we go. If we don't both agree, we'll keep talking until we do."

"I hope to hell we have that kind of time. If I manage to have us come out at the right place, I think things will go pretty fast."

He leveled his gaze at her. "Lara, I've been working with a partner for years. There's always time for some level of communication. Besides, there's work to be done before we can go anywhere. Do you have any idea where Trevor might be in the *Dreaming*?"

She shook her head.

"Have you spent any time thinking about how we might find him?"

Lara shook her head again, heat rising to her cheeks. "Uh, no. Guess I figured the amulet would lead me to him."

"Humph. Hadn't considered that angle. It's good, though. We'll need all the help we can get, since the hardest part will be locating him." When she nodded her understanding, he went on. "You've been there. Tell me everything you remember."

She'd been speaking for a few minutes when he held up a hand. "Wait. Be right back."

He returned with a few sheets of paper, a pencil, and a large book to write on. Once he sketched out what she'd already described, he motioned for her to go on. Lara talked until she couldn't think of anything else. She felt so tired her words were slurring together.

Turning the drawing her way, he asked, "How's this?"

She dragged the candle over and examined his rough rendition of the part of the *Dreaming* she'd seen. "Not bad. Move those rocks a bit over that way. The stream actually came from this direction." She pointed. "The stone castle was more toward that hill. And then the mouth of the cave was just so…"

After a time, he held up a second drawing. "Is this close to what you remember?"

When she nodded, he said, "Okay, next question. Do you have any idea how much more there is to the *Dreaming* than the part you saw?"

"Not really." She sucked in a ragged breath as understanding dawned that she really didn't know enough to be embarking on the path she'd chosen. Not yet, anyway. Trevor could be anywhere. Even with the amulet's help, it might take *days* to find him. Which meant they needed to pack provisions.

She spread her hands in front of her and exhaled an anxious breath. "Raven told me the tree, the rock cairn, the stone castle, and the waterfall are the primary landmarks. He seemed to think I couldn't get lost so long as I could locate one of them. Wouldn't that argue the place isn't all that big?"

Brad's forehead wrinkled in thought. Finally, he said, "Maybe. Depends on how the Sidhe see things. In the little time I've spent with them, it seems they interpret distances differently than we do."

"I guess we should take packs with food and overnight gear."

Brad shot her a look worthy of Raven. "Of course. Weren't you planning to do that?"

Her face got even hotter. Lara felt desperately out of her comfort zone.

"It could take days to figure out where he is." Brad spoke succinctly, folding the drawing and placing it in his shirt pocket. "We'll have to remain hidden, so we need warm clothing, food, water. Maybe a compass, though I'm not so sure it would work there." He shrugged.

"Yes," she mumbled. "I came to the same conclusion five minutes ago. About it taking days, that is. Not so much about what we needed to take."

"Any significant tree cover? Otherwise, we'll be sitting ducks the second we materialize."

"The place looks like the Scottish Highlands."

"I haven't been there." His voice held an impatient edge that softened with his next words. "So you'll need to describe it."

He's used to having men who obey him. And quickly too. "The castle sits right out in the open on top of a small rise. Ground cover's mostly scrubby little bushes. There are a few stands of trees, though. And there's the cave behind the waterfall. That's where Raven said the Sidhe were."

Brad frowned. She knew he was processing what she'd told him.

He was accustomed to taking men into danger…and bringing at least some of them out again. *Good thing he's here. If it were just me I would have gone off without so much as a crust of bread.*

She started to get up, then remembered and held out her wrist. He looped the rope around it, knotting it securely. "Night," she said. "Hope I can sleep. God knows I'm tired enough."

"I hope you can too." He'd stopped frowning, and the look on his face was so tender, it tugged at her heart.

"Don't," she murmured brokenly, dropping her gaze to her hands.

"I'm trying, Lara. Don't worry. I'd never do anything to hurt either one of you."

Despite her extreme fatigue, Lara felt restless the first part of the night. The baby was moving more, which didn't help. It was such an unfamiliar sensation, it brought her back to consciousness if she wasn't under too deeply. While tossing and turning, she asked Psyche to help her find Trevor, hoping to get some clues about where the Goblins had sequestered him.

The next time she opened her eyes, the moon was high in the sky. She figured it must be past midnight. *Please,* she begged Artemis. *Please. Tonight of all nights, I need to find a path to Trev.* Finally, she drifted down, deeper and deeper, and she knew the dreams she sought would come at last.

Time dripped past before the bizarre imagery of the dream world surrounded her. Trevor sprawled in a tangle of arms and legs. The sight of him warmed her, and she drank him in for a moment or two, her lips curving into a warm smile.

He wasn't in his cell anymore. Realizing they must have moved him, she scooted close and peered curiously at a comfortable room with rounded walls. *Like a hobbit hole. Must have been a Sidhe's home before the Goblins invaded.*

She extended a hand, trying to touch Trevor, concerned her mere presence in the room hadn't woken him. Some sort of barrier stood in the way. Unlike the time in his cell, whatever stood between them was invisible. As she reached forward again, she stared at her hands.

My body. How did my body come along? I was tied. Gazing at her naked wrist, she understood she must have undone the rope in her sleep.

No, I wouldn't have done that.

Well, a different inner voice inquired. *If not you, then who?*

Deciding she'd puzzle that out later, she pushed toward Trevor again, but the same obstruction stopped her. Lara slid her hand around the amulet and asked for help. The magic moonstone rose to her need, and seconds later her other hand slid through. She touched Trevor, emotion sluicing through her at her first contact in many days. She blinked back tears and willed the lump in her throat to go away. Not knowing what would happen if she let go of the amulet, she knelt and shook Trevor with her free hand. He didn't stir.

"Trev," she whispered. "Trev, you've got to wake up." When he lolled back and forth at her touch, she rocked onto her heels. "Jesus Christ, what have they done to you?"

The tenor—or maybe it was the pitch—of the amulet shifted. She understood it as the warning it was meant to be. With a last, longing glance at Trevor, she pulled the dream shards around her and thought of home.

And then she stopped.

"Maybe I can bring him back," she muttered, starting forward again to settle her arms around him. "I'm here. He's here. Should just be the reverse of what I did this afternoon. I have to try. I have to."

She shut her eyes, concentrating hard as she held him close to her, but nothing happened. Lara repositioned herself so she could grip the amulet with one hand. When she shut her eyes again and began to chant, rather than sending strength into her, it began the thrum that meant *danger, danger. Leave while you can.* It had done the same thing before Gradoxst swept her out of her office and onto that goddess-forsaken beach.

Fear quickened her heartbeat. She prayed to any deity who might be listening for help and set the incantation to return them in motion again.

"L—Lara." Trevor's voice was thick and muddy. His body stiffened in her arms. "You have to go. Gradoxst is close. Even I can feel him. Leave, love. Go."

Why'd he come around now?

Lara realized she'd jammed the amulet against his neck and understood it was unweaving the spell holding him comatose. She looked at him with alarm, her own terror fed by the specter of his fear.

His voice steadied and his blue eyes, darkened to midnight with anxiety, stared back. He pushed her. Hard. "Bloody hell, Lara. Go back. Now."

A rising wind screeched discordantly in her head. Gradoxst's form shimmered at the edges of her vision. Trevor was still pleading with her to leave, panic stamped on his dear face. Desolation swept over her. *He's right. No point in us both being trapped.* She clutched the amulet and thought of home. "I love you," she cried as the *Dreaming* disintegrated around her.

The bedroom blazed with light. At least it felt that way to her dark-adapted eyes.

Brad, who'd apparently been pacing, his face hard as nails, spun the second she found herself back in her bed. The rope was wound around one of his hands several times. "What the fuck?" he demanded, shaking the fist that held the rope at her.

Fighting disorientation from her dream journey, Lara shook her head, feeling dazed and wounded. In seconds, he loomed over her, wearing his fury—and his fright—like a hair shirt.

"I asked you a question."

"You're yelling at me. Stop it." Anger and pain and confusion and loss rose to the fore. She'd been so close. She'd almost had Trevor. He'd been in her arms, goddammit. Blinking against the glare in the room, she drew her knees up to her chest and wrapped her arms around them.

"Lara." His voice was a shade less abrupt, but not much. "Why'd you untie the rope?"

"I didn't." The answer rose to her lips so quickly, it had to be the truth.

His eyes widened. "I tie good knots. And I didn't loose you."

Gunter ran in from the hall. Obviously delighted to see his mistress, he took a running leap and landed on her bed, where he proceeded to lick her face and hands.

"I'm telling you, I didn't untie the fucking rope. Once I realized my body had come along with my dream mind again, I damn near panicked."

"Oh." The word sounded small and inhibited, balanced against his earlier rage. When she glanced at him, he looked like a sail with the wind knocked out of it.

Understanding the storm was over, she unwound her arms and dropped her legs over the side of the bed. "I'm going to the bathroom. Then I'm going to come back here, and we can figure out what happened."

The sky outside the bedroom window was getting lighter by the time she finished telling him about her journey to the *Dreaming*. He sat cross-legged on his bed while she paced, too overwrought to settle down. Rain streaked the windows and beat a steady tattoo on the roof one story above them. She was able to describe where Trevor was in enough detail that even Brad seemed satisfied, though he said it was unfortunate she hadn't had a chance to see the outside of the place Gradoxst was holding him.

"So." The detective clicked things off on his fingers. He was all business once again, perhaps to cloak any residual discomfiture from his earlier meltdown. "We know Trevor's still alive. We know he's been moved out of his prison cell. We know Gradoxst has him, probably as a lure to draw you."

"And we know he's damned scared," she added. "Scared enough to send me away. We also know that the magic I thought would bring him back here isn't strong enough."

"No. We don't know that." Brad pursed his lips together. "Look, I may not understand magic, but I do understand following protocols. You went to that place in a different way than you'd have gone if you'd done that incantation thing you picked up from the book. Maybe that makes a difference."

Maybe it does, she thought, feeling a smidgeon more hopeful. "That leaves the problem of the rope," she said, leveling a measured glance his way. "Out of all of this, that's by far and away the most unsettling. At least to me."

"No one came in here," he pointed out. "Dog would've warned us."

A sudden idea—and not a pleasant one—intruded. "Did you examine the rope?"

He looked at her. "No. Why would I have done that? It's still in one piece."

She held out a hand. He'd blown out two of the three kerosene lamps while she was soaking her face in cold water and peeing. When he dropped the rope into her outstretched hand, she walked it over to the one remaining lamp.

"There," she said, pointing. "And there."

He limped over to her, curiosity about whatever she'd seen stamped on his face. A low whistle escaped him. "Not much of a detective, am I? Seems I've gotten rusty in these few short months." He stroked the unraveled spots at one end of the rope. Black marks, looking almost like burned places, marred the rough fibers.

"Let me see your wrist."

Puzzled, she held out both of them. He grasped her right wrist and turned it first one way, then the other. "You've got black on your skin. Just like what's on the rope."

The amulet, which had been quiescent since it led her out of the *Dreaming,* thrummed merrily against her chest. *You!* She wound her other hand around the stone. *You wanted me to go. So you freed me.*

"You're probably not going to believe this, Brad, but…"

"What?" He was still examining the black marks on her wrist, holding the rope close for comparison. "Definitely looks the same." He glanced at her. "What am I not going to believe?"

"I guess I did untie myself—in a backhanded sort of way." She ground her teeth together. "It was this." She pulled the moonstone from under her thick top. "It just told me—"

"Maybe you ought to lie down," he said softly, looking worried.

Of course he'd think I'm nuts. I sound crazy. "For some reason, the amulet thought my trip to the *Dreaming* tonight needed all of me," she persisted, her voice soft. "Lillian told me it would get stronger—and more independent—as I used it, and we became better attuned to one another."

"Uh, Lara." He cast a sidelong glance her way.

"I know how preposterous it sounds." She shrugged. "But I also know that's how the rope got untied. The thing I can't figure out is why the amulet wanted to make sure I ended up in Gradoxst's stronghold. Christ, the moonstone's supposed to be on *our* side." She tapped on the stone with her index finger, noticing her fingernail had broken and left a jagged edge.

He avoided her eyes. When he finally looked up, he said, "Only thing I can figure is the amulet believes you belong with Trevor. Maybe it thought if it led you there, you'd be able to bring him back."

"Yes, but why wouldn't that argument hold if you and I went after him? Don't you suppose the moonstone could help us find—? Oh-ho." She clapped a hand to her forehead. "We're making this way too hard. The stone was mined in the *Dreaming*. It wants to go back there. Maybe it decided it wanted to return *tonight*, so it made sure I'd bring it along."

She screwed her face into a wry grin, totally lacking in humor. "Not that I like the answer very much, but at least that mystery's solved. Now, about getting back… If I couldn't weave a spell strong enough to bring Trev and me back, how the hell will I manage to transport all three of us?"

When Brad looked at her with his clear, ice-blue eyes, his face was set in an expression she'd seen on soldiers in movies. Stoic. Determined. Dogged. "I still believe you might've gotten different results with a more normal protocol. If it truly comes down to you not having enough power, though," he said, his voice very quiet, "you'll leave me behind. The Sidhe will help me find a way back."

Like hell they will, she thought. Raven had wanted to jettison Brad as soon as his daughter was buried. She bit back the protest that rose to her lips, moved to tears by the sacrifice he was willing to make on her behalf—and Trevor's too.

Her eyes stung as she mumbled, "Come on." Her throat was thick with unshed tears, and she didn't know what else to say. "We have lots to do to get ready."

CHAPTER 9

Trevor cringed in a corner of the room. He was free enough of the Demon's spell to try to escape, but he also understood his adversary would be back, probably within seconds. The air stank of Demon magic. It made his skin crawl, and his arm still ached from being burned.

Insofar as he knew, only one doorway existed to get in and out of the underground dwelling. Since he didn't have enough time to race out the door without running squarely into the rogue Sidhe—who'd be furious—Trevor held his ground, fear eating into his guts like a rabid animal with sharp teeth. Thank Christ Lara had gotten away in time. There were a few seconds when he'd been afraid she'd refuse to leave his side. He pulled a curtain over his thoughts. Maybe he'd get lucky, and Gradoxst wouldn't deduce Lara had been there.*s*

Not very bloody likely.

"You disobeyed me." Gradoxst's voice, shrill with outrage, preceded him into the room.

Because it was pointless to either protest or argue, Trevor sat where he was, trying to latch onto a calm place within where he could ride out Demon's fury. *I've had a decent meal. If he wants to toss me back into the slammer, it wouldn't be so bad.*

A blood red coruscation formed in the air. It cracked open and deposited Gradoxst into the room amid flames and a strong sulfur smell.

Maybe I should've tried for the door, since he doesn't seem to use it.

The Demon's clothing, which hadn't been any too clean to begin with, was clotted with mud and gore. Dirt streaked his pasty complexion. His long, white hair hung in greasy tangles mingled with debris. His hands were raised in front of him, fingers curled into claws. Once he'd fully materialized, his gaze zeroed in on Trevor.

Humph. He looks surprised I'm still where he put me.

"Who was here?" A quiet menace replaced Gradoxst's overt rage, and it felt far more unnerving.

Trevor shrugged and worked at appearing innocent. "I'm sure I don't know what you mean."

The Demon stomped closer, scenting the air like a dog. A cunning look washed over his face. "Ah, I understand. Your lady love came to rescue you. But you are still here." He began to cackle. "Which means she was not strong enough to both break my binding and extricate you. Tsk. Tsk. Training is everything." He looked hard at Trevor, his dark eyes shrewd. "And I fear she has had precious little." His laughter escalated, a hungry sound that scoured Trevor's nerves. "No matter. I shall simply plan my next trap better."

Trevor's heart lurched into overdrive. He had to escape. If he didn't, it would only be a matter of time before Lara's visits ended up being her doom.

His captor offered a travesty of a grin that looked more like a sneer. "Perhaps you understand now why I left the fold. I wanted access to *real* power, not that pale substitute that appears to mollify the likes of Lillian—or Raven, false god that he claims to be."

Gradoxst cocked his head to one side, a complacent smirk on his face. He'd apparently moved past wanting to mete out punishment for Trevor's disobedience. "You will heat water. I would bathe."

"Is there a tub, uh, sir?"

The Demon's face took on an odd, knowing expression. He waggled his fingers toward one side of the dwelling and a wall shimmered. Once it reformed, Trevor saw an opening that hadn't been there before. Skittish it might be a trap and the Demon would imprison him in some new way once he crossed under the lintel, Trevor edged cautiously toward the opening.

"Come now." Gradoxst's voice held an irritable undercurrent. "If you do not move a bit faster, it will be tomorrow before my bath is ready. That is not acceptable."

Something fiery grazed his arms, almost like the popper of an unseen whip. Trevor sprang forward into what turned out to be a short hallway leading to an alcove with a deep tub. Off to one side, he saw a room with a generously sized bed and *another door.*

Of course there had to be more than one, he lectured himself. Picking up a bucket sitting near the tub, he draped the handle over his good arm and then trudged to the kitchen to build up the fire in the stove. From the looks of things, it would take so many buckets to fill the tub, it was likely water from the earliest fillings would have cooled long before the bath was ready for use.

After his third trip traipsing past Gradoxst, who'd seated himself in the front room with a book of poetry, Trevor stopped long enough to ask, "Can't you heat water without the stove?" The Demon just looked at him, so Trevor stumbled on. "Even Lara can heat water, and you just said she wasn't nearly as strong as you are." *There, that had just about the right touch of flattery.*

"Of course I could warm my own water. But why should I? You are here and in need of work. Idle hands—" A hint of a smile played over his old, cracked lips.

"Got it."

Dumping the third bucket into the tub barely brought it to one quarter full. Trevor headed back to the kitchen for more. His arm throbbed dully, but he ignored it.

Trevor lost count of the number of trips. Though it wasn't particularly warm in the hobbit hole dwelling—except in the kitchen

—sweat ran down his sides. At last he stood, panting slightly, in front of Gradoxst. "Ready, sir," he said with a slight bow.

The Demon sprang to his feet. He smelled so rank, Trevor had a hard time maintaining a neutral expression. The rotten-meat miasma had gotten far worse. "You will attend me," Gradoxst announced, as if he were conferring a great honor.

Nooooooo…

"Certainly. How might I assist?" Thanking whoever might be listening for his twenty-seven years of *coffee-tea-or-me* training, Trevor backed away a pace or two. Gradoxst stepped out of his clothes, leaving them in a filthy heap on the inlaid stone floor.

The sight of the Demon's ancient body was revolting. Without clothing, he looked like the thousand-year-old creature he was, his skin loose and sagging with knobby joints and pustules where the skin had split because it was so thin. Trevor had seen enough of the Sidhe without clothes to understand they didn't age like the specimen in front of him. *He may have gotten power, but at what price?* Remembering the danger, Trevor clapped a quick lid on his thoughts.

"Attend me." Gradoxst's command tore into Trevor's efforts to look anywhere but at the Demon's broken-down body.

"Coming, sir."

Trevor walked into the room with the tub just about the time Gradoxst settled himself into the water. Looking about, he saw soap on a nearby ledge and a scrub brush. Wordlessly, he handed both to the Demon, waiting for what would be expected of him next.

For a time, Gradoxst scrubbed himself. The water took on first a gray, then a black hue. Trevor wondered if he'd have to fill the huge tub all over again.

"As long as you chose to mention Lara." The Demon grinned at Trevor, baring uneven teeth. "Do you think she has settled in with the detective now that you are, shall we say, absent? He is quite a fine looking specimen. Confidentially, that is why I selected him to persuade your lovely wife to locate his missing daughter."

Gradoxst snickered nastily. "Women. They are always searching out a strong, well-proportioned protector. Nicht stimmen Sie?" The Demon morphed into accented Swiss German.

Trevor's hands balled into fists of their own accord. "I'm sure I don't know, sir. I'm scarcely there to ascertain whether my wife has developed an interest in my friend."

"Yes, yes." The Demon's voice was silkily suggestive. "But surely you have considered the *possibility*. Both of them are young. They have appetites. Even *I* have them, but they do become less pressing when one is my age."

"Can't say as I've considered any such thing," Trevor muttered through clenched teeth.

"The three of you have lived together for a few months," Gradoxst pressed on, still grinning. "Surely you managed an experiment or two? After all, as I recall these things are far more stimulating with more participants."

"I wouldn't know." It was getting more and more difficult to gin up civil answers. The Demon's focus on sex was kicking up a welter of sick feelings he remembered with stomach-churning clarity from watching his father rape his little sister over and over again.

"Oooooh, anger. I love anger. It is such a *powerful* emotion. Come closer, you can wash my back."

That did it.

"Wash your own fucking back," Trevor spat and spun on his heel to return to the kitchen. The muted glow from the mead had long since worn off. He wanted to replenish it by drinking some more—lots more. Something viselike caught him across the middle. It felt like a pair of giant arms. He couldn't move. Even breathing became a chore. Panic flared. He didn't think Gradoxst would kill him until he had Lara—but he wasn't sure.

"Not your choice," the Demon snapped. "I said, come here and wash my back. You will be very sorry if I am forced to repeat what is really a very reasonable request for a third time." The Demon's voice felt like hot nails—each word pounded individually into Trevor's brain. Something sharp scored his body. He would've looked down to see what was stripping the flesh off his bones, but he couldn't. Even his vocal chords were paralyzed, keeping his cries of pain locked within his throat.

"I am going to release you, and you are going to be a good boy."

Trevor tried to nod. The needle-like sensation ceased abruptly, and he dragged himself to the tub, looking for the scrub brush. The water was so dank it was impossible to see through it.

"Well?"

"I'm, uh, looking for the back brush."

"There is a cloth hanging on the wall. I think I would prefer the feel of your hands on my body."

Trevor's stomach lurched, but he pulled a small cloth off its peg. Then he dragged it through the disgusting water and made a show of at least moving the grime on the Demon's shoulders and upper back around a bit. At least the tepid water wasn't hot enough to kick his burned arm into a pounding lump of jelly.

Touching his captor's split, diseased skin was repulsive. Trevor glanced about for a weapon. Something, anything, he could use to beat that hoary skull into a paste. What was worse was that Gradoxst, apparently oblivious to Trevor's thoughts—or maybe feeding off them —was practically purring.

"They used to take such good care of me at the Institute," he murmured, eyes closed, head thrown back. "Between the acolytes—ah, rather students—and the hired help, I wanted for very little."

Trevor started to ask why he didn't go back there, but bit his tongue. He hoped against hope the Demon wouldn't start back up with his earlier ménage à trois theme. Or anything sexual, for that matter.

"That is quite sufficient. No need to remove my skin." Gradoxst captured Trevor's hand, guiding it lower in the water.

Understanding all too well what was coming next, Trevor tried to pull away, but the rogue Sidhe's grip was like iron. "I suggest you cooperate," he said smoothly, "or I'll make you use your mouth."

Trevor's hand closed around a shockingly erect member. Frozen in place, he controlled his roiling guts with difficulty.

"Come now. I'm sure you know what to do. It's the same thing you've done for yourself thousands of times." The Demon cupped his hand around Trevor's and forced it up and down his shaft.

Fighting a sickness that threatened to obliterate him, Trevor pulled at the ancient flesh, willing it to spew so he could escape what had turned into his worst nightmare.

"Perfect," Gradoxst gasped. "Your emotions are just what I need. Harder, now. Yes. Yes. Yesss…"

Sweat dripped down Trevor's face and ribs. He smelled his own revulsion and fear as he put everything he had into bringing the vile old Demon to orgasm. Soon enough, the cock in his hand bucked. A high, thin shriek of satisfaction filled the room. At least the tub of filthy water masked the pungent scent of semen.

Trevor stepped back, panting almost as hard as Gradoxst. *I should've let him kill me before I acquiesced.*

"Ah, but you didn't." The Demon laughed. "That was delightful. We shall have to do it again soon. Maybe next time, I can reciprocate. Gather up my clothing and see that it is laundered."

Unbearably relieved to have an excuse, any excuse, to get out of the damned bathroom, Trevor bolted for the door.

"Bring me a robe," floated after him.

Trevor stepped into the neighboring bedroom, nausea dancing so close to the surface he was afraid he'd puke. Struggling to keep desperately needed calories inside himself, he pulled the wardrobe door open. Robes hung in a neat row. Apparently the previous inhabitant of these quarters had favored them. Selecting a black one, Trevor looked longingly at the door he assumed led to freedom, then shook his head. It wasn't the right time. Retribution would be swift if he were caught. And he was certain he would be. Resolutely, he stopped back by the bathtub, hanging the robe on a handy hook. With a, "Here you go, sir," he strode back to the living room to collect Gradoxst's clothing.

In the kitchen, he upended the mead bottle, sucking down the liquid as if it were the only hedge between him and death. It had an amazingly salutary effect. Even more so than he remembered. Opening a second bottle, he drained off a quarter of it as well, trying to block out what had just happened. Still feeling sick and shaky, he dumped the Demon's clothes into a large kettle, added water and a generous handful of soap, and heated the revolting mess on the stove. It took a long time before the smell got better. He had a feeling it was the open sores on Gradoxst's body that lent such a rotten odor to everything that touched him.

Wonder if I'll start smelling like him too? Trevor shook his head from side to side to dispel the feel of the Demon's ancient cock straining against his hand.

"Attend me."

Trevor missed the solitary quality of his cell more and more with each passing moment. He pushed the kitchen curtain aside. "Yes?"

Gradoxst was back in his customary chair. He'd shrugged into the robe, but hadn't tied the sash. The garment fell open, exposing aged, wrinkled flesh and withered genitals. Trevor's guts tightened.

Not again. Oh, Jesus, God, not again.

"Come in. Come in. You needn't stand there in the doorway like a guest. Why we are practically family."

Yes, I know all about families. Trembling began in his belly and extended to his limbs. Trevor wondered if his legs would give out. "I need to finish your clothing, sir. It's nearly clean, and then it will need to be rinsed, wrung out, and hung."

"Never mind that, my boy. Pull it out of the pot and damp the stove." A pause, then the Demon added suggestively, "I can heal that burn of yours. You'd like that, wouldn't you?"

"Certainly." Trevor ground his jaws so hard he was surprised his teeth didn't crack. "Give me ten minutes, sir?" At the Demon's nod, he retreated to the kitchen, whistling an old Gaelic tune to cover his thoughts.

I don't know how much longer I can do this. If that old bastard wants me to touch him again, or worse suck him off, I'll tear him to bits with my bare hands, and then he'll probably kill me.

That would be better than letting him use me again, another inner voice stated flatly.

Where the fuck was Raven, anyway? He hadn't heard anything since moving here, where Raven had intimated it would be far easier to free him. He worried about Lara and her visits for the first time in hours.

He was just rinsing Gradoxst's clothes at the pump in the sink, when the unmistakable tang of magic zinged through the air. Goblin magic, so it meant they had company. A reprieve.

Maybe he can have it off with one of his men.

Trevor continued rinsing, wringing, and hanging. He did a slipshod job as he favored his sore arm. By the time he'd finished and dumped the filthy water down the sink, he settled in to eavesdrop. That had been hard to do while he'd been clanging about the kitchen. Absently, he patted the pocket that held his silver shavings. His knife retained so little silver, it probably wouldn't even deter a Goblin child at this point.

"Master, I am telling you we must leave," a rough voice snarled menacingly.

"Yes," another, more guttural, voice chimed in. "They are slaughtering us. It is the spirits of the half-dead Sidhe. We cannot kill them."

"Kill them," a third voice rang out. "Bah! By the tits of Aerot, we cannot even slow them down. We cannot fight what we cannot see."

An argument had apparently been escalating over the few minutes since Gradoxst's men arrived. The Goblin tongue had lots of consonants and a tense edge to it anyway, but the verbal exchange on the far side of the curtain sounded positively feral.

Too bad one of the doors doesn't exit from the kitchen. I could slip out of here and they'd never notice.

Gradoxst screamed at his men and they yelled right back. At least one battle wing had already left. The remaining two were packing up.

The old fart will never leave me here. He'll probably try to take me with him to wherever he lives when he's not here. Either that, or he'll kill me. He's not going to leave a potential hostage behind. Or lover.

Trevor's stomach lurched again.

Odd lights blazed from the next room, reminding him of his battle with the Goblin the night Lara had gone with the Sidhe to rescue Adriana. Trevor glanced frantically around the kitchen, seeking another of those magic door panels Gradoxst had opened off the living room, but he didn't find a thing.

Gently rounded walls mirrored the contours of the hillock outside the home, without a break or a shimmer to indicate another hidden door. Taking a desperate chance that Gradoxst and his henchmen were too preoccupied to notice, Trevor cried out for Raven with his mind. But no one answered. Next he tried Artemis. He'd no sooner thought her name, than a silvery moonbeam flittered across the neat kitchen floor, disappearing into the corner near the cold box.

Confusion filled him, and then he girded himself for a desperate flight against strong odds. There were no windows in the kitchen, or anywhere else in the neat dwelling, to allow moonlight inside. Surely Artemis was showing him a way out of this hellhole—if he had the guts to follow her lead. His heart leaped into his throat, and his palms slicked with sweat.

He dropped to his knees an instant later and followed the goddess's light. Behind the cold box, he found the welcome outline of a trap door, conveniently illuminated by the moonbeam. As he watched, the door swung inward, groaning a bit on unseen hinges. Trevor understood that part of a stream was diverted to keep the food cold. This must be the service gate to fix the flow if something went wrong.

Without stopping to consider the wisdom of his actions, he slithered through the small hole on his belly, practically dislocating a shoulder in the process. He considered leaving the door open a touch, since his only light source was the kitchen.

Nope, got to chance it.

Pulling the door shut, he latched it firmly, wishing it had a lock. At first the small space was totally dark, but then he spied a small, flirtatious moonbeam dancing ahead. He followed it, moving as fast as he could. His clothing soaked through in seconds, since he was crawling through an underground streambed. At least it numbed the pain in his arm.

Seeing daylight ahead, he slowed dramatically. No point popping out in plain sight of a Goblin regiment. According to the brave boys back in Gradoxst's purloined quarters, they were all leaving, so he'd have to be extra careful. He gripped the edges of the underground culvert and tilted his head back to peer out cautiously. Trevor turned to give himself a three hundred sixty degree view. The grassy vale was empty. A single stand of trees stood about fifty yards distant. If he could get to them, he might buy himself some breathing space.

A shout rang clearly over the noise the water made. From the combination of anger and angst in that cry, Trevor understood his absence had been discovered. The fifty yards suddenly looked much too far. Not seeing any other possible cover, he ducked back into the culvert. His breathing escalated to a fever pitch until the edges of his vision grayed and his head spun.

"Come on, man," he spat through chattering teeth. "Get a grip. If I pass out, I'm done for."

He heard the tromp of booted feet and more shouts. Risking a quick peek out the top of the culvert, he saw Gradoxst, his now-belted robe flapping grotesquely in a stiff breeze, and four Goblins gesturing to one another. They stood in plain view, only about thirty yards away, in the opposite direction from the stand of trees. Trevor assumed they'd fan out to look for him. He heard one say quite clearly. "Stupid human. We shall be able to hunt him down easily. Let us loose the curaets."

Curaets... Lara had told him about the red-eyed, marmot-sized rodents with wings like bats. She'd encountered the hideous creatures on one of the Goblins' worlds.

Trevor understood he had to do something. He wondered about

the advisability of retreating to the kitchen. It was probably the last place anyone would think to look for him. He even started climbing back down the passage, but every foot closer to the place that stank of Gradoxst felt like another fetter looped around his soul.

Better to die a free man… He stopped and collected his flagging reserves. There has to be something, he told himself. Something beyond giving myself up to certain death out in the open or going back into that miserable hellhole. He retraced his steps upward. Enough daylight filtered through the opening of the culvert for him to examine the moss slick walls.

And then he saw something.

Off to his right was an area where the moss grew far more thickly. As he grappled with the cold, slick vegetation, a side channel came into view. Because it was the only possible route left to him, he crawled into it. His arm throbbed and burned as rocks scraped against it, but he pushed the pain to a far corner of his mind.

The claustrophobia that had always bothered him in caves swooped into high gear. He did his best to ignore it. Rocks tore at his pants and his flesh, but he kept going because the only other choice was to retreat right back into Gradoxst's clutches. After about two hundred yards, moving by feel in a darkness that had become pervasive once he rounded a bend, he saw a faint glow up ahead. The ground was sandier and the passageway opened into a respectably sized cave lit by small, glowing places in the walls.

"This is just like in that dream," he murmured, amazed, and wondered if he'd stumbled into the root structure of the Tree of Life by some strange accident of space and time.

Doesn't matter what it is, his inner voice pointed out acerbically. It's a bloody dead end.

CHAPTER 10

*L*ara worked off the list Brad had jotted down, shuttling back and forth between the house and the shop as she added to their small pile of provisions. She'd sliced the last couple loaves of bread he'd made and set the slices in the oven to dry out. She'd also spread out the contents of a few cans of fruit on cookie sheets, hoping the heat from the woodstove might create an approximation of fruit leather. As she moved from task to task, Gunter raced along by her side. The dog clearly understood something was afoot. The thing that obviously hadn't occurred to him was that he wouldn't be included. When Lara looked at him, all lolling tongue and forward-pricked ears, she felt a pang of guilt.

I sure hope he can take care of himself if we don't come back.

On their way back to the house from milking the goats, a task she'd forgotten earlier, the dog stopped dead, ears swiveling in the direction of the bridge that crossed Troublesome Creek. Driven by multiple generations of inbred guard dog training, he barked, placing his body between Lara and the bridge. She grappled for the amulet, but it wasn't doing anything special.

Good. Not Goblins.

Brad ran onto the porch, shotgun in hand. "Lara." His voice held an urgent note. "Get up here. Now."

She sprinted for the porch, driven more by his anxiety than her own. "Not Goblins," she said, scooting through the door he held open.

"How can you…? Never mind." He shook his head and got the same expression he always had when magic might be in play. "If not Goblins, then what?"

"I have a feeling we're about to find out. Don't close the door." Turning, she glanced back into the yard. "Look, Brad, it's two children." Lara pointed to a scraggly pair making their way toward the front door. "Uh, no, maybe one of them is a small adult."

"Looks like a mother and a kid. Maybe early teens. I'm going to see what they want."

She watched from the porch while Brad walked briskly down the steps and out onto the gravel-strewn parking pad. The ungodly mess of Goblin bodies from the previous night had been gone this morning, leaving gore-streaked muck as a grisly reminder the attack really had happened. Brad raked everything over, but she could see crimson blotches in places he'd missed.

While grateful they'd not had to bury—or burn—all those bodies, their disappearance was unsettling. Raven had tried to explain why Goblins couldn't remain on Earth for very long— living or dead. But the explanation included vibrational fields and other physics concepts she didn't quite grasp. He'd warned her that having too many Goblins breach the veil between their worlds and this one could change all that. And not for the better.

"Thank God you're here," the woman said in a cracked voice. "Our car broke down a ways down the road. My husband's sick. Need to get him to where a doctor can take a look at him. Wouldn't have thought to turn down your side road, but Johnna heard your dog barking."

"Where'd you come from?" Brad's deep voice rumbled. He held the shotgun at half-mast.

The woman just looked at him. Something shifty in that look

alerted Lara that she was likely lying. Apparently, Brad felt it too because he added. "Answer my question. Now."

The woman's shoulders slumped. She appeared to be in her forties, dark hair streaked with gray. Slightly built, she was dressed in grease-stained blue jeans and an oversized wool shirt. Tired hazel eyes skirted away from Brad.

"Can we come in?" the girl, who might've been about ten, asked. "We're tired. Been walking since the middle of last night." She had the same dark hair as her mother and red-rimmed blue eyes that made Lara suspect she'd been crying.

Lara had just opened her mouth to say *of course*, when Brad said, "No." Gunter, still sticking close to Lara, seemed to agree with the detective, since he hadn't raced down the steps to greet the newcomers.

Lara drew her brows together and went to stand next to Brad. "You do need to tell us who you are and why you're here. We have a busy morning planned and not much time to just stand around."

Of all the mornings for strangers to show up. It's almost like something's afoot that wants to keep us here.

"It's a pretty long story—" the woman began.

"Shorten it," Brad suggested, curtly. "Like my wife here just told you. We haven't got much in the way of time today."

The girl, who seemed older than Lara had originally thought, maybe as much as thirteen or fourteen, tugged at her mother's arm. "Let's go, Mom. They don't want us here. And they ain't gonna help."

"But we've been walking for hours," the older woman protested. "This is the first house we've come to."

"There aren't any others farther in, either," Brad said and added, "Your daughter's correct. Either tell us what you want or leave."

"I want you to come see if you can't get our car going. I already told you my husband's sick." Something chilly slid beneath the woman's words, almost a threat, but not quite.

"What sort of sick?" Brad's voice held a guarded undercurrent.

"If you ain't gonna tell 'em, then I will," Johnna announced defiantly, taking a few steps nearer to Lara and Brad. "Dad was in the State Reformatory in Monroe. He busted out. A bunch of the guards got dragged off to help fight in the Seattle riots, so Dad just sort of walked out of there. We were waiting for him nearby."

The girl's eyes welled with tears, but she shook her head and went on. "Guess the guards shot him—Anyways, he took a bullet in his arm. Not enough of the law left to chase us down. They didn't even try." She paused to take a breath as she brushed tears off her thin cheeks.

"There's more," Lara suggested gently. Like Brad, she recognized half-truths when she heard them.

"Yeah. Mom remembered this place from when she was really little. 'Cept we had a hard time finding it. Mom had it marked on the map and all, but we kept walking in circles. Plan was for all the guys who busted out of Monroe to show up here."

"What?" Lara broke in, her voice incredulous.

"That will *not* happen." Brad spoke so low in the back of his throat it sounded like he was growling.

"Course it will," the woman said almost cheerfully. "'Cause that's how I planned it. Never figured someone else would already be here. Place was deserted for years."

"Your name?" Brad asked.

"Jane."

"Jane what?" he persisted.

"I don't have to tell you."

"You're right. You don't. Now, this is private property. It's been in our family for close to a hundred years and you're trespassing. For your information, I'm a cop." Reaching into his back pocket, he flashed his badge.

The woman's eyes widened. "Thought you were squatters, just like us."

"No. We have a right to be here," Lara confirmed. "You don't. So while I'm sorry about your husband's bullet wound, you still have to leave. There's a pharmacy in Skykomish where you might get antibiotics."

"Tried that," the girl muttered. "They wanted over two hundred bucks just for penicillin."

"And the pharmacist insisted on looking at Warren. Knew we couldn't do that, so we left," Jane added.

"How far away is your car?" Brad asked.

"Only 'bout a mile," the girl admitted.

"So you haven't been walking half the night? Why'd you want to come inside, anyway?" Lara asked, suspicions flaring.

"We were walking for quite a while. Like I said, we couldn't find the right driveway. If it hadn't been for the dog barking we'd prob'ly have missed your turnoff again." The girl hesitated. "I asked to come in 'cause it looks real nice in there, and I ain't never seen the inside of a really nice house." A sullen undercurrent ran through her last words.

"Wait here," Brad instructed. Turning to Lara, he said, "Come inside. We need to talk."

Behind a firmly closed door, Lara grabbed a shawl and pulled it close. It wasn't all that cold, but the conversation outside had chilled her to the bone. When she looked at Brad, worry tied her gut into a knot. "Jesus Christ, I wonder how many escaped prisoners are planning to converge on us. Once upon a time, I worried about refugees from Seattle stumbling on this place. This is far worse."

"Yeah, I'm concerned about the same thing. Even if we send these two packing, they'll just meet up with the rest of the bunch. They'll probably have gotten guns from somewhere since convicts are pretty proficient at that sort of thing. It would be really bad if a dozen of them threatened us at gunpoint to leave."

"Whatever warding Raven and the Sidhe did at least slowed them down—" she began.

"But it didn't stop them," he cut in. "Since the shielding seems to primarily work against Goblins, I don't think it will help us much with the current problem."

"What do you think we should do?" she asked. Apprehension made her nauseous and set her teeth on edge. "We can't just shoot these two."

"It does go against the grain," he admitted. "Even for me. But we could."

Lara narrowed her eyes. "All of them? This bunch and whoever else shows up? Once we start down *that* path, we're no better than they are."

He turned away from her and paced the length of the large room. After a couple minutes he said, "I'm open to suggestions here, Doctor. What do *you* think we should do?"

"I honestly don't know. One thing is abundantly clear, though. We can't both leave here."

"Glad you figured that part out," he mumbled.

"Maybe if you offered to help with their car in exchange for them finding somewhere else to hole up?"

"Yes. That might work if they were normal, decent people. These are criminals. I know how they think. You give them an inch and they decide they're entitled to a foot." He ran a hand through his shaggy hair in a gesture so reminiscent of Trevor it made her heart ache. "Wouldn't surprise me if they're casing the outbuildings while we're in here talking."

"Okay," she said evenly. "Maybe that means we need to go out there and tell them we're sorry, but they have to leave. And not come back."

"I'll do that." He picked up the shotgun and pulled the door open. "Stay inside," he instructed. "Nothing much you can do." A second later she heard him swearing.

"What?" She stuck her head out the door that hadn't yet closed.

"They're gone."

"Maybe you should check the other buildings," Lara said, suddenly worried about her chickens, goats, and their two horses. Securing the shawl tightly around herself, she started for the front steps.

"Uh-uh. You wait here." Brad's voice held a sharp edge. Gunter wiggled past her and raced after him, eager to offer German

Shepherd guidance and protection. Brad was back in a very short time.

He joined her on the porch and said, "They really did leave. Their tracks are pretty clear, both in and out of the driveway." He hesitated. "Unfortunately, they detoured past the barn and snared two of the hens."

She pulled the door open wider for him and muttered, "Damn it."

Back in the living room, Brad bent to toss more wood into the fireplace. "We did talk about this with Raven," he reminded her, kicking off his muddy boots before coming to sit next to her on the sofa.

"I remember." She nodded. "He said no one had come by in all the years he'd been here. Except he wasn't here all the time, so maybe he missed Jane's family. And perhaps a few others. This was a pretty well-known hot springs in the thirties, forties, and fifties. I looked it up on the net once I knew we'd be moving here. It said people still came to Garland Mineral Springs as late as the seventies and eighties, but that formal operations ceased years before that."

"Raven wasn't dealing with large numbers of people driven out of the cities by food shortages and riots, either," Brad pointed out. "That shifts the equation considerably. And not in our favor. It's unlikely this ragtag group is going to be the only one with fond memories of the springs."

"Mmph." She thought about their plans to rescue Trevor. They couldn't possibly leave the house unattended for more than a few hours, certainly not for the days they'd planned on being gone. "If we leave here," she said slowly, "and someone else has settled in while we're gone, it might be impossible to reclaim it."

"Not to mention that it will be hard enough to hang onto it even if we *are* here, and a large enough group storms the fortress."

"Well, we obviously can't both go to try to bring Trevor back," she said. "So that means I go alone."

He reached a hand toward her, his heart in his eyes. "I do *not* think that's a good idea. You've already discovered that using your magic as a weapon drains you. Do you really think you can go there, kill Goblins, and have enough power left to return?"

When Brad said it aloud, the truth in his words was harsh—and incontrovertible. "Not yet," she muttered, her mouth set in a hard line. "But if I wait much longer, Trevor may be dead." A lump formed in her throat and she swallowed around it. "I've been working as hard as I can on my magic. Looks like I'll have to work harder. Christ! What a fucked up mess this has turned into." She sprang to her feet, unable to sit still, and walked in a tight circle, hands clasped behind her.

"Who would've guessed Raven and the Sidhe would desert us?" she demanded sharply. The amulet, clearly not liking her last sentence, sent a wave of chilly disapproval into her. She toyed with tearing it off and letting it find its own way back to the *Dreaming* where a more deserving acolyte could pick up the banner. Maybe *their* teacher would stick around long enough to be useful.

At another stab of discomfort from the moonstone, she gripped it hard and said, "Stop that."

"Why don't you see if you can raise Raven?" Brad suggested softly. "Tell him about this latest problem. And see if maybe he's been able to help Trevor."

She closed her teeth over her bottom lip, understanding she was mired in feeling sorry for herself—and feeling helpless to boot. Not a good combination. "Could you check on the stuff in the oven?" Seeing him nod, she turned toward the stairs, hands folded protectively over her belly.

Lara knew she had to calm down to have any hope of connecting with either Raven or Lillian. When she was overwrought, she wasn't able to focus her magic to do much of anything. Her lessons in even the simplest spell casting always begun with structured breathing to empty her mind of competing priorities.

Because the library was her favorite of the second floor rooms, she settled there, lighting a scented candle and shutting the door firmly against intrusions from the outside world. She toyed with drawing the curtains, but the light calmed her, so she left them alone. When she scanned the yard, it was still empty. For a moment, she wondered about Jane and Johnna. Who were they, really? Where had they gone? Was their unseen husband and father really wounded, or was he just waiting until either dark came or his buddies showed up to launch an attack to wrest the farmhouse from them?

She stripped off her clothing and shivered. The library was cold, but she didn't want to take the time to build a fire. It had been Trevor's idea to use an ancient Celtic love charm to facilitate a connection with Lillian. After a bout of pagan abandon, where they screwed like bunnies in front of the old stone fireplace in the front room, Lillian had indeed appeared. Highly amused, the Sidhe informed them it took her back to Beltane where people truly appreciated the old rituals and proper care and feeding of magical beings like herself. Once she stopped chortling, Lillian informed Lara that simply removing her clothes would have been sufficient to summon her. Sex was icing on the cake, but not necessary.

Settling into a soft chair, she emptied her mind and called for Raven and Lillian. Vapor from the lavender-scented candle soothed her frayed nerves. After a time, she no longer noticed how cold she was. It seemed as if a very long time passed, but time moved differently when she was in a trance state, just like it did in the *Dreaming*. The amulet warmed where it nestled between her breasts, humming gently along with her meditative chant. She must have dozed because she started when she heard Raven's voice.

"Child."

"Raven." She was awake in an instant, intent on preserving the delicate trance state and its link to him.

"Much has happened."

She waited, knowing he'd tell her what he wanted her to know.

"The Goblins are leaving. Gren's tactics were highly effective. Gradoxst's field marshals decided his desire to re-establish himself as lord here comes at much too high a price." He snorted and, for a moment, he sounded like the old Raven: a big, bearlike demigod who was gruff, yet full of life.

"Trevor?" The word tore out of her. Projections tired Raven, and she didn't want him to leave before he told her what he knew.

"He managed to escape from Gradoxst."

She waited, heart in her throat; her fingers clutched the chair's fabric and the amulet so hard, her knuckles turned white.

"I can tell you that he yet lives. Aside from that…" the mage sighed. "It's strange, daughter. We understand how he foiled Gradoxst well enough. He crawled through a culvert designed to divert water into a dwelling.

"What we don't know is where he went from there. It's a good bet he didn't travel overland, since there's no sign of his passage. When I hunt for him with my mind, I run up against a barrier. The odd part is that the obstruction is of our making: Sidhe-forged, not made by Goblins. None of us can identify it more specifically. Many died in this battle, though. It's possible the one who carries the secret of this making has moved on to the Summerlands."

Raven's ability to project himself over distances never lasted long, so Lara hurried to get the next part in. *"You must return,"* she said. *"At least one of you. And sooner rather than later."* Launching into an abbreviated version of the morning, she told him about Jane and her daughter.

"One of us will be with you before nightfall," he promised grimly. "Is there anything else?"

"Yes." She detailed how she'd found Trevor the previous night. And that he forced her to leave, fearful of the Demon's imminent return.

"Good to know, daughter." His voice grew weaker. "It means Trevor's sojourn behind the mysterious barrier has been brief."

"Should I try to find him?"

"Were you even considering such an ill-advised course?" The rest of Raven's statement died away, and she knew he was at the end of the energy that held him near enough to talk.

"Well, yes," she mimicked Raven's speech pattern. "Now that you mention it, I was, indeed, considering precisely that *ill-advised course.* Furthermore, I haven't totally given up on it."

Lara stretched. Her body was stiff from what had likely been hours in the soft chair. As her trance receded, she shivered, then gathered her clothing and dressed quickly. That done, she glanced out a window at the westering sun and realized dusk was close to hand.

I spent hours in here. No wonder my body feels like it's been on a rack.

The front yard was empty and the house quiet. An idea took form in her mind. The more she thought about it, the more she knew she'd never get another chance to help Trevor. The amulet would help her find him.

Why not? she asked herself. *Brad's here in case Jane comes back with that group of thugs.*

She considered going downstairs to tell Brad she was leaving, but thought better of it. He'd try to talk her out of going, just like Raven. Heart thudding against her chest, Lara grabbed the amulet and began the incantation that would take her to the *Dreaming*.

The swirling mist parted. Fighting disorientation, it took her a few moments to realize she was in the same place she'd found Trevor the previous night. The place reeked of Goblin. Reaching out with her magic, she didn't sense anyone else in the cozy dwelling with rounded walls.

The room she was in was thoroughly trashed. Furniture had been tipped over and scrolls tumbled off the shelves. *Gradoxst was looking for something,* she surmised. *He didn't find it and lost his temper.* The extent of the damage chilled her. The fallen Sidhe was arrogant enough to not take kindly to interrupted plans. She peeked through a curtained alcove leading to a kitchen area. The amulet thrummed hotly against her chest, so she stepped through. All she found were still-damp clothes hanging off open cupboards.

Knowing she could easily be trapped in the hobbit-like home, Lara went back to the main room, intent on using the door she'd seen to go into the *Dreaming*. Despite the amulet's suggestion in the kitchen, it was clear Trevor wasn't here anymore.

The air hummed in warning. The amulet's tone changed

dramatically right along with it, alerting her of danger. The air in a corner of the room took on a shimmery, incandescent look.

Got to leave. I've got to get out of here. Now.

Lara chanted, but nothing happened. Horror filled her as Gradoxst's form solidified across the room. She clutched the amulet so hard, blood welled. Lillian's voice echoed in her mind. *Blood consecrates all.* Indeed, her blood gave the amulet what it needed to strengthen her spell. The walls swirled away to nothingness, and Gradoxst's cries followed her into the ether.

"Whore. I will get you. It is just a matter of time."

Panting and crying, Lara landed in a heap of tangled limbs on the floor of the library. She was shuddering so hard her teeth rattled. *Raven was right. That was fucking stupid,* she berated herself as she lurched to her feet, sucking air.

Still badly shaken, she let herself into the hallway, stopped by the bathroom to throw cold water on her face, and went down the staircase, intent on finding Brad. He was in the kitchen, sitting at the table reading a book. Both the shotgun and the Hoch and Keckler lay within easy reach.

He smiled when he saw her. "Ready for dinner?" he asked. "You pretty much missed lunch." The smile turned to a frown. "Jesus Christ. You look like hell. What happened?"

Gunter, who'd been lying in a corner, jumped up and ran to her. Hunkering down, she took the dog's head between her hands and kissed him between the eyes while she smoothed his fur back, murmuring endearments.

"Dinner would be good." Once he'd mentioned food, her stomach reminded her how empty it was. Over leftovers and dried bread smeared with fresh butter, she told him what Raven had said. Brad didn't say much, but she could tell he was listening intently.

Should I? Gathering her courage, she detailed her brief trip to the *Dreaming.* Even through mostly downcast eyes, she couldn't miss the abrupt change in his expression.

Brad leaped to his feet, wincing as he weighted his hurt leg. "That was fucking stupid." He pounded a fist into his open palm. "You thought you'd accomplish what?"

"I thought I could find him. The Sidhe can't seem to." Tears filled her eyes. She brushed them away angrily.

His next words were softer. "You should have told me."

Lara nodded. "Yes. I should have. Sit back down. Your dinner's getting cold."

"Mmph." He landed heavily in his chair and focused intently on his plate. Where he clenched his fork, his knuckles whitened.

Time dripped by as they ate in silence.

Finally, Brad looked up. "Sorry I lost my temper."

"I understand. I probably would've too."

"Good they've got those bastards on the run," he mumbled around a mouthful of supper. "Where do you suppose Trev's got himself holed up?"

"Why do you believe he's holed up anywhere?" Lara asked, surprised. That idea hadn't even occurred to her. When she'd gone looking for him, she'd assumed he was on the run.

"Simple." Brad finished chewing and swallowed before continuing. "Raven told you he didn't walk out of the *Dreaming*. Which means he's still there. He's alive, so he must've gone to ground, likely behind some sort of magical screen built by one of the Sidhe killed in battle."

"But the battle's over. Why wouldn't he just come out?" She took a swallow of some mediocre wine they'd found in one of the outbuildings. It hadn't aged well and was decidedly sour.

"Maybe he doesn't know the fighting's over. Or maybe the magic has him trapped in some way." Brad looked at her, his blue eyes serious. "I'm not the one to ask. Didn't Raven say one of them would be here soon?"

The words had barely left his mouth when the air across the kitchen shimmered. Lara jumped to her feet, dinner forgotten. As soon as Lillian stopped glowing, Lara lunged for her, practically throwing herself into the other woman's arms.

Not wanting to be left out, Gunter ran to her too, wagging his tail frantically in an enthusiastic bid for attention.

"There, there now, child," Lillian crooned, gathering Lara close. "This has been very hard. If the goddess is good to us, I shall not have to leave you again for a very long time." On his hind legs, the dog licked her chin. Untangling one hand from behind Lara's back, Lillian stroked him.

Lara pulled back, swiping impatiently at tears that wouldn't stop welling. "Trevor," she managed. "Do you know anything else about him?"

Lillian shook her head. When Lara really looked at her, she saw concern etched into Lillian's timeless features, and sadness mirrored in her clear, green eyes.

"Raven and Elidora are hunting for him, along with several others. Most of the Goblins have left, yet Gradoxst remains. We fear he too, is searching for Trevor." Her face took on a grim cast. "We must ensure we find him first.

"Is there enough dinner to share?" Lillian glanced at the table. Whispering in Gunter's ear, she convinced him to put all four paws on the floor.

"Of course," Brad replied. "I'll make you a plate."

"While we eat," Lillian said as she looked hard at Lara, "tell me in detail about who was here today." She pulled a chair out and sat down. "Don't hover, child. You need to finish your supper as well."

"You sound just like Trev," Lara grumbled, but a half-smile tugged at the corners of her mouth.

"Well," Lillian said with her distinctive asperity, "someone has to look out for Elizabeth."

Brad, who'd long since finished his meal, busied himself with his guns. In response to a questioning glance from Lara, he shrugged. "I've just got a feeling," he said softly. "And my instincts about people are hardly ever wrong. That bunch of misfits will be back. I don't know when. But they will be."

Lillian favored him with a rare smile. "I do believe you're right,

Detective," she said before digging into the food he'd laid in front of her. After a time, she glanced at Lara and adopted a matter-of-fact tone, "You have something to tell me."

"Uh, why would you think that?"

"Because it's blazoned across your mind. Whether you want to tell me or no, we must talk about what you did today."

Trevor pulled himself to his feet. The center of the cavern was more than tall enough for him to stand upright. The lights flickered more brightly, as if sensing his presence. Looking about, he saw a smooth floor, inlaid with good-sized flat stones. Water trickled down one wall, and someone had built a small bench out of wood, placing it next to a pile of rocks not too far from the entry passageway. *What was this?* It looked like caverns he'd seen in the Deep South that had housed runaway slaves. In some ways they'd been much the same, with an underground tunnel leading away from one of the grand, old manor houses.

"Why would any Sidhe need a hiding place in the *Dreaming?*" His voice echoed slightly off the walls, and the glowing places took on an amber hue. Curious, he walked closer to examine one and found a tiny sprite in an enclosed space. He tapped gently on the clear surface, but the creature inside cringed.

Trevor murmured, "Sorry, didn't mean to bother you," as he backed away. *They're little living things,* he marveled, even more certain a Sidhe had built this place. Likely the one who'd lived in the rooms below.

Too bad I never asked Raven or Lillian anything about the Dreaming, he reflected, knowing they might not have told him much, even if he'd had the foresight to inquire.

Settling on the bench, he took stock of himself. He was chilled, mostly because his clothes were soaked. He considered stripping down, but the damp fabric had a better chance of drying on his body than off. A shiver ran through him, and he examined the cuts and scratches he'd gotten during his scramble through the culvert. Nothing looked overly serious, other than his burnt arm.

Being away from Gradoxst was an unbelievable relief. Though he'd held himself together, the time he spent with the Demon had eroded him until his nerves felt like frayed rope. The wretched old creature just kept baiting him, delighting in the uncomfortable emotions he dredged up.

I've certainly got more than my share of ugly memories for that pervert to feed on. The minute the thought crossed his mind, Trevor understood how true it was. Gradoxst *had* been feeding off him—draining him— to keep his worn-out old body going. No wonder the Jung Institute had worked out so well for the old bastard. Psyche fueled such intense dream energy, it was likely no one even noticed when Gradoxst siphoned off what he needed.

Trevor got up to pace a bit, hoping to speed the drying process for his clothing. He'd been walking back and forth for a few minutes, when he heard a muted explosion. Fear bit deep, and he raced for the far side of the cavern, threw himself on the floor next to an overhanging wall, and curved his arms protectively over his head. Out of nowhere a vision of Gradoxst, sans clothes, head thrown back in ecstasy as he came, filled Trevor's mind. He felt ill all over again, sick and disappointed he hadn't taken a stand—even if it meant the Demon would have killed him. Another boom rocked the cave.

What the bloody fuck?

In a flash of unpleasant insight, he thought he knew. Unable to locate him, Gradoxst must have blown up the culvert. "Mary, mother of God, I'm fucking trapped in here," he moaned. "I'll never be able to dig my way out." Another rumble crashed against his ears, louder this time. Dirt drifted down from the rounded ceiling. Rocks clacked against one another. As he cowered near the wall, his eyes squeezed tightly shut, Trevor feared for the integrity of his shelter.

With his teeth chattering from a sudden shot of adrenaline, he stayed hunkered in place for a very long time. Finally, the dirt shower slowed, and the only sound was the thud of his heart, loud against his ears. Trevor unfolded his body and assessed if there'd been any significant damage to the cave. Aside from new piles of rocks, he couldn't find any.

The sprites glowed red. *They're either scared or angry,* he thought, wishing he could talk with them. Rapidly escalating panic at the thought of being trapped made it hard to think. His muscles felt tense, uncooperative; bile burned the back of his throat.

He walked close to one of the glowing walls. The sprites hissed at him, waving their tiny hands in a universal gesture that meant *hit the bricks.* Apparently they saw him as the source of the current problem.

"Yes, well, I'd certainly leave if I could," he told them, bowing slightly, then felt foolish.

In spite of himself, a ray of hope dangled tantalizingly. "I don't actually *know* that I'm trapped. I only *think* I am. Perhaps I should find out." Buoyed somewhat by the sound of his own voice, Trevor looked again at the glowing creatures. Could he carve a couple of the cylinders out of the wall? It would be useful to have a light source in the tunnel.

He dragged his knife out of a pocket. The remaining silver glowed faintly in the strange light in the cave. Examining the wall, he saw that some of it was solid stone, but parts were dirt. He plunged the point of the knife in between two of the sprites, sawing with a downward motion. The blade was sharp, cutting through the pounded dirt easily. In no time, he held one of the small creatures in his hand—safe within its dirt-crusted cylinder. He was midway through reassuring the tiny thing he meant it no harm in Celtic Gaelic, when he broke off, feeling like an idiot. It probably couldn't understand him.

He considered freeing another, but he'd need one of his hands to balance himself in the tunnel. Since he couldn't figure out how to lash the cylinder to his forehead like a headlamp, he decided to make do with what he had. Besides, the sprite seemed so distraught, changing colors every few seconds, he didn't want to upset any more of the magical beings.

He dropped to his knees, then to his belly, to begin a reconnaissance of the damage done to the tunnel. Pain flared in his arm as he crawled forward, but he ignored it. He didn't have to go far. The passage was only open to the bend. Grateful for the sprite and its glow, which had developed a greenish cast, he examined what looked like hundreds of tons of dirt and rocks blocking his way. Heartsick, he back-crawled into the cavern, pushed the sprite gently into its spot, and sat on the bench once again.

He gazed about the cavern, trying to think what to do, but his heart felt like a winged fury. It was beating so fast, he wondered if he was about to pass out. He heard the rapid rush of his breath and smelled his fear. Sour and acrid, it burned his nostrils with its intensity.

"Come on." He spoke as evenly as he could, since catching his breath was a struggle. "Settle down. I need to think, not panic. Won't figure anything out if I can't calm down." He forced himself to take nice, deep breaths, just like Lara had taught him. Thinking about her helped. If he lost it, he'd never see her again. After a time, he got up and walked over to where water flowed down the wall. Cupping his hands to gather liquid, he slurped noisily. Trevor hadn't realized how dry his throat was until the cold liquid slid down it. The water tasted sweet, almost as if it had been spelled by the Sidhe. He stuck his arm under the cold flow and was rewarded by an almost instantaneous reduction in pain.

Having drunk all he wanted, he swiveled his head from side to side to ease the iron bar of tension sitting between his shoulder blades. He was about to drop his chin to his chest when his eyes opened wider. The flickering sprites were creating waves of single colors. First a wash of amber, then of blue, then of green. All the waves pointed to a single spot. When he stared at it, his heart vaulted.

To the left of where water dribbled down was an opening—and a damned big one at that. Trevor rubbed at his eyes, willing them to focus more sharply. Even with the light from the sprites, it was still quite dim in the cave.

"Think, old man, bloody think," he exhorted. Trevor knew he'd been blessed with an uncanny sense of direction. Focusing that ability, he tried to remember just how far he'd been from the surface when he'd taken the side tunnel leading to the cavern. Next he closed his eyes and reconstructed his journey through the dark tunnel. It had been quite flat without any significant ups or downs. So that meant he was only about ten feet from freedom, assuming the cavern hadn't been excavated into a hill he didn't know about.

Glancing up, he estimated the ceiling of the cave to be seven feet at the center and something slightly less than that where he'd seen the opening. "So," he breathed, still talking out loud to steady his nerves, "all I have to do is figure out some way to climb up to that hole, and I should be able to dig my way through dirt until… Well, until there isn't any more. And that shouldn't be very bloody far."

Scooting over to the wall where the waterfall was, he tried kicking steps in the dirt, but it had the consistency of clay, and his boots didn't make a dent. He got out his knife and tried carving steps, but as soon as he stepped into the footholds, they shattered under his weight. He wiped sweat out of his eyes with the back of one hand. When he stopped working to consider what to do next, he was panting from tension and exertion. So close, but still so far.

After another half hour with virtually no progress, Trevor understood he needed to come up with a better plan. He dragged the bench over next to the wall. That gave him a bit of help. He could reach the rough edge of the opening easily. After several heart-wrenching tries, though, he found he couldn't support his weight. His burned hand and arm shot pain darts every time he tried to use them. Hoping for inspiration, he stared at the sprites. Their shifting colors had nearly mesmerized him when an idea blossomed.

The cylinders.

They were firmly embedded in the wall. If he edged them out an inch or so, that should be enough to give him a rough ladder. There'd still be several inches sticking into the hillside, so they should be stable enough.

Tamping down wild hope tearing through him, Trevor worked slowly and methodically, one cylinder at a time, until he thought enough of them protruded to allow him to stem his body into the chimney-like opening and jam himself between the narrow walls like he'd seen rock climbers do. Sitting on the bench, he removed his boots, tied the laces together and hung them around his neck. It would be much easier to climb the slick wall barefoot. He held the knife in his hand, considering what to do with it. Finally, he shoved it into a deep pocket where, hopefully, it wouldn't stab him if he had the bad luck to fall.

Trevor walked to the water. He drank, more to forestall having to actually test his newly constructed ladder than because he was thirsty. The clear liquid was far more refreshing than water had a right to be. He soaked his arm and hand again, hoping the effects would last until he was safely through the opening above him.

He sucked in a few raspy breaths, then made a concerted effort to draw air deep into his lungs. Taking another look at his impromptu ladder, he realized he was afraid to test it because if it failed, he was dead out of ideas. "No time like the present," he said, trying to infuse confidence into his voice. Swinging onto the bench, he repositioned his boots so they hung behind him. The laces crossed his windpipe, but the pressure wasn't bad.

Besides, I'll be out of here in a trice.

With half his body in the chimney, one foot slipped, shattering a cylinder. A high-pitched scream filled the cavern; it had to be the sprite dying. The rest of the cylinders glowed red. The ones he was touching were suddenly blistering hot. Agony shot through his burned hand, but if he let go he'd fall, and the cave would become his crypt.

Trevor's breath came fast. Adrenaline surged. Terror shot through him. His burned fingers cramped and slipped off a heated cylinder, and his heart stuttered in his chest. He felt himself starting to fall—beginning the trajectory that would end with him lying on the cave floor, likely with his back broken—when he managed to grab onto a root embedded in the wall. Pain surged through his arm as the wood dug into his flesh, but he clung to it and pressed upward.

Now that he knew what to look for, he curled his stinging fingers around another root, and then one more. His feet weren't faring much better than his hands since he was barefoot. The smell of singed flesh joined the stench of his fear. By the time he passed the last of the cylinders, he could barely believe it. Panting raggedly, his arm, hands, and feet screaming in pain, he realized he'd judged right, and his spirits soared.

Enough of his body was finally in the opening to shove his back against one wall and his bare feet against the other. Reaching up, he dragged the bootlaces away from his throat since they were choking him. Remorse for the dead sprite dogged him, but he told himself not to think about it. At least not until he was safe.

Using his arms and legs, he inched upward. The chimney had a bend in it after only a few feet. It led to a flat spot, but the passageway —that someone had definitely carved out of dirt and rock—kept going. Excitement coursed through him as he looked at gouges in the walls that had to have been made by a man—or a Sidhe.

On a patch of sand just ahead, he spied the most welcome glow he'd ever seen. *Daylight!*

Finally sure he wouldn't fall, Trevor collapsed, sucking air like a bellows. He cradled his aching arm against his body, willing it to stop hurting. When his breathing stabilized, he took stock of blisters on his fingers and feet from the super-heated glass cylinders. Guilt washed through him. He'd killed a sprite by destroying her home. "I'm sorry," he called softly back down the tunnel. "Truly I am."

Despite wanting to scooch forward until he could feel the sun on his face, Trevor made himself put his boots back on. He pulled the knife out and crept cautiously toward the opening.

No point in doing all this if I'm just going to run back into Gradoxst's arms.

"Trevor!" Raven's worried voice reverberated in his mind, so loud it practically deafened him.

"Yes—" he began, then remembered he wasn't supposed to answer out loud. "Yes. I'm almost out of that God awful cave above the house where I was imprisoned."

"Aha! That's why we couldn't locate you. I know exactly where you are now. Thank the goddess. We've all been frantic trying to find you."

"Is it safe?"

"Quite safe." Raven used his real voice. "In fact, I'm right here. Come on out."

A shadow played across the patch of daylight. Trevor pulled himself the last short distance. Heaving his body out of the hole, he lay on his belly, shell-shocked. His weary mind couldn't quite grasp that his ordeal was over. *It's Raven, not Gradoxst. I've got to pull myself together.* It took two tries, and help from Raven, to get his feet under him because his legs shook so badly.

The sun was setting, casting rays of gold across the horizon. Trevor realized how many hours it had taken him to get out of the cave. He started to say something, but Raven pulled him into a hug. Trevor hugged back just as hard as he could, forgetting about his burned arm until pain shot up it. "Arrrgh," he moaned. "Hurts. What happened? Where's Gradoxst?"

Raven smiled grimly. "That, son, is one of the mysteries we're still trying to solve. *You* were the other. Here, let me take care of that." Raven laid wonderfully cool hands on Trevor's arm. In minutes, the pain improved. Once it was down to a bearable level, he tried to pull his arm back, but Raven shook his head. "Wait until I'm done."

Nodding tiredly, Trevor lost track of time. When Raven finally let go of him, he stumbled and would have fallen if the mage hadn't reached out to steady him.

Looking around nervously, half-expecting Gradoxst to jump out from behind a rock, Trevor finally met Raven's gaze. "Take me home, please. I'd go on my own, but I don't know how."

The mage skewered him with such an intense glance that Trevor looked away. "Aren't you even a bit curious about where you were?"

Trevor laughed weakly. "Sure, but I figure you can tell me about that any old time. Right now, what I want more than anything is Lara."

Raven laughed. The sound of his booming mirth filled Trevor with joy—something he'd not felt since his capture. "All in good time. Elidora would never forgive me if she couldn't lay eyes on you. And Gren too. He is but spirit, yet he still can see. In truth, his ideas are what saved us. And there are others who would meet you as well. Follow me."

"I thought Gren was somewhere here that the living couldn't access." Trevor's brain felt like it was made of mush, but he did recall Elidora keening about Gren being lost to her forever.

"The gods recanted," Raven explained, "after Gren came up with the idea to use his energies, and those of spirits like him, against the Goblins, Shape Shifters, and other Demons."

Trevor trailed across the heath, half delirious with the knowledge he was really and truly free of Gradoxst. In spite of that, he found himself glancing over his shoulder as the sun set in a blaze of red. Though lovely, the bloody color cast a sudden chilly premonition.

This is just a respite. We're not out of this yet. Not by a long shot.

"Perspicacious of you." Obviously reading his thoughts easily, Raven looked back over one shoulder. "But for now, we shall enjoy our victory. The *Dreaming* is ours once again. And it shall stay that way. I doubt even Gradoxst will be able to convince his minions to return here anytime soon."

"Has it been under attack before?"

"Certainly. Why do you think Celan built the cave you just crawled out of? And shielded it with magic."

"The one whose quarters were below?"

The Sidhe nodded. "Just this way, now."

Trevor cocked his head. He heard water. A lot of it, cascading over rocks. Twisting his head, he saw a beautiful waterfall glowing iridescently in the rays from the setting sun. To his surprise, Raven walked right through it. Though he girded himself for a drenching, Trevor didn't end up any wetter than he'd been. He found himself inside another passageway, similar to one he'd just left, except this one was tall enough to stand and walk normally. The same curious light illuminated things.

"What's in those?" Trevor pointed at a tiny cylinder.

"Air sprites."

Noticing that they changed to a soft blue when Raven walked past, Trevor asked, "How do they survive?"

"Their Sidhe imbues them with magic. They can last a thousand years, living on air."

"I—uh." Trevor cleared his throat. "I'm afraid I killed one getting out of that cave."

Raven stopped walking and turned to face Trevor. "I'm sorry to hear that. Things will not go well for the next person who sets foot in there. These small creatures have long memories."

"I figured they wouldn't welcome me, but why take revenge on another?"

"To even the score."

An eye for an eye…

Trevor followed Raven down a gentle slope. He was sad about the air sprite and extremely weary—it surprised him he was able to keep going. After what felt like a very long time, they came to an open cavern.

Elidora ran to him, laughing and crying at the same time. Gathering him close, she said, "Hale, sweet boy, aye an' I'm so glaid we fand you. I were fearin' for your life, laddie. We searched and searched, but we couldna find you. Silly o' us no' t' 'ave minded Celan's cavern. He built it for just such times as these. 'Twas shielded so no magic could penetrate the walls. A body hiding within is all but undetectable."

"'Twas th' hand o' th' midder led him thennis," another woman said, sounding stern. Pulling away from Elidora, Trevor looked into golden eyes so like Gren's that he started. "Aye, an' I be Gren's syster, Bean," the woman murmured, inclining her head slightly. "If ye shut up thine een, ye'll sense Gren. He'll be nere by."

Obediently, Trevor shut his eyes. Soft as butterfly's wings, he felt something brush his face and he heard Gren's voice deep within his mind. *"'Twas mony a sair day's kemping, my lad, yet thaut whit be guid i' th' warld sall lange dure. Get thee haim t' thy gudwife and bairn. Ye hae no' yet done wi' th' kemp agayne th' mirker. An' ye may nevir hae. But th' saal within you be strang and schynand brycht. Gae thee wi' my blissing, lad."*

"Such a brave thing you did, closing the Goblins out from our world," Trevor murmured. "I wanted to be able to thank you. And now I can."

"What neid it mair. 'Twas behuvit. No mair thair is."

When Trevor opened his eyes, all the Sidhe in the sacred cave had come close. Everyone introduced themselves. The mead went round —and round again. After a time, Trevor wondered giddily just how many bottles they'd drunk. He wanted to go home more than anything, but didn't want to risk offending the Sidhe by asking if he could leave.

When he was tottering on his feet from exhaustion, Elidora finally said, "I will take you back, laddie. I would see my other laddie." Catching his eye, she winked. The gesture was so bawdy and so typically Elidora, that Trevor laughed.

"Come on, then," he urged. "I'd like to catch Lara whilst she's still awake."

"Oh aye, I suspect she'll open those coal-dark eyes for her bonny laddie, no matter what the time." Coming close, Elidora closed her arms around Trevor. "Ye shall follow me. We could part from here, but 'twill be mair eith if we stand 'neath the goddess's sky."

"Wait." His gaze sought Raven's. "When are you coming?"

"Soon enough. Give that wife of yours a kiss for me."

Once they'd reached the other side of the waterfall, Elidora pulled him close. "Hold on, now," she whispered in his ear. "Quick as a wink, ye'll be hame."

A swirling sensation filled him. The bottom dropped out of the world, and he fell into nothingness. It wasn't unpleasant, more dreamlike than anything else. His feet hit something gently and, when he opened his eyes, the welcoming walls of the living room rose about him. He felt the sting of tears and understood he'd never really believed he'd see his home again.

Or Lara.

Fighting vertigo, he heard Elidora say, "'Twill pass, laddie," as he forced his unsteady feet toward the stairs. Gunter raced in from the kitchen, threw his paws on Trevor's midsection and licked him furiously. Since he was dizzy anyway, Trevor fell over in an untidy heap with the dog lying on top of him, whining.

Feet clattered on the stairs. Lara knelt down and threw her arms about both of them, crying softly. "Aw, Trev… I never thought I'd see you again. I was so frightened that monster would…would… Never mind, it's not important. You're home. Thank the goddess, you're back." She held on so hard it hurt.

Reveling in her closeness, he lost himself in her familiar scent: lavender mingled with something uniquely Lara.

Trevor lay on the floor, his arms wrapped around the woman he loved more than anything in the world. His heart flooded with relief. Something twisted tightly within him ever since Gradoxst had dragged him to the *Dreaming* began to ease.

Meantime, Gunter's cold nose and warm tongue worked on his arm. The dog managed to ferret out bare flesh through a rent in his shirt. "Yes, yes," he told the dog. "Daddy's back. Let's just move over a touch so he can give Mum a better hug." As if he understood, the dog sat back on his haunches, tongue lolling, a knowing smile on his canine face.

Trevor pushed himself to a sitting position. "Lara." He spoke her name softly, almost reverently. She repositioned herself to sit across from him. He placed a hand on either side of her face. "You're the most beautiful thing I've ever seen," he murmured, his voice choked with emotion. Eying his hands, he winced and reluctantly drew them away. "I'm filthy. I shouldn't be touching you. Not until I've had a proper bath."

"Well, come on then." She smiled at him through her tears. "Let's go upstairs. I'll draw one. Fact, I'll even wash your back."

A vision of Gradoxst's ancient, disgusting back—and what had come next—ratcheted through him. Trevor shivered involuntarily.

"What?" Lara looked so tender and so concerned it broke his heart.

He shook his head. "Nothing, love. Just bad memories. I'm sure they'll pass."

"We shall make certain of that." Lillian's dry voice cut through his melancholy.

He told himself to get a grip. *I'm home, for chrissakes. Home. It could be so much worse.*

Gratitude welled in him. When he looked up, he saw Lillian standing next to Elidora over by the fireplace. Brad was on Elidora's other side with an arm draped around her waist. He hooded his eyes, but not quickly enough. Trevor saw love and longing in them as the detective dragged his gaze away from Lara. He also saw a weary resignation.

Trevor drew an unsteady breath and looked hard at Lara. "What the fuck?"

"Not now," she said quietly. "We can talk upstairs."

"Let's see if I stand up then," he suggested and shot another glance at Brad. Color stained the detective's cheeks, a declaration of shame if Trevor was any judge.

Brad's in love with her. When the bloody fucking hell did that happen?

The disorientation in the wake of traveling back from the *Dreaming* had eased, and Trevor managed to scramble upright. He held out a hand to Lara. Once she was by his side, he twined an arm about her shoulders, and they started up the stairs, leaning into one another. Gunter padded alongside them, like a shadow frightened of being left behind again.

"I'll bring you something to eat presently," Lillian called.

CHAPTER 12

*L*ara tightened her arm around Trevor's waist. He'd stumbled several times on their way up the stairs, and she could tell he was almost at the end of his reserves. When she pulled open the door to their room, he froze, his body stiffening.

"What the bloody hell, Lara?" He straightened, half turning so he looked right at her. "Why are there *two* beds in this room?"

"It's all right," she murmured, meeting his gaze head on so there could be no mistaking the truth in her next words. "The other bed is here because, after I disappeared the night you'd been kidnapped, Brad tied a rope around one of my wrists and held onto the other end all night, every night. He did it so my body couldn't leave again." She hesitated, picking her words carefully. "If there'd been anything going on, there'd only be one bed in here. You're not thinking clearly."

He shook his shaggy head, and a blush crept from his torn collar to his filthy face. "I saw how Brad looked downstairs. It was rather like me coming home was the worst thing that could have happened—at least for him."

Sensitive to the pain in Trevor's words, Gunter pushed past Lara, shouldering his way into the room just before she pulled the door shut. The dog walked to Trevor and rubbed against him, whining softly.

"There's a good boy," Trevor murmured, reaching down to pet him.

As she listened to his very-carefully-enunciated British accent, Lara understood how rattled Trevor was by this latest development. She could scarcely blame him. After everything he'd been through, to come home to Brad's poorly-concealed affection for her had to be damned unsettling.

She laid a hand tenderly over his shoulder, rubbing gently. "Let's not dissect this just now. Why don't you start getting out of those clothes? They'll need a turn through the washer, but not tonight. I'll get a bath going for you. You can clean up and then we'll go to sleep. There'll be time to talk in the morning."

If we don't get attacked by that passel of convicts tonight.

"I thought Lillian was bringing food up here."

"I'm sorry, Trev. Now it's me that's not thinking. You must be hungry." Lara felt contrite. *Of course he'd be. He must have been half starved where he was.* "Do you want food before your bath? I can go get some—"

"Nah," he interrupted. "I'm so bloody tired, I don't know what I want, other than to wrap my arms around you and never, ever let go again."

The joy that had bloomed in her heart once she realized he was truly back, expanded. "Yes, well, I'd like that too, but let's get some of that Goblin filth off you first." Crossing the room, she shoved the curtain aside and flipped on the taps to start the tub filling.

Gunter retreated to his favorite corner of the bedroom and curled up in a ball. He kept his eyes on Trevor, though, alert and ready to take on anything that might threaten his daddy.

When Lara turned to face him, Trevor's blue eyes looked so wounded her heart ached. She wanted to scream: *What did that bastard do to you?* but held her peace. He'd tell her in his own time. Tonight if he just got cleaned up and some food into him, it would be enough.

Trevor folded his body accordion-fashion until he was on the floor. Once there, he worked at untying his boots.

"Why don't you sit on the bed?" she asked. "It'd be more comfortable."

He shook his head. "Too dirty," he mumbled. "Don't want to get anything on the sheets. And I stink. I can smell myself, so I know you must be able to smell me."

"I wouldn't care if you'd been rolling in an offal heap," she said. "Dirt washes off."

"Maybe so." Trevor sounded resigned. "'Fraid It'll take more than clean clothes, a washed body, and a full belly to fix what transpired in Gradoxst's lair. Sorry, love, but it's the truth."

Lara's heart clenched. She wanted to go to him, but he was stripping off the rags clinging to his emaciated form, and getting him clean felt more important than telling him everything would be all right—especially when he knew different. Turning back to the rapidly filling tub, she grasped the amulet, placed her other hand in the water, and began to chant. As soon as the water warmed, she motioned for him.

SHE DRAINED the water and refilled the tub twice before Trevor finally felt clean. He was bruised and scraped, but none of his injuries, including a residual mild reddening where his arm had been burned, looked serious enough to dress. He was just wrapping his old, blue robe around him and shaking water droplets out of his blond curls when a tap sounded on the door.

"Must be Lillian," he mumbled. Raising his voice, he called, "Come in. I'm decent, and I am hungry."

The door flew open, except it wasn't Lillian but Brad standing there, a tray balanced on one large, splayed hand. "Told her I wanted to bring it up," he said, avoiding Trevor's eyes.

Off to one side, Lara watched the two men. Her stomach

tightened, and she had to make an effort to unclench her jaw. She flirted with grabbing the tray from Brad and shooing him out of their room, but told herself the men needed to talk sometime. If they had to mount a defense against the escaped convicts later on, there couldn't be unresolved tension hovering between them.

Trevor looked warily at Brad. If he'd been a dog, his hackles would've been standing on end. Brad just looked sad—and determined. The detective walked to the far side of the room and placed the tray on a dresser.

"Did you poison it?" Trevor asked grimly and furled his brows.

Brad spun about, the movement so abrupt Trevor's hands flew up, balled into fists. Brad just shook his head, looking desolate. "Do you really think I'd do that to you?" His voice had an odd catch in it, and he cleared his throat.

"I'm not sure of much of anything," Trevor growled. "Why don't we start with this one: when did you fall in love with my wife?"

Brad laughed hollowly. "Probably the first time I laid eyes on her. You're not very observant if you haven't noticed before. Although the lady in question," he waved a hand in Lara's direction, "tells me there are holes in my, ah, defense mechanisms that didn't used to be there. So maybe I'm not as good at hiding things as I once was." He shrugged helplessly.

"Oh, I see, then. Certainly. A psychological explanation. Isn't that bloody fucking convenient?" Trevor paced up and down the room, blew out an annoyed sounding breath, and then another.

Lara struggled with wanting to go to him, but it would be better if she didn't interfere. Not yet anyway.

"I would never do anything to hurt either of you," Brad said, looking hard at Trevor. But Trevor set his mouth in a tense line and didn't say anything. He did stop moving, though, and turned to face the detective, scowling.

"Do you think this is easy for me?" Brad went on, his voice cracking. He clasped his hands in front of him, the knuckles white from pressure. "You're the closest thing to a friend I've ever had. I *care* about you. You've been kind to me. Helped me, even after I sold Lara out to that unspeakable monster. I—I can't help the way I feel about her. Don't even know where it came from. But I'd never do anything about it. Never. You have to believe me."

"He offered to come with me to rescue you," Lara said softly. "And to stay behind in the *Dreaming* if I only had enough magic to bring two of us back here."

Trevor's gaze never left the detective's face, as he sifted Brad's words, no doubt seeking truth behind them. After a few moments, he exhaled raggedly. Lifting his head resolutely, he said, "All right, Brad. I believe you. But I'm too tired to talk about this tonight."

Brad nodded, the harsh set of his shoulders relaxing a bit. "Thank you. We don't ever have to talk about it again if you don't want to." The detective hesitated, exchanging a glance with Lara.

"What?" Trevor looked from one to the other, the line of his jaw tightening. "If there's another shoe, drop it now, goddammit it."

"It's possible a group of escaped prisoners from Monroe might show up here sometime before dawn. Lillian, Eli, and I should be able to handle them, though." Brad snorted. "Now that I think about it, I'm sure the women could manage just fine without any help at all from me."

Trevor scrubbed his hands down his face. "How would you know hooligans are planning to come here? I thought this place was warded." Trevor swung to look at Lara. "You didn't—"

"No," she broke in firmly. "I didn't tell you about it. And I'm not going to talk about it now, either. You're going to eat, and then we're going to get some sleep." The baby chose that moment to do a somersault. She laid a hand over her midsection. "Trev," she motioned. "Come feel."

Stepping close, he placed a hand over her belly. A look of wonder washed over his face, and he asked, "When did you first feel her?"

"About the time Brad's leg got caught in that trap. I didn't have a chance to tell you because so much else was happening. But she's getting a whole lot more active." Trevor closed his hand more tightly around the mound of her stomach.

She met Brad's ice-blue gaze in a silent plea for privacy. He nodded and slipped out the door, tugging it shut behind him.

"Come on," she said. "Let's get some food into you." But Trevor pulled her into his arms, his mouth coming down hard on hers. She twined her arms around him and kissed him back. All the pain and desperation she'd lived with ever since his capture added fuel to their embrace. Scarcely daring to believe he was really and truly back in her arms, she clung to him and strung kisses all over his neck and face. With her heart full, she murmured his name over and over, while her blood ignited with need.

"The food will keep." Trevor's voice was rough with barely suppressed emotion. He scooped her up as if she weighed nothing and laid her tenderly on the bed. His robe puddled on the floor around him as he shrugged out of it. Pulling at her clothing, he settled one hand on a breast, the other on her belly.

"Let me help you," she said breathlessly, her fingers busy with the drawstring she'd fashioned to hold up the pants she couldn't zip anymore. As he lay down next to her, she slid one leg out of her jeans and reached for him. "I need you," she murmured, her breath coming fast. "Now. Fancy can come later."

"Ach, love. I was so afraid I'd never see you again." Tears glistened in his eyes.

She tightened her arms around him, pulling him close. With an inchoate moan, Trevor buried his face in her neck, his body trembling. He wound his hands in her long hair and rained kisses on her breasts and belly, then lower still. Crying, Lara moaned his name as release rocked her and then took her again.

Time stopped as he covered her body with his own and drove himself inside her. She wrapped her legs around him and held on, urging him to love her with everything she had. Maybe she couldn't heal him with words, but there was magic in the dance their bodies did, twined together by desperation and passion.

BRAD SAT next to Adriana's grave. He'd been talking with her for over an hour, telling her he missed her and how sorry he was he hadn't been able to rescue her in time to save her life. He'd been in the house for a while after leaving Trevor and Lara, but the unmistakable sounds of their lovemaking drove him outside. It wasn't that he was jealous, or maybe he was. He ached for someone to love, and for someone to love him. Between his fucked up mother and his equally fucked up marriage, he'd never had either.

"I made my choices," he muttered," but they weren't very good ones. Now I guess I've got what I deserve."

"An' are we feelin' very sorry for ourselves?" Elidora's soft brogue interrupted what was, indeed, a spate of self-pity.

"Yeah, I suppose I am. It's not a crime." Brad bristled.

"An' I am no' sayin' that 'tis. My, ye are a bit on th' tetchy side tonight. I might not be th' one ye're a'wantin', but I left th' *Dreaming* t' hold you in my arms. Is that no' th' way o' things? Love is so often at cross purposes, eh?"

Brad scrambled to his feet, searching the darkness with his eyes. Elidora's black-clad form would've been hard to pick out if he hadn't just been talking with her. Striding close, he pulled her to him and settled his mouth over hers. His cock stiffened when he pressed against her, but his heart wasn't in it. Not tonight, anyway.

Pushing away, she laid a gentle hand on one side of his face. "We will beg th' goddess's blessings, but let it no' be tonight. I ken mair 'an ye think. 'Tis just tha' I have lived far longer an' I understand about takin' comfort where it's offered. Even lives long as mine can feel short betimes."

"Let's go back inside," he suggested. "Did Lillian tell you about our unexpected visitors from earlier today?"

"Aye, that she did. Curious, is it no', tha' they were able t' find th' house in th' first place. I checked th' wardings an' all were still in place."

"I found it," Brad pointed out.

"Aye, but ye cheated by followin' Lara an' Trevor," she reminded him gently, an undercurrent of humor in her words.

"Mmph," he snorted, acknowledging the truth in her statement. "I think it was the dog barking," he added. "At least that's what the woman said." Brad took hold of Elidora's arm, turning her gently to face him. "I don't want you to think I'm not grateful, or that I don't enjoy what we do together. I do. It's incredible, really. I didn't think passion like that existed…well, anywhere." He hesitated, feeling uncomfortable, but plowed ahead anyway. "You've opened a part of me that I feared was dead."

"Aye, laddie. I know all o' that, and more. Just no' tonight. 'Tis probably for th' best." She laughed, and the rich sound bounced off the evergreens. "Ye may not know it, but the two o' us are bound. When ye trifle with a Sidhe, we get under your skin in th' most unusual ways."

Taking his hand in one of hers, she pulled him toward the house. "If there are to be problems, Lillian an' I must ready ourselves. 'Tis far easier t' mount a defense at th' front end of things than in th' middle."

Brad nodded thoughtfully as he walked toward the well-lighted house, side-by-side with the Sidhe. He knew all too well from his years of police work that it was best to be prepared and get a jump on things before they got out of hand. "If the convicts show up, do you want me to do anything? Or would staying out of the way be best?"

Elidora laughed again. "Och, you humans! Best to let Lillian an' me take care o' things. We can ensorcel. All ye can do is kill. "'Twould be best if those who come here have no memories o' this place to share with others."

They reached the steps. At the top, Brad held the kitchen door open and motioned Elidora through. Turning to him, she bowed slightly. "Manners. I have always approved o' those in a man."

It was Brad's turn to laugh. "I'll bet. Far too many of us don't have any."

"Get in here." Lillian's voice held an irritated edge. "Another ten minutes and I would've dragged the two of you out of whatever bed you'd found for yourselves. With the exception of the two upstairs—whose need is understandable and blessed by the goddess—this is not a time to be indulging ourselves." She looked pointedly at Elidora.

"Bosh." The witch woman threw her hands in the air. "Just because Raven's still in th' *Dreamin'*—"

"Enough," Lillian snapped. "I am *not* sharing my private life with mortals."

So there is *something between the two of them,* Brad thought with satisfaction. He'd assumed so, since Raven and Lillian had the feel of a long-married couple.

"Dinna fash yersel'. No harm done. Ye will be keepin' your mouth closed about this?" At Brad's nod, Elidora pulled up a chair and sat at the kitchen table. "Where's th' mead?"

Lillian dropped one of the green glass bottles in front of her. Elidora took a long drink, then passed the bottle to Brad, who was still standing next to the table wondering what he should do.

"I can leave if you'd like," he offered, holding out the bottle so one of the women could take it.

"Sit down." Lillian sounded about as friendly as an alley cat defending its territory, but Brad sat, took another swig of mead, and passed the bottle to Lillian. Silence stretched between them.

After a time, he glanced at the wristwatch he hadn't been able to give up. It was past midnight. "Can either of you sense anything?" he asked.

Lillian looked as if she'd forgotten he was there. "No," she said, her voice curt.

"The wards mute what we can sense," Elidora said. "They shield our presence from others, but it works t'other way as well."

Didn't seem to work worth a shit when Gradoxst sashayed past them and nabbed Trevor. Brad hesitated since Lillian seemed to be in such a foul mood, but curiosity got the better of discretion. "Could either of you tell me how Gradoxst defeated the wards so easily."

Elidora shot him a look that made him sorry he hadn't kept his mouth shut. "Because that goddess-be-damned traitor is still one of us," she snapped.

Heat rose to his face. "Of course," he muttered, understanding he should've been able to figure that out on his own.

The click of Gunter's claws on the floor provided a welcome reprieve. Last time he'd seen the dog was in Lara and Trevor's room. "Need out, boy?" he asked. Standing, Brad walked to the door.

"If he goes, you go with him," Lillian snapped. "Keep him quiet. In fact, when the two of you get back in here, I'll have a little talk with him." The dog's ears had been pricked forward. They drooped when he heard Lillian's sharp tone. Tail hanging low, he scuttled out the door Brad held open for him.

"Women. They get angry quicker than lightning," Brad said conversationally as he walked the dog around the yard. Gunter woofed once—but softly—almost as if he'd understood Lillian's admonition. Brad glanced at the moonless night. High, scattered clouds drifted past; a few stars shone silver against the deep black of the sky.

Wonder what it'd be like to be like the Sidhe?

Brad hadn't even believed in fairy tales as a boy. To have real-life magicians only a few feet away felt damned unsettling—if he let himself think about it. A wry grin split his usually serious face. He did think about magic, just not very often. Every time he thought about it, so many questions he couldn't answer popped up that he backed away in the interest of preserving his sanity. The reality of other worlds, some inhabited by bad guys and some by good, took some serious getting used to.

He clucked to the dog, since he was roaming a bit too far. Gunter turned and looked back at Brad, his tail pluming, but he didn't come. "Now," Brad spoke firmly. The Shepherd, who'd been digging at the edge of the yard, finally trotted back with something clamped in his jaws. Expecting a rabbit or a squirrel, Brad's eyes widened once the dog got close enough for him to see. "What's this?" he asked, tugging at a small doll dangling from the dog's mouth. Gunter growled softly, hanging on.

"Okay then, bring it with you." Brad ran up the risers, taking them two at a time. Gunter scooted through the door, his treasure dangling from his mouth. Brad locked the door, and then strode into the kitchen, thinking he really needed to get some sleep. He stopped dead at the expressions on the women's faces, goodnight words dying on his lips.

"Where did he get this?" Lillian held the bundle of cloth gingerly between her thumb and index finger.

"In the side yard, over by the barn. Why? It's just a child's toy, isn't it?" Of course not. Otherwise they wouldn't be staring at me as if I'd brought something unspeakable into the kitchen.

"'Tis a location charm," Elidora said through clenched teeth.

"Huh?" Brad felt confused. "You mean like a GPS chip that transmits information?"

"You two aren't speaking the same language." Lillian sounded tired. "What this means is the Demons have returned. At least one of them, probably Gradoxst—since we never did chase him down in the *Dreaming*—is just biding his time."

"So two possibilities exist, in terms of who might attack us?" Brad asked, feeling like he'd been kicked in the guts.

"At least," Lillian answered dryly. Whistling sharply, she summoned the dog. "Good boy," she said when he trotted over. "Good that you found this." She waggled the charm gently. Gunter, sensing a game, lunged for it, but she said, "Uh-uh," and he subsided, looking quietly pleased with himself.

Brad fell into a nearby chair. "I've always felt uneasy this place wasn't farther off the highway," he mumbled. "Figured when things got bad enough, there'd be roving bands of people looking for something, anything, they could use to stay alive. The roads to get back here aren't all that hard to drive on."

"Aye, an' that is why we set wards…" Elidora began, but lapsed into silence at a pointed look from Lillian.

"Yes, too bad they're not a shade more effective—or predictable." Irritation twisted Lillian's mouth downward. "I'll take first watch. Get what rest you can, Eli. I'll wake you in a while."

"What about me?" Brad looked at her. His eyes felt hot and gritty. He understood how badly he needed to close them, at least for an hour or so.

"Settle on the couch in the living room," she told him. "That way you'll be close if we need you."

revor swung the splitting maul, bringing it down hard on a pine round. The wood shuddered. Droplets of moisture flew up from its whorls splattering him in the face. Shaking water out of his eyes, he tightened his belly and swung again. This time, the wood shattered into several jagged pieces. He dropped the maul, bent to pick up the wood, then carried it into the shop, where he added it to a tier he had going against one wall. At least it was drier in the shed, so the wood might actually be able to burn at some point without magical intervention from one of the women.

Sweat dripped into his eyes. It stung and he drew his sleeve across his forehead. It had been three weeks, more or less, since he'd gotten back. Despite Lillian and Elidora stomping about with expressions that could curdle milk, there'd been no visitors—mortal or otherwise. Gunter had unearthed three more of the strange dolls, though. Since someone had glued hair on them and sketched a parody of a face, it was clear each was supposed to be an approximation of one of them. They had yet to find the Brad-doll.

The detective had smirked knowingly when doll number four was added to the lineup in the kitchen window because it wasn't him. "Maybe some lady Goblin has eyes for me," he joked, but Elidora had belted him in a less-than-funny fashion. Lillian followed that up with a terse admonition to not voice such things aloud.

As if he could sense Trevor's thoughts, Brad strolled around the corner, his shirtsleeves rolled up. From the looks of things, he'd been mucking out either the barn or the paddock or both. "Want a hand with the wood?" he asked, a broad smile lighting his gaunt features.

"Sure. That would be splendid." Trevor raised his arms over his head and rotated his torso from side to side trying to get the kinks out of his back from hefting the heavy maul over and over again. After a few tense days, an easy camaraderie had re-established itself between them. Brad really was useful. Not that Lillian and Elidora couldn't have helped out, but even with their magic, they weren't quite as handy as another man.

"It's odd no one's bothered us," Brad said conversationally as they moved back outside into the drizzly afternoon.

"I've thought the same," Trevor agreed. "After all that fuss the night I came home, I thought sure I'd wake the next morning with bodies to bury."

"Not if they were Goblins, you wouldn't. Remember, they don't stay around any too long."

Trevor nodded. "True. Do you suppose that Monroe crew got picked up by the law after all?"

The detective shrugged and coiled his fingers around the maul's handle. He kicked a round into position and whaled on it. Trevor bent to gather the pieces. "This will work," he said. "You split. I'll stack."

The men worked in silence for long enough to finish one tier and begin another. When Trevor came back outside after stacking his last armful, Brad had pulled a handkerchief out and was mopping his face with it. "Hard work," he panted. "That thing," he pointed at the splitting maul, "gets heavy after a while."

"Tell me about it. What do you suppose happened to the convicts?" Trevor turned the conversation back to his earlier query. "It's odd we haven't seen a trace of them since those two women picked their way through Raven's warding."

Brad sat on a round of wood, looking uncomfortable. "Ah, I haven't wanted to say anything, since there's nothing we can do about it—and last time I was dead wrong when I went chasing after things I thought were a threat—but lots of nights I'm up and about late. Never did sleep well."

Trevor laughed bitterly. "You and me both."

"Anyway, some nights I've seen lights in the distance. Once I was pretty sure I heard rifle fire. I asked the women about it. They came outside and did whatever it is they do with their hyped-up senses, but both of them just shook their heads. Then Eli dragged me off to our bed and tried to drug me into insensibility with sex." Brad dropped his eyes, color flooding his pale skin.

Trevor laughed. Aping the Carlisle witch-woman's accent perfectly, he said, "Oh aye, laddie. An' there's naught but a wee roll in th' hay canna mend."

Brad began to chuckle. In moments, he was laughing right along with Trevor.

"What's so funny, boys?" Lara came round the corner of the shed, holding her skirt up out of the mud. Her belly was growing so fast she wasn't able to get into any of her pants anymore. "Tell me. I could use a good laugh."

Gunter trailed after her, nipping at her hem. "Stop that," she scolded, pulling the heavy wool out of his mouth. The fabric snagged on his incisor, and she bent to untangle it. "Well?" Putting her hands on her hips, she looked from Brad to Trevor.

"We were trying to figure out why we've not seen hide nor hair of the Monroe bunch," Trevor said. "Then Brad said he'd seen strange lights—"

"Oh, brother. Not again." She glared at the detective. "Last time—"

"I remember what happened last time all too well," he cut in. "And I haven't gone chasing off after anything. But that doesn't mean I haven't wanted to."

"Anyway," Trevor went on, "Brad asked the Sidhe to check things out, but they couldn't sense anything."

"Which means what you've been seeing has to be something produced by humans—if it exists at all." Lara looked pointedly at Brad. "That's obvious. But I don't understand where the joke was. What did I miss?"

"Humans." Angling his head, Trevor sidestepped Lara's question and looked at Brad. "We should've figured that out."

Brad nodded. "Means we can flush them out and persuade them to move on." He drew his brows together. "Doesn't explain those voodoo doll-things, though."

Lara looked alarmed. She folded her hands protectively over her belly. "Why not wait until Raven gets back? The women say it'll be soon. It's not like whoever's out there is hurting anything." She hesitated, shaking her head. "You don't even know how many there are."

Almost as if he'd been listening to their conversation, Gunter's ears swiveled toward the bridge. A low growl vibrated in the back of his throat, and his hackles rose, quivering. He was on his feet in an instant.

Trevor made a grab for the dog's collar just in time. "Stay," he said, gripping the homemade leather band. "Forget all that German Shepherd programming. Mum would never forgive me if you got yourself shot."

"Well, it was your idea to teach him to hunt—" she retorted.

"Otherwise he'd have starved," Trevor said softly. "You may recall we had precious little in the way of food here for a while. And our stocks are getting low again."

Another problem. Bloody bollocks. Will we ever get to the end of them?

Brad said, "Ssht," sharply, then told Lara, "Go in the house. Take the dog with you. Tell the women to come out here, but to cloak themselves or whatever it is they do. I think I saw something move out there."

"Guns?" Trevor whispered.

"Both inside. Doesn't matter, we're damn near out of ammo—again."

Lara grasped the amulet. In seconds Lillian and Elidora came flying around the corner. Brad looked confused. "I called them," Lara said softly. "Don't worry, I'm going inside. I understand how vulnerable I am. Can't run much faster than a waddle these days." Taking hold of the dog's collar, she muttered an incantation that would include both of them, shimmered, and was gone.

"What?" Lillian sounded irritated. "I was close to figuring out where those damnable dolls came from."

A shot zinged past, thudding into the wall of the shed.

"Get down," Brad shouted, hitting the dirt with Trevor right behind him.

"Och aye, this is ridiculous," Elidora spat. Raising her hands, she began to chant. Soon a numinous shroud circled the four of them. More bullets followed the first one, but the shells bounced off their shield.

"'Tis only a group of pesky humans." Lillian sniffed derisively. "Should I turn them into toads? Or would you prefer gnats?"

Trevor sat up, feeling foolish. He tried to brush the mud off himself, but it was thick and sticky, and he only succeeded in smearing it around with this hands. "Whatever you can do to make them go away would be brilliant," he mumbled. "For good."

"A tall order." Elidora winked at Brad. "You can—"

The next bullet penetrated Elidora's curtain and pinged off the shed's low metal roof.

"I dinna ken how they managed that." She glanced at Lillian, her dark eyes fencing with Lillian's green ones.

"Maybe they teamed up with whoever left us those dolls," Lillian speculated darkly. "Regardless, we need the house. Its magic strengthens our own. Trevor, come close."

"An' I will be takin' Brad." Elidora opened her arms, beckoning him to her. Getting to his feet, he came into her arms.

Trevor slithered over to where Lillian stood. "I don't understand," he said, looking at her.

"I need Raven," she spat. "The masculine half of the energy is missing. It limits what I can do. Come closer. I'm not worried about getting dirty."

The air held a metallic zing, not so different from Goblin magic. It felt cleaner, but an electric edge made the fine hairs on the back of his neck stand up. Lillian closed her arms around him. Her melodic chant filled his ears, and the familiar walls of the shed whirled away to nothing.

LARA PACED BACK and forth in the living room. She'd heard the gunfire. Though she kept telling herself Lillian and Elidora could handle most anything, she was still frightened—and angry. Gunter kept running to the front door, scratching at the wood. Long gouges from his claws scraped through the paint.

"No," she snapped. "You cannot go out there. Do you want to get yourself killed?" Instantly contrite, she went to the gangly, adolescent dog. "You're worried about Daddy. I am too. We just got him back. But I'm glad you're in here with me."

As she stroked the dog, she thought about Trevor—and Gradoxst. Trevor had been back for a few days before he'd told her anything. It seemed like he wanted to talk to her, but never quite got around to it. Knowing something was bothering him—and badly—she'd ferreted the truth out of him. Though she tried to help him understand what happened wasn't his fault, Trevor steadfastly believed he should have died before servicing the Demon. The last time she brought up the subject, he told her he wasn't interested in talking about it anymore. The therapist part of her was worried, but there wasn't much she could do.

Trevor, Brad, and the women materialized in the kitchen. Lara tried to sprint for that end of the house, then settled for a fast walk when her stomach bounced uncomfortably. "What happened?" she asked. The rattle of gunfire punctuated her question.

"It's still happening," Brad noted as he ran for the corner of the living room where they kept the guns. "Damn." He slid a magazine into the automatic rifle, then held up another. "Last one, and we're dead out of black powder. We need to go to Monroe. Don't think Skykomish has a gun shop."

"We still have shotgun shells," Trevor pointed out. "But we're running out of them too."

"They don't do enough damage unless you're right on top of whatever you're shooting at," Brad replied. "Wish I'd brought my service revolver."

"Wish we'd brought a lot of things," Trevor muttered.

"Whoever's out there has us right where they want us," Lara said through clenched teeth. "We're in here and most all of our food—what little there is of it—is out there. We played right into their hands —again."

"Where are you going?" Trevor asked sharply, his eyes on Brad who was heading for the back door.

"To shoot as many of them as I can," he said.

"Stop it." Lillian thundered. "Eli, come with me. The rest of you stay within these walls."

Lara watched magic channels weave between the two Sidhe. About the time she wondered if the house could contain all that power, the two women disappeared. The amulet warmed against her skin, thrumming in time to the spell Lillian had woven.

"I don't like any of this," Brad muttered. When Lara looked closely at him, he was practically quivering.

I just bet you don't, she thought. You're used to taking charge and going after the bad guys.

An idea formed, and she turned toward the stairs. "Where are you going?" Trevor asked. "Why does everyone want out of this room so badly?"

"I'm going to try to find Raven," she said. "I heard Lillian tell you she needed him."

"Magical eavesdropping, huh?" He quirked an uneasy eyebrow.

"What else? You can come with me, but I need to hurry. As much as I can, anyway." Holding tight to the amulet, she dragged her bulk up the stairs, thinking it would be a relief when the baby finally came. *Library or bedroom?* Deciding the library was a safer bet because that's where she'd raised the mage last time, she hastened toward the far end of the hall. Lara bolted through the door and shoved it hard, hoping it would latch behind her.

"Whoa. Practically took my nose off," Trevor complained, as he squeezed through the small space between the heavy door and its frame.

"Sorry. Didn't know you were right on my heels. How about you take one of the chairs over here?" She jabbed an index finger toward the far corner of the room. "I need to concentrate."

"Look, if you'd rather I left—" He sounded upset.

She twirled to face him. "Trevor, I do not need this right now. Lillian and Elidora are out there fighting to save us. I'm trying to help. Stay or go. But let me do what I can here."

Ach Christ, I've hurt his feelings.

Looking troubled, Trevor made his way to the far side of the library. She noticed he was watching her sidelong, though. The magic held a draw, and no one was immune to its pull.

She stripped off her clothes, letting them drop where they would. Touching the amulet with one hand and a candlewick with the other, she drew magic to light the fragrant taper, chanting softly. The amulet hummed along with her incantation, and her trance state formed and deepened. The *Dreaming* blossomed around her and she called for Raven.

He didn't come at first. She looked around the empty heath, picked out the waterfall hiding the sacred cave, and moved toward it. She wasn't exactly walking. It felt more like gliding, since she had no sense of touching the ground. Afraid to split her concentration, she allowed herself a very small moment of satisfaction that she was coming closer to figuring out how to travel the spirit paths without always dragging her body along.

"Raven," she called again.

He burst through the waterfall in an incandescent shower of droplets. "Lara. What's wrong?" Two Sidhe men followed him out. As striking as Lillian and Elidora, their faces were ageless, their features perfect.

"We're under attack. Lillian needs you. So does Eli." Lara sucked in a breath. It was difficult to both talk and hold herself in the *Dreaming* at the same time. Clutching the amulet harder, she urged it to give her strength.

Raven cocked his head to one side, gray eyes closed. His long hair danced around him in a wind that only blew where he was standing. The others—one man dark like Raven, though more slightly built, the other with hair red as Lillian's—bent their heads together.

Raven opened his eyes slowly. "I see," he breathed. "Goblins and humans have teamed against you."

"We could accompany thee," the other dark-haired man suggested in courtly, old-fashioned English, eying Raven speculatively.

"Gradoxst?" the third man spat, making the Demon's name sound like the curse it was.

Raven snorted. "Perhaps. Probably. Come." He reached out a hand for Lara, but her magic was at the end of its tether. She felt herself being dragged toward her body waiting in the library. A moment of disorientation jostled her as spirit and flesh reconnected. Disappointed—and annoyed—she hadn't managed to stay longer, she got to her feet, pulling on her scattered clothing.

"You weren't gone long. What happened?" Trevor rose and handed her a shirt she'd tossed over a chair.

"Raven should be right behind me," she panted, feeling as if someone had drained all the grit out of her.

The air took on a glow, forming a portal. Raven stepped through, along with the two other Sidhe she'd seen in the *Dreaming*.

"You must learn to pace yourself better, daughter." Raven shook a finger at her. "No time to explain now, but later." Turning to the other men, he said, "Olafr, Bron. One more jump here." The three of them seemed to ooze out the second story wall.

Trevor ran to the large windows overlooking the front of the house. "Bloody Christ, Lara. They're running toward the bridge with power blazing from their hands."

Lara collapsed onto a chair, still breathing hard. "That's so much more difficult than they make it look." She gestured toward the windows. "If I try to do more than one thing, it's like sand running through an hourglass where someone made the hole bigger. I get this feeling I'm living on borrowed time. Hurrying makes it worse."

Trevor nodded, looking sympathetic. "I think I felt much the same when I was trapped in that cave. I knew I had to keep working until I was free—or until I died trying. My whole body was shaking. If I would've fallen either of the times I slipped, I'm not certain I'd have had the starch to have another go at it. Assuming the fall didn't finish me off."

"Come here." She patted the front of the chair between her splayed legs. Once he was sitting on the floor, leaned back against her, she wrapped her arms around his shoulders.

"That's nice, Lara," he said pushing his head and shoulders against her belly. "Baby's growing really fast. I know it's not possible, but I could swear you're twice as big as you were when I came home."

She laughed. "It must be possible, because I am. I asked Lillian about that yesterday. I was afraid I might have something like gestational diabetes where the baby grows so big they can't be born easily."

"Well?" He reached back over his head, laying both hands on her stomach. "What'd she say?"

"It seems Sidhe pregnancies don't last quite so long as human ones. And since I'm part Sidhe, it's likely Elizabeth will come sooner rather than later."

"That seems like good news," he said cautiously.

"To me too. I feel so awkward right now. Everything's a struggle. Even something simple, like getting out of a chair."

He half turned to look at her. "I should go down and try to do something. Brad's down there."

"Not outside, he's not," she countered. And then she wondered if she was right. Brad had looked like a tightly wound spring when she'd left the living room.

"Not so sure I'd take bets on that," Trevor murmured.

The rattle of gunfire intensified. "What do you suppose is happening?" she asked.

"Don't know." He scrambled to his feet, holding out a hand to her. "I'm going to get some food together. There's not much, but I'll bet everyone's hungry when they come back inside."

If everyone comes back... Lara reached for his hand and got clumsily to her feet. She shook her head. "Phooey. It's like my center of gravity is off by about a foot."

"That's because it is," he retorted and nearly tripped over Gunter lying right outside the library door.

"So that's where you were, snookums," Lara said, reaching down to scratch his ears.

"Better in here than out there," Trevor said as a burst of something caught the rays of the setting sun and lit up the sky. "Sodding hell. What the bloody fuck are they doing?"

CHAPTER 14

Brad stood in a corner of the living room for a few minutes after Lara and Trevor left, watching Gunter trail behind them up the stairs. He laid his Hoch and Keckler down. Then he picked it back up. "Jesus Christ," he growled. "I can't just mill around in here like a damned old woman." He knew he ran a risk if he went outside, not just to himself, but to everyone else out there. One of the essential ingredients in any sort of group attack was that the players on the same side had a plan. He assumed Lillian and Elidora were able to keep track of one another. If he went outside, he'd have no way of either figuring out where the two women were, or of alerting them to his presence. He might shoot one of them by mistake, or they might take him out with their magic.

He paced, rifle cradled under one arm. Ammunition was a problem. Food was getting to be—again. The cars were parked behind the springhouse at the far side of the property. He considered what sort of chance he'd have if he tried to drive over the bridge and out the dirt road leading to Skykomish. He knew if he could just get a couple miles down the main road, he could turn off on the spur roads he'd discovered earlier and lose himself in the forest. Then he'd have a fair shot at going for ammo and food. He wished he had his police cruiser. At least it had bulletproof glass.

Cocking his head to one side, he listened, but didn't hear much except bursts of gunfire. "Not going to know if I can make it out of here by standing in the house," he muttered, as he considered what he'd need for a trip back to civilization. Money, that was for sure. His police ID… He gathered items as he thought of them. In less than five minutes, he slipped out the back door, halting at the bottom of the steps to glance from side to side. The yard was empty. He'd figured it would be, since all the noise was coming from the area closer to the bridge on the other side of the house.

Taking a deep breath, he sprinted across the open area between the main house and the outbuildings, flattening himself against the barn when he arrived. He waited, forcing himself to watch the second hand on his watch sweep through three full rotations.

Okay. Three minutes and no one's charging over here.

Brad looked around, choreographing the least exposed route between him and the cars. He'd decided to take his own car, since the Ford sedan was far more maneuverable than Trevor's truck. He'd considered Lara's BMW, but didn't want to take it into a situation where it might end up with bullet holes, at least not without asking her first. He patted his jacket pocket to make sure he had the keys and that the wad of cash hadn't fallen out when he raced across the yard.

He felt just the right amount of adrenaline humming along his nerve endings. A wry smile split his face. Brad *liked* danger. It was why he'd been first a soldier, then a cop. That simmery, gritty edge to things was almost like an aphrodisiac to him. Infinitely better than sitting in that house hoping for the best.

Dodging past the barn, he skirted the wood shed and moved from tree to tree as he scuttled closer to his objective. If he got to his car without incident, he was going to put his head down and go for it. The women would know it was him in the car, so all he'd have to deal with were the escaped criminals. Truth was, he hated lawbreakers. If he hit one or two with his heavy car, so much the better. His smile stretched into a grin.

After a measured breath, he took a good, hard look at his penchant toward violence—at least where bad guys were concerned, but didn't come up with much.

Best thing about martial law is I get to tromp on that scum without having to answer to Internal Affairs.

He was just pulling his keys out of his pocket when a voice from somewhere off to his right drawled, "Where ya think you's goin', bud?"

Not Gradoxst. Trevor said he's got a German accent. Besides, if it was him, he'd have killed me on the spot without the benefit of conversation. "Why do you want to know?" Brad crouched down, placing his car between himself and where he'd heard the voice.

"Oh, ah tol' the bossman someone'd come 'long to fetch one o' them cars. He said ah was full o' shit, but ah come over here anyways. Damn if ah weren't right." High-pitched, braying laugh burst out of whoever was over there. He sounded young, his voice still cracking. "Why don't ya toss that piece out here?"

Fat fucking chance.

"How about if you come on out and show yourself like a man, instead of hiding like some weak-kneed pussy?"

"Toss yer piece, and I'll come on out."

He's by himself and they don't have radios. Brad began stealthily edging back the way he'd come, half creeping. He'd had enough conversation with hero-boy by now to have a pretty good idea where he was. Sure enough, a skinny blond kid with greasy hair plastered to his skull crouched behind Raven's ancient Model A. Hesitating only for the second it took him to decide if the stupid jerk was worth any of his precious bullets, Brad swung his rifle into position and fired, aiming for the neck to cut off the possibility of any vocalizations beyond a gurgle.

The sound of movement must've gotten the kid's attention because he'd just begun to turn, gun questing for a target, when Brad's shots nailed him. He fell, flailing, in a shower of blood. He got off a shot before hitting the ground, but it went skyward.

"Damn," Brad swore. He'd barely touched the trigger, but the automatic weapon had still fired more than one round. Diving forward, he pried the gun out of the kid's hand and fished through his clothes for ammo, but didn't find any. Now that he got a good look, that the kid was scarcely more than a boy. Despite his earlier bravado, Brad felt vaguely ill. Killing children wasn't part of his programming. Never mind he'd done it in the Middle East when they'd come at him with bombs strapped to their little bodies. It didn't help that this kid wasn't quite dead yet and squirmed whenever Brad touched him.

Convinced nothing of worth was in the dying youth's pockets, Brad started to get to his feet when a searing pain shot through his wrist. Startled he looked down. The outlaw had buried his teeth in his lower forearm. Instinct took over. Raising the pistol, Brad slammed it down on the young man's face. All it took was once and his jaws went slack.

"Christ!" he growled, examining the wound. He'd have to get it cleaned out fast. Human bites were chock full of toxic bacteria. He thought about the first aid kit in his car and promised himself he'd stop to use it just as soon as he got a safe distance from the house.

Brad held up his new acquisition, squinting at it. "Hmm. Colt Forty-Five Combat Elite," he muttered. "Where the hell did he get hold of one of those?" Brad smiled grimly. If the gun store didn't have anything for his rifle, surely they'd have forty-five caliber bullets. They were common as goose grass.

Wiping his bloody hands and wrist on some low bushes, Brad stepped over the youngster he'd killed and went to his car, keeping a close eye on things. If anyone had been listening, they would've known the rifle fire wasn't from one of their guns. But no one came rushing over. Brad hoped the women were giving the bastards a run for their money. It felt *good* to have helped out, even if he'd only taken out one of the outlaws.

Brad threw himself into his car. Having secured the pistol was a great boon, since it meant he could fire out the car windows. Even through the glass with such a big bore weapon. He held up the gun, checking the sights. They seemed sound, and he blessed Colt Manufacturing for making indestructible firearms.

Turning the key, he nosed the car out from behind the springhouse and jammed his foot down on the accelerator.

THE MOMENT she set foot on the ground floor, Lara knew Brad wasn't inside. Maybe it was her magic. Or maybe she keyed into the amulet as it sounded a subtle warning vibration. It didn't matter how she knew. What mattered was the detective had left the relative safety of the house. "Trevor..." She moved out of his way as he cleared the bottom step.

"Not here, huh?" he said. "Somehow, I didn't think he'd be. He's not the type to just sit about whilst there're windmills to joust at."

"Not funny."

"I wasn't trying to be." Gunter whined at the front door. "He probably needs out, Lara."

"Do you trust him not to take off after one of the bad guys if he senses something?" she asked worriedly.

"Not entirely," he admitted. "How about the dirt floor in the basement?"

"I'll take him. You can start something cooking. I really am hungry. Eating for two and all." She laughed, but with zero humor. She was worried about Brad. And about the Sidhe too, even though the odds had likely improved with the addition of Raven and those other two, whose names she couldn't remember.

Time passed slowly. She and Trevor made small talk while he tossed rice into boiling water and sautéed some wilted wild onions with grease from a rabbit they'd killed the day before. As it grew later, far more silence than conversation moved between them. She could tell he was just as anxious as she. Occasional bursts of bright, white light lit the sky outside the kitchen windows, but it was hard to see much else through the first floor glass.

Trevor had just mixed some cornmeal into a rustic polenta when she heard footsteps on the back steps. Leaping to her feet, Lara lumbered toward the door.

"Wait." Trevor's voice was sharp. "We don't know who's out there."

"Oh yes you do." Raven's deep baritone preceded him as the key turned of its own accord and the door opened.

Lara blew out a breath, and then another. "Thank the goddess…"

"By all means." Lillian's dry humor reasserted itself after days of absence. Slipping around Raven's bulk, she stood next to him. "We needed all the help we could get out there. Thanks to you too, child, for summoning him." Pushing straggling hair out of a begrimed face, Lillian jabbed an index finger into Raven's thickly built torso.

Elidora and the two other men crowded into the kitchen. The witch woman held a body cradled in her arms. Stooping, she laid it tenderly on the floor.

"Oh my God. It's the girl who came here with her mother the other day," Lara exclaimed. "The convict's child." With a bit of difficulty, she sat next to Johnna, stroking soft, dark hair back from a face that had most of the skin singed off it. The girl moaned incoherently.

Elidora sat on Johnna's other side.

"I don't see why you didn't leave her out there," Lillian snapped. "The girl is dying. Stock she came from, I say all the better."

"Th' lass is but a wee child," Elidora protested.

"You cannot save all of them," Raven countered. "Yet, so long as she is here, I shall assist in seeing she travels to the Summerlands when the time comes and not…elsewhere." Levering himself down next to Lara, he murmured. "Eli and I will take care of this. If you could make me a bowl of something and set it just here," he tapped the floor next to him, "it'd be a great help."

Johnna's blue eyes opened. Her body thrashed from side to side. "Dead," she moaned. "All dead." Those unsettling eyes—far older than their years—found Lara's face and clung to it. "You're the lady from the house," she gasped. "So I—I'm not dead after all?"

"No, dear." Lara took one of her hands. "But you are safe, and we'll do everything we can to help you." Feeling like a rat deserting a foundering ship, she moved the girl's hand from hers into Raven's big paw. "He'll take good care of you."

Johnna whimpered. "Hurts," she groaned.

Lara rose to her feet, stepping over a pool of blood spreading under the girl. Sadness filled her for the youngster who'd never had much of a chance and now had none at all.

Taking a deep breath to steady herself, Lara peered behind everyone. "Where's Brad?" she asked quietly.

Elidora swung her head about. "What on airth do ye mean, lassie?"

"He's not in here," Trevor said. "So we assumed he was with you."

Raven drew his brows together, and he rubbed the heel of one hand across his forehead. "I suppose that means I must hunt him down."

"No, what it means is you'll eat something first," Lillian said firmly, moving past Lara to dish some food up for him. "It won't take so long as all that. Besides, you have chosen to sit Morrigan's watch over this youngster."

"Food would be good for all of us," one of the men said, in a strong Norse accent. He sounded subdued as he scooped a bowl off the sideboard and went to help himself.

In the ensuing confusion of everyone getting a dish and milling about near the stove, Raven sat in the middle of the kitchen like an ancient sentinel. He ate methodically, shoving food into his mouth with a flat-bladed knife he'd drawn out of his belt. When he wasn't eating, he and Elidora chanted a refrain Lara had heard before: the dirge for souls entering the Summerlands. Lillian was right. Johnna was indeed dying. After a few weak moans, she was still, the sound of her tortured struggles for breath replaced by a silence so loud it battered Lara's ears.

Reaching for one of the mead bottles, Raven upended it and drank for long moments. Lurching to his feet, he walked to stand behind Lillian, settled at the table with her own food. Laying large hands on her shoulders, he bent close to her ear and murmured something in Celtic Gaelic. At her tense nod, his bearlike form first shimmered and then faded from the kitchen.

Elidora touched Johnna's eyelids, drawing them closed with practiced fingers. "She will need burying." The witch woman sounded sad as she stood.

Lara looked at Trevor and asked, "What did Raven say?"

"He's gone to hunt for Brad," Trevor explained. "But you could've figured that out without me."

Lara smiled forlornly. "You're right. Why can't all of us be together for more than a few minutes? That's why we moved all the way out here in the first place. To avoid violence and danger..." Her voice faded. *Ach, I sound like a lost little girl.*

"Maybe it's why *you* moved," Lillian said, her clear, green eyes drilling into Lara's dark ones. "I suspect danger is part and parcel of yon detective. He thrives on it."

Elidora looked up and nodded. "'Twas him in that car I heard. An' here I was thinkin' it was one of those rascals we chased off. Since th' car was leavin', I thought we'd done some good. If only I would ha' known."

"Even if you had," Lillian observed dryly, "there was precious little you could have done. I remember when we heard that car engine. The two of us were sore pressed. You couldn't have left me then. It would've been disastrous."

"How about if you back up a bit?" Trevor set his fork down. "I'd like to know what happened out there. I'm sure Lara would too." He shifted his gaze to the two Sidhe men. "Raven said your names, but I don't remember what they were."

"Ursäkta mig," the dark-haired man jumped to his feet and bowed low before taking his seat again. "Det anses väl ohyfsat av mig att äta eller dricka innan jag introducerar mig själv. Jag heter Olafr. Till din tjänst." Though he had the lithe build of a young man, lines carved deeply into his features. And his eyes, green as Lillian's, held hard edges.

"I am Bron," the redhead said, inclining his head slightly at Olafr's words. His eyes were dark and he seemed younger than Olafr, but with the Sidhe it was hard to tell. "And we are *both* at your service."

"Thank you for coming to help," Lara said.

"Yes, quite decent of you," Trevor added, smiling as he held out a hand to each man in turn. Though they looked a bit taken aback, they shook hands before going back to their meal.

Lillian looked at Trevor. "Not one of our customs," she explained. Trevor started to apologize, but she waved him to silence. "Shush, no harm done."

Lara laid down her fork and met Lillian's eyes. "What happened out there? Is everyone dead? Or did some of them leave? If that's the case, will they come back?"

Lillian held up both hands to stem the tide of Lara's questions. "Some are dead, including yon child's parents." She gestured toward Johnna's body, making the sign of the goddess with two fingers. "Others we, ah, persuaded to leave. I doubt they'll be back since Elidora does a wonderful ghoul impersonation. Scared them half to death."

"Aye, they were more scared o' me than o' Gradoxst and his remaining minions," Elidora added around a mouthful of food.

Lara's heart sank. "So that goddamned Demon is still dogging my tracks," she muttered. "Christ. Why can't you kill him off?"

Bron snorted, made a grab for the mead bottle, and drank. "We have been attempting to *kill him off* for years, young lady. If effort were sufficient, he would have been dead long since."

"Han är en slug en," Olafr nodded, holding out a hand for the mead.

"Och aye, it dinna help that he can command our magic as well as that o' the Goblins. He bends our spells an' they bounce back at us." Elidora rolled her eyes eloquently.

"How many were out there?" Trevor asked.

Lillian cocked her head to one side and counted on her fingers. "Let's see, Johnna and her mother—and eleven men. We killed half a dozen of them, plus a few Goblins. Eli found another dead man over by the cars. The others we chased off."

"Over by the cars," Lara echoed. "Brad must have killed that one on his way out of here. Wonder why he left?"

"To get ammunition and food," Trevor said as he got up, carrying dishes to the sink. "You'll have noticed we ate everything I made, and I suspect everyone's still a wee bit hungry. I know I am, but there's nothing more to make unless I go out there and kill something. Or boil up more grain."

"Vi skall nu ta och gå," Olafr said formally as he stood.

"Yes, there is no cause for us to remain. Thank you for sharing your limited provisions with us," Bron added.

"Do you live in the *Dreaming*?" Lara asked curiously. The moonstone jabbed her, so she presumed the question was considered off limits. She caught the gem in her hand to hold it away from her skin.

"Bit you, did it?" Bron asked, eyebrows quirked in his timeless face.

Olafr laughed. "Ingen bor i *Drömmen*. Vi kommer bara dit för att tacka gudinnan."

"We go there for respite from whatever world we inhabit. As well as to protect the *Dreaming* itself," Bron clarified. "'Tis the heart and soul of our kind. So long as it prevails, so shall we."

"What about those like Gradoxst?" Trevor turned away from the sink to face the two men. "He used to be one of you. Does the *Dreaming* welcome or spurn him? From the looks of things, he seemed to be thriving there whilst holding me captive."

Anger flashed from Olafr's eyes, but he hooded them quickly. "*Drömmen* försöker hjälpa alla fe. Därför får han alltid återvända. Det spelar ingen roll hur korrupt han blivit."

Lara held up a hand and looked helplessly at Trevor. Nodding, he explained, "The *Dreaming* tries to repair damage to any Sidhe. So it would always allow Gradoxst to return, no matter how corrupt he'd become."

"The mother wastes her energies on that one," Bron spat. "Come Olafr, we should have been gone long since. We shall take the child with us and bury the other dead afore we leave." Hoisting Johnna to one shoulder as if she weighed nothing, Bron sketched a door in the air. He and Olafr jumped through. The glittering outline remained until Lillian raised her hands and barked a few words in Celtic Gaelic.

"What did he mean about the *Dreaming* being your mother?" Lara asked, looking from Lillian to Elidora.

"We are of the Earth, child," Lillian replied simply. "As are you. The Earth is our mother, and mother to the *Dreaming* as well."

The baby shifted. Lara laid a hand on her belly. Noticing, Elidora smiled knowingly. "The little one is dancing, eh?"

Lara winced. "Guess that's one word for it. She's certainly active these past two or three weeks and growing so fast it's almost like there're twins in there."

Trevor turned to the witch woman, looking concerned. "Lara told me her pregnancy would likely be shorter than nine months. How much shorter?"

Elidora shrugged. "Mayhap less than that, mayhap more. Each bairn is different for us. They grow in their own time. But lookin' at things," she got to her feet, walked over, and laid practiced hands on Lara's distended abdomen, "I would say only a few more weeks afore this new spirit will be ready to join us. She's a strong one. I can feel her life force."

"So soon?" Lara frowned. "Won't she be premature?"

"Nay. I have already told you, such things are different for us." Elidora looked right at Lara and winked. "There's only one bairn in there. It only feels like an entire army."

Moving away, she snatched up a bucket from beside the sink, filled it with water, and bent to clean Johnna's blood from the floor.

CHAPTER 15

Still reeling from how easy it had been to just drive away, Brad realized he was surprisingly close to Skykomish. Whatever was going on between the escaped convicts and the Sidhe must have been up the road in the other direction. He'd thought about trying to help Lillian and Elidora, but decided he'd be more of a liability than a boon. He knew how it was when you were in the midst of a fight. Anything that diverted your attention could be fatal. The women weren't expecting him, so he didn't want to chance a split second moment of surprise that might spell disaster.

Slowing the car, he turned right onto Highway Two. He debated stopping at the market in Skykomish. Shopping was permitted once a month, but since it was just him, he'd only be allowed food for one. *Eh, probably not worth it. I'll stop in Monroe, right after the gun shop.* Brad grimaced. It hadn't helped their food situation that there'd been five of them sharing dwindling rations for the past few weeks.

He'd almost cleared the town's western limit when flashing lights appeared in his rearview mirror. Brad pulled to the shoulder, frowning. *I was going the speed limit. Registration's not expired. I didn't stop in their town. What the hell do they want with me?*

He glanced at the Colt on the passenger seat and the bloodstains on his shirtsleeves. Never mind the Hoch and Kechler in the back seat. Brad shoved the Colt under the seat in a fluid motion, moving to unlatch the glove box immediately afterward. If the cop asked, he'd just say he was getting his registration and insurance certificate.

Brad peered at his side mirror and groaned. Sheriff Smoley was working his way out of his cruiser, looking every bit as much out of shape as he'd been a few weeks before.

Eventually, he managed to drag his bulk out of the car and walked doggedly up to Brad's window. "Detective," he said. "Thought it was you. Then I ran your license. Figured you'd have been back through here long since."

"I'm just back from visiting my wife. Did I do something wrong?" Brad asked, his tone carefully neutral.

"Huh?" Smoley looked genuinely puzzled. "No. Of course you didn't. I pulled you over because I could use your help."

Brad swallowed hard. That would be a reason for one law enforcement officer to flag down another. Worse, his acquiescence would be a foregone conclusion. "What seems to be the problem, Sheriff?"

The other man blew out a beleaguered breath. "Shit. They took over half the guards from Monroe to help out in Seattle. Prisoners have been just walking out of there ever since. There're about twenty holed up down by the river east of town. Think there's another batch of the bastards out thataway." He jerked a thumb to the north, the direction Brad had just come from. "But they're not the ones causing all the ruckus. There's only me and Jackson here. He and I talked it over on the radio. We figured with three of us, we could tackle that group by the river." He paused to wipe his nose with the back of one hand. "Got to do something. Every night, they come into town and help themselves. Townspeople are plenty scared."

Almost in spite of himself, Brad's police instincts rose to the fore. He felt himself getting sucked in. "Have they hurt anyone?"

"Not yet. But that's sure to come. We ain't got none too much here as it is. Soon as the easy pickins is gone, they'll start breaking into houses."

"Have you complained to the state prison system?"

"First thing I did." The sheriff laughed hollowly. "They told me wasn't nothin' they could do since things is so much worse in Seattle than they are out here. Bet they'll be glad to have you back. From what I hear, they need every man."

A twinge of guilt coursed through Brad, and he wondered how many more of his men had died while he'd been indulging himself.

Not fair, an inner voice protested. I've helped Lara, and Trevor.

Yes, but I could've been doing so much more.

"Tell me what you need me to do," he said. "I'd planned on pushing through to Seattle this afternoon, but it won't make that much difference if I don't get there till tomorrow. Things were so chaotic when I left, I doubt a few hours one way or the other will make much difference."

"Say—" Smoley looked closely at Brad's shirtsleeves. Reaching out a finger, he tapped one of the stains. "Looks like blood. Did you run into some problems?"

Brad took a deep breath and blew it out. "Now that you mention it, I did. Drove through the last part of the night. By morning I was spent. So I pulled off on that first dirt road to the east right before town. I'd just drifted off when some hoodlums started banging on my window. It's a long story, but I killed one of them. From what you just said, I suppose he was an escaped convict. Rest of 'em scattered after that."

"Good you got one at least. How far in were they?"

"Maybe five or six miles. Place where I pulled off looked deserted, so I figured it'd be safe enough." Brad shrugged. "Nowhere's safe anymore."

"You got that right."

"What do you need me to do?" Brad asked again.

"Wait here. I'll go get Jackson. Might take me an hour. He's taking care of something on the other side of town. "

Brad glanced around him. A yellow sign up ahead denoted another side road. "How about if I pull off there?" He gestured. "Could still use that nap."

Smoley smiled. "Sure Detective. You do that. Be back for ya by seven. More rain's coming in. Should give us good cover. And hey, thanks for helping out."

"You'd do the same for me."

"You betcha." The Sheriff flashed him a grim smile before waddling back to his car.

Brad thought about what he'd agreed to as he pulled his sedan down the dirt road fifty feet ahead, brought it to a stop off to the side, and switched off the ignition. What he'd said had been right. If Smoley were in Seattle and the police asked for his help, he'd give it. And gladly. It was part of the training. Other police officers were like your brothers. You stood by one another, no matter what. The guilt that had pricked him earlier returned in full force.

What the fuck was I thinking? I know I went a little crazy when Adie died. But why did I ask if I could stay? Was it just to be close to my daughter for the next thirty or forty years?

Unable to sit still, he pushed open his door. Eying a small stream, he walked to it, turned back his sleeve, and immersed his abraded flesh in icy water. That done, he fished the first aid kit out of his car and doused the bite with Betadine. He considered a bandage, but thought it might be better to leave the wound open. Still feeling rattled, he started down the road on foot to clear his thoughts. His mind was such a muddle, he didn't remember until he was about thirty yards away that he hadn't locked his car. Reaching for the clicker, he pushed it and heard an answering *ding* from the Ford.

"What in the goddess's name do you think you're doing?

Brad started at the unmistakable sound of Raven's voice. "What does it look like I'm doing?" he asked irritably. "I'm taking a walk and trying to think."

Raven moved from behind a large tree and caught him up. "You did not answer my question, human. Why are you out here and not back at the house? Everyone's worried about you."

Maybe it won't be such a bad thing to have someone to talk this through with.

"I left to get more ammunition—and food. There hasn't been enough of either since we got here. On my way through town the local sheriff stopped me. He remembered who I was from when Lara and I came to Skykomish to get antibiotics and groceries."

Knowing the hard part was yet to come, Brad set his jaw and forged ahead. "Seems there are a bunch of those escaped convicts wreaking havoc here. The sheriff asked if I could help him and his partner." Brad stopped walking and spun to face Raven. "I said I would."

Raven looked thunderstruck. He thinned his mouth into a harsh line, and fire blazed from his gray eyes.

"Didn't see how I could refuse." Brad drew himself up, squared his shoulders, and looked Raven right in the eye. "He needed help."

"While I understand why you agreed to help this stranger, you promised not to leave the farmhouse." Raven drew his thick brows together. "You may recall that was one of the conditions—"

"Of course I recall," Brad snapped. "If I hadn't left the first time, I'd be dead. No medicine there. And none of you, either." He felt his temper heat. Listening to Raven, he remembered how high-handed the mage was. "While we're at it, both you and Lillian promised to help us. And then you got diverted by your own war. Well, now I'm being diverted by mine."

Raven opened his mouth, then closed it again. Brad knew him well enough to understand the mage was struggling not to scream at him or use magic to pound him into the dirt.

Good that he's at least trying to be reasonable.

"So long as you're thinking about this," Brad went on, fighting to control his own anger. "There's the added problem that I seem to have fallen in love with Lara. Oh, I can keep it under wraps, but it's a bit uncomfortable with the three of us under the same roof since Trevor knows—and so does she."

"I thought you and Elidora—" the mage began, looking flummoxed.

Brad shook his head. "I enjoy her body," he admitted. "And she enjoys mine, but there're too many differences between the two of us. I'm human and she… Well, there's not the common ground you need to build a relationship."

"Really." Raven's voice dripped mockery. "And this observation comes from your vast experience with the fair sex?"

Brad exerted a great deal of effort to keep his voice pleasant. "Now that you mention it, yes, it does. Maybe I learned something through all those miserable years with Barbara. One of which was to not link my star to women who don't love me. Elidora's heart belongs to Gren, and I suspect it always will."

"All right." Raven narrowed his eyes, seemingly done with sarcasm and anger. "If I'm understanding you, you're requesting to be released from your agreement."

Is that what I'm doing? Brad thought long and hard. "What I really want probably isn't possible," he said after a few moments of silence.

"To come and go?"

Brad met the mage's gray eyes and nodded.

"You're correct that you cannot do that. Come, walk with me." Raven folded his hands behind his back.

Brad fell in next to him, grateful they'd moved beyond being furious with one another. He felt curious about what the mage wanted to discuss, but knew better than to feed him a bunch of questions.

"How much time do we have before yon Sheriff comes to collect you?"

Brad glanced at his watch. "At least an hour, maybe as much as two."

Raven nodded. Then he glanced at Brad, quirking an eyebrow. "That will give me time for the long version then."

Brad waited, but it was apparent the mage wasn't going to begin until he'd sorted out what he wanted to say. After a time, he spread his hands in front of him and began talking. His voice was so low that Brad focused intently on the bearlike man, straining to not miss anything.

"When Lillian first became aware of Lara, I cautioned her that we needed to remain aloof from human affairs as we always have. For such is the goddess's will. But Lillian was quite taken with Lara. For a time, most of our conversations revolved around the training Lara would need in the face of escalating Demon and Goblin threats." He paused. "Though you have suspected the two of us are bound, we have not confirmed that such is true. I am telling you now that it is. And that, much like Elidora and Gren, we tried for years—hundreds of them—to have children of our own.

"In many ways, I indulged Lillian in her desire to help Lara because I understood she saw her as the daughter she never had. In spite of the fact that dabbling closely in human interactions makes me uncomfortable, I reminded myself Elidora lived for years in proximity to humans with no ill outcomes. At least none that I knew of.

"So when Lillian pressed for Lara and Trevor to take up residence at my house, I tried to lay my concerns aside."

"What were those concerns?" Brad asked.

Raven turned to face him. "It'd be best if you could wait until I'm done to ask questions," he said mildly. "Though I'm sure that's not the way you were trained by those who uphold the law."

"No." Brad exhaled sharply. "It's not. But I'll keep quiet. Go on."

"Getting Lara to understand time was of the essence if she and Trevor were to relocate was difficult. I'm certain she still didn't fully appreciate the concept of psychic windows of opportunity on the night Lillian and I pushed her out of her house and into her car. Because she didn't leave in an auspicious fashion, channels remained open that could have been tied off had she left sooner, and with a more willing spirit."

Brad started to say something, but choked off the comment.

"Good." The mage laughed softly. "You're learning. While I'm not blaming Lara for Gradoxst's continued harassment, nonetheless, neither is she guiltless in that regard. When that goddess-be-damned rogue Sidhe kidnapped your daughter, he did so with full knowledge it would pull all of us into the in-between to try to rescue her, leaving Trevor by himself."

Raven shook his head, his eyes troubled. "Had Trevor not curried favor in Artemis's eyes and been as nimble-minded as he is, Gradoxst would have cast his mischief, and Lara would have returned with Adriana only to find her true love dead."

Brad swallowed hard. He leaned toward Raven, anxious for his next words.

"Sometimes," Raven spoke deliberately, "when you tamper with things that should have been left alone, unfortunate outcomes ensue. Lillian pushed hard to have Lara by her side. She became even more determined once she knew Lara was pregnant.

"I recognized Lara—and Trevor too—would need assistance for at least a full year. I understood food would be a problem, and I wondered how the two of them would adapt to such a different lifestyle. It didn't help that the rains came right after they moved, making it impossible to consider growing even winter crops. Then you showed up.

"I still believe it was a mistake to allow you to remain. You shifted the energy in the house, making it less predictable. Oh, you did good things too. Like standing by Lara's side while Trevor was held captive in the *Dreaming*. But now it appears you were scarcely motivated by noble principles."

Brad considered protesting, but understood the mage had nailed him dead to rights. "I would have done what I did regardless," he mumbled.

"I'm certain of that." One corner of the mage's mouth turned downward wryly. "Of course, it didn't hurt that you were feathering a possible nest—just in case Trevor didn't make it back."

He took a measured breath before continuing. "I don't expect you to fully understand, but that's what I mean about energy. When we do things with a pure heart, and without subterranean motives lurking about, it pleases the goddess. When we do not..." Raven extended his hands, palms upward. "It's then we find ourselves beset by escaped criminals and renegade Sidhe."

When several minutes passed without Raven saying anything further, Brad asked, "Is it all right if I ask questions about some of what you said?"

At Raven's nod, he dove in. "One of the things you inferred was that Lillian's motivations were, ah, well-meaning, but scarcely altruistic. Sort of like mine, actually. Does that mean the outcome of encouraging Lara and Trevor to move was doomed from its inception?"

"Maybe not doomed, but likely to be fraught with tension and problems, yes."

"Have you told them this?" Brad's stomach tightened. His hands clenched into fists, and he understood how worried he was about his friends.

"Of course not."

"Why not?" Brad demanded. He swung the larger man to face him. At the shocked expression on Raven's ageless face, he realized he'd crossed an invisible line and drew his hand back, mumbling, "Sorry."

Raven, who'd raised both hands into the position he used to call magic, slowly lowered them. "Never touch me again without my invitation," he growled.

"Yes, yes, I get that. And I am sorry." Brad unclenched his teeth. *No I'm not. Not really. What I'd like to do is...*

Remembering the mage could read his mind, he clamped down on mental imagery that had him flattening Raven's nose into a river of blood. He'd played Lara and Trevor like puppets—in fact, he still was.

Taking a deep breath, Brad said, "You need to tell Lara and Trevor what you just told me. They have a right to know."

In that moment, Brad understood how much he loved Lara and Trevor. Fury raced through every sinew as the full extent of how the mage had manipulated them by withholding key information sank in.

A pulse pounded in one temple, and he balled his hands into fists again.

"I'll take it under consideration. But now, we must talk about you. And then I shall go. Your choices, human, are two. Either you return with me, promising to remain no matter what. Or I leave you in your own world. Trust me when I tell you there will be dire consequences should you try to find my home on your own uninvited."

Oh, I do believe that.

Blowing out a ragged breath, Brad made a conscious effort to relax his hands. "May I return once to say goodbye? I'd come right after whatever goes down here tonight."

"No. It's too risky. You might be followed, which would create other problems. I haven't been vigilant enough in honoring the goddess's will as it is." Raven cleared his throat. "I'll be honest. Things have gotten so far out of hand, I don't know if Lara and Trevor will be able to remain. Yet I promised Lillian I'd make every effort to calm the forces threatening their ability to make a home with me." He paused, sadness flaring from his eyes. "Lillian understands this. She and I have talked."

"I see." Brad's heart ached. He cared more for Lara and Trevor than he had for anyone in a very long time, except his daughter and she was dead. With his jaw set in a resolute line, he met Raven's gray eyes with his ice-blue ones. "You knew, didn't you? What I'd choose."

"Yes." The mage inclined his head. "I don't know if this will help, but it would've surprised me had you not left at some point. It's one of the reasons I didn't want you to bide there at all."

Brad gripped his hands together so tightly that they hurt. Unclasping his fingers, he said, "Please tell the others I'm doing what I was trained to do. And I suppose what I was born to do as well."

Raven smiled. "Yes. You're a warrior. At least the modern day version of one. You and I have that in common. It's why I knew a life tucked away from danger wouldn't work for you, at least not for long."

"Plenty of danger dogged your place—" Brad began, thinking about Gradoxst and the Goblins.

"But not the right kind," Raven broke in. "You need human enemies, not magical ones."

Once he heard it spoken aloud, Brad recognized truth in the mage's words.

"Will you…?" Brad's voice ran down as he struggled against a lifetime of suppressing his feelings. *Come on. Just spit it out.* "…tell them I—I love them? Trevor too. Be sure he knows how much I respect and value him. And Elidora—she really is quite a remarkable woman."

Raven nodded solemnly. "I will make certain your feelings are known. Anything else?"

Brad thought for a moment, then inclined his head. "Yes. Tell them if they leave, they can find me in their house on Queen Anne. As long as it's still standing, I'll spend the next few months there. If they haven't shown up by the end of this year, I'll assume they found a way to stay out here, and I'll close up their place and go back to my own."

"May the goddess bless you, human." Raven closed his arms around Brad, drawing him close. Energy flowing from him soaked into Brad, warm and soothing.

Raven murmured a few words in Gaelic before stepping away. Sketching one of those doorway contraptions, he stepped through and was gone.

Brad stared after him. *Christ! Hope I did the right thing.* Walking back toward his car, an idea took shape. *It's risky,* he thought to himself, *but I'm going to do it anyway.*

CHAPTER 16

*L*ara woke from a half doze. She'd moved to one of the living room sofas after Olafr and Bron left, and then her eyes had shut of their own accord, telling her how worn down she was. The low buzz of Raven's voice coming from the kitchen roused her. She shook her head from side to side to summon the remains of a dream. Psyche's sendings had been few and far between since Trevor's abduction, and Lara welcomed their return.

She replayed the dream in her head. There hadn't been much, really. But then she'd only been asleep for a few minutes. *Let's see. I was back in my office, sitting in a rocking chair with Elizabeth cradled in my arms. A fine mist hung in the air, but it felt soothing, not like Gradoxst had come back. I was talking to a client, but not one I recognized. In fact, she looked like a fairy, sort of translucent, with delicate, patterned wings. Wonder what that means? I'm certainly not planning to ever return to Seattle, much less go back to work…*

Feeling confused, she drew the backs of her hands across her eyes to rub the otherworldly dream sequence from behind her lids. She realized she had to pee and dragged herself to her feet. The baby jabbed her bladder with a little hand or foot, and Lara hurried up the stairs. *If what I do at this point could be labeled hurrying.* She laughed softly, feeling like a beached whale as she lumbered to the bathroom.

She pulled on another sweater before going back downstairs, since the house felt chilly. When she walked into the kitchen, everyone looked up. Trevor jumped to his feet and put an arm around her shoulders. "Did you get a bit of a nap, love?" he inquired solicitously.

In spite of his kind words, something about his expression was unsettling. Cold fear pierced her. "What?" she managed. "Did something happen to Brad?"

"Not so bad as all that, child," Lillian murmured. "He made a decision to return to his world."

Lara transferred her dark gaze to Raven. "Did you help him along?" she asked boldly, suspicion rising. "As I recall, you didn't want him here in the first place."

"He left here all by himself without any prodding from anyone." Raven's gray eyes sought hers. "Once I found him, I gave him a choice. He could return—or not. What he couldn't do was go back and forth. This place may feel as if it's part of the world from whence you came, but it's not. Not since I claimed it for my own. That's why humans cannot come and go anymore. It disturbs the energies binding the house and confuses things."

"You came and went. And for years, if what you told me is true," she pointed out, certain Raven had more to do with Brad's absence than he was owning up to.

"I'm not human. Different rules apply." Raven's voice sounded strained, as if he were keeping a tight rein on his temper.

"Does that mean I could come and go?" she asked, curious.

"You might be able to," Lillian answered cautiously, "once your ability to control your magic is much stronger."

"As things stand, you can travel freely to the *Dreaming* and back," Raven added in what sounded like an attempt to be conciliatory.

We're getting far afield here. "Tell me what happened," Lara demanded. She moved from under Trevor's arm, walked to the stove, and poured hot water into a cup. After adding a few leaves to brew tea, she settled at the table, resting her head on an upraised hand.

The telling didn't take long. Tears sheened Lara's eyes when Raven described Brad's decision to return to being a police officer and his farewell to her, Trevor, and Elidora. "That's all?" She looked hard at the mage.

Raven nodded, innocence cloaking him like a banner.

With instincts honed from long years as a psychotherapist, Lara grappled with the uncomfortable feeling he'd left something out. Something important. *Watch it. He can read my mind.* "Did Brad say exactly where he was going?" she pressed.

"Just back home to his old job once he's done helping out in Skykomish."

Lara pinched the bridge of her nose between her thumb and forefinger. When she looked up, she stared intently at Raven and asked, "What if he changes his mind?"

"He can't do that, and I told him so. It was either return tonight with me or not at all."

"I see." Lara drained off the last of her tea and glanced at Trevor. "Are you ready to come to bed?"

He looked surprised. "Certainly, love. If that's what you want. It is getting on here. And it's cold. I was just thinking I should feed the fire in the front room if we were going to stay up much later."

"Good night, child." Lillian looked up from a muted conversation she'd been having with Elidora in Celtic Gaelic. Though she generally hid her feelings behind a brisk sarcasm, tonight the caring she felt for Lara shone warmly from her eyes.

Impulsively, Lara rose to her feet, walked around the table, and bent to hug the old woman with the ageless face. Reaching up, Lillian hugged her back.

Straightening, Lara looked at Elidora. "I'm sorry. You'll miss him, won't you?"

The Sidhe's full lips parted in the softest of smiles, and her dark eyes met Lara's. "Och aye, that I will. But not so much as all that. The one I will miss till th' end o' my days an' beyond is Gren, an' I think th' laddie knew as much. 'Tis one o' th' things that made it easier for him t' leave."

Lara half turned, feeling Raven's gaze on her. She raised her eyebrows. "What?"

"Sleep well. You and the child both."

Trevor held out a hand to her. She took it, her mind a riot of thoughts as she walked toward the stairs. Usually, the dog followed them, but not tonight. Lara stopped and turned back toward the group sitting around the kitchen table. "Where's Gunter?"

"With me," Lillian called back. "He's still nervous from all the gunfire today."

So we're all here. All except for Brad.

As she walked up the stairs and into their bedroom, Lara replayed her dream. Given Brad's return to what she'd taken to calling *the other world*, perhaps it had more significance than she'd thought.

SHE LAY on her side in bed with Trevor snugged against her back and murmured, "He didn't tell us everything."

"Huh? Oh, you mean Raven?" Trevor sounded half asleep already.

"Uh-huh."

"Yeah. I thought the same myself," he said. "You missed the first half hour after he got back."

"Tell me."

Trevor pulled her closer with the arm cradling both her and Elizabeth. "Well, he fairly blew back into the house. You know how sometimes he's more subtle about it?"

"Yes, I know. What happened after that?" Lara turned over so she was facing Trevor. Moonlight streamed through the window, and she could see him clearly.

"The women fairly mobbed him. He just raised those huge hands of his and shook his head. Then he said, 'He's not coming back, and it's for the best.' After that the questions flew thick and fast." Trevor snorted. "Good thing I've been practicing my Gaelic, else I'd not have caught even half of it."

Yes, a very good thing, since I can still only pick out a phrase or two. "If you had to synopsize it?"

Trevor nodded. "Basically, Raven was saying *I told you so,* and the women were adding their two cents' worth. You do remember it was you and I who wanted Brad to stay right after we buried Adriana? The others wanted him gone. So I got to hear all the reasons he should have left then."

"Even Elidora?" Lara was surprised. She'd assumed the witch woman cared for Brad, since she was sleeping with him.

Trevor sighed. "Yes, even her. Apparently he'd turned her down a time or two here of late and she didn't like that much." Letting out a sound between a snort and a grunt, he rolled his eyes. "Now that I think about it, I don't ever recall anyone telling her *no* before. I'm sure it didn't sit well."

"So." Lara blew out a breath. "It's all good riddance as far as they're concerned?" She felt sad as she said the words. Brad was a decent man with a good heart. Even though his feelings for her had created tension in their household, she knew she'd miss him. *It's because he's human, like us,* she realized with a start, understanding dawning just how strange the Sidhe truly were.

Trevor's brow furrowed, so she guessed he was considering what she'd said about good riddance. "That might be putting a colder edge on it than is needed," he murmured after a time. "It's not that they don't have any compassion. I think it's that they view how the world works in a very different way than we do. It's all about balance and energy and timing and goddesses—and I suppose gods as well, since that's what Raven truly is. They live for so long, I don't think they consider us much at all." He chuckled softly. "Hope that made sense. It's been a long day."

"Yeah, Trev. It did. I'm thinking. And I'm not very happy with what I'm coming up with. It's like we're just game pieces on some sort of board. Except Raven and them haven't bothered to explain the rules."

"I don't think it's quite as bad as all that," he protested. "If it weren't for them, we'd be stuck in Seattle. Hell, we'd like as not be dead right now. Just like poor Arabel."

Oh my, I haven't thought about her in weeks. Lara folded a protective hand around her stomach. Arabel's soft southern drawl reverberated in her head, as she remembered her wonderful receptionist hoping for a little one to dandle on her knees. "I miss her." Lara's eyes filled with tears. "She was part of my life for so long. The real one, before things got crazy and we let Raven and Lillian talk us into abandoning everything."

"Come here." Trevor held out his arms and she scooted closer. "Lara." His mellow baritone rumbled against her hair. "It was really, really hard those few months before we left Seattle. I had to scrounge for food. Power was off better than half the time. Bloody hell, love, I had to kill…" He stopped for a few moments, his fingers digging into her shoulders betrayed his emotion. "Do not make the mistake of romanticizing how wonderful things were back on Queen Anne Hill."

"Guess you're right." Her voice was muffled against his chest. "It's been one thing after another ever since we got here, though. There hasn't been much of a chance for this to start to feel normal. I wonder if it ever will."

He just held her, stroking her hair and murmuring wordless endearments. After a time, she fell asleep.

ADRIANA CAME to her in a dream, crying for her father, her long, blonde hair swirling round her. On the heels of that dream came another. She was back in Seattle again—this time at the University, and her students were gathered close. Some of them were screaming at her and some were crying. All of them accused her of abandoning them when they needed her most, since Ryan's prophetic dream had come true and no one was left to help them.

"That does it," Lara muttered, clawing her way back from Psyche's realm and getting up to go to the bathroom. She was so tired her eyes felt swollen and gritty, but she didn't particularly want to go back to sleep. Not if she was going to have dreams like that.

"What do you want from me?" she asked Psyche softly. Having returned from the toilet, she stood in the bedroom window looking out at the moonlit yard. "Just tell me what you want, and I'll try to do whatever it is." She eyed the moon. "Artemis. If you ever talk to Psyche…" Lara ground to a halt, feeling foolish. As if the gods would pay one whit of attention to someone like her.

Ach, goddesses, dreams, Sidhe… Poor Adie knows her father's left her for good. That's what that dream means. But why can't she haunt him instead of me? He's the one who left, for chrissakes. The other one's an extension of the dream I had earlier. Am I dreaming of our old life because Brad went back to it, or because Psyche's trying to tell me something?

Elizabeth rolled over—or tried to in what had to be increasingly close quarters—and Lara plodded tiredly back to the bathroom. It didn't take much to stimulate her bladder these days. Because she couldn't think of anything better to do, and because she truly was dead on her feet, Lara went back to bed. Trevor was sleeping more soundly than usual, his soft snores comforting.

She planned to just shut her eyes for a few moments to rest them, but when she opened them again, daylight streamed into the cheery room, and Trevor was already gone.

"Thank God. No more dreams," she mumbled as she pulled on the clothes she'd worn the day before. Getting into anything was becoming more and more of a struggle. For a moment, she envied Arab women with their shapeless burkas and then she laughed. It was a welcome respite from the dark place she'd been the previous night.

The aroma of fresh-brewed coffee hit her the minute she started down the stairs, and she wondered where it came from. They'd been out for a while. *Maybe Raven felt guilty, so he brought some provisions.*

Lara kicked herself. No matter what transpired between Brad and Raven, the mage had been kind to her. And to Trevor too. He'd been telling the truth when he said he'd offered Brad a chance to return.

What more do I want here? Lara wasn't sure as she rolled the question around in her head. When Trevor met her in the kitchen with a cup of coffee in hand, she smiled at him, took the coffee, and sat down.

"Thanks." She sipped appreciatively from her cup. "Where'd we get coffee from?"

"Not sure." He smiled back. "It was here when I got up, along with a bunch of other food."

"Where are Raven and the Sidhe?"

He shook his head. "Haven't seen any of them yet. But Gunter was curled up in the kitchen. I let him out."

"Mmph." Lara drank more coffee and cocked her head to one side. "Well, it has to be either one of the Sidhe or Brad who left us food. Since Raven's barred Brad from returning, that means—"

"Not necessarily. If the Sidhe left during the night, Brad could've snuck back to tell Adie goodbye and leave us those things. They're most of the food items we've been missing. Like fruit and vegetables. Whoever left them knew what we needed."

"If it was Brad, do you think we should hide the new stuff?" Lara was suddenly worried about Raven's wrath if he discovered Brad hadn't complied with his wishes. Thinking back to her restless night, she added, "You could be right, I had a dream about Adie. She was crying for her daddy, so maybe he did manage to tell her goodbye."

"Interesting." Trevor inclined his head. "Given the data, who do you think left all this?"

"I'm sure we'll find out soon enough," she muttered, taking another long drink from her mug. "My, but that's good. Didn't realize how much I missed it."

"Crikey, Lara. We only ran out a couple weeks ago."

"What with all that's happened here, it feels like longer than that." She offered up a weak smile. "What's for breakfast?"

He pulled a pan out of the oven. "Omelet and cornbread. I kept it warm for you. And here's an apple and an orange."

As she tucked into her food, Lara had a hard time keeping her mind quiet. It didn't help that Elizabeth was doing flip-flops.

"Tell me more about your Adriana dream." Trevor sank into a chair across from her, clasping his own mug between his hands.

"Nothing more to tell," she said around a mouthful of eggs. "Something got her spirit riled up enough it felt the need to rattle some cages. Now that I think about it, Brad sitting with her to tell her he was going back to the police force might have been enough to do the trick."

"I see." Trevor set his mug down.

"Did you already eat?" she asked. At his nod, she said, "I figured as much. I didn't plan to sleep so late."

"No need to apologize. You need rest, love. Food too. Finish your breakfast and then we'll talk."

At a muted scratching from the kitchen door, Trevor got up to let Gunter in. When he pulled open the door, Brad stood right behind the dog. Trevor's eyes widened. "Thought you weren't supposed to be here."

Lara's head shot up. She lumbered to her feet. "Brad… But Raven said—" she sputtered as she walked over to give him a quick hug. Stepping back, she looked at him. Soot tracked down one cheek and across his high forehead. Rolled up shirtsleeves showed a jagged cut and a bruise down the lower part of one arm. He smelled like sweat and gunpowder.

"How'd you get past the wards?" she asked, curious.

"Clocked the mileage on my odometer when I drove out of here. It was easy." Brad looked pleased with himself; a lopsided grin tugged one corner of his mouth upward. "A really thick mist obscured pretty much everything, but I found where the turn had to be and took it. Once I got over the bridge, everything looked normal again."

He raised a hand to forestall more questions. "Can't stay long. I saw them leave just past five this morning. Figured they'd be gone for a while, since they generally are when they draw that doorway thing. Seems to mean they're going a distance. Anyway, I've been hanging around in the barn, waiting till both of you were up. I need to be sure you know some things Raven told me. Then I'll be on my way.

"First off, did Raven let you know I'm going to stay in your house on Queen Anne for the next few months?" Brad blushed, then hurried to add, "If that's okay with you guys that is."

Lara shook her head. "No. He didn't tell us that. And yes, you're welcome to stay there."

"I thought as much." The detective sucked in a quick breath. "Well, if he didn't tell you that part, he probably didn't tell you the rest either. You see..."

Ten minutes later, Brad shook Trevor's hand, gave Lara a quick kiss on one cheek, and hustled out the door. "Do what you can to make sure Raven doesn't turn me into a toad," he called over his shoulder, laughing grimly. "Didn't matter what he wanted, I had to say goodbye to my Adie. And warn the two of you. Remember, I'll wait for you until past New Year's, maybe a little longer." He clattered down the porch steps. When his feet hit the dirt of the yard, he started running. Lara heard his car door slam and the muted roar of an engine.

"Well," she said dryly, pulling the kitchen door shut. "*That* was interesting. Feeds right into what I said earlier about us being game board pieces."

"Certainly does, love," Trevor agreed, coming up to her and placing both hands on her shoulders. "Lara, look at me."

She did. What she saw in his blue eyes drew her up short. He looked as fierce as she'd ever seen him, almost as intense as he'd been the day he'd told her about finding his sister dead in his barn back in Carlisle.

"We need to be very careful here, since Raven and the Sidhe can read our thoughts," he said. "Regardless of how you're feeling about

Raven and Lillian right about now, Lillian cares for you. Raven probably does too, though to a lesser extent. And Elidora is fond of me. She's known me since I was born. We will do whatever we need to so we can stay here until after Elizabeth is born. I want you to have Elidora and Lillian by your side. I trust them far more than I'd trust some doctor we don't know." He stepped away from her and raked his fingers through his hair in a gesture Lara knew only too well, before adding, "God only knows what shape the hospitals are in at this point."

"What about Helen Morgan?" Lara asked, reminding him of her old friend who was head of the obstetrics and gynecology department at University of Washington Medical Center.

"If she's still alive and the hospital is still doing deliveries, that's probably fine. But there's no way for us to know any of that. If there've been more riots—and it sounds as if they've been continuous since they're tapping prison guards to augment the police force— seems to me most hospitals would reserve their beds for the injured. As you've pointed out, pregnancy is scarcely an illness. Where I grew up, most women had their babies at home."

Lara scooped up her coffee mug, carried it to the stove, and poured herself another jot. Her temper *had* flared listening to Brad. Raven and the Sidhe were treating them like children, circumventing them where important decisions were concerned. But she could see Trevor's point too. Her first instinct had been to gather up a few things, jump in the cars, and go home, but she understood how much help she'd need to deliver her baby. At forty-six, she wasn't the best candidate to be having a first child. Worry nagged at her, and she caught her lower lip between her teeth, biting hard enough to hurt.

Making a concerted effort to calm down, she eyed the rounded hump of her stomach. "Let's see," she counted on her fingers. "It's either early or mid-April. The way I figure, I have about three months to go. But I'm so huge, I can't imagine the pregnancy lasting that long. If the baby gets too big, she won't come out except by C-section."

"Didn't Elidora say Elizabeth would come when she was ready and that the timing for their births is different?"

Lara nodded. "Something along those lines, yes. It was actually Lillian who said that. Not that it really matters." She reached for his hand.

"Okay. So we bide our time and wait." He tipped her chin up so her eyes met his. "Are we agreed on that?"

"Yes."

"No temper tantrums. Just be sweet and, uh, as normal as you can when they all get back here."

"I'll do my best." She gritted her teeth. Trevor was right. When she was riled, her anger had a tendency to get the better of her. "Don't you think Raven will be able to figure out Brad was here?"

Trevor shrugged. "Maybe. We'll just have to wait and see. If he's as egotistical as I think he is, he'll just assume Brad would never dream of going against one of his edicts. And if Raven's not looking to find evidence, perhaps he won't."

"I hope you're right." Tamping down a desire to get the hell out of Raven's guesthouse—forever—Lara stomped back to the stove and spooned more breakfast onto her plate.

CHAPTER 17

Trevor was in the garden, carefully transplanting seedlings he'd nurtured for weeks in the shop. Brad's instincts had been good, since a month had passed with no sign of Raven or the Sidhe. Lara, who'd been diligently practicing her magic skills, was able to communicate with Lillian fairly easily through the amulet now. She'd told him the previous night that at least the women would be back quite soon. "And a good thing too," she'd said, "since I don't think this baby's going to wait much longer."

He grimaced, and breath whistled from between his teeth. Lara did look as if she felt perfectly wretched. Her breasts were swollen to twice their normal size, and it didn't seem as if the skin over her abdomen could stretch another centimeter without tearing. Nonetheless, she didn't complain, even though it took her a couple tries to get up out of most chairs, and her stomach got in the way of everything.

For the first few days after the last go-round with the convicts and the Goblins, Trevor had been more than a little edgy. He'd kept the shotgun next to him pretty much all the time. At least ammunition wasn't an immediate worry anymore. Along with coffee and produce, Brad had also managed to come up with shotgun shells, cautioning Trevor these ones weren't spiked with silver. He'd begun to launch into an explanation of how he'd smelted the silver into pellets, but Trevor, concerned Raven might return at any minute, had waved the detective to silence and said, "I'm sure I'll figure it out."

Now he was sorry he hadn't gotten a fuller explanation. *Twenty-twenty hindsight. Nothing quite as sharp.* Trevor laughed ruefully at his foray into philosophy. He'd taken a good look at the rustic kiln Brad rigged up. He'd even tried to fire it, but it hadn't gotten nearly hot enough to melt the silver spoon he laid in the tray. Something elemental was missing, but he hadn't found time to dissect the problem.

"Humph," he snorted. "One more thing to do. Right after I get these tomatoes and peppers and zucchini planted. And the potatoes, carrots, and onions after that." It had finally stopped raining every day, but the growing season wouldn't be all that long. He knew he had to take advantage of every day of it if they were going to have something to eat next winter.

Assuming they stayed put.

He and Lara had talked about returning to Seattle, but without much in the way of resolution. Arguments bounced back and forth on both sides of the stick. Sometimes it was her longing for the relative comfort of their rambling house on Queen Anne; sometimes it was him. "Things have likely changed quite a bit since we left," he murmured, pushing the last seedling into a mound of dirt. "And not for the better. Bloody hell, for all I know, the place could have burned to the ground, or it might have turned into a haven for scum like those young toughs that tried to kill me."

And then he remembered Brad was there—at least for now. Assuming the detective hadn't managed to get himself killed, likely their house was safe enough.

"Talking to yourself?" Lara's cheery voice preceded her into the garden. "You need to watch that. They say it's the first sign you've gone off your rocker."

Trevor sprang to his feet, brushing his hands off on his pants. "I suppose a psychoanalyst would know these things." He grinned at her.

Lara folded her hands over her belly. "Perhaps. Oooph. There's barely enough room left inside me to breathe. And my lower back's started hurting."

Something clicked in Trevor's mind. "When did you say Lillian and Eli would be here?"

"Later today, I think. Why?"

Spreading his hands in front of him, Trevor looked at her. "It's just something my Mum used to complain about when she was about to go into labor. Her back would hurt."

Lara's eyes widened and then she shrugged helplessly. "I should've thought of that. It's in that midwifery book I found in the library." Reaching behind her, she rubbed her tailbone and winced.

"Uh, maybe you should tell Lillian they need to show up sooner rather than later." He thought for a moment. "Until one of them gets a look at you, you probably shouldn't eat anything else."

"I *knew* that part," she said, sounding irritated, but Trevor understood she was probably more scared than anything else. "Another thing I learned from that book—or maybe I already knew this—is that first babies take their time. Is there anything I can do to help out here?"

Trevor shook his head. "Nope. Just finished with this part. I've got to prep some more beds for the root plants before I can plant them. Right now the dirt's like clay. Needs aerating."

Gunter, who'd been digging in the mud, looked over at them. His nose was coated with damp earth, and he gave a little yip before going back to his excavations.

"Looks like you've got a helper," she observed.

"Yeah. Too bad I can't get him to dig where I need him to. Right now he's damned close to undoing some of my work. Hey," he clucked to the dog. "Yes, you. Come on over here."

Ever obedient, Gunter got up and shook himself. Dirt flew every which way, and he trotted to his daddy's side. "Until I get the fence finished," Trevor lectured the dog, "you have to stay out of here." The Shepherd, head cocked to one side and tongue lolling, started for the house. "Good boy," Trevor called after him.

"I'll go too," Lara said. "I've got bread rising, and I'll just give the Sidhe a bit of a heads up." Frowning, she reached for her lower back again. "It doesn't exactly hurt. But it sure does smart."

"Would you like me to do anything?" Trevor felt worried. He still knew next to nothing about how to help a woman in labor, despite spending hours thumbing through the book Lara had unearthed from upstairs.

Lara, one hand clutching the amulet, seemed lost in thought, so he went to stand by her side, waiting. She'd moved beyond the point where she needed the library and nudity to communicate with the Sidhe. He assumed she was talking with them now.

She stayed in her trance—or whatever it was—for quite a while. Maybe five minutes. When she opened her bottomless, dark eyes, they looked worried.

"What? Aren't they going to come?" Alarmed, he jumped to the worst imaginable conclusion.

"No, silly. They'll be here. And really soon. But they want us to go inside and make sure the dog's there too. Apparently there's been more trouble with Gradoxst. Lillian is worried he'll be hot on their heels. Also, she finally told me what they've been up to. Guess they've gathered the others. You know," she gestured, "human-Sidhe hybrids like me. They're all in some old castle in the Scottish highlands. Lillian says I need to come as soon as I can after the baby's born, but she didn't say exactly why."

Trevor rolled his eyes. "Where does that leave me?" he demanded, but Lara just looked at him, palms turned upward. After a pause he sputtered, "On other fronts, I was hoping we were shut of that slimy old rogue Sidhe."

"As was I," she agreed, her mouth set in a grim line. "And for him to show up when I'm in labor would be just like him. I'll probably be helpless as a kitten for hours—maybe even days. And Trev, about that

Scotland thing— I'm not going anywhere without you. We're stronger together. So unless Lillian says we can both go, well then, neither of us will."

He drew her as close as her stomach would allow. "Thanks, love," he murmured, kissing her forehead. He thought about how many silver bullets he had left. Not liking the answer he came up with, Trevor ran his hands through his hair in frustration. It had been days since he'd brushed it out and his fingers caught in his tangled curls. "Is Raven coming?" He remembered how hamstrung Lillian had been without Raven's magic to shore hers up—at least against Goblins.

Lara nodded. "Come on, we may as well both go in."

"Got to milk the goats. Then I'll lock them in the barn. Be there directly." He took off across the yard at a fast trot thinking about their two horses in a distant paddock. They'd eaten all the grass in sight, so Trevor had moved them further afield the previous week. *Nothing to be done about that now,* he told himself, hoping against hope they weren't in for a siege.

"Maybe we should go back to the city," he mumbled gloomily. "I far prefer human enemies to Gradoxst and his ilk." While his hands were busy with goat udders, Trevor's thoughts turned reluctantly to his time with Gradoxst in the *Dreaming*. He tried to think of something else—anything else—but the knowing leer on that ravaged old face filled his mind until he couldn't stand it anymore. Stomach tied in knots, he let go of the goat, who *baahed* indignantly, and rubbed his eyes until the familiar barn walls came back into focus. Fighting a chill that settled in the pit of his stomach, Trevor glanced about warily half-expecting the fallen Sidhe to pop out from behind something.

He waited through three long breaths, the silvered knife he'd slipped out of his boot in hand. When it was apparent he was alone and his imagination was working overtime, he bent to finish the milking, intent on getting back inside the house as fast as he could.

LARA BENT over a mound of dough spread on one of the kitchen counters. The rocking motion of kneading relieved the pain in her back. She wondered what was taking Trevor so long. He'd said he was going to milk the goats, but it was closing on an hour since she'd retreated to the house.

For that matter, where are the Sidhe?

Pinching off generous balls of dough—something between large rolls and small loaves—she laid them on a baking sheet, looked toward the woodstove, and willed the embers to come to life. "Too bad I can't figure out how to use magic to get the wood in there too," she muttered as she lumbered over to toss a few sticks of damp wood into the stove. In spite of Trevor working on their wood supply almost constantly, it never really had a chance to dry out, so all their fires were smouldery messes unless she focused a trickle of magic to help things along. She'd just draped a dishtowel over her finished dough when he blew back into the house, shucking his jacket as soon as he was inside the back door and shaking it out. Gunter, sensing a game, tried to grab the moving cloth in this mouth.

"Raining again, huh?" She stepped close and turned her face up for a kiss.

"Uh-huh. Pouring, actually. Surprised you didn't notice."

"Now that you mention it, I can hear it," she admitted. "Guess I've been lost in my own thoughts."

"How are you feeling?" He laid a hand over her swollen abdomen. And then he grinned. "Wow! She's pretty strong. That kick nearly took my hand out."

"Tired. Heavy. Wondering what's keeping Lillian…"

The air across the vast downstairs room shimmered, and the outlines of a doorway took form.

"Well, that answers one question." Leaning away from Lara, he shook water out of his curls.

Yes, it certainly does. Fighting irritation that they hadn't rushed to her side the moment she called, Lara moved her baking tray to the back of the woodstove for a final rise and turned to greet the Sidhe.

Elidora was first to stop fading in and out. Draping heavy, black braids over her shoulders in a gesture reminiscent of Lillian, she strode briskly to Lara and laid both hands on either side of her stomach. Eyes closed, she said, "Hush now, child."

Lara, who'd opened her mouth, promptly shut it. The baby quieted under Elidora's knowing touch. In a bit, the witch woman opened her eyes. "Not quite yet," she pronounced. "But soon. In fact, very soon."

"What does that mean?" Lara heard a whiny tone in her voice that she didn't particularly like.

Elidora patted her cheek, but it was Lillian who answered as she walked close to give Lara a hug and feel her belly. "A day or two. Not more than a week."

Lara groaned. "Ach, Christ. A week. I'm not sure I can do this for that much longer." Then, to her horror, she started to cry. Brushing away tears in exasperation, she blurted. "What's wrong with me?"

"Oh aye, ye are just very pregnant. All women feel as if th' end will never come. Do no' be afeard, lassie, that bairn will find her way out. They all do." Elidora smiled, the lines at the sides of her eyes crinkling with pleasure.

Gunter raced about the room, barking and whining. Lillian called him to her and bent to whisper into the dog's ear. Whatever she said calmed him, because he immediately positioned himself at her feet, looking up at her adoringly.

"Isn't anyone going to give me a hello?" An edge sharpened Raven's deep voice, but Lara knew he was teasing. She plodded over to wrap her arms around the mage's bearlike bulk.

"There," she said. "Is that better?"

"Much." When he smiled at her, his teeth were very white against his black beard. "Now go on with you." He let go of her, then held out a hand to Trevor.

"I was starting to wonder if I'd ever see you again." Trevor's eyes shone as he pumped the other man's hand. "So long as you're here, maybe you can help me figure out how to get the kiln in the shop going, so I can melt more silver."

Raven drew back, his lips curled in a distasteful expression. "So long as I don't have to be there while you're smelting it, of course I can help."

"Don't worry." Trevor extricated his hand, meeting the Sidhe's gray eyes with his blue ones. "All I need is more heat for the forge."

"That, son, is something I can definitely provide." Raven looked around hopefully. "Is there anything to eat?"

"There will be in an hour or so." Trevor looked at Lara, who nodded her confirmation of his time estimate. "Until then, how about if you come outside with me? If there are Goblins afoot, I need more silver bullets."

"Not really, since you have us," Raven retorted.

"Yes, but you have a nasty habit of disappearing and not coming back for weeks. Coming?" Trevor held the door and beckoned with one hand. He clucked to the dog, who trotted over then slipped through the open door.

Lara felt something wound tight within her begin to relax as she watched the men walk out the kitchen door. In an odd way, Raven and the Sidhe had taken the place of the family she'd never known and, in spite of the secrets they'd held back, she drew comfort from their presence. Mouth turned up in a half-smile, she plodded across the kitchen to pop her bread into the oven.

"What else are we having?" Lillian asked.

"Aye, an' can we be doin' anything to hurry things along?" Elidora added.

Lara straightened, closing the oven door with a small *thud*. Glancing at Lillian, she shrugged. "There's part of a goat we slaughtered the other day in the springhouse. We could finish that off and hunt up some wild onions to sauté along with it. I found some mushrooms the other day, but I wasn't sure they were safe to eat—"

"Mushrooms?" Elidora interrupted eagerly and moved quickly toward the door. "Come on then, lass, and show me."

"I'll get the meat going," Lillian offered, sounding tired. "See you two presently."

Lara stopped short at the door. "I thought you told me to stay inside," she said, looking back at Lillian. "That it might not be safe."

"That was *before* we got here, child." Lillian smiled grimly. "There's safety in numbers. Go on. Get moving. None of us have eaten today."

As she picked her way through the nearby woods, her skirts pulled up in front of her to make a rough basket for the bounty they were collecting, Lara asked about the gathering in Scotland. "So how many others like me are there?" She found she was curious. Other than her Aunt Mary, Lara had never known other humans who had any magical ability at all.

"Well now, an' that's hard to say, exactly," Elidora mused. "Because sure and there are many that have escaped our notice. Like that relative of yours, as one example." Reaching down, she plucked a fat bunch of mushrooms, dropping them into her own skirts. "Ye can eat these ones, lassie. Look close so ye'll remember what they look like."

As Lara bent to examine the newly plucked mushrooms, she said, "But these are different from those ones." She pointed to another mushroom Elidora had dropped into her impromptu basket.

The witch woman laughed. "There are several kinds that are fit to eat."

"How many?" Lara demanded.

"Mushrooms?" Elidora's brow furrowed.

"No, others like me."

"We have nigh onto a hundred, but some are too young and most far too old t' be o' much help against th' Dark." She sighed. "Mostly, they are wantin' t' go home, which is why Lillian asked for you t' come. They are afeard o' their magic, see. Mayhap ye might help wi' that."

"Why did you call them together?" Lara reached toward an enticing mushroom, but Elidora grabbed her hand before she could touch it.

"Not that one, lass. See, it has a brown border 'neath th' cap. Those ones are poisonous."

More to this than there appears.

Lara felt chagrined, convinced she wasn't going to be adding mushrooms to their diet anytime soon, unless one of the Sidhe went gathering with her. As she sliced off a bunch of wild anise with a pocketknife and pulled a few onions, she prodded, "Well?"

Elidora looked momentarily confused. "Och! Ye be worse than a dog with a bone. But th' long and short o' it is that things were quiet for a bit after Gradoxst's ill-conceived attempt t' wrest th' *Dreamin'* from us. We heard from one o' our spies—"

"You have spies?" Lara stopped walking and turned to stare at Elidora.

"An' how else would we be gatherin' information?" the witch woman asked indignantly. "There, lass, grab those mushrooms just near your right foot."

Having made the mistake of squatting, Lara held out a hand for Elidora to help her up. "I forget I can't do things," she mumbled, irritated by her ungainly bulk. "I think we probably have enough for dinner. What was it you heard from your spies?"

The two women retraced their steps. Along the way, Elidora replied thoughtfully. "It seems there is a complicated plot, conceived by Gradoxst an' other Demons." Blowing out a disgusted breath from between gritted teeth, the witch woman went on. "This is no' unlike human wars, lass. Your conflagrations never end. An' neither do ours. There are lulls o' course, but th' Goblins an' other Demons are always tryin' t' get th' upper hand. This time they've targeted those like you, since they believe you are far more vulnerable an' more easily managed than those like us."

"Well, that's true, isn't it?" Lara drew her brows together as she assimilated the implications of Elidora's words.

"Yes…and no. Most of you are quite clever. Look at how your Trevor managed t' extricate himself from Gradoxst's very clutches— and his claim to old blood is quite weak." Elidora chuckled before her face turned serious again. "Your forebears were an alien race. Th' Demons' scheme involves capturing as many o' you as they can. They believe they will be able t' gather sufficient information t' conquer th' worlds from which you came. There are…things they can do with your blood t' make it appear as if they are th' aliens returned home. Once on a distant world—mayhap yours—they think t' infiltrate themselves and do much harm afore their charade is revealed."

A chill ran down Lara's spine despite the relative warmth of the afternoon sun. They crossed the clearing and mounted the steps leading into the house. "So it doesn't really matter where we are," she said, fighting a bone-deep fear. "Gradoxst, or others like him, will always be breathing down our necks. If Lillian had told me that, I'd probably have stayed in Seattle. At least—"

"Och aye, but it does. Matter, that is," Elidora interrupted, turning to impale Lara with her dark gaze. "Here ye have th' goddess's protection. But even She cannot keep th' Dark from attacking. All She can do is help you when they stir their mischief. Just dump those there, lass." Elidora pointed to the sideboard. "I'll be cleanin' them afore I cook them."

Shaking bits of vegetation out of her skirts, Lara was surprised when she felt Elidora's arms circle her from behind. "Ye'll be feelin' more like yersel' once th' bairn is here," she murmured, as she lay her soothing hands on Lara's stomach.

"I sure as hell hope so," Lara sputtered. "Because I don't like how I'm feeling now at all." She sighed, relaxing into Elidora's touch. "My, but that feels good, especially over there on my right side."

"Aye, the bairn is turned so she's pressing more on that side than t'other. Not much longer, dearie." She patted Lara soothingly before letting her go and turning to pump water over the vegetables.

The smell of roasting meat had reached Lara long before she entered the house. It smelled rich and good. She realized how hungry she was. "Wonder where Lillian is?" she mused as she walked over to the stove and broke off the end of one of the loaves Lillian had rescued from the oven.

"Right here." Lillian's voice drifted into the kitchen from the direction of the stairs. "Shall I tell the men dinner is ready?" she asked as she strode into the kitchen, her long skirts rustling.

"Sure. Probably in about fifteen minutes since we need to cook the vegetables." Lara fell heavily into a chair. "Are you sure it's okay for me to eat?" She looked at the two Sidhe who were busy at the sink.

"Why wouldn't it be?" Elidora half-turned to stare at Lara, incredulity stamped on her ageless features.

Lara thought about telling the witch-woman about the midwifery book, but decided against it. If Elidora thought she shouldn't eat, Lara was convinced the Sidhe would be the first to tell her so. "Never mind," she murmured and reached hungrily for the bread she'd placed on the table.

*L*ara wasn't sure what woke her. Not that she'd been sleeping all that soundly. In fact, it was incredibly difficult to find a comfortable position. More often than not, the baby kicked hard enough to disturb her after she'd managed to finally drift off. "Ah crap," she mumbled, realizing she needed to pee again. Walking toward the bathroom, she felt something shift inside her. Warm fluid gushed down between her legs. At first she thought her bladder had let go, and then she understood her water had broken.

It's finally happening, she told herself as she sat on the toilet, shivering with anticipation and fear. *No reason to wake anyone else yet. This will likely take a while.* When she was done, she took off her soaked nightgown and drew on a robe. In the meantime, the amulet had begun shooting out something that felt untamed. Lara thought she'd been exposed to just about all the magic moonstone's varied moods. *Guess I was wrong,* she told herself as she gripped the large gem, trying to draw energy from its exuberance.

She'd just settled back in bed when the first labor pain hit. It felt as if someone stabbed her in the kidneys with a sharp knife. Unable to control herself, she yelped.

"Lara?" Trevor asked sleepily. "What?" Turning toward her, he looked at her in moonlight spilling into the room. "Are you in labor?" he croaked, sounding much more awake as he laid a hand on her abdomen.

She nodded. "My water just broke and..." her voice trailed off as she ground her teeth together to suppress a moan. "I thought this was supposed to start with *easy* contractions," she managed, struggling against panic. "There's only been one, but if it was easy, I don't think I'll be able to live through the hard ones." She tried to smile at Trevor, but failed utterly. "I'm scared," she mumbled, looking away, embarrassed by her lack of courage.

Get a grip. Women have been delivering babies for thousands of years.

"I'll go find Elidora." Trevor sprang out of bed. Lara heard him calling for Lillian and Elidora the minute he cleared the door of their room.

Gunter uncurled himself from his customary spot and jumped onto the bed next to Lara, licking her face. Reaching out to the dog, she buried her fingers in his rough coat, drawing strength from his simple, animal presence. Another contraction rocked her. The dog grunted when she clutched him. "Sorry. Sorry," she mumbled, letting go. The dog hopped down, whining softly. When she glanced over, she saw he was licking her amniotic fluids from where they'd spilled onto the floor. Lara started to tell him not to, but decided they couldn't hurt him.

Elidora swept into the room just as another contraction ripped through her. Lara grunted, trying not to scream. The witch woman grasped her arms, pulling her upright.

"What are you doing?" Lara struggled against Elidora's iron grip. "I need to lie down."

"Oh no, you don't." Lillian, who must've entered the room on Elidora's heels, hovered above her. "What you need to do, child, is walk. Eli, you get one of her arms and I'll get the other."

"I'm not sure I can," Lara protested. On her feet, she swayed between the Sidhe.

"Ye can and ye will," Elidora pronounced. "'Twill hurry things along."

Raven stood in the doorway, bushy eyebrows raised. Lillian looked at him and shook her head. "Not yet," she said. "Take him." She pointed at a very pale-faced Trevor. "You might pour some mead into him."

"Come on. Get some clothes on, man." Raven looked pointedly at Trevor's mostly-bare legs.

"Okay. Uh, yeah." Bending, Trevor sorted out a pair of jeans and a sweater from where he'd dropped them over a chair. In a few moments, he glanced at Raven. "Better?"

"Yes. Now come with me. You won't be needed here for quite some time."

Trevor gaze settled on Lillian and Elidora walking up and down the bedroom with Lara supported between them. "Lara?" he said tentatively.

"It's fine," she managed, panting slightly. "You can come back when the baby's closer to being born." Because she was looking up, Lara saw something pass between Lillian and Elidora. "What?" she asked, panic layering itself over fear and apprehension.

"From the looks o' things, it willna be all that long," Elidora murmured, pulling her forward. "Keep moving. Once th' men have left, we'll go out into th' hall. It's longer."

Lara walked and walked. Up the hall, then back down it. Every once in a while, one of the Sidhe handed her a mead bottle, but the liquor didn't help much. Pain was like a living thing, clawing at her. It was so intense she almost couldn't breathe. Once she raised a fist to clobber Lillian when she dragged her faster than she felt she could walk, but Lillian just laughed at her. When the gray light of dawn lightened the upstairs windows, Lillian murmured something indistinct to Elidora, who nodded.

"Come, child," Lillian invited. "The hardest part is nearly over."

Just about the time Lillian's words registered, Lara felt something change. Added to the ever-present contractions was an unrelenting urge to push. "C—can I?" she asked as the two women helped her onto the bed. "Can I do this?"

"O' course." Elidora's rich brogue was indescribably soothing. "In truth, your bairn's nearly here. Push, lass. Push as if your very life depended on it."

Propped on lots of pillows, legs splayed, Lara squeezed her eyes shut and pushed. Someone had thrown a thick blanket down atop the bed and the rough wool rubbed against her skin. The pain did seem a little better. Hope swept through her that she might survive after all. Once that thought surfaced, she understood how frightened she'd been that she'd die in childbirth. She pushed again because she had to, carried along on a cresting wave with a mind of its own.

Trevor's dear face swam into view the next time she opened her eyes. "I can see her head," he said. "Ach, love, just a little more and Elizabeth will be here." Tears glistened on his cheeks. Lara extricated her hand from Lillian to reach out to him.

"One more," Elidora exhorted. "Just one more and I'll have her."

Lara felt the small body slither out of her. She heard a thin mewling and her eyes flew open again. Letting go of Trevor, she reached out with both hands. All the love in the world felt concentrated inside her, and she was full to bursting. "Let me see," she begged. "Oh, let me hold her."

Elidora, a broad smile on her face, handed the tiny, red infant, umbilical cord still attached, to Lara. "There, lass. Just for a moment. I need to clean th' birth matter from her. Then ye can hold her forever."

"Trev, oh, Trev, come look. See what we made." Lara cradled her daughter in her arms, kissing the top of her small, wet head.

"S—she's wonderful." Trevor's voice caught in his throat as he reached out a hand to gently stroke Elizabeth's arm, still coated with creamy vernix.

"Yes, she is," Raven's deep voice agreed, as he stepped close to lay an index finger on the infant's forehead. Eyes widening in surprise, he murmured, "And strong. My, this one will be strong."

Elidora closed a hand firmly over the cord, seemed to come to an internal decision, and took a knife from one of her many pockets. After holding it in the flame from a kerosene lamp for a few moments, she quickly cut through the cord close to the infant's stomach, laying the hot edge of the knife on the cut end. "'Twill seal it," she said.

"You're not quite done, child," Lillian bent close. "Another push or two. We need that placenta. Raven prepared a special, hidden place to bury it earlier. This birth honors the goddess who stood by you and helped us this night."

Looking at Elizabeth, Lara thought her daughter was the most perfect thing she'd ever seen, and she started to cry as a complex array of emotions pummeled her. Soon, she felt something else slide out of her. She drew her streaming eyes away from her baby for long enough to see Lillian carry the placenta over to the window, where she turned it over carefully. "What are you looking for?" Lara asked, curious in spite of her exhaustion.

"Only that there are no tears and it is complete, which it is." Smiling, Lillian handed the small basin holding the placenta to Raven, who left the room, chanting softly.

Elidora took Elizabeth. "Just for a moment," she said. "I need t' clean her up a wee bit." When the Sidhe picked up the baby, the little one opened her eyes. "Oh aye, blue, just like your daddy's," the witch woman murmured. "And red hair from your mother."

"You can sleep soon," Lillian said gently. "For now, you need to take another turn or two up and down the hall. It will speed your healing. I'll freshen your bed while you're gone."

"Shall I take her?" Trevor asked, emotion plain on his face. At Lillian's nod, he went round to Lara's side of the bed and helped her up.

"You were amazing," he whispered. "Stupendous. Brilliant. You've done an incredible thing. Birth and death, well, they're not many degrees of separation betwixt the two. I was plenty scared."

"So was I." Lara laughed weakly. "And now I feel as if I could sleep for a week." Meeting his eyes, she said, "I love you."

Covering her mouth with his, he answered with a kiss.

With an arm around her, Trevor led her back into the long hallway. "Would you like to throw some water on your face?"

"Sure. And I'm hungry."

"Will you be all right if I leave you in there?" he gestured toward the bathroom. "I could go down and make you a bit of a snack."

Lara laughed. The sound was stronger this time. "Yes, Trev. Somehow I think if I could make it through what I just did, I'll be fine for a few moments here at the sink."

"Ye need to walk." Elidora's voice floated out into the hall.

"You heard the woman." Trevor was still beaming. "So we'll walk, and then I'll make you something to eat."

TREVOR COULDN'T REMEMBER EVER FEELING QUITE so elated. The steely grip he usually kept on his emotions fled completely as he bounded down the stairs to create something for Lara, his Lara. For a moment, he wished he had access to all the exotic foods they'd left behind in the city, and then he just shook his head. *She'll be happy with anything I make for her,* he reminded himself, throwing a few sticks of wood into the bed of coals in the stove.

He'd just loaded a tray with leftovers from supper, spring water, and mead when Raven let himself into the kitchen. Actually, he materialized rather than using the door, but Trevor had moved beyond being surprised by magic. The mage was smiling, full lips curving until they were lost behind the curtain of his thick, dark beard.

"It's a glad day," Trevor offered, balancing the tray on an upraised hand. For the first time, he understood why new fathers handed cigars about. It gave them something to do to address the unutterable pride swelling through them.

"That it is," Raven agreed. "I'm grateful the wards held."

"Huh?" Trevor felt momentarily confused before understanding dawned. "Ah, it wasn't that Gradoxst *isn't* out there. It's that you did something." At the mage's nod, Trevor thought guiltily about his half-finished silver bullet project. "How many besides him?" He set Lara's tray on the sideboard.

"Hard to say, since they come and go." Raven blew out a breath. "There are energies afoot linked to borning and dying. They make it easier for all magical creatures to move about. Us too." He smiled wryly, cocking his head to one side, eyebrows furled in a gesture Trevor had come to know well.

Something nagged at Trevor. "But the wards won't keep Gradoxst out." He eyed Raven. "You know, because of his Sidhe blood and all."

Raven's face darkened. Trevor drew back. He'd seen enough of the mage's temper to not want to set it off. "That may be true." Raven bit off each word, enunciating precisely. "We kept him too busy to tamper with them, though."

Trevor waited, hoping Raven would tell him more. After silence reigned for a span of time, Trevor nodded. "I'll just run this food upstairs, then I'll come back down."

"No need. There's naught to be done at the moment." Raven had that closed look that meant he wasn't about to say any more.

Trevor heard the click of heels descending the stairs. "There you are." Lillian's voice held an undercurrent of annoyance. "I wondered what was taking you so long." She exchanged a meaningful look with Raven. "I'll just take that." She shouldered Trevor aside, grabbed the tray, and walked briskly toward the risers leading upstairs.

Raven snorted. "She's always been temperamental," he muttered under his breath, as his form faded from view.

Looking at the empty place where Raven had been, Trevor shook his head and turned to give the kitchen a once over. That done, he followed Lillian's path up the stairs, trying to be quiet in case Lara and the baby were asleep.

Trevor stood in the doorway for a moment, gazing adoringly at his wife and child. His heart was so full, he was surprised he didn't burst. Elizabeth, small mouth attached to Lara's breast, nursed hungrily and Lara was eating as if she'd never seen food before. Trevor cleared his throat and stepped into the room. Glancing at the almost empty plate, he asked, "Would you like more?"

Lara met his eyes. "No. Part of me thinks I should sleep, but the rest is too wound up. Besides, I'm afraid if I go to sleep, all these wonderful feelings," she made an expansive gesture with her hands, "will have gone away by the time I wake up." She grinned sheepishly. "Guess I feel sort of like Cinderella. I don't want to miss anything. And I don't want that clock to strike midnight, either."

"Know what you mean, love." Trevor thought about the cold-water effect of Raven's revelation just a few moments before. Coming close, he placed a finger on Elizabeth's cheek. The baby turned toward the sensation, losing Lara's nipple in the process. It registered that she'd lost her food source, and she began to cry.

Lara shifted the baby to her other side. "How about this one?" she crooned, guiding the infant a bit clumsily. "Babies' mouths are awfully tiny," she observed, maneuvering her nipple into it.

Trevor realized the Sidhe weren't in the room. "Where did Lillian and Elidora go?" he asked. "And where's the dog?"

"The Sidhe left after Lillian plopped my food on the bed. Said they'd be back and that I should rest." Her forehead creased. "Seems Gunter followed Raven, but I can't remember exactly when that was. Might have been when he left with the placenta."

Humph, bet the women met up with Raven. Gunter's probably outside somewhere. Hope he's okay.

Trevor felt torn. He didn't want to burden Lara with the knowledge that Demons were about. A part of him felt he should try to help the Sidhe. But that would mean leaving Lara and his baby alone, which might be risky if he had to go any distance from the house.

He angled his head to one side, listening. If fighting was going on out there, it had to be a long way away since he couldn't hear any evidence of it. Mentally throwing his hands up, he thought, *Yeah, like I'd be anything but an impediment to those three, even if I could find them.*

Hell, for all I know, they're off in some parallel world I couldn't get to anyway.

He moved the empty tray off the bed, kicked off his shoes, and lay down gently, an arm curved around Lara and Elizabeth. "How are you feeling?" he asked, settling a corner of the quilt over himself.

"Exhilarated. Like I could conquer anything," she said, edging closer to him. Wincing, she murmured, "and quite sore too."

"You have every right to be." He kissed her forehead. "Do you feel like talking for a bit, love?" He felt her head nod against his shoulder, so he went on. "Did the women say anything more about that trip they want you to take to the Old Country?"

Lara paused before she answered. He wondered if that meant she was picking her words carefully, or if it was just that she was tired. "They did. But I don't think there are any plans till the baby's at least a month old. They want to use me as an example that humans can open themselves to magic and still survive, or something."

A month. Everything will be growing by then. Someone will need to be here to tend to the crops, or there won't be any food next winter.

"It would be better," he spoke slowly, "if we didn't go until after the harvest. It won't be possible for both of us to leave during the summer. Not unless we want a winter like this last one. You'll be nursing for at least a year. So you'll need lots of calories."

"I suppose you're right." She sounded thoughtful, then asked abruptly. "Do you still want to try to go back to Seattle?"

"I don't know," he replied, considering the question. They'd talked about the possibility, but never come to any decision.

She pulled away from his embrace. The baby had fallen asleep, and Lara slid a finger into the rosebud mouth to detach her from her nipple. A muted squeak of protest escaped the newborn, then Elizabeth was quiet where she lay between her parents, breathing softly through a half-open mouth.

"Just a minute." Lara pulled a tiny coverlet close about Elizabeth, patted her back, then leaned over the side of the bed to where a cradle stood. "Sleep well, little one," she murmured, laying the baby tenderly in a nest of blankets.

"We do need to figure out which way we're going," she said, as she settled back into Trevor's arms.

He chuckled. "I keep hoping if we wait long enough, the choice will become obvious. Sort of like it did for Brad."

"That's because most of who he was lived back in the other world," Lara pointed out. "That used to be true for us, but not anymore."

Trevor wasn't so sure about that, but figured now wasn't the time to dissect just where they belonged. Or if they belonged anywhere anymore.

Sucking in a breath, he told her that Demons—and maybe even Gradoxst—were lurking nearby, held at bay by Raven's warding. He'd decided she had a right to know, especially if something horrid happened, and Gradoxst eluded the Sidhe's efforts to keep him contained.

"I wondered what became of him," she muttered, frowning. "And here I was thinking how lucky we'd been that he left us alone until after Elizabeth was done being born. I suppose that's where Raven and the Sidhe are. Fighting Goblins and Demons?"

He nodded. "Like as not. They don't tell me about their comings or goings."

"Know what you mean." She snorted softly. "They don't tell me, either."

"So" he said, "there are Demons here and back in Seattle too."

"At least here, we have some level of protection, or maybe that's illusory." Her voice faded. He felt her shake her head from side to side. "Think the adrenaline, or whatever it was, finally wore off," she mumbled. "Suddenly, I can't hold a thought in my head. Sorry, Trev. We can finish this conversation later." Her eyes closed and, within moments, she was snoring.

Trevor pulled her close. He hadn't had much sleep the previous night, either. Exhaustion tugged at his lids. With a great deal of effort, he looked out the window. It appeared to be past midday from the angle of the light. He thought about the goats and the horses, knowing he had to do some things before he could sleep. *And the calendar too. Need to make sure I know what day it is, so we know which one is Elizabeth's birthday.* For a moment, he thought wistfully of Brad's wristwatch, with its date and time functions. When he began to drift off, he forced himself back awake.

Kissing Lara fondly on the forehead, he levered his arm from under her head. She murmured in her sleep before turning over. "I'll only be gone for a short time, love," he whispered, comforting himself with the thought that he'd be close enough to hear her if something went wrong.

Like Demons, for example... Besides, I need to get my shotgun and what I've got for silver bullets before I'll be any good protecting anyone.

For the briefest of moments, he considered just staying. But the thought of the goats with their distended udders roused enough guilt that he forced his tired body into action. Bending a bit creakily, he kissed his child before picking up his shoes and padding silently out the door.

CHAPTER 19

$\mathcal{L}$ara dreamt about a shimmery, golden goddess that looked a lot like Brigid. Before she could find out why the goddess looked so stern—and worried—Elizabeth demanded her attention. After changing the newborn from a stack of clouts Elidora had left folded at the end of the bed, Lara settled back against the pillows, baby at her breast. Her sleep-fuzzed brain worried for a moment about rolling over and crushing the little one, but sleep reclaimed her before she could return the child to its cradle.

The next set of dreams was far less pleasant. She found herself in the well-appointed Sidhe home Gradoxst had commandeered in the *Dreaming*. Trevor was there, but try as she might, she couldn't rouse him. She had hold of his arm and was tugging hard on it, pleading with him to wake up, when the baby's cries roused her again. Opening gritty eyes, she fought a disorientation that came from having been deeply asleep. Then her eyes widened. Her hands flew about the bed in a panic, and she bolted to a sitting position.

Elizabeth! Where was Elizabeth? Not in her arms anymore, that was certain.

Wait, a part of her brain urged. *I hear her crying. Look that way.* Frightened she'd somehow knocked the helpless infant to the floor,

235

Lara raked her gaze through the shadowed room. It was apparently early evening. Not yet fully dark, but moving in that direction.

Lara zeroed in on Elizabeth and leapt from the bed, shying away from what her eyes told her. The child's shrieking escalated. Lara's screams joined hers.

"Give her back to me," she cried, catapulting across the room to where Gradoxst stood holding Elizabeth between his gnarled hands. He wore an old-fashioned black linen suit, with a cloak draped elegantly over his shoulders. The ends of his long, white hair curved over Elizabeth's head.

"Stop right there." He shook his head in clear warning. "One step closer and I'll strangle her." His hands moved closer to the baby's neck.

"You wouldn't." Lara, hands held out, stared at the Demon through narrowed eyes. "Even scum like you must have children. If you killed them, you'd all die out."

"So sorry to be late," he continued, as if she hadn't said anything at all. "I really did want to be here for the birth."

"You weren't invited," she snarled. The amulet sent alternating waves of heat and cold through her. *"Lillian, Raven,"* she called in mind speech, clutching the moonstone.

"None of that, either." Gradoxst's voice was sharp. Lara dropped the magic moonstone, her mind racing a million miles an hour. *What can I do? There's got to be something.* The baby was crying in earnest, little gaspy sobs that tore at Lara's heart.

"You're hurting her," Lara shouted. "Stop it right now."

"Or what?" he asked in a mocking tone. "Seems you're scarcely in a bargaining position at the moment. Oh, and don't expect to be rescued. I have seen to it that your friends are, shall we say, otherwise occupied."

"What do you want with me?" Lara made her voice cold to mask the desperation sweeping through her. She hoped Trevor wouldn't come barging in, because she was certain the rogue Sidhe would kill him on the spot. "What did you ever want with me?" she asked again, trying to divert him.

He looked down his aquiline nose. "Why, my dear, the same thing I've always wanted: your power. Except now there are two of you, so it is even better." He pulled the baby right up against his body. Elizabeth whimpered. "She'll be much stronger than you ever dreamed of being."

Gradoxst began to laugh; the crazed edge set Lara's nerves on fire. "Come." Uncurling one of his fingers from Elizabeth's body, he beckoned to her in an odd parody of an invitation.

"No." Lara planted her feet firmly beneath her, grimacing as her sore nether regions rearranged themselves.

"Well, I am leaving. Since I am taking her," he shook the baby as if she were a rag doll and she yelped, "I assumed you'd *want* to come with us."

Cringing inwardly, Lara wondered how far she could push him. Or if she could push him at all. *Not much to lose,* she decided. "Only if you give my baby back to me," she said, standing as tall as she could. "Do that, and I'll come along. Just let me get dressed."

Gradoxst looked at her. Lara saw calculation in his eyes. She figured he hadn't laid hands on her because he couldn't. It might have something to do with the amulet and its magic. She just wasn't sure. Lara knew she was much stronger than she'd been when the Demon had swept her into the in-between months earlier.

Her mind raced, dredging for what was real. For something she could latch onto and use against him. In a corner of her mind, she wondered what would happen if she jumped him and started swinging. Or drew power with the amulet and focused its killing force. *I can't do that with him holding Elizabeth and he knows it. Bastard!*

"Well?" She stared at him.

"You drive a hard bargain, Dr. McInnis. Go ahead. Gather some clothes."

"Give me my baby. And turn around." Elizabeth was clearly tiring; her cries were thin and pathetic, her face a blotchy red.

Wordlessly, Gradoxst held out the child. Ugly marks showed where his long nails had grazed her delicate skin. "I will not be turning around," he informed her. "Get used to it. I've admired you from afar for far too long, *liebchen*. This is the barest beginning of what I hope will turn into a charming affair."

Like hell it will, she thought, her stomach churning at the thought of the vile old mage coming anywhere near her. She clutched the baby to her, gratified when Elizabeth quieted almost immediately. Thoughts still racing wildly, Lara tried to come up with something she could do to help them both.

"I can read your mind," he said, a chill edge in his tone. "Just like your other Sidhe friends. In fact," he went on, silkily, "mayhap it would help if you looked at me in the same light. After all, we come from the same blood."

"And that's where the similarity both begins and ends," she snapped.

Laying the baby on the bed, Lara grabbed clothes randomly, stepping into thick socks with heavy boots last of all. *Maybe I'll get a chance to kick him.* Stuffing a stack of diapers and a few of the little blankets she'd lovingly stitched for her child in a cloth bag, Lara tossed her long hair over her shoulders and settled the child at her breast.

"I'm ready," she said through clenched teeth, thinking nothing could be farther from the truth. "Where are you taking me?" The amulet was so distressed it was practically stabbing her, but she ignored it.

"You will find out soon enough." He held out his hands, making wings from the long cloak that covered his dark suit. "Stand here," he gestured with his head.

Reacting to an impulse she recognized as stupid even before her feet took flight, Lara spun and ran for the bedroom door. She made it three steps before her limbs became paralyzed. As if from a great distance, she heard, "Tsk, tsk, Doctor. Not a good idea. Did you think I would just stand here and let you fly away? I'm disappointed. I had so hoped you were something more than a brainless slut."

He cuffed her hard on the side of the head, making her ears ring.

"Now, shall we try this again?" he asked evenly.

Lower lip clamped firmly under her front teeth, Lara nodded. When she tested her legs, she found she was able to walk. Turning, she marched to where Gradoxst stood. His eyes blazed with rage. With a sinking heart she understood it wouldn't be possible to protect her baby and fight the Demon at the same time.

"Don't worry, my dear," he chortled. "I do like my women with a bit of spirit. But too many little tricks like that last one and you will come to regret them."

Lara slunk under the edge of his cloak and felt the world drop away. Before it faded to nothingness, she heard Trevor's frantic voice calling for her. Desolation hammered her as she wondered if she'd ever see him—or her home—again.

Trevor debated whether to do the goats first or the silver bullets. Or whether he should start with the horses and work his way back toward the house. A pathetic bleating from the barn made up his mind for him. He wondered for the hundredth time how the animals had managed when Raven only dropped by every month or two. He'd just finished with the goats, draped a cloth over the milk pail, and started for the barn door, when something caught his attention and he froze.

It had been almost eerily quiet in the yard, aside from the goats' cries, when he'd first left the house, reinforcing his belief the Sidhe had taken off again for parts unknown. He'd whistled for the dog, and even he hadn't come. A clicking noise grated against his ears. It was subtle, just barely audible, but a wrongness to it chilled him and made the fine hairs at the back of his neck rise. A shiver traipsed down his spine like an abandoned waif seeking shelter.

He pushed against the barn door, but it wouldn't slide open.

Thinking it must have stuck, he shoved harder, but it still didn't budge. He set the milk down and looked for something he could use pry the door open. His eyes lit on a pitchfork he didn't remember ever seeing before and, all of a sudden, he was back in the barn in Carlisle. Blinking hard, Trevor cried out, "Nooooo," but whoever was choreographing things apparently didn't care what he wanted. Eyes drawn upward against his will, he saw his sister swinging from one of the rafters, her neck bent, her pregnant stomach grotesquely swollen.

"This can't be happening," he growled. "It *isn't* happening. Those bloody, goddess-be-damned Demons have trapped me in here." His hands curled into fists as they beat impotently against the rough wood of the barn door.

Lara. Gradoxst was after Lara. The bastard had always wanted her.

Bloody blazes, I played right into his game. Bastard's smarter than I gave him credit for.

Trevor scouted the gloom of the barn with frantic eyes. It didn't have any windows. The door was the only way out. Avoiding looking at the spectral form of his sister, he examined the barn's sliding door. "Think I can get it apart," he muttered, pulling at one of the pieces of hardware. "All I need to do is unscrew this plate, and that one, and the door should fall right off."

"Boy! Yes, you."

It was his father's voice. Trevor ignored it. If Gradoxst could gin up a simulacrum of Lizzie, why not his father?

"You worthless sack of dung. Look at your poor sister. You killed her, you did."

"You're not real," Trevor spat through jaws clenched so hard it felt as if his teeth would shatter.

"Well, that's a fine one." The thing masquerading as his father laughed as Trevor rustled for a screwdriver in the toolbox he kept in the barn. "I suppose you're going to do me in with something other than a pitchfork this time around. Something closer and a tad more personal."

Don't listen to him, Trevor told himself. *It's all part of a plan to keep me in here. To slow me down. Christ, what's he doing to Lara—and my baby?* Feeling desperate, he stopped to listen for noises from the house, but the father-thing kept nattering at him.

"Shut up," Trevor finally shouted. "Just shut up."

"You will show some respect, you young pup. Come over here and fight me like a man. Not like you did last time."

That did it. Trevor twirled to face his father's leering face. "You never deserved respect. Not then and not now. Go back to where you came from."

I'm losing my mind. He's dead and I'm talking to him.

Trevor pulled a stepstool over to the barn door and began to dismantle it. Suddenly, his vision blurred. He swiped a sleeve over his eyes, but it didn't make any difference. Motion from behind him caught his eye. Jumping down from his precarious perch, Trevor turned. Lizzie and his father were gone, but something that looked like a giant screen had taken their place. As he watched, scenes played themselves out, one after the other.

Lillian, Raven, Elidora, and others he didn't know were engaged in battle. The air was thick with shouts. Blood flowed freely. Magic sizzled through the air. Because he could only see clearly when he looked directly at the vision, Trevor stared intently, trying to determine where the Sidhe were.

Not Earth, that's for sure. Couldn't have found them if I'd tried.

Then the screen shifted and he saw Brad, covered in soot and gore, wearing riot gear. He was leading a pack of other policemen into a grotto that looked like something out of a third world news clip.

Drawing back, shocked, Trevor wondered if the rest of Seattle looked like that. "There's no way we could ever go back there," he muttered, before he remembered he was trapped in the barn, and there might not even be a *we* by the time he managed to free himself.

As if in answer to his question, the next scene was from the University of Washington campus with its fine old nineteenth century buildings lying in piles of rubble. A sense of urgency rose in him.

This can't be real. Just like Dad and Lizzie aren't real.

Trevor turned his head away from the visions. The minute he did so, his sight darkened, and he was effectively blind. Heart pounding, bile rising in the back of his throat, he looked at the screen again. And saw Lara. Hair flying around her, Elizabeth clutched to her breast, she looked like one of the Furies. Then he looked closer and saw Gradoxst with his head thrown back, laughing.

Trevor ground his fists into the dirt of the barn floor, shouting helplessly. Adrenaline shot through him making him feel crazy. As he hurled epithets at the screen, he saw what was unfolding in his bedroom, just a hundred feet across the way. It tore mercilessly at him.

"I never should've left," he screamed. "Never. Fuck the bloody goats." He felt tears on his cheeks and knew he was crying. Lara tried to make a run for it. For a scant moment he felt hopeful, but Gradoxst did something that brought her to a halt. After that, she walked toward the Demon with an expression on her face that broke his heart.

The barn door creaked, sliding on well-oiled hinges. Trevor felt his way toward it and shoved hard. Fresh air blasted him in the face. Grateful his vision was clearing, he stumbled across the yard shouting Lara's name. Gunter came out of nowhere, but Trevor ignored him. Running for all he was worth, he dashed into the house and up the stairs. By the time he reached the bedroom, breathing hard, it was empty. The stench of evil magic hung in the air, but Lara and Elizabeth were gone.

Not recognizing the agonized sounds tearing out of him as anything human, Trevor sank to the wooden floorboards. As his fists crashed into the floor over and over again, he knew he had to get himself under control. In the end, it was the dog's whining that brought him back into himself.

When he finally focused on Gunter, Trevor saw that one of the dog's paws was bleeding, and he had streaks of gore in the fur around his neck. Pathetically grateful for something he could actually manage, Trevor examined the German Shepherd carefully and finally understood one of the Goblins must've tried to harm him.

"What did you do?" he asked Gunter, as he held the dog in his arms. "How did you escape? Yes, yes. Never mind. Let's go downstairs. We could both do with something to drink, and I can clean those wounds." *And take care of my hands. Bloody stupid of me. Not to mention self-indulgent.* Trevor looked at the bruises beginning to form on the sides of his hands and his knuckles. He felt like an idiot, and a weak, ineffectual one at that.

"Those theatrics will *not* get her back," he lectured himself, as he pumped water at the kitchen sink, filling a bowl for the dog and a glass for himself. Thirst slaked, he knew his throat would be sore for days from all the shouting he'd done. When he closed his eyes, Lizzie and his father filled his mind. He shook his head hard from side to side to clear their presence.

Grabbing some lengths of linen, he dipped one in the hot water bubbling on the back of the stove and went to work on Gunter's injuries. It seemed the dog had been far more resourceful than either he or Lara. He was just finishing when the air in the farmhouse kitchen took on a shimmery hue.

Trevor jumped to his feet, looking about wildly for a weapon. The shotgun was in the living room, not close enough if the portal disgorged something from the dark side. Remembering his silvered knife, he slid it out from his boot, wincing as he closed his sore hand around the hilt. Then he glanced at the dog. Gunter's tail was wagging and Trevor relaxed. No way the animal would be greeting anyone who smelled like those who'd injured him.

Sure enough, in moments, a tattered Raven emerged into the kitchen, hands raised in case he had an immediate need to draw power. His eyes lit on Trevor and the dog. He furled his eyebrows questioningly.

Trevor knew what the mage was asking. "Gone," he snapped. The word burned his tongue, feeling bitter and alien. "They're bloody, fucking gone. Lara and my baby. Gradoxst—"

Raven shook his head to still the tide of words tumbling out of Trevor. "We feared as much," he said gently, stroking the dog circling round him. "They trapped us. Naught we could do to return in time."

"Where did he take them?" Trevor demanded, shoving the knife back into his boot.

Sadness shone from Raven's gray eyes. "Wait till the women get here."

Elidora was next to materialize, followed by Lillian. Both women wore grim expressions. For once, they looked aged and careworn. "It is as we suspected," Raven told them in Celtic Gaelic. Lillian's form began to shimmer again, but Raven snaked out a hand fast as lightning and grabbed her arm. "Not yet," he snapped. "We need a plan."

"But she's like a daughter to me," the Sidhe protested, red braids twirling about her head as she spun to face Raven. "I must go. And the babe—"

Raven drew her close. It was the first time Trevor had seen an overt display of affection between the two. "'Twill do no good for you to throw your life after theirs," he said gruffly.

"But we have to go after them," Trevor said, hearing anguish in his voice. "We have to." Repeating the words made him feel worse.

"And we shall, lad. Do not be afeard on that count." Elidora's dark eyes were full of something he didn't have a name for. Something feral and primitive. Even though he'd lived with the Sidhe for months, in that moment Trevor understood he didn't know them at all. That they were capable of things he could grasp only dimly.

"You must tell us what happened here," Raven urged, letting go of Lillian and turning his intense gray gaze toward Trevor.

As he tried to pull the jagged parts of himself together, Trevor shut his eyes. Like Lillian, he wanted to leave to go after Lara and Elizabeth —right this very minute, even though he recognized the wisdom in Raven's words of caution. Trevor exhaled sharply. He knew the Sidhe would do what they could. His best bet to hurry things along would be to give them what they asked for. And so he began to talk, haltingly at first, and then the words wouldn't stop.

CHAPTER 20

*L*ara lost all sense of time. The vertiginous sense of falling dissipated long before they stopped moving, and she understood she'd adapted to the sensation. Elizabeth dozed, worn out from the time she'd spent screaming in Gradoxst's hands. Her occasional movements were a great relief. *At least she's still alive,* Lara thought. When the bedroom had first dissolved about the two of them, she'd been frantic the journey to wherever they were going would kill her newborn. Even the amulet had settled down a little. It was still protesting, but not as intensely as before.

The gray-black around her finally gave way to stone walls. When she touched down gently on the inlaid stone floor of a smallish chamber, Lara looked about her. For a moment, she and Elizabeth were by themselves. But then Gradoxst materialized near the door to the room. He took shape just about the time she noticed the door and had begun moving toward it, intent on flight.

"We have arrived," he announced unnecessarily, with a flourish that made his cloak flutter. "There are things I must attend to. I shall leave you to your rest." Lara stared intently at him. He seemed tired. She wondered if she could capitalize on whatever energy he'd lost transporting the three of them to God-only-knew where.

"This chamber is bound by magic," he said, his shrewd dark eyes not leaving hers. "If you try to run off, I shall know. Besides," he cackled unpleasantly, "escape is not possible. You are farther from home than you can possibly imagine...*liebchen.*" The endearment sounded like a curse. A murky mist enveloped him—opaque gray and damp as a cellar. When it cleared, he was gone.

Lara took a measured breath, relieved he'd left them alone. She looked at her surroundings. The main piece of furniture was a large bed, piled with dusty looking pillows and blankets. A canopy frame that had probably once held bed draperies was so grimy, the black metal looked gray. The room was rectangular, with a window high in the far corner. It would be difficult to climb up to, and it didn't look as if it opened, even if she could reach it. Sconces lined the walls at intervals, with curious globes of reddish glass set into them. When she looked closely, Lara saw that the entire room was paneled in smooth, gray stone. The pieces fit into one another precisely without any mortar between them.

Whoever built this place was quite the craftsman. It couldn't have been Gradoxst. He must've stolen it. Just like the hobbit house in the Dreaming.

Elizabeth in her arms, Lara walked around the room thinking about Demons and the tenuous relationship they must have with one another. Irritated, she chided herself. *This is nothing like Lord of the Rings. These bad guys are real, not fictional characters. I have no idea how they feel about one another.* Then she remembered what Trevor told her about his time with Gradoxst and decided her first assumption—that her captors were probably at one another's throats—was at least close to the truth.

Gradoxst must've found a way to rise above the squabbles, though, since someone had helped him kidnap her and Elizabeth. Other Demons had no doubt kept Raven, Lillian, and Elidora busy, so the rogue Sidhe could do his dirty work. And made certain Trevor stayed out of the house.

Lara blew out a frustrated breath. Why the hell would anyone—

even other Demons—do anything for Gradoxst? He was such scum. *They liked him well enough at the Jung Institute,* she reminded herself. Lara hated to admit it, but she'd actually been taken in too. Wincing, she recalled her trans-Atlantic telephone conversations with him before one of her visions warned her the good Dr. Himmelschaun wasn't quite what he seemed.

As she walked around the small room, Lara flicked aside curtains that covered two alcoves. The first held a privy and a sink with a pump. The second, a sunken tub affair with brackish water streaming into it. Holding out one hand, she ascertained that the water was lukewarm and wondered if it would be safe to wash in, let alone try to drink. Continuing her circuit of the room, she saw a basin and ewer on a stone stand cunningly built into one corner. The water in the pitcher looked cleaner than the stuff coming out of the wall. Because she was thirsty, Lara tipped it backward and drank. As she set the porcelain pitcher down, she noticed its fine workmanship.

"If the water's going to kill me," she said to the silence of the room, "I'd like to find that out. I'll be here for far too long to avoid it." She looked about her again, checking to see if she'd missed anything that might help her. A small inlaid wooden table stood next to the door.

Not sure what tipped her off, Lara was suddenly certain the room and its contents had been designed by Sidhe workmen. *So at least I'm somewhere that was once in the hands of friends.* She found the thought comforting, even if the Sidhe involved had probably been gone for several human lifetimes.

Walking to the bed, she sank down onto it. A cloud of dust wafted up from the covers. Knowing she was shielding herself behind meaningless activity to avoid thinking about Trevor and home, she jumped up, laid Elizabeth on one of her blankets in a corner of the room and addressed herself to shaking out the bed covers. They seemed clean enough, but it might've been years—or centuries—since anyone had used them.

As she picked up her baby, changed her, and set her to nursing,

Lara couldn't quiet her thoughts. Questions buzzed around in her head like a horde of nattering insects.

Where am I? Is this where he keeps prisoners? Does the fact it's so unused mean the other prisoners are somewhere else? Or that there aren't any others? Most important of all: How can I get us out of here?

The Persephone myth ran through her mind. With it came an idea. Gradoxst spent years at the Institute. Maybe if she could engage him around mythology or Jungian philosophy, he'd drop his guard and begin to trust she wasn't waiting for a chance to kill him. She gripped the amulet with the hand not curved around her daughter, seeking its soothing power. It felt different somehow, so she tilted it up to look at it. The incandescent surface appeared dull and, for once, the magical moonstone wasn't doing anything at all, its gentle hum absent from the stone room. "Maybe it doesn't work here. Or maybe Gradoxst did something," she mumbled half to herself, wishing she knew more about magic than she did. The library swam into view in her mind's eye, and she cursed herself for not taking the time to study its contents more thoroughly. Over the months since she'd moved to his farm, she'd learned at least as much from Raven's books as from him or Lillian.

Still, she could've done far more.

Shifting Elizabeth to her other breast, Lara's eyes begin to close. She tried to force herself to stay awake, but gave it up for a lost cause. *Maybe Psyche will help me,* she thought, as she drifted into blackness.

It wasn't Psyche, but Brigid who came to her in her dreams. The goddess with the long, blonde hair and golden eyes looked regal, robes swirling about her tall figure. Her multihued fairies were with her as well, just not so many as Lara remembered.

"Daughter, why pass you here?" Brigid sounded stern. She was even shaking a finger at Lara.

"I was brought against my will," Lara replied, a thin flicker of hope flaring. "Can you help me?"

"Mayhap." The goddess looked at her for a long while before continuing. "But first you must find ways to help yourself. I will be watching to see if you are worthy. It is troublesome you are here at all."

Lara felt like crying. Had there been a test back in her bedroom that she'd somehow failed. Was it possible Gradoxst couldn't have transported her without her assent? *If I would have refused, he might have killed me—and Elizabeth too.* But would he have? The rogue Sidhe hadn't had the least bit of difficulty sending her to the in-between without her cooperation. Was today's journey different because she'd gone so much farther? Or to some other world? Frustration nagged at Lara. She had a lot of questions and very few answers.

Even in her dream state, Lara understood the goddess wouldn't approve of either pleas or tears. Brigid needed to see strength from her. Since begging for help wasn't an option, Lara remained silent, which seemed to please the goddess.

"You are learning temperance as well as wisdom, child," she said before fading away.

The dream had been so real that Lara woke as soon as the goddess left her. Light from the window was muted, cloaking the room in a dusky gloom. The lantern sconces glowed dull red, lending the stone an eerie, bloody cast. The baby was still sleeping. Lara bit down on her lip to keep from dissolving into tears. There had to be rules that governed these magical creatures. She just didn't understand them.

"Yeah. The good guys won't ride to your rescue if they think you don't deserve it." She spoke aloud to steady herself.

She remembered something Brigid had said in the sacred cave: It has come to this. We are reduced to rescuing humans from their folly. Humans who have ceased to pay homage to us.

Was that the problem? Did Brigid see her as one more pesky human needing to be rescued from her own foolishness? Unable to sit still, Lara got up carefully, making sure her daughter was positioned in the center of the bed, surrounded by pillows. Pacing up and down the small room, she forced herself to think. When she pushed the privy curtain aside, a strange glow emanated from the corner of the little enclosure. Lara bent closer, then realized it was one of Brigid's fairies. She held out a finger and the tiny creature lit on it for the briefest of moments. When it touched her, the amulet thrummed once. Heart soaring at this unexpected boon, Lara murmured, "Thank you."

Wish I knew how much of my thoughts he can discern, she mused, tugging the curtain closed.

"Practically all of them, my dear." Gradoxst's voice preceded him into her prison as the heavy door swung inward noiselessly. He'd traded his suit and cloak for blood red robes. A heavily-carved golden ankh, hung from his neck.

Stilling her thoughts, Lara strolled over to the bed and picked up her daughter. "What's next?" she asked casually, peering at her captor in the reddish light from the sconces. Lara knew she had to shield her mind, so he wouldn't find out about Brigid or her fairy. "By the way," she said in a conversational tone, "the architecture is lovely. This was built by the Sidhe, wasn't it?"

"Perceptive of you." His sharp tone cut off thoughts of further discourse, at least along those lines.

Lara waited, watching him and hoping against hope for clues about how to defeat him.

"I thought you might be interested in some supper." He snapped his fingers. A cowed-looking figure crept into the room holding a plate. He was probably only middle-aged, but looked much older. Bent, with downcast eyes, he was definitely human. "Put it down," Gradoxst commanded. "Then leave us."

"Where, my lord?" The man's voice was creaky, as though he didn't use it often.

"Anywhere. There aren't any curaets about."

Lara tried to control her expression. She remembered the beasts from the in-between. Gren had called them Goblin pets. The servant stooped, placed the plate on the floor and crab-walked back through the door.

"Close it," Gradoxst screeched after him, moving to retrieve the food, which he placed on the table next to the door. "Sorry," he shrugged. "It is difficult to obtain decent help.

"Well," he scowled at her. "Aren't you hungry?"

Lara *was* hungry, but she didn't think she'd like what was being served. It smelled of rancid fat and other things she couldn't identify. "How do I know you won't poison me?" she countered, thinking about the rats Trevor had eaten to stay alive.

He laughed wickedly, favoring her with a twisted grin. "You don't. It took me a great deal of effort to get you here, though. While I may tire of you at some point, we have yet to get to know one another. I believe you may be safe from poison for at least a few weeks." The leer following those words was unmistakable and, between the smell of the food and fear that the rogue Sidhe might actually try to touch her, Lara's appetite fled.

"If you're planning on raping me—" she began, shutting her mouth with a snap as he closed the gap between them in a few steps.

"If that was all I wanted, you would still be with your precious Trevor," he shouted, mouth so close to her face he sprayed her with spittle. "I need a queen. You will do perfectly."

"W—what?" She was certain she hadn't heard him correctly. "Surely there are women here…"

"My tastes are far more cultured. I was once a Sidhe lord. In fact, I still am. I require something other than a mere Goblin mate. They really are quite uncouth." His nose wrinkled in distaste.

Following a sudden instinct, Lara began recounting a myth. Maybe, with his time at the Jung Institute, this will help him see what he's done.

"…And Hades, dark god and King of the underworld, stole Persephone, enslaving her in the netherworld for half a year. As you know," Lara favored Gradoxst with a glance, "Persephone was the daughter of Demeter and Zeus. While Zeus bargained for his daughter's freedom, Demeter, goddess of Earth and the harvest, mourned. Winter fell upon the Earth. The people worried about their crops and feared warmth would never return. The only reason Persephone was allowed back—"

"Yes, yes, I know that story," he interrupted, a wistful smile on his ravaged face. "Come now. Do try to eat something. Even Persephone ate six pomegranate seeds."

She shook her head. "It smells wretched," she said. "Isn't there something like bread here? Or fruit?"

"You are fortunate I am feeding you at all," he snarled, his mood shifting so abruptly it startled her. Drawing his arms upward, then together, in a gesture that made his robe look like bat's wings, he vanished from the room as quickly as he'd arrived, ignoring the door.

Lara shook her head. From kind to haughty to angry. She'd do well not to underestimate Gradoxst. That much at least was becoming clear. A sad, knowing smile spread across her face. "He's insane," she muttered. "He didn't sell his soul for the dark magic, he offered up his mind. Wonder if he even knows what he lost?" She laughed bitterly in the bloody light of her chamber. "I should be able to figure him out. After all, it's what I used to do for a living."

Elizabeth was still sleeping, so she laid her daughter gently back on the bed. Feeling at loose ends, she wandered over to the food, poking at it with something that looked like a chopstick. The slender wooden wand had been laid on the side of the plate. Seeing something she was almost sure was a carrot, she popped it into her mouth and was surprised by how well spiced it was. The food was greasy, but perhaps it would be more edible than she thought.

As she stood over the plate picking at it, she turned over how she could get past Gradoxst's iron guard. It was hard to know what to say to him, as innocuous things set him off.

Maybe not. I did criticize the food he brought me. If I'm more subservient and grateful, maybe…

Lara didn't like all the *maybes* in her mind. She washed down the contents of the plate with some more water. Then she went to look in on the fairy. *"Can you talk?"* she sent, but the green, glowing creature was silent, hovering in its corner.

Probably just as well. Might not be safe.

The day's light had faded from the room. Lara thought about lying down and at least attempting to get some sleep, but she decided to try something first. Walking briskly to the door, she pulled on it. Surprise bloomed on her face when the latch snicked, and the solid piece of polished stone canted inward. Moving hurriedly to the bed, she snatched up Elizabeth and walked out into a stone hallway lit by the same sconces—except these were blue alternating with green. As she stared up and down the long hallway, dotted by identical doors at intervals on both sides, Gradoxst shimmered into view.

"What is the meaning of this?" he demanded. "Ungrateful wretch! I told you to remain within your chamber—"

"I was lonely." She took a chance and interrupted him. "I didn't think the door would actually open, so when it did, well, I…" Lara let her voice trail off. She was of a height with her captor, but she kept her eyes on the floor. "I ate my dinner," she added, in an attempt to be conciliatory. "It was better than I thought it would be."

"Back in the room." His voice was brusque and he clapped his hands together. "There are curaets about. You would have no protection from them."

Her downcast eyes caught the moonstone. It was glowing again, and she heard its subtle song. *Gradoxst must have spelled the room to stymy it,* she deduced, as she turned and walked slowly back into the stone chamber.

"Yes, the room shields you. It is why I placed you here."

Still trying to divert him, Lara walked meekly over to the pitcher, where she tipped the last of the water into her mouth. Then she held the delicate porcelain out to Gradoxst.

"In there," he gestured at the privy enclosure. "There is a pump with clean water."

"I'll get some later." She tried to smile at him, but her heart rate accelerated. The last thing she wanted was for him to go in there and see the fairy. It might have ways of hiding itself, but she wasn't sure.

"No more trips out of this room without me. Do you understand?" he asked abruptly.

Once she'd nodded, he turned, his robe swirling around him, and stomped out the door. Lara heard him chanting something as he went. She surmised it was a spell to keep the stone panel more firmly in place.

Lara changed the baby and the rag between her own legs too, rinsing both in the tepid water that ran perennially both into and out of the sunken tub. Remembering the soiled diaper from earlier, she washed it as well, her mind feverishly turning over plans to trounce Gradoxst and escape.

When she finally lay down, her last thought before sleep took her was gratitude that the food hadn't upset her stomach. She'd need all her strength—not to mention her wits—to have a prayer of outfoxing Gradoxst.

CHAPTER 21

The baby awakened her from time to time, but Lara was surprised how refreshed she felt when she finally opened her eyes. The fairy hovered about her, gossamer wings brushing against her skin. "Maybe you're why I slept so well," she said, smiling at the tiny creature.

Then the reality of her situation caught up with her, and Lara turned her attention to more practical things. Light poured into the room from the high window. Scootching carefully out of the bed so she wouldn't disturb her daughter, Lara walked to the wall directly underneath the window, the stones of the floor cold against her bare feet. Closer examination verified something she'd suspected the day before. The window was a good foot above her outstretched hand, even standing on her tiptoes, and the surface of the wall so smooth it wouldn't provide any purchase for climbing. Casting about, her eyes lit on the small table that still held the plate from her supper. If she dragged it over, she'd at least be tall enough to look out the window and examine it more closely.

Lara stopped by the privy, her thoughts churning. Gradoxst would be furious if he caught her moving the furniture around, especially since he'd figure out immediately she was working on finding a way out. "Better to wait," she mumbled, "until just after he visits me. At least then I should have some time before he comes back."

It was a long while, though, before the dark mage chose to come to her again. She'd filled the pitcher from the pump a couple times. Hunger nagged as the hours marched on. Judging from the angle of the light, the afternoon was on its way out. In spite of efforts to stay calm, her enforced imprisonment was starting to gnaw at her when the door flew open.

"*Liebchen*, did you miss me?"

She just looked at him, glittering in dark green velvet robes, and was uncertain what to say. If she was too gushy, he'd know she was lying. "Uh, not exactly," she stammered. "But I am hungry."

"That," he announced grandly, "shall be taken care of shortly. Would you like to go on a little walking tour of your new home?" In a travesty of civility, he held out an arm to her. Lara started for the bed to pick up her child.

"Uh-uh," he waggled a finger at her. "She stays here."

"Then I do too," Lara said flatly, sitting on the bed next to Elizabeth. "I am not leaving a two day old baby by herself."

"I presumed you'd say as much." A cunning smile played about Gradoxst's face. "So I brought along a *kinderhütter*." The beaten-looking man from the night before stood next to the doorway, seemingly reticent to enter the room.

A babysitter. Lara guessed the word easily enough from the context. "Nope." She looked at him resolutely. "I don't care if you brought Dr. Spock himself, I am not leaving my child."

"Dr. Spock?" Gradoxst looked confused.

"Never mind. He was a pediatrician who was a child expert in the nineteen-fifties. It's just an expression. Either Elizabeth comes with me, or I stay here."

"If you wish to eat, you will accompany me."

Swallowing down her fear, Lara scooped up the baby and walked toward the rogue Sidhe, her eyes downcast in mock submission.

After a long hesitation, he beckoned with one long-nailed finger.

"Very well then." An exasperated sigh escaped him. "But you must behave yourself. You are about to meet some of your subjects."

Lara nodded, muting down the triumph surging through her. *Maybe, if I play into his delusion...* Seeing the layout of the building could be very helpful. If she was on the umpteenth floor, there'd be no point in struggling with the window. Who knew? Maybe she'd find something that would complement an escape attempt. At least she still had her mind. Gradoxst hadn't beaten her senseless or turned the curaets on her. Not yet, anyway. She edged toward the door, but he hissed, "Stay behind me. You, Delgran, get in back of her. Alert me, if need be."

"Yes, master." Fear vibrated behind those two words.

Walking down a long corridor, Lara looked carefully from side to side trying to get her bearings. She wanted to ask questions, but was certain Gradoxst wouldn't take kindly to anything like an information-gathering effort. So she kept her eyes open and maintained a tense silence.

At the end of the hallway was a set of steps. They'd been carved into one end of the building and, as she followed them down, Lara counted. When she hit twenty, she knew the window in her room would be far too high off the ground to risk jumping. At sixty-three, they reached the bottom. There had been landings on the way down that she presumed led to other floors. It was clear enough that the stairs ended on the ground floor, since thick, wavy windows revealed an odd landscape beyond.

It looks like a photographic negative of the Dreaming.

Where the Sidhe's home was full of life and color, the land outside had a gray dullness about it. Rolling terrain with shrubbery and trees reflected the same uninspired colorlessness. The sky had a touch of a bluish tint, but even it was mostly gray. She didn't see any other buildings and wondered if the stone edifice was the only structure in this bizarre land.

Breath rattling in her throat, she caught a glimpse of something oddly familiar. Not wanting Gradoxst to chastise her, she reluctantly pulled her gaze away from the window and followed him down another long corridor. As she walked, something clicked in her mind. What she'd seen looked just like the waterfall hiding the entrance to the sacred cave in the *Dreaming*.

Lara examined thoughts as they rampaged through her head and tried to figure out what the connection could possibly be between the Sidhe's home and where she was. The two places seemed to be mirror images of one another. What did that mean?

"In here." Gradoxst's rough voice broke into her musings.

"Sorry," she mumbled, entering under a carved archway. As she walked beneath runic symbols, her amulet thrummed once. *What?* Lara demanded, but the moonstone lay placidly between her breasts. Shaking her head, she wondered if the pendant had chimed to acknowledge something in the runes, or as a warning.

When she glanced up, surprise shot through her. A large hall fanned out, lined with wooden trestle tables that had been set for some sort of meal. A few Goblins scurried back and forth, but the seats were empty. One of the Goblins tripped, the stack of bowls in his hand shattering on the stone floor. Another Goblin clonked him over the head with a mace. The clumsy one collapsed in the middle of the pile of broken crockery groaning.

Horror spread through Lara, intensifying when Gradoxst chuckled. "Just the boys, having a bit of fun, my dear. No need for concern."

"Since when is it fun to have someone beat you with a club?" *Shit. Need to keep my mouth shut.*

Gradoxst turned to her. "That will be enough out of you, slut," he hissed, laying one hand on her forehead and the other on Elizabeth. The baby began to wail, and Lara's stomach tightened. She could easily imagine the fallen Sidhe backhanding her child to shut her up. But Gradoxst was doing something even worse that claimed his full attention. Lara felt him drawing power from her. She imagined he was doing the same to Elizabeth.

Fear filled her that he'd kill her child with his machinations.

Panicky, she tried to pull away. Heat blasted through her, and she heard his voice in her mind. *"Hold still or you shall both die."*

Lara closed her eyes, feeling herself grow weaker by the moment. Just when she thought her legs would crumple beneath her, Gradoxst removed his hands. Staggering backward a pace, she forced her lids open, shocked by how feeble she felt. Gradoxst looked absurdly pleased with himself. When she glanced about the hall, she was amazed to find it filled with an assortment of humans. None of them paid the slightest attention to her. They were shoveling food into their mouths as fast as they could pick it up with their fingers.

"W—where did they come from?" she managed.

"Another of your friends' plans that I have foiled," he purred. "They shall be our subjects. Come."

Trailing after Gradoxst, Lara wondered about the strange assortment of folk. Had they just been captured? Or had they been in some sort of magical holding tank? She remembered what Lillian had told her: *Nothing human can survive in the Goblin realms without a lengthy time in the in-between.*

Maybe I'm closer to Earth than I know.

The puzzle of the similarity between the *Dreaming* and where she found herself rose to taunt her again. Dragged back to the dining room by a jolt from the amulet, a slow horror spread through her.

Taking advantage of her apparent inattention, Gradoxst had snaked his hand out; it hovered inches from the moonstone. Lara tried to turn away, but he grabbed her arm advancing on the amulet with his other hand. Once he got to within a finger's breadth from the moonstone, he shrieked, cursing in German as if it had burned him. Taking a step back, he let go of her.

"Oh, so you can't touch it," Lara smirked, remembering her vow to be subservient a shade too late.

The same hand that had reached for the moonstone smacked her solidly across the face. Lara twisted sideways from the force of the blow. Shielding her baby as best she could, she grunted against the unexpected pain.

"Whore." He hit her again. This time, she staggered before falling to her knees, body curled around Elizabeth. "Get up," he hissed. "What will people think?"

Blinking through hot tears, Lara got her feet under her and stared at the assembled masses. None of them had so much as missed a bite, and she knew with a sudden, blinding clarity just how commonplace violence must be to them. Looking more closely, she realized with a shock that they weren't even paying attention. It was as if she were invisible.

Maybe it has nothing to do with violence. It's almost like they're all in some sort of trance, she thought, puzzled by the same blank expressions on every face.

"Sorry," she managed, determined not to make the same mistake again. The moonstone, however, seemed positively delighted. It was thrumming and humming and dancing against her chest. Lara saw Gradoxst eyeing it and dropped it back inside the folds of her top, hoping it wouldn't provoke him if it was out of sight.

"Give it to me," he demanded, holding out a gnarled hand.

"I can't. It won't let me."

"You will give it to me." He advanced threateningly toward her, hand raised as if to strike her again.

The amulet gave a little leap, and Lara understood it would be able to take care of itself. She drew it out slowly from under her clothing and pulled the golden chain over her head. Holding the stone cupped in one hand, she extended it toward him, watching through narrowed eyes.

Gradoxst tried a time or two, but wasn't able to get any closer to the magical moonstone than when it had been around her neck. Visibly agitated, his face red and a vein throbbing in one temple, he shouted something in Gaelic before reaching for the stone again. Whatever he'd said didn't change a thing. He'd get to within about two inches of her outstretched hand, but the stone always stopped him.

Lara felt the moonstone grow warm against her hand. She could've sworn it was enjoying itself.

"Delgran!"

"Yes, master." The beaten-looking man was beside Gradoxst in a flash.

"Take that necklace out of her hand."

Delgran dragged his gaze up off the floor for long enough to take in Lara, the baby and the amulet that had begun streaming with light. A look of sheer terror washed over his face. His eyes opened so wide the whites showed all around his pupils. He quivered with indecision, and then he turned and raced out of the hall as if the dogs of Hell were nipping at his heels. Even though Gradoxst shouted after him, the man's pace never slowed.

"Cretin," Gradoxst roared. "I shall have you flogged."

As surreptitiously as she could, Lara slipped the golden chain over her head. Elizabeth had begun to cry, so Lara half-turned away from the crowd in the hall and offered her a breast. The baby latched on, her small fists swinging wildly.

"Ssht… Hush, it will be all right," Lara crooned. Elizabeth quieted as soon as she began to nurse. Lara tried to relax so her milk could flow. It wasn't easy since she was expecting another blow at any moment. Nonetheless, she tried to pretend she was somewhere other than the cavernous stone hall.

Long moments passed. When she dared look behind her, Gradoxst was gone. Shifting the baby to her other breast, Lara draped part of her loose top to provide a bit of modesty. She really was hungry and edged closer to one of the trestle tables to locate something she could use to serve herself from the community pots.

Try as she might, the only dishes she saw were in front of each of the sad-looking people seated at the tables. Finally, she sidled toward an old woman who seemed to have finished eating. "Might I share your bowl?" she asked softly. "I'll give it back as soon as I've had something to eat."

The woman looked up at her out of rheumy, blue eyes, but at least the blank, hypnotized stare was gone. Maybe Gradoxst needed to be present to keep this many people in thrall. The old woman said something in a language Lara didn't think she'd ever heard before. It sounded vaguely Slavic. *If Trevor were here, he'd be able to figure it out.* As soon as she thought of him, her stomach clenched. He must be worried half to death about her and feeling helpless on top of that. It wasn't like it had been when Gradoxst had kidnapped him, and she could at least study which magics she'd need to rescue him.

Trevor rescued himself. The reminder bit deep, urging her to try harder to get something nourishing into herself. She'd never figure out how to leave—or much of anything else—if she couldn't provide fuel for her body.

The old woman was still looking at her. Lara pantomimed eating with the hand not supporting Elizabeth. The woman nodded once and pushed the cracked crockery she'd been using in Lara's direction.

"Thank you." Lara figured even if the woman couldn't understand the words, maybe she'd pick up their inflection. She tried a half smile, but the woman shook her head and dropped her gaze to her lap.

Though she didn't find much in the large cauldron in the middle of the table, Lara tipped it and used a disgusting looking ladle caked with food to gather what little was left. Dinner had been a thin gruel with bits of meat and vegetables added to a watery broth. Something that looked like flatbread sat next to the pot, so she took some of that too. Settling herself into an empty chair, Lara emptied her mind as she ate. There didn't seem to be anything to wash down the tasteless concoction, so she made do without, as she listened to the ebb and flow of several different languages. By the time she was done, the room was half empty.

"What the hell am I supposed to do now?" she muttered, swiping a finger around her bowl to clean the last dregs of food out of it. Once she handed it back to its owner, the woman rose to her feet and shuffled toward the door. Acting on impulse, Lara walked after her. The woman had been kind, and Lara didn't want to be alone again. She thought she might be able to find her way back to her room, but wanted to make the most of her unexpected taste of freedom before Gradoxst showed up to remove any possibility of choice.

"Where are you going?" Lara asked, having caught up with the collection of black rags that clothed her benefactor.

The woman, long white braids trailing down her back, shook her head again and tried to walk faster. Lara noticed the knuckles of her hands were swollen and assumed the woman probably had rheumatoid arthritis. *Damn it,* Lara thought. *She's human. All of them are—except Gradoxst and a few of the servants.*

A burst of the same Slavic tongue rattled from Lara's other side. When she swung about to locate its source, a middle-aged man with dark skin and a hawk's beak of a nose made shooing motions as he went to the old woman's other side and took her arm.

"Go away," he mumbled in heavily accented English, his brown eyes ominous. "We want no trouble. You are trouble. You stay gone." His words were punctuated by a grimy index finger stabbing the air in the general vicinity of her chest.

English. He speaks English. "How did you get here?" Lara asked eagerly. "At least tell me that much."

"Twice we have been spirited off by strange magic. First by those pretending to be kind. Now by a madman. Leave us alone." The man, long, dark hair flying behind him, hustled his mother—or maybe his grandmother—away as fast as he could propel her forward.

Lara walked up and down the long hallway outside the dining room. She searched for a door, but couldn't find one. Examining the windows didn't help. They didn't have latches. She tapped on one hopefully, but it seemed to be a somewhat clearer version of the windows on the ground floor of Raven's house. It would take something large and sharp to fracture it.

Hoping that perhaps there'd be an exit from the large hall, she headed back that way. It was empty of people. She looked carefully at each pot, taking what was left, as she searched for a way out. Feeling tired and thirsty, she sat down, laying Elizabeth on the table in front of her. The baby was sleeping. She was also wet, but Lara couldn't do much about that.

As she rested her head on her upstretched hand, understanding blossomed that Gradoxst had left her alone precisely because escape was impossible. If her prison had been built with Sidhe spells, perhaps the doorways required incantations before they showed themselves to you. And what had that man meant by his statement that he'd been captured not once, but twice, by magic?

"If it's a mirror world, maybe you enter it through dreaming," Lara mused half-aloud. Her eyes snapped open. Could this be the collective unconscious? While he was at the Institute, had Gradoxst figured out some way to summon souls to the collective, trap them there, and then use their energy to fuel his plots?

"But I'm not dreaming," she muttered. And then she remembered she had been asleep, wakening—or perhaps not—to find the dark mage in her bedroom holding her daughter. "Christ. If I am in the collective, how the hell do I get out?"

"You are very bright, Doctor. I like that in my acolytes." Gradoxst's unmistakable, braying voice caught her by surprise. She swiveled to one side and saw him standing at the far end of the room, a smug smile on his face. The old-fashioned black suit was back in place, with his black cloak draped over it.

"I could be brighter," she suggested, with what she hoped was a warm smile. "You taught at the Institute for many years. Perhaps you could teach me?" Gathering her baby, Lara rose to her feet and walked toward her captor, stopping a few feet from him.

"Why would I want to do that?" He furled bushy brows in her direction. "You have not behaved particularly well since you have gotten here."

She thought quickly. "You say you miss the Institute. Well, so do I. The best part of my years there were the discussions. I'm sure you see me as a bit inferior at the moment. If you were to teach me…" Lara let her suggestion hang in the air, hoping he'd fill in the last few words for her. When he didn't, she stumbled ahead. "If I had even a small part of your extensive knowledge base, I'd be a far more interesting companion." She held her breath. Would he take the bait? Was he narcissistic enough to believe her?

Astute dark eyes drilled into her. Lara did her best to shield her inner thoughts. The amulet warmed. She hoped it was helping her.

After a long moment, he smirked. "Now that you mention it, I do miss teaching."

Staring at her down his aquiline nose, he added, "Back to your room. I am certain you have determined by now that jumping out the window is not a possibility."

"I'm not sure I can find it," Lara lied smoothly. "Never did have much of a sense of direction." She paused before adding, "I'm intuitive, not sensate."

She was rewarded when Gradoxst chuckled. He closed the distance between them, gripping her arm firmly. "This way, my dear. As we walk, think of a myth you can tell me once we reach your quarters. Mythology is a platform for learning. Did not your Jung say that?"

Not exactly. Thank God the old bastard seems to be in a good mood again. "Something quite close, I'm sure," Lara murmured as she racked her brain for a myth that would help her find a way out of her imprisonment.

revor was frantic. Lara and Elizabeth had been gone for three days. Raven and the Sidhe had gone off in pairs to look for her, always leaving one of them with him, but they'd returned empty-handed from each foray. He'd encouraged all three of them to join forces, figuring it might help bring Lara back. But having lost one human, they were determined to keep a close eye on him.

A bit like closing the barn door once the cow's fled. But he kept that thought to himself.

Lines of strain carved deeply into Raven's face. Elidora had taken to cooing over Trevor, much as she'd done when he was just a lad. Lillian had stopped even trying to make polite conversation. Gunter clung to his side like a shadow. All in all, the mood was bleak. And it didn't seem likely to change, since with each passing hour the probability of Lara's return ebbed just that much further.

He finished up in the barn, carried a pail of milk into the house, and poured it into containers. He had absolutely zero appetite, but knew he had to force himself to eat. He wouldn't do anyone any good if he collapsed. Toward that end, he tilted the milk pail and poured the last of it into a glass that he swallowed hurriedly. He'd just wiped his mouth on his sleeve when he saw a doorway begin to form in the air. The dog yipped once, then stood quivering.

Must be Lillian and Raven coming back, he told himself. Trevor realized he was clutching the glass so hard it might shatter, so he set it down on the counter with a *thud*. Would Lara and Elizabeth be with them? *Oh, please God, let them be,* he prayed to whatever deity might be listening to a poor sod like him. He stared hard at the portal, willing Lara to be there.

Elidora, apparently drawn by the feel of magic, glided silently to his side where she took hold of his arm. "Mayhap…" she whispered hoarsely as she gripped her amulet—a twin to Lara's—with her other hand. "Mayhap, laddie."

But Lara wasn't there. Raven and Lillian looked more weary and drawn than Trevor could ever remember seeing them. As soon as he was through the portal, Raven shuffled over to one of the kitchen chairs and fell into it. "I just don't understand," he growled. "We've looked everywhere. And asked all those who spy for us. No one has seen her or the child. No one."

"No one's seen that goddess-be-damned rapscallion, Gradoxst, either," Lillian swore. Not bothering with a chair, she collapsed in a heap on the floor, pushing her braids back over her shoulders. They were badly askew, giving her a disheveled look. Elidora joined her friend, rubbing the other woman's back and shoulders.

Something tight in Trevor's chest made it difficult to breathe. After Lara had first been abducted, he'd been sure the Sidhe would be able to locate her. As time had passed, though, a sick frustration ripped at him, carving off chunks of his soul. Unable to stand still, he turned on his heel, heading for the stairs with Gunter hard on his heels. No one called after him, which make him feel even worse. Raven and the Sidhe knew how desperate Lara's situation was. *Bloody hell, they know far more than I do.* The fact that they weren't trying to humor him or reassure him, as they'd done the first day and a half, was disturbingly telling.

"They don't think they'll be able to find her," he mumbled, as he fought down an urge to curl up in a fetal position and shriek his angst to the universe. Slamming the heavy library door against its stops, he told himself to breathe. He was going to try something that had come to him the previous night when he'd lain awake for hours tossing and turning. He'd wanted sleep to come more than anything, hoping Lara would be able to communicate with him if he could just dream her. But he hadn't slept and, with the dawn, he'd gotten up and gone for a long walk with the dog.

Elidora hunted him down, chastising him roundly for not telling her where he was going. She'd looked utterly inhuman—not like the Elidora he knew at all—her black hair unbound and whirling around her, as she shook a finger at him, hurling imprecations in Gaelic. After a time, her anger apparently spent, she'd hugged him and herded him back to the house.

It's the only thing left, he told himself, gazing intently at the books. I'll cull through all these magic books for something a mortal might do to find his one true love. I probably won't stumble onto a bloody thing, but I have to do something. I can't just sit here hoping for a miracle. Trevor's jaws ached. He made an effort to unclench them.

One thing he knew was that life without Lara and his baby wouldn't be worth very damn much. He couldn't imagine never seeing her again and, for a moment, panic blurred his vision. Desperately sucking down air and trying to do what Lara called structured relaxation, he was relieved when the room swam back into focus.

All right, then, old chap. Sinking to his knees, Trevor perused the section of the library devoted to magic. Gunter curled up right next to him, occasionally reaching out to lay a paw on Trevor's leg. He'd skimmed the table of contents of about thirty-five books, and was close to giving up, when he finally found something that looked promising. Moving from his knees to a cross-legged sit, Trevor flipped to a chapter he hoped would teach him how to project himself through time and space to find Lara.

The disclaimer at the top of the page was so sobering, he didn't bother to finish it after reading the first few words. The book was old, so old that the cover was leather-covered wood. The pages looked to be parchment and were hand lettered, which probably meant it pre-dated the printing press. A previous owner had made notations on some of the pages. The book was written in a Gaelic dialect, but Trevor didn't have any difficulty translating. Since the notations were in the same script, he assumed this particular iteration of the language had been in common usage at some point.

My mind is wandering because the stipulation at the front made me feel as if a ghost just took up residence in here—a malevolent one.

His gaze found its way back to the heading. No, he lectured himself sternly. *Let's call it what it really is: a warning. If I were smart, I'd slam the book shut, go downstairs, and ask Raven and the Sidhe if there's anything I can do, rather than running off half-cocked on my own.*

"But I never have been smart that way," he answered himself, as he began to read aloud:

Be warned, mortal. This book will give you knowledge that, once drawn, cannot be eschewed. You summon dark secrets at immediate risk to yourself. While you may accomplish your desperate goals, it will not be without enormous cost. You will likely perish, trapped by the magic that will sear you irrevocably.

As if he could understand Trevor's Gaelic, Gunter launched himself into his master's lap, effectively blocking Trevor from reading further. The dog was panting and visibly disturbed. He whined and reached up to lick Trevor's chin.

"It is a bit unsettling, isn't it?" Trevor said, as he stroked the dog's heaving flanks. "You must sense something even beyond the words." His eyes were hot and swollen from lack of sleep. He shut them as he urged his weary brain to weigh the advisability of his chosen course. The book sat in his lap like a stone. He thought the leather cover felt inexplicably cold and then pushed the notion away as an impossibility.

It felt as if time were passing oddly. He pushed feebly at Gunter a time or two, but the dog growled at him and refused to budge. Finally, Trevor took Gunter's head between his hands and looked into the Shepherd's eyes. "Look. I understand you're trying to protect me. That's what your breed does. But I have to try to do this. It may be Lara's only hope. And Elizabeth's too."

At the sound of his mother's name, Gunter whined again, tail thumping softly against the carpeted floorboards.

"So," Trevor continued, still holding eye contact with his dog, "you have to move. I understand this is dangerous and that, apparently, there will be no turning back after the next few sentences, but I have to do this. My life's not worth a shit without Lara and my baby, so…"

With a final, mournful sound, Gunter slid off Trevor's lap onto the floor. He got up, shook himself, and went to lay by the door. When Trevor looked down, he saw a damp spot on the open page and understood the dog had been so distraught he'd peed on the book he saw as a threat to his master.

Heart knocking hollowly in his chest, Trevor lowered his eyes and continued reading.

Lara racked her brain as she wound her way back up the stairs. It didn't seem possible to find a myth that embodied what she needed. She'd thought of and discarded Cassandra, Cupid and Psyche, and Pandora. The amulet thrumped softly and her eyes widened. *Of course,* she thought, with a burst of hope. *Inanna is perfect. Wonder what he knows about that one?*

Gradoxst barked a sharp word in Gaelic, and the door to her room swung open. He gestured for her to enter, then pulled the door shut behind them both. "Well?"

At the challenge in his voice, she turned to face him, Elizabeth held firmly against her body. "I'm going to change my baby first," she ventured conversationally, "but what would you think of the Inanna myth?" When he didn't so much as twitch an eyebrow, she hurried on.

"That's definitely a tale about descent and redemption. In fact, it's the original one, after Parsifal, that is."

"Get on with it," he said gruffly, settling himself on her bed. "But if you are likening your current state to Inanna's descent into the underworld, you had best pick another tale."

Moving about the small space, Lara felt his eyes on her. A frisson of fear for the fairy skittered down her spine, as she pulled open the curtain hiding the tub alcove, but the little fairy was nowhere to be seen. Once the baby, who'd been mewling softly, was resettled at her breast, Lara moved the basin and ewer off their stand and boosted herself onto it. She'd be damned if she'd sit next to him on the bed.

"Did you ever teach that story?" Lara asked, wondering what he knew about the ancient Sumerian tale.

"Of course," he spat. "My patience is not bottomless, mortal woman. Either begin, or I shall leave you."

If he goes, I lose any chance of finding out anything useful. "Very well." Lara closed her eyes, coaxing the story out of memory.

"Inanna was the Sumerian Goddess of Love. She abandoned heaven and Earth to descend to the underworld where her sister, Ereskigal, ruled. Before her journey, understanding the need to protect herself, Inanna gathered seven things: a crown, earrings of lapis, a double strand of beads, a breastplate, a golden hip girdle, a lapis measuring rod, and a royal breechcloth."

Lara opened her eyes to glance at Gradoxst. He seemed to be listening intently, leaning slightly forward. "Surely there is more," he protested.

He doesn't know the story... At least not well. Maybe I can make something up to help myself. "Of course there is," she said soothingly, just as she'd calmed many patients over the years. "I was wondering if you wanted to discuss the Jungian implications during the tale or after."

"We may not discuss them at all," he smirked, mimicking her voice tones. "You serve at my pleasure, not the other way around."

Nodding, Lara went on, aware of sweat beading in her armpits. Her body's reaction reminded her what a perilous game she played.

"Inanna had a faithful handmaiden, Ninshubur. Inanna told her to wait three days and, if she did not return, to beg to the gods for assistance. The faithful Ninshubur represents a model of women's deepest reflections. She is egoless, simply carrying out Inanna's wishes, though it is she who ultimately saves her mistress."

"Tell it in order."

Guess he doesn't want the Jungian side of things. "As you will." Lara nodded in his direction. "When Ereskigal discovers Inanna at the outer gate—in all her glory and wearing the garments of her power—the Goddess of the Underworld isn't pleased. Enraged, she's like Lilith, ruthlessly destroying all she doesn't deem true."

"Lilith is not a part of the myth." Gradoxst came to his feet, pacing.

"Sorry," Lara murmured, though she wasn't at all. "This is how it was told to me. I wanted to be sure not to leave anything out." She waited while he continued to charge up and down the room without speaking.

Maybe if he gets agitated enough, he'll slip and tell me something.

"Each of Inanna's seven raiments represents one of the Kundalini chakras. Inanna is systematically stripped of one after the other, and so loses her roles as queen, holy priestess, and woman. Finally, she creeps naked and abased before her sister, who turns her over to the Annuna, the judges of the underworld. Ereskigal fastens the eye of death on her sister. She strikes her and turns Inanna into a corpse, which she hangs from a hook."

"What else did Ereskigal do?"

Lara glanced sidelong at her captor. A feral smile lit his face, and he was rubbing his hands together delightedly. Her stomach turned so sour, she was afraid she might vomit up her dinner.

"She mourned." Jumping down from the table, her sleeping child held close, Lara advanced toward the self-styled Demon. "Her sister was part of her. So in killing her sister, she also destroyed part of herself."

"Tripe," he announced smugly. "That was not in the version I studied."

"Perhaps not, but it is in many commentaries written about this story over several thousand years." Lara took a measured breath. To her dismay, her next words slipped out with a mind of their own. "Look. I know you've come up with a way to shanghai souls into the collective. How will you manage to keep all of them here?"

"The rest of the story," he pressed, ignoring her question.

Anger that had been jockeying with her fear, grabbed the upper hand. "I'm sure you know it as well as me. Besides, I'm tired."

"*You* are tired?" he snapped. "You have no appreciation for the energy it takes to maintain this illusion."

"I'm sure I don't." She met his eyes, hoping hers reflected a compassion she was far from feeling. "Why don't you tell me about it?"

Yes, by all means, please tell me something I can use to get myself out of here.

He opened his mouth, and then closed it so abruptly she heard his teeth clack together. In an attempt to soothe his mood, which seemed to be turning foul again, she picked up the threads of Inanna.

"Three days passed and the faithful Ninshubur went to the gods. The first two said Inanna had gotten what she deserved, but the third offered to help. Enki, God of Wisdom, scraped the dirt from under his fingernails and created two creatures that he sent to the Underworld with specific instructions."

When she looked up, Gradoxst had at least stopped moving. He stood stock-still, head tilted to one side as if he were listening for something. She thought about the fairy, then wiped the image from her mind.

"The creatures find Ereskigal in terrible shape. She's thrashing and moaning because of what she has done to her sister—and paradoxically to herself. They join with Ereskigal in her grief, and eventually talk her into freeing Inanna. The creatures then sprinkle the food and water of life on Inanna's corpse and she lives again. The Annuna are not pleased. They tell Inanna that she can leave only if she provides another from above to take her place."

"She was better off with the dead."

Lara turned her eyes toward Gradoxst. "Why would you think that?" she asked, truly curious since everyone else she'd discussed this tale with believed Inanna belonged with the living.

"You do not see the true meaning of this story," he pronounced, his voice tones patronizing.

"Why don't you tell me," she invited, shifting the baby to her other arm.

"It is a story of death, not of redemption. Death at the hands of the gods. What could be nobler?"

He sounds positively delighted. Despite it being only a story, Lara felt fear bite deep. "It's a story of the divine feminine," she offered. "While it doesn't feature the triple goddess, it does—"

"Silence." His voice wasn't loud, but it cut through the still air of the room like a scythe. Lara backed against the nearest wall, eying him. Her heart was beating faster, but she tried to maintain a neutral expression.

"You want to know about where you are, don't you?" An unpleasant gleam hovered behind his eyes.

Lara didn't react. He was so volatile she wasn't sure what he wanted out of her. She thought of a dozen placating statements, but bit her tongue. Yes, he was disturbed, but he wasn't her patient. This wasn't her office, and she was far from safe.

"I will tell you something," he went on, looking pleased with himself. "I found a way to shift the energy of the *Dreaming* while I was there. What remains for the Sidhe," he spat on the floor, "is but a shadow of their sacred place."

"Are you sorry you left them?"

He bristled. "Why would you even ask that?"

She shrugged. "Seems you never got very far away from them. That's all."

"They did not understand. They could have had what I have. Limitless powers. They are nothing but a pack of spineless idiots. My people and their misplaced loyalties." He grimaced, and then he was on the move again, and Lara knew he'd almost forgotten about her.

I know how to do this. How to fade into near invisibility as I feed questions that don't sound like questions. "You miss them." She made it a statement, spoken barely above a whisper.

"The Sidhe are brilliant. The closest I have come to feeling an affiliation with others since leaving the Old Ones was at the Institute, but my kin destroyed that. Lillian and her...her..." he sputtered, rage overcoming his ability to find words. His face took on the mottled redness it had earlier, just before he hit her.

"No. You interrupted your tenure at the Institute by going after me." Lara paused, understanding she'd be far better off keeping her mouth shut, but finding she didn't care. "The Institute is still there. I'm sure they'd welcome you back." Her voice was silky and as inviting as she could make it. "They'd be very interested in how you've been able to control the collective." *If that's what he's really doing.* "Even Jung couldn't do that. You'd be a hero."

"Tricks." He cut her off abruptly. "You're playing tricks. All you analysts do that. You are nothing but trained charlatans."

Fury trod just below the surface. She wrestled with it briefly before her next words took form. "And you think you're something better?" Her tone was incredulous. "You've ripped me away from my home. From Trevor. And for what? So I can entertain you? So you can dispose of me once you tire of your games? Bah." She considered spitting in his face, turned her head at the last possible moment and spat on the floor. "If that's your plan, get moving with it. Maybe your next *queen* will be a bit more cooperative."

That wasn't very smart. She cringed against the wall, waiting for him to backhand her again or send lightning to finish her off. When she realized her eyes were shut, she cracked them open to look at him. What she saw shocked her. He looked distraught, as if her words had been a surprise.

He can't have believed that fairy tale he spun about shoving me onto a throne next to his.

A ghastly shriek burst from his lips, and he left the room in a sheet of flame. The second he was gone, she went hunting for the fairy, comforted beyond reason when she found the tiny creature, wings beating double-time, under the bed.

Her legs trembled so violently, she was surprised she didn't tumble to the floor, Lara steadied herself by placing a hand on the bed. In a few moments she lay down, a sleeping Elizabeth held firmly against her body. Her head was pounding. The food she'd eaten earlier sat in her stomach in an undigested lump. She ordered herself to concentrate on her ragged breathing, to get her shattered emotions under better control. As soon as she closed her eyes, Trevor's dear face formed behind her lids and she felt like crying.

"I have to get out of here before Gradoxst kills us," she moaned. "But how?"

CHAPTER 23

Lara knew she was dreaming, but she felt very much awake. Her limbs were heavy, weighted against the mattress so she couldn't move. Even breathing was a struggle. It felt as if hundreds of pounds were smothering her, and she began to panic. Trevor wavered into view. He was sitting cross-legged on the floor in the library with a thick volume open in his lap. As she watched, he raked his fingers through his blond curls in a gesture so familiar it ripped at her heart. His mouth formed words, but she couldn't hear what he was saying. He talked, then closed his eyes and said something else. Then he glanced down at the book again.

It's as if he's memorizing something, she realized. Before she had time to conjure up which book might have commanded his attention—she was certain it had something to do with her abduction—the scene before her shifted dramatically. Brigid, lantern and all, stood off to one side staring at her. Along with the goddess came a lessening of the pressure holding her down. It was still there, but at least she could take shallow breaths.

"So, mortal woman." Brigid's voice was cold and stern. A chill entered Lara's chamber that settled in her bones. Elizabeth curved her small body closer to Lara's as if she too, felt the temperature change.

"It seems your beloved has taken it upon himself to change the texture of Gaia's weaving. It has been long years since any mortal has chosen that path." Her voice softened slightly. "He must love you beyond hope and reason."

Lara's mouth went dry. She told herself she was dreaming and that none of this was real. Seconds later, she understood she was deluding herself. "What has Trevor done?" she asked, her voice tremulous.

"He treads the path of the gods at incalculable risk to himself."

"Can you stop him?"

Brigid shook her head. "No, child. 'Tis far too late for that." Eons of sadness reflected from her golden eyes.

"Can you get me out of here? Maybe I can do something." Even as she said the words, Lara wondered what she could do to turn back the wheels Trevor had apparently set in motion.

"We do not meddle in the affairs of mortals." The goddess's timeless face was set stubbornly.

Lara realized she wasn't dreaming anymore. Unaware of when the transition from sleep to wakefulness occurred, she pushed herself to a sitting position, struggling against a residual heaviness in her limbs. "But you're here," Lara pointed out. "There must be a reason for your visit." The tiny fairy rose out of the dusky gloom near the floor, fluttering around Lara's head.

"So that is where you have been." Brigid crooked a finger. "You ought not to have left my side."

In a burst of what Lara was sure had to be uncharacteristic defiance, the fairy came to rest on her shoulder, small wings beating a tattoo against her neck.

"You refuse me?" The goddess took a menacing step forward, then her outstretched hand fell to her side, and she shook her head sharply. Her long hair shimmered about her like an iridescent shroud.

"I must think well on what this means," she said, before slowly fading from view.

Lara's head dropped to her chest. She pinched the bridge of her nose between thumb and forefinger to clear her thoughts. "Thank you," she breathed to the fairy, wishing they shared a language.

What had Trevor done? He was likely working on rescuing her, but why weren't Raven and the Sidhe taking care of that? For that fact, why hadn't they stopped Trevor, if what he dabbled in was so dangerous?

Probably because they don't know.

"Of course they don't. If they did, they'd…" Lara stopped, aware she'd been talking to the fairy. And also aware it wasn't beyond imagining that Raven and the Sidhe wouldn't lift a finger to stop Trevor. After all, they'd practically shoved Brad out, with nary a thought his return to Seattle could sign his death warrant.

"If I get out of this," she muttered through gritted teeth, "Trevor and I and the baby are going back to Seattle. I've had enough of the Sidhe. And enough magic to last a lifetime. We'll take our chances with the mortals. At least I *understand* them."

The air flickered oddly. For a second, she thought it might be the goddess returning, but the fairy knew better. As soon as the little creature dove into one of the curtained alcoves, Lara understood with a sinking feeling that Gradoxst would soon be in her bedchamber again. *Could he have sensed Brigid?* Hastily closing her eyes and turning to one side, Lara feigned sleep.

"That charade does not become you," the rogue Sidhe shouted, his voice grating like the rough edge of a saw blade. "Get up."

"Mmph." Lara tried to maintain the illusion of being half-asleep. Searing heat blanketed the back of her head, smoke stung her nostrils, and the odor of burnt hair filled the room. *Thank God the baby's on my other side.* Lara instinctively rolled her head against the pillows to put out any residual flames. She tasted blood and knew she'd bitten through her cheek.

"I said get up." The cold, dispassionate edge to his voice frightened her far more than his rapidly-shifting moods had earlier.

Is this when he murders both of us? And Trev will have thrown his life away—or whatever he's mixed up in—for nothing. Lara tried to think. Was there anything she could do to divert Gradoxst? Spitting blood on the floor from her lacerated cheek, she made up her mind.

"I thought you'd returned for a bit of love play," she murmured, positioning herself to face her adversary, Elizabeth tucked behind her. "Surely you don't want to harm me before I've had an opportunity to do what you brought me here for. What was that you used to call me on the phone? *Liebchen*, wasn't it?" She held her breath. Her tone hadn't been all that inviting despite her best efforts.

"You must be desperate," he sneered. "I am all too aware the touch of my flesh is anathema to you. No. I have come to my senses. You shall live out your days with the others who are trapped in my web. I find the energy of so many is useful to my plans." He paused and leveled his dark eyes at her. "Get up."

She raised her eyebrows. "What if I refuse?"

"Then I shall burn you and your precious child to cinders where you sit."

So he does need my assent to move me. Christ, wish I'd have known that back in my bedroom. "If you murder us, you'll lose our psychic energy. You said yourself that Elizabeth will be far more powerful than me." Lara met his eyes in silent challenge. She was fighting to stay alive. Her only weapons were her mind and her tongue.

"There are others where you came from."

That unnerving coldness hadn't left his voice. It didn't give her anything to work with. Elizabeth picked that moment to begin wailing. Lara's heart plummeted. Even if Gradoxst might reconsider, a crying child could be enough to shift things in the other direction. As she watched warily, he began to chant in a guttural language that certainly wasn't Gaelic. His hands came up slowly. A deadly gleam shone from his eyes.

"Wait." She sprang to her feet.

His eyes met hers. "What?"

"I really am lonely." Lara held out her arms. She didn't want him to touch her, but it seemed a small enough price if it kept her and Elizabeth alive.

Something like confusion crossed his stark features. He shook his head, muttering in German. "You are stalling for time." He glared at her, as if he expected her to go along with his plans to banish her to wherever he kept the others without any kind of pushback.

"No, really—" Her mind worked feverishly. What could she do to stop him?

What the hell have I got to lose? Unsure if her power would work at all, since the amulet's magic was so truncated in her stone cell, Lara grasped the moonstone with one hand and began the incantation that would call up the power to destroy. Even though the moonstone felt inert, a fire bolt materialized in her other hand faster than it ever had before. She hurled it at Gradoxst and called another.

His cloak caught fire. He screamed with disbelief and rage. Surprise must have queered his aim, because Lara easily evaded the lightning erupting from his hands by ducking to one side.

"You think to defeat me?" he cried, lobbing bolts of electric death her way.

"I stopped thinking when you dumped me in this room," she snarled back. Grabbing her crying child, Lara feinted right and laid Elizabeth on the floor in the alcove she'd seen the fairy take refuge in. With a hasty prayer to the fairy to watch over her child, Lara spun, dropping the heavy curtain back into place. Her hair smoldered where it had caught fire. She cursed herself for not having it braided and out of the way.

Girding herself for a fight to the death, she called on whatever unknown source was helping her and hurled power as fast as she could draw it. She should be petrified, but there wasn't time to think. Barely time to react as her body filled with magic, vibrating with the effort of channeling so much energy.

The small room filled with the smell of burning flesh, hair, and cloth. Lara coughed reflexively to clear her lungs of smoke. Her watering eyes made it hard to focus on her target. She smiled grimly, assuming Gradoxst was similarly handicapped.

Searing pain tore down her face. She ripped burning fragments of something out of her jaw, tossing them aside. Desperate, she wished she'd taken more time to study the varieties of defense in Raven's books. Because she only knew how to do one thing, she kept heaving strikes at Gradoxst, praying most of her magic would find him in the smoke-filled room. Dizzy from lack of oxygen, she staggered. Something lashed itself about her legs pulling her off balance. Arms flailing, she crashed to the floor sucking air. At least it was easier to breathe lower down. Lara peered through the sooty air looking for Gradoxst.

Something launched itself atop her. Knowing it had to be him, she twisted like a mad thing, trying to get her hands around his neck.

"No, *liebchen*," he panted. "I liked your first idea much better. On your back. Let us get this over with."

Get what over with?

Gradoxst barked a word. Her arms pinned themselves against her sides. Her legs spread of their own accord. Much of his clothing had burned away. His revolting penis was fully erect, sticking straight out from his body. Fingers scrabbled at her waistband, trying to push her pants out of the way. Realization flared that violence excited him. *Of course. Why wouldn't it?* Elizabeth's squalls rose in intensity, pounding at Lara.

An idea came to her. It was sick and disgusting, but she pounced on it. With a throaty laugh that she hoped to hell sounded seductive, she said, "Let my arms loose. I'll touch you—and help with my pants."

She didn't think he'd fall for her ploy, but the invisible bonds holding her arms in place fell away. Lara channeled the same energy she'd been using to pull fire from the Earth. Grabbing his cock, she focused the power within her—and let it go.

Thick, viscous liquid spurted onto her hands, as his anguished howls filled the chamber. Lara leaped to her feet. She asked for more power, determined to finish him off if she could. There'd be no second chance. Once he pulled himself together, he'd kill her. Someone must have been listening because fire blazed from her hands.

"Stand aside, child." Brigid's unmistakable voice came out of nowhere and everywhere.

"And you, scum that you are. Get on your feet." Brigid kicked Gradoxst, who staggered upright.

Shocked, Lara stood rooted to the spot, the power she'd called pouring through her. A thunderclap rattled her brain and made her ears ache. Fire blazed all around her. Not sure if it came from the goddess or the Demon or herself, she dropped to her knees, rolling out of the way. Pain registered in a dim corner of her mind, and she looked down at blackened palms. Two fingers on her right hand were incinerated down to bone. The sight of her ruined flesh brought searing pain front and center.

"I told you. Stay out of the way." Brigid twirled past Lara, moving so quickly she appeared nothing more than a flash of multihued light.

Stuffing the remains of a sooty sleeve into her mouth to keep from screaming at the agony spilling from her ruined hand, Lara half-crawled and half crab-walked to where Elizabeth screeched her dismay. Once she'd gathered up the inconsolable babe, Lara scuttled into a corner. She thought about trying to let herself out the door, but Gradoxst was in the way.

He and Brigid circled one another like uncaged beasts, but the pathway to the door remained blocked by either one or the other. Brigid glowed with a white heat, while the air about Gradoxst was tinged with red. They were both panting with effort. In between throwing liquid fire and wounding one another, Brigid talked with her adversary, her voice rich and low. Though Lara didn't understand the language, it sounded like a confessor chiding her parishioner.

Gradoxst's replies were furious at first. After a time they developed a whiny edge. It was apparent he was tiring. His greasy hair was mostly burned away. He'd long since shucked his cloak. The clothing beneath was charred, as were large patches of his wrinkled skin. He'd apparently shoved his cock out of harm's way after Lara's assault, because it was nowhere to be seen.

Brigid was burned as well. Unless her magic could undo the

damage, her hands and face would carry scars from this battle, marring her perfect beauty. Her hair had fared better than Lara's, since it was braided in many tiny rows tight against her head. The long part of the braids disappeared beneath her clothing.

Pain throbbed from Lara's hand in white-hot waves that threatened to annihilate her. Even above the crushing discomfort, she wanted to know what the two—goddess and rogue Sidhe—said to one another. Elizabeth gradually quieted against her breast. Lara held her child carefully. Her other hand was burned too, just not as badly.

After a final unintelligible comment that sounded decidedly hostile, Gradoxst turned on his heel reaching for the door handle. He never made it. Brigid said something, her voice as chill and sere as his had been earlier. Something so bright Lara couldn't look at it left the goddess's hands. Gradoxst wavered for a moment or two before his wizened form vanished from the room. As the unholy brightness faded, Lara stared at the afterimage in hope and disbelief until it winked out of existence.

Brigid's hands dropped against her sides. Lara heard her take a deep breath in and then blow it out. Scarcely daring to look at the goddess who'd saved her, Lara ventured, "Thank you."

"I would not be so quick with your thanks," the goddess muttered caustically. "After all, you are still here are you not?"

"B—but I assumed... I mean, since you were able to kill..." Wrapping Elizabeth carefully in her blankets, Lara lurched unsteadily to her feet. Moving a few steps, she laid the baby on the bed.

Brigid turned her golden eyes on Lara. After trying to meet that relentless gaze and giving up, Lara looked at the floor, waiting.

"He is far from dead," the goddess said, sounding resigned. "I may have injured him sufficiently that he will not bother anyone for a few millennia, but I do not take life. I tried to convince him to return to the Sidhe. To walk a path to expiate his many sins. He refused."

Silence prowled through the room like an uninvited guest. At length, Lara dredged up what was left of her courage and asked, "Can you help me find a way back? And the rest of those unfortunates he dragged here against their will, they need to find their homes as well."

The goddess stalked to the alcove where the fairy was. This time, the tiny creature came to her mistress, hovering about her head. "I may assist you in returning to your proper place," she said after several moments, as much to the fairy as to Lara. "There is a balance that must be restored."

"The others?" Lara found if she didn't move her hand, the pain wasn't as devastating. Other hurt places clamored for her attention. A gingerly exploration of her face revealed skin torn from forehead to jaw line. She felt as if a truck had run over her.

"The reason I helped you," Brigid informed her haughtily, "was because you fought bravely to save yourself."

Lara's anger flickered which surprised her. She'd thought herself far too battered in body and spirit for her characteristic ire to flare. "Does that mean you'll help Trevor? Whatever it is he's done, he did it to try to save me. And none of those poor, wandering souls imprisoned here deserve their fate, either."

"Does anyone ever get the fate they deserve?" The goddess's rich voice was low. It vibrated with suppressed emotion. "That is a myth promulgated by you humans."

"Maybe so," Lara replied, weary beyond imagining as adrenaline leeched from her system. "But I've always believed it."

Brigid chuckled, the sound so unexpected Lara's head snapped up. "I will return you to your home, child. But first I must untangle what that pesky Sidhe has done to the *Dreaming*. I can barely move between the energy fields holding his illusory world in place." The goddess made a disgusted moue, then threw her hands upward in irritation. "This castle used to be part of the *Dreaming*. I have no idea what mischief Gradoxst spun to move it to the shadow side of things."

She quirked an eyebrow Lara's way. "If you can figure out how to free those *unfortunates*, as you called them, before my return, you have my permission."

"But—" Lara began.

Brigid waved her to silence. "Another regrettable human trait. Given the opportunity, you would all talk things to death. I shall return presently."

"Trevor—" Lara tried again, but the goddess was gone.

TREVOR CAME AWAKE WITH A START. He was still sitting on the floor in the library with the heavy book on his lap. Gunter whined softly from his place by the door, and Trevor understood the dog probably wanted to go outside. As he laid the book to one side, a tingling from his feet told him both of them had fallen asleep. Readying himself for unpleasantness, he struggled upright, using a nearby chair for assistance. Pins-and-needles coursed up and down his lower legs. When he took a step toward the door, he nearly fell over.

"Bloody hell. What the fuck is wrong with me?" Trying again, Trevor found he could shuffle along. Just not easily. Passing a break in the bookshelves lining most of the room, he glanced at his reflection in a mirror and came to a dead halt. He rubbed at his eyes and then looked again.

Could the book have done that to me? Hands shaking, he drew them up, laying his palms against the sides of his face. The face he expected to have about ten years from now, that is. His blond curls were definitely grayer. A webbing of lines that most certainly hadn't been there before he'd fallen asleep etched his face.

"And when was that?" he muttered, wondering if he'd somehow stumbled into a variant of the Rip Van Winkle story. Turning slowly, the problems with his feet forgotten, Trevor gazed out the window and was unspeakably relieved to see it was still daylight. *Yes, but is it still the same day?*

He didn't see how it could be. But surely Raven, Lillian, and Eli wouldn't have let him sit upstairs for years while they went about their business. The dog barked once. Trevor turned away from both mirror and window. That the dog was still there argued not much time had passed.

"Time to go downstairs," he told the Shepherd. "May as well face the music. The minute they get a gander at me, they'll know I got into something I shouldn't have." As he paced the length of the long upstairs hall and moved down the risers, Trevor took stock of his body. It wasn't his imagination. He didn't just look as if he'd aged. He felt it too. His joints ached, and walking took more effort.

Wonder if whatever this is might be reversible. After I go after Lara. A grim smile split his face. He had gotten that much from the book. He was fairly certain he knew how to go about finding her and Elizabeth. He just needed to prepare a few things and get something Lara had worn next to her skin and some hair from her brush. After that, a fairly straightforward cookbook of instructions he was sure he'd jotted down before he passed out, detailed the rest. Patting his pants pockets, he was rewarded by the crinkle of a folded sheet of paper.

He was just unlatching the door to let the dog outside when he heard a muffled expletive from behind him. "You have not—" Raven began, a horrified expression on his normally impassive face. "I told the women I should try to find you, but both of them said you were *tired*. That I should let you alone. Goddess be damned, son. Of all the magics for you to meddle with, you had to choose *that* one."

The women crowded into the front room, alternately chiding him and clucking over him. At length, Trevor took a step back and asked, "Why are the lot of you so unhinged? All I did was ferret out a way to find Lara. And I'm going to go after her, if it's all the same to you." Trevor swallowed hard. "I fear she'll be dead soon. That monster will kill her before you figure out how to rescue her."

"Ach, son." Raven's deep voice rumbled against Trevor, his gray eyes inexplicably sad. "You may have found a way to locate her, but what you have traded is your own life, or most of it anyway. Did you not read the bargain mortals must make for knowledge such as you acquired?"

Trevor shook his head mutely, fear gnawing at him. "Uh, no.

Didn't get that far. You see, I fell asleep before I came to the end of that section. A warning of some sort was at the front of the chapter, but I'm afraid it wasn't terribly specific."

"'Tis not attached to a section," Elidora murmured. "If I recall, 'tis at th' very beginnings o' th' tome. 'Twas th' thick one bound in creased, tan leather, was it not?"

He nodded once, curtly, unable to meet the witch-woman's dark eyes. His mouth was suddenly dry. A desperate need for haste swept through him. "Tell me," he spat through clenched teeth. "But be quick about it. If I haven't got much time left, I want to use it to get my wife and child back."

"The trade," Lillian replied, her voice strained, "is a day for a month. So for each day of your life that passes, you will age a month. Though it'll feel like more than that at the beginning as the magic takes root in you." She met his eyes with her clear, green ones. "And no, there is no counter spell."

Trevor cocked his head to the side, acid biting into his guts. "Whoever's charging the tariff does seem to be getting ahead of themselves since I look years older than when I went up those stairs." He gestured behind him, aware that if he thought too hard about what he'd done, he'd sabotage any chance he had of rescuing Lara. He tried to do the mental math that would determine just how many months he might have before death claimed him, but his mind shrank from the task.

"Och aye, lad. That would be th' shock o' introducin' you t' magic in th' first place," Elidora murmured, seconding what Lillian had said a few moments before.

Raven interrupted Elidora, leveling his intense gaze on Trevor. "Such things were never meant for humans. But since you have gone thus far, let us ready you for what lies ahead."

"Why haven't you been able to find her?" Trevor blurted, unable to stop the words.

"Because that bastard Sidhe scum has perverted the *Dreaming*. It's the source of our power," Lillian snapped, looking uncomfortable as

Raven shot her an unmistakable look that meant she'd said far too much.

"I don't care." She looked defiantly at Raven, tossing her thick red braids out of the way. "The lad has sacrificed much. The least he deserves is the truth."

~

TREVOR STOOD in the kitchen about to set his spell in motion— the one he hoped would bring him to Lara and his baby. He gathered the last of his provisions and slipped the straps of his pack over his shoulders once he had everything.

After Lillian's last comment, he'd run out into the yard. For once the sun was out, though it failed to warm him. It hadn't taken long before he'd ferreted an old daypack out of the shop, returned to the house, and filled it with what the spell book told him he'd need: a T-shirt of Lara's and strands of hair from her brush. He tossed in a water bottle and some cheese and bread, although his stomach was in such an uproar, he wondered if he'd ever be able to eat again.

"Och aye, and I wish ye'd rethink this lad—" Elidora began, walking to his side and laying a hand on his shoulder.

"Yes, it would be far better if you could wait till we can accompany you," Raven broke in. "Perhaps if you don't expend any of that magic you paid so dearly for, it might alter the outcome."

"Maybe so at that," Elidora echoed. "I canna recall the last time a human tampered with that binding."

"I can," Lillian said dourly. Something in her tone made Trevor's guts clench.

He shook his head, resolute now that his decision was made. "If I don't go now, there's no point. Lara's in mortal danger, I feel it here." Trevor tapped his breastbone.

He sang the notes of the incantation that would carry him into the unknown. His throat was so dry, he had to do it twice, since the first set of notes was so off-key. The last thing he saw, before the kitchen swirled away to mist, were Raven and the Sidhe, concern and something else that might have been guilt, stamped on their familiar faces.

The *Dreaming* congealed around him. It had a slimy feel to it that stank of Goblin magic. It didn't take Trevor long to find his bearings, although the castle that had sat on a far hill wasn't there anymore. *How could that be?* Not willing to waste his time worrying about it, he saw the waterfall that led to the sacred cave and took off running. His body felt as if he were slogging through thick honey, but he propelled himself forward, breath sticking in his throat.

"*Lara,*" he screamed in his mind, hoping she'd hear him. "*Lara. I'm coming. Hang on.*"

CHAPTER 24

*L*ara considered lying down next to Elizabeth. As the adrenaline retreated, pain registered every time she moved. But she told herself she needed to do what she could to help the others out of Gradoxst's prison. Without his magic holding things together, it might be easier. Hope flared quick and bright, giving her the energy to get going.

She made her way to the pump. Steeling herself for pain, she stripped out of her burned clothing and pumped cool water with her less-injured hand. It took a while, but she managed to clean the worst of the soot and burned spots. Taking a good look at the fourth and fifth fingers of her right hand, she cringed. Bone showed down to the second knuckle. At least Brigid's fire had effectively sealed what was left of her flesh, since she wasn't bleeding. As she struggled to treat her injuries, she kicked herself for never taking even a basic first aid class. Brad would've known what to do, but she didn't. Settling on a clout as the only clean cloth in the room, she tore strips with her teeth, clumsily securing them to cover the worst of her injuries.

It was taking such a ridiculously long time to do anything, Lara felt like she was sleepwalking. Finally, she made her way back to the pump and dunked her head under it. The cold water pummeling her did revive her somewhat. She used some bedding to soak up the water from her dripping hair and salvaged what she could of her clothing. Lara wound a sheet around her shoulders, knotting it so it would stay in place. It would serve as a jacket, covering the holes in her burned top.

Got to get going. Lara knew if she gave in to the inertia tugging at her, she'd fall on her face. That thought scared her. Brigid had provided an opportunity. Lara wanted out of Gradoxst's enchanted castle more than she'd ever wanted anything. Except seeing Trevor again. And those two things were closely related. She picked up her baby and padded softly to the door. Taking hold of the latch, she had a moment of panic. *What if it doesn't open?*

But it did. Moments later, she let herself into the stone hallway and retraced her steps from earlier that day. Lara found the lower level easily enough and the large room where she'd shared food with the others. The building was eerily silent. At length, she raised her voice to call out, but her, "Hello, hello. Is anyone here?" was met with an echo.

"At least a hundred people were here," she mumbled. "They can't all have disappeared." She tried to recall the name of the mousy, little man who'd defied Gradoxst. It had been Del something or other. So she tried calling, "Del? Del?" He didn't answer. Remembering Gradoxst's warning about curaets, she glanced about warily for the carnivorous beasts.

No curaets, no people. What does that mean? Where could they all have gotten to? Must mean there's a way out of here. Mystified, Lara kept walking. Elizabeth had fallen asleep at her breast, so Lara gently detached her. She started to shift her to her other arm, but hot, shooting pain from her wounded hand stopped her.

"Miss?" The voice was wispy and weathered. Lara twirled to see Gradoxst's servant standing about fifty feet behind her.

"Where are the others?" she asked.

"N—no others. Just me," he said nervously, hesitating before speaking again. "D—did you get rid of master?" A hopeful note that he tried to squelch ran through his voice. He looked about fearfully as soon as the words were out. "The others—his henchmen—just sort of vanished 'bout an hour ago, along with those hellish beasts."

Lara's heart bled for the man. She tried to smile reassuringly. "Everything will be all right," she said, hoping she was telling the truth. "Gradoxst is gone. And I suppose the rest of the Goblins—and the curaets—left right along with him." She paused. "But what do you mean there are no others? What happened to all those people? I talked to them. Ate with them. Where have they gotten to?"

Del blew out a tense breath, then seemed to come to some internal decision. "They're down at the river." He hesitated. "I never seen 'em before earlier today. Master must've done something to summon all of 'em. Probably, they ain't even real." Making a sign against evil, he muttered what sounded like the first line of the Lord's Prayer.

"Show me where they are." *Maybe he knows how to get outside…*

Del stared at her for several long moments. Then he said, "Follow me."

Stairs wound down from a doorway at the back of the dining hall. Lara watched as Del positioned his fingers just so on the stone wall. Once he did, and held them in place, a panel opened inward, revealing the exit she'd been hunting for. Memorizing where the man had placed his fingers in case she had to go back inside, Lara hurried after him down the single flight that led to the world outside. It was brighter than she'd expected it would be, and she squinted against the glare.

Once her eyes adjusted, she looked hard at the rolling scrublands, mentally comparing them to what she'd seen out the windows of the stronghold. *There's more color,* she told herself. *Maybe because Gradoxst is gone and Brigid is trying to fix things.* Lara spun in a slow circle. When she saw the stone building from the outside, it looked enormous. She realized it truly was the castle from the *Dreaming,* just like Brigid had said. Why was it in this drab hinterland? What sort of magic had

Gradoxst manipulated to move such a massive structure? Or was it all psychic smoke and mirrors?

"Missy," Del called from about fifty feet away. "Are you coming?" He turned away from her, then abruptly turned back. "Do you have magic?" he demanded.

She nodded. "Some."

"Can you find a way back for me?"

Lara felt the man's eyes on her, watchful and wary, yet hopeful at the same time.

"How long have you been with Gradoxst?" she asked as she walked to where Del stood.

He shook his head. "Don't know. He took me from my farm near Monroe. That's in Washington State," he clarified. "Anyways, I was coming back from the barn one night. It was spring, but still cold, see. I'd gone to check on the animals." He barked a disgusted sound. "Never made it as far as the house. He just come up out of nowhere with all these unnatural lights. And a wind to boot."

The man sighed heavily. "Seems like years ago. But it might not have been so long as all that." His face twisted in an unpleasant grimace. "Don't know why he picked me to wait on him when others could've done better. Guess he took a shine to me." Del squeezed his eyes shut and shuddered. "Wife probably thinks I run out on her."

Lara laid a hand on his arm. "He really is gone," she said. "Truly. And I will see if there's anything I can do to help you."

They walked until they came to the waterfall Lara had thought was twin to the one in the *Dreaming* that led to the sacred cave. Given what Brigid had said, she was certain a connection existed between the *Dreaming* and where they were.

"Have any of you tried walking through the water?" she asked, eying the small knots of people sprawled on dirt and patches of grass near the rapidly flowing creek.

A cacophony of languages erupted, most of which were incomprehensible. She asked, "Do any of you speak English?"

A small group of elderly men wearing kilts stepped forward. "Aye an' we do," one bent fellow with long white hair said.

Lara came close, remembering what the man with the accent had told her after she'd tried to engage his grandmother in conversation. "Where were you before you were here?" she asked, curiously.

"Loch Barrough castle, well enough," the man replied. He looked about him, then lowered his voice. "An' we got dragged there, we did. Was told we had some sort of special abilities. Pah!" He spat on the ground, showing a mouthful of yellowed teeth. "If you was to ask me, if we hadna been taken to th' castle—and held there like prisoners, mind you—we'd not be here, neither." Straightening his bent spine as much as he could, he crossed his arms across his chest and glared at her as if she was responsible for the current turn of events.

Not the collective unconscious. Oh my God, this must be the group the Sidhe pulled together in Scotland. My kin. Other humans with Sidhe blood.

"Have any of you tried walking through the water?" she asked again, pointing at the waterfall, as she worked to still her tumultuous thoughts.

The man shook his head. "Now what sort o' sane person would be doin' somethin' like that?" he demanded, his voice shrill.

"I think it might be a way out of here," she said softly. The old man looked at her as if she'd lost her mind and herded his small group back to their spot next to the streambed.

Lara glanced at her sleeping child. She had no idea if there would be a cavern hiding behind the falls, but she knew she had to look. Some of the people had noticed her and were pointing her way and talking softly with their companions. When she looked at the rolling terrain again, it had gained still more color, almost as if it were wakening after a long sleep. The amulet thrummed against her skin, and a half-smile played about her mouth. The stone had an affinity for the *Dreaming*. Maybe it knew it was close to where it had been mined.

"I'm going to try to go under the water," she told Del. "I believe there may be help for us on the other side."

He knit his brows and held out his hands. "I can hold your babe."

His gesture was so sincere, Lara knew there had to be at least one child left behind in the farmhouse with his abandoned wife. "Thank you," she murmured. "I think my magic will protect us."

Shielding Elizabeth's head and face with her wounded hand, Lara pushed through the water. Unlike the falls in the *Dreaming*, these drenched her, and she wondered if her hunch was only wishful thinking. Then she was through and in a cavern black as pitch. The amulet was singing, actually chiming like temple bells. All at once, the walls of the cave came alive with the living lights she remembered from the passageway into the *Dreaming*.

And from my cataclysmic dream too, she reminded herself. The dream that dragged Trevor and me away from Seattle.

Lara let out a tightly held breath. The cave's floor pitched downward and similarities to the *Dreaming* intensified. By the time she reached the bottom, Lara was certain she'd find the same sacred space she knew so well. When she got there, though, she wasn't sure. A large, open cave marked by stalagmites, and a pool that sort of looked like the same one, were there. But the cave seemed smaller, truncated somehow. And she didn't see a matching passageway leading upward on the other side. She'd just assumed she could find her way to the *Dreaming* because of how excited the amulet was.

Lara sat down heavily on a chunk of rock, startled by how cold it felt through her wet clothing. Movement from a far corner of the cavern startled her. "Show yourself," she cried out, instantly on alert.

"Just me, Missy."

The tightness across her shoulder blades relaxed once she understood Del had followed her.

"Thought you might need a hand," he said conversationally. "Right surprised all this is down here. How'd you know?"

"It would take too much to explain," she mumbled, racking her weary brain for what to do next. The baby stirred in her arms, and Lara realized the infant was both wet and soiled. Pulling a clean clout

—the last one she'd brought with her—out of a pocket, she changed her baby while Del hovered a few feet away.

"May as well go back," she said at length. She knew she'd have to sleep before she could think of anything else. Maybe Brigid would be back by then, but Lara had a hunch the goddess wouldn't go out of her way to help the people huddled above. As she started back toward the long upward-curving passageway, the amulet protested vigorously, thumping against her chest.

Lara stopped moving. She curved her injured hand about the amulet with difficulty. "What?" she asked. "If you know something, goddammit, find a way to tell me." The moonstone warmed against her skin. Her pain receded to a manageable level, and she hoped the stone might be healing her. After a time, with no further clues forthcoming, she turned again to begin the trek back to the river. If she didn't go now, she'd fall over. An immediate blast of cold from the stone made her hand ache unbearably.

"All right," she muttered, turning back. "I'll look more closely, since that seems to be what you want."

Del drew away from her. It was too dark in the cave to see the expression on his face, but Lara assumed he probably thought she was mad.

Yes, fey and talking to myself.

Stumbling from exhaustion and the uneven floor, Lara made her way to the nearest wall and started walking clockwise, examining it closely. The lights recessed into the stone brightened as she came near, dimming again once she'd passed by. She was so tired she nearly missed the slender break between dirt and stone, but the moonstone jabbed her, and she forced her sandpapery eyes to focus more intently.

When she investigated closely, she saw an inch wide crack that began at floor level and extended beyond where her eyes could see. Letting go of the amulet, Lara wedged the two uninjured fingers from her right hand into the opening. She tried pulling, then pushing, but all she got for her efforts was a resurgence of white heat from her hand. She'd just turned to lay Elizabeth down when Del materialized at her side.

"I'll take her." His voice wavered. Lara guessed his time with Gradoxst hadn't created any comfort level with magic-wielders.

Marshaling what little energy she had, she tried to tell him about the amulet and the *Dreaming*, but everything came out muddled.

"It's okay, Missy," he said after a few minutes. "Like as not I wouldn't understand anyways."

Nodding, Lara considered what to do next. She needed both hands. One to hold the amulet and the other to coax the gateway into existence. It was either lay the baby on the cold, rocky ground or let Del hold her. *If he was aligned with Gradoxst, I'd have sensed it,* she told herself as she reluctantly handed her baby to him.

"Bran' new, ain't it?" he asked, a wistful note in his voice. "Wife, she was in a family way again, and we had two others." He sounded embarrassed by the emotion he'd let slip.

Lara relaxed. Something reassuring ran beneath his words. Del would hold onto Elizabeth as though his life depended on it.

Gripping the amulet, she closed her eyes and emptied her mind. That last part wasn't hard since she was so tired it was challenging to hold even a single thought in place. For a few minutes nothing happened, and then a vision took form behind her closed lids. Just as she thought she had something she could work with, the image flickered, then faded. She slid to the floor like a marionette whose strings had suddenly been cut. Pain from her hand seared her. Her head spun. She was afraid she was going to pass out.

"Missy?" Del's worried voice cut through the fog her brain had become.

With a great deal of effort, she opened her eyes. "I—I thought I knew what to do," she mumbled. "But then it was gone." The hopelessness in her voice revealed how exhausted she was.

I can't give up. All those people out there are counting on me, even if they don't know it.

She held out her less injured hand, and Del helped her to her feet.

Thinking movement might clear her head, Lara walked in a tight circle a few times as she took deep, ragged breaths. Her wet clothing clung to her like a winding sheet, leeching heat from her body. She came to rest in front of the place the amulet seemed drawn to. Murmuring quick prayers to Brigid and Artemis, she took hold of the magic moonstone and faced the wall opening—all her senses questing toward whatever was locked within it.

Rather than a vision, words filled her mind. She chanted softly. Nothing happened. Desperation filled her. Lara sank to her knees on the uneven floor, the chill seeping into her bones. She shivered uncontrollably, teeth chattering as she forced her tired brain to do something other than run in circles. There had to be a way through to the other side. Why couldn't she find it?

Elizabeth started to cry. Lara reached for her, but Del shook his head. "You're not strong enough, Missy. Here, let me help you up again."

She struggled to her feet, blown away by how much effort it took.

I thought when Gradoxst disappeared, the rest would be easy, she thought, just before pain from her hand wiped everything else from her mind.

"Oh, but I am far from gone."

Gradoxst's unmistakable Swiss-German accent brought Lara's heart into overdrive, and she spun in the direction his voice came from. "You can't be here," she hissed. "Brigid said you were gone—for millennia."

Light from a blood-red mage light illuminated his bent form, burnt clothing, and charred hair. He leered at her and shrugged. "It would appear she was incorrect." He strode toward her, and his face twisted into an unholy smile. "I notice she is no longer by your side."

Lara's stomach tightened. She cast a thought to where Del had faded into the cavern's deeply shadowed recesses with Elizabeth, grateful she didn't have to protect her daughter and fight too. The amulet throbbed hotly against her breast, and for the second time in as many hours, she turned to face the rogue Sidhe. Weakened, all she could hope was that he hadn't recovered his full powers, either.

She squared her shoulders and faced Gradoxst. "We will finish this," she growled. "I'm not living the rest of my life running from you."

"Brave words, *liebchen*. If I have my way, the rest of your life will be measured in minutes."

He launched himself at her, driving her to the ground in a cloud of smoke and flames. Rocks cut into her back, but at least she didn't hit her head on the way down. Too spent to struggle with magic, Lara pummeled him with fists and nails, each beat sending agony up her injured hands. He ignored her. Just kept his hands firmly planted on her shoulders. In a horrified flash of insight, she understood he was draining her essence. She tried to erect a barrier, but it crumpled before her once, twice, and a third time.

He angled his head until his cunning, dark gaze settled on hers. "Do not bother, Doctor. You are mine now, whether you wish it or not. Since you were far too much trouble alive, I will take what I can before I leave your body in this cave."

With her consciousness ebbing, Lara frantically called for Brigid and hoped to hell her feeble efforts against Gradoxst were noteworthy enough to earn the goddess's help.

TREVOR PASSED UNDER THE WATERFALL. Banking on instincts that had rarely failed him—and the magic he felt coursing through him—he didn't question his chosen destination. Numinous lights floated in the gloom. Suddenly the passageway blazed as all the air sprites turned a fiery red. Shame for the sprite he'd killed swept through him. "I truly am sorry," he said in Celtic Gaelic. "If there was a way I could bring her back, I would."

To his surprise, the red faded to a gentle blue, almost as if they understood. *Well, maybe they did because of the magic,* he thought, as he pelted down the long corridor.

Moving as fast as he dared down the familiar subterranean grade, it still it took far too long to make the bottom. His heart pounded in his chest. Sweat dripped down his face and sides. Lara had to be down here. He felt it in his bones.

Not just here, but in deep trouble. He sensed her life force, but it was weakening by the moment.

Trevor came to a halt. The cave looked different somehow. It was smaller than he remembered. Forcing himself to take some deep breaths so he could think, he dredged up memories of the night he'd been here. Nodding, he realized the far wall had been moved inward. Maybe it was illusion, but he didn't think so.

He pulled Lara's clothing and hair out of his pack, holding them between his hands as the book had instructed. Next, he read out loud from the paper where he'd taken painstaking notes. Though he waited hopefully through five long breaths, nothing happened.

"Bloody fuck," he muttered, "did I throw my life away for nothing? Do the Sidhe cheat those who sacrifice everything?" A muted rumble filled his ears, and a small rock shower cascaded down, far too close for comfort.

Frantic, Trevor racked his brain. What was he missing? Trusting his instincts, he moved closer to the place the cave's wall had shifted. From his new vantage point, he reached out a hand, touching the dirt and stones of the wall that shouldn't be there, and repeated his incantation.

The sound of rocks grating against one another filled the subterranean space. To his amazement, a hidden door swung open, revealing what he'd known had to be there: the rest of the sacred cave.

"Lara!" he screamed, shoving his body through the opening just as soon as it was big enough to accommodate him. It took a moment before he made out her and Gradoxst grappling with one another on the cave's damp floor.

Trevor didn't stop to think. In one fluid motion, he pulled his silvered knife from a sheath that hung from his belt, launched himself at Gradoxst's back, and drove the knife deep between his ribs. Not satisfied, he pulled it back and stabbed again and again and again. Black ichor spattered his hands, smelling rank, like sulfur and dead animals.

Lara slithered from beneath them and rolled to one side where she lay still as death.

Grunting with pain, Gradoxst twisted beneath Trevor, amazingly alive considering the extent of his wounds. Magic jabbed Trevor, but whatever he'd garnered from the book protected him. Gradoxst's attack felt like bee stings, nothing more. Because the rogue Sidhe faced him, Trevor brought the knife down into his eye, driving it on through into his brain.

"Die, you manky bastard. Die." Fury drove Trevor's hand. When he yanked the knife back, ready to put out Gradoxst's other eye, the dark mage rolled his head to the side.

"Enough," Gradoxst burbled in a rush of blood.

"It'll never be enough until you're dead." Trevor grabbed a hank of burned hair, twisted Gradoxst's head back, and thrust the knife through his other eye. He was panting with effort, but it felt good, goddammit, every time the knife went in.

More black blood rushed from Gradoxst's mouth. To make certain the job was well and truly finished, Trevor pulled the knife out and plunged it a final time directly into the Demon's chest. When his body developed the insubstantial look Goblin bodies had before they disappeared, Trevor turned to where Lara lay on the ground.

He crawled to her and cradled her against him, grateful beyond words when the soft sound of her breathing rustled against his ears. "You're safe, love," he crooned. "I've killed him. He can't hurt you ever again."

Her dark eyes flickered open. "Trevor. Oh, Trev. I know, I watched most of it."

The sound of her dear voice filled him with unutterable joy. He murmured her name again and drew her close. "Where's our baby?" he asked, hoping against hope Elizabeth was still alive.

"Safe. She's safe." Lara pulled back from his embrace and called, "Del. You can come out now."

A stranger walked out of the gloom and stood next to them, holding Elizabeth. Trevor thought about asking who he was, but decided it wasn't important. He reached for his baby, and the man handed her to him. With Lara and Elizabeth in his arms, tears poured down his face. He repeated Lara's name over and over again. And told her how much he loved her.

Lara was crying too, as she clung to him. He rained kisses down her face. She sagged against his body.

"There now, love. Let's see if we can get you on your feet." Keeping an arm around her shoulders, he stood and then helped her. "Let's get you out of here."

Lara's mouth was set in a resolute line. She shook her head. "Not yet." She turned to the stranger. "Go get the others," she said. "Freedom's just that way." She pointed the direction Trevor had come.

He was about to ask what she meant and why they couldn't leave, when the sound of boots trampling over stone made his head snap up. "What the hell?" he began, pushing away from Lara and tucking Elizabeth into her arms, in case he had to fight.

Raven slithered through the hole in the wall, sweeping both of them into a heartfelt hug. "The barrier that held us out of the *Dreaming* fell not long after you left," he said. "I feared it might be a trap, but Elidora insisted we come anyway."

"Thanks, but I had things under control." Trevor spoke stiffly. Raven's presence reminded him of the bargain he'd struck.

"You'll have to tell us what happened," Raven said gruffly, seeming close to tears himself.

"Yes, and Lara must pay closer attention to her lessons," Lillian added dryly from the opening between the caves before running lightly to where they stood and lacing her arms around Lara. "Ach, daughter. It's good to hold you in my arms again. I feared—"

Elidora strode briskly to them, adding her tears and good wishes to the rest. They traded hugs for a long time, bathed in blue-green light from the air sprites.

"Missy?" A cautious voice broke into the greetings.

Trevor raised his face from Lara's hair, peering behind her. "It's the bloke who had our child. Who is he?"

"A man Gradoxst imprisoned. His name's Delgran. In fact," Lara sucked in a breath, disentangling herself from Trevor, "there are about a hundred more behind him. Gradoxst figured out a way to transport the human hybrids secreted away in that Scottish castle. They're all here. Hopefully," she eyed Raven and the Sidhe meaningfully, "you'll give them a warmer reception than you did in that God-awful castle you stuck them in."

"Blast it." Raven sounded thunderstruck. "How could he have moved them?"

"I have no idea, but we can't just leave them here," Lara argued. "And you can't take them back to Scotland, either. Damn it! They have homes, families—"

"You dare to tell me what I—" Raven began, breaking off when Lillian jabbed him. Even in the dimly lit cave, his face took on a blotchy hue.

"Yes," Lara snapped. "I do. They told me you were holding them prisoner. Christ, how could you have done such a thing?" Her voice broke and she looked close to tears. "I hate to even think this, but it makes you not much better than…than…" Her voice ran down.

"They were not detained against their will," Lillian's voice held an odd undertone, and Trevor, who really didn't like the way this was going, wondered why she was bothering to dissemble.

Turning to face the red-haired Sidhe, Lara inhaled angrily. "They thought they were," she said, her voice still as death. When Lillian dropped her gaze, Lara turned toward Delgran. "Is everyone here?" she asked.

"Yes, Missy." A chorus of voices in several languages echoed through the large cavern and the throng pushed forward, anxious now that escape seemed at least a possibility.

Turning back to Raven, Lara said, "I plan to invite these people above ground on the *Dreaming* side. All that's over there," she gestured behind her, "is the stone castle, though I haven't any idea how Gradoxst could've moved it from the *Dreaming*."

Raven raised his eyebrows as he took in Lara's statement. "So that's what the traitorous bastard did—"

Lara waited. When he didn't say anything further, she prodded, "What? You need to say more because I don't understand."

"He split the *Dreaming*," Lillian answered carefully, avoiding Lara's forthright gaze. "The castle used to be a part of it. And a very important part, mind you. The roots of our power lay deep within its stone foundation. It's why we couldn't reach our magic. It was hidden with guile and cunning. Still on this plane, yet drained of all life."

"Only one with our blood would've known how to do that," Raven hissed, looking like he wanted to tear something apart with his bare hands. "I should've killed that lying, scheming scum fifteen hundred years ago when I had the chance."

"We could let them sort this out," Trevor suggested, stepping forward and looping an arm around Lara's waist, "whilst you and I walk topside. Here, I'll take her."

Lara laid the baby in Trevor's arms, wincing. "Sounds like a good idea," she murmured "I want to lie down in the grass and sleep for a week."

"You're hurt." Trevor's tone was solicitous. "Let me help you."

"I think I'm hurt inside as much as out," she mumbled wearily. "It's hard to think about Raven and the Sidhe playing god with human lives. Even though I know they've done the same thing with ours."

"Right, then." Trevor wanted to change the subject before he blurted out what had transpired in Raven's library. "What happened to your hand?" He gazed at the primitive wrappings, wondering what sort of wound lay beneath.

"Burned," she replied. "And pretty badly. But Trev." She stopped walking and turned to him. "You killed for me. You killed him." Tears welled; she blinked them away. "I never thought I'd be glad to see anyone die, but I was wrong, I needed him dead. Needed to see him die." She shrugged uncomfortably. "How bloodthirsty is that? Never mind. Don't answer. How in the goddess's name did you find us?"

"It's a long story," he said, not wanting to ruin the joy of their reunion with the truth. He waited to see if she'd probe deeper, but mercifully she was too tired to do more than grasp his arm and walk with him up the long passageway toward daylight waiting for them above.

CHAPTER 25

As soon as she and Trevor emerged from the waterfall, he led her to a lush patch of grass and sat with his back against a convenient rock, cradling Elizabeth against his chest. Lara lay next to him with her head in his lap. She drifted off immediately, wet clothes and all. The din of many pairs of feet woke her. She was certain she hadn't been asleep for more than a few minutes when the first of Gradoxst's captives poured out into the warmth of a late afternoon sun.

Brigid's warning about Trevor tampering with something he should have left alone rattled about in the back of her brain, but Lara was so exhausted, she pushed it out of the way. Trevor was with her, so everything would be all right now. It had to be.

"Guess I spent most of the day down there," she murmured sleepily, trying to get her time sense back.

"So there's another place that's linked to the cave?" Trevor asked, sounding curious. "Someone built a wall to keep it separate?"

"Yes, it's like a mirror of the *Dreaming*, but dull and colorless." Lifting her head, she looked around. "There must still be some sort of shielding. Otherwise you'd be able to see where I was from here. It looks like a medieval castle.

"It was much cooler there and the land had a grayish hue. But it was getting better—more like this side. Ach." She pushed herself to a sitting position. "I'm rambling. The long and short of it is that it's the stone castle from the *Dreaming* that somehow got separated from it."

The baby whimpered softly and Lara took her, settling the tiny thing at her breast. "She was really good." Lara looked at Trevor. Her eyes stung as she fought back tears. "I was so afraid we'd both die there. That I'd never see you again, or be able to tell you how much I love you. Or how sorry I was about letting that bastard sucker me into leaving." She moved her bandaged hand to a more comfortable position. Then she remembered Elizabeth screaming in Gradoxst's grip and knew she'd really had no choice.

Her face felt hot. Lara recognized how angry she was at her own lack of knowledge. She brushed away a tear that spilled over. "I'm going to read every single book in that goddamned library until I know all of them by heart. Maybe if I'd done that before, I'd have been able to figure out a way to...to..."

"Hush." He moved so he could drape an arm around her. "Hush. All that's over now. We'll be home soon."

"Maybe not quite as soon as all that." Lillian walked up behind them, and she spoke with her trademark asperity. "We have to ferry this group of people to about twenty different places. That will take time."

"You're going to take them home." Lara twisted so she could see Lillian. "Thank you," she breathed, gratitude and relief washing through her. "They are my kin, you know."

"Yes, child. I know that," Lillian said, a rueful smile on her face. "Our intentions were good. It's just that most of them were as ambivalent about their magic as you used to be about yours."

The air behind Lillian developed a three-dimensional aspect. The Sidhe clearly felt the shift and spun, hands raised, ready to annihilate whoever might be threatening them. Something caught in Lara's chest, and she knew how close she was to the end of her emotional reserves.

Brigid emerged from a glowing portal, lantern held high. Another regal-looking woman, dressed in a snow-white robe, followed her. Where Brigid was fair, her companion was dark with masses of hair piled atop her head in intricate braided patterns. Sky blue eyes shone from a lined face.

Brigid rounded on Lillian. The phalanx of fairies surrounding her scattered in the soft breezes that always seemed to blow in the *Dreaming*. "You are aiding humans?" she asked dubiously. "Ones you do not even know."

Lara expected Lillian to roll her eyes and come up with a cynical rejoinder, but the red-haired Sidhe surprised her by falling to one knee, grasping the goddess's outstretched hand and kissing it. "What would you have us do?" she asked without a trace of sarcasm. "They were brought here against their will by one of our own. It is proper for us to undo at least some of the harm Gradoxst caused."

While Lillian was talking, the other woman moved to Lara's side. Bending, she brushed a long, delicate finger across Elizabeth's cheek. The baby stopped nursing for long enough to turn her head toward the sensation. Murmuring low in Celtic Gaelic, the woman arranged her robe and settled on the ground across from Lara.

"What did you say?" Lara asked, hoping the question wouldn't be considered rude.

"That the babe is a beauty," Trevor answered, an odd, wistful note in his voice. "That she is a promise that life shall not cease on Earth."

"That is right. You know our ancient tongue," the woman said in heavily-accented English.

"You must be another of the goddesses—" Lara's voice faded. She wasn't quite sure what she wanted to know.

"Do you not recognize me?" The woman tilted her head to better meet Lara's eyes. "You prayed to me for years. And in turn, I have watched over you."

Eyes widening, Lara felt herself drawn toward the woman. "It can't be," she whispered.

"If Brigid can be real, why cannot the same be said for me?" A soft humor skirted beneath the surface of her question, with a suggestive undertone that could have convinced hostile armies to lay down their weapons.

"Psyche?" Lara reached out with a trembling hand.

"You knew it was me even before you asked, child. I endured much, and so I understand suffering. Remember, once I too, was mortal. Were it not for the mercy of the gods, I would have perished at Venus's hands." Her blue eyes developed a hard edge, and the goddess took Lara's outstretched hand. "I fear your trials are not yet over, but I shall stand by you, as I have through the short years of your life. The child is my gift to you. My promise that life on Earth shall not die out. It is the least I can do after the vision I sent."

"The one where the Tree of Life fails?" Lara looked speculatively at Psyche and the goddess nodded.

"Dreams are metaphor, child. You of all people should know that."

The amulet pulsed joyfully where it lay nestled between Lara's breasts. Elizabeth reached out a hand and batted at the gold chain almost as if she could feel energy radiating from the magic moonstone.

Mulling over Psyche's words about trials to come, confusion boiled through Lara. Trevor had found her. They were going home. Gradoxt was dead. Too tired to sort things out, she just sat, babe in her arms.

Lillian and Brigid were still talking. Their conversation eddied around Lara as she half-dozed, leaning against Trevor.

"You aided Lara." Lillian's voice edged a notch or two higher. "Why are you so opposed to us helping the rest of these wretches?" Lillian spread her arms wide to encompass the people that had spilled out of the entrance to the sacred cave. "What would you have us do?" she repeated.

"Lara fought Gradoxst." Brigid said coldly, as if that explained everything.

"So did I." Del had snuck round behind Lillian, obviously

eavesdropping on the conversation that would decide his fate. The mousy little man looked scared, but willing to stand up to anyone if it meant getting home to his wife and children. "Master killed many. And would have starved and beat this bunch of people, if he was still here. He set those horrible bat-things loose and laughed when they bit us."

With his story spewing out of him, Del sidled in front of Brigid. He held his hands rigidly at his sides with his fingers balled into fists. Eyes downcast—apparently looking right at Brigid was too much for him—he kept talking. "And he made me do things to him. Sex things. It was pain that gave him his jollies. Not his, mine." Del made a gagging sound and spat.

Trevor's body stiffened against her as he listened.

Lara glanced at Psyche, asking a silent question, and the goddess nodded. Handing her sleeping child to the one who had been her mentor ever since she'd begun to study depth psychology, Lara pushed to her feet and went to stand next to Del.

She bowed her head briefly in Brigid's direction. "Thank you for coming back to help me," she began, picking her words with care. "I no longer need that help, but there are others here who do. What if I give you my word I will try to reestablish shrines to you?" A light shone deep in Brigid's golden eyes, so Lara hurried on. "The world is such a shambles that now might be a good time for some to decide to return to the old ways.

"I cannot make you any promises beyond my own actions, but if you return these people to their loved ones, I'm certain at least some of them will sing your praises."

"It might be a start." Lillian linked arms with Lara and the two stood looking at Brigid. Half turning toward Del, Lara held out her other hand to him. He took it gently, respectful of her injuries.

The goddess's stern face softened; a smile curved the ends of her full lips. She made an expansive gesture with her hands. Obviously understanding, the fairies flew in twos and threes to the small knots of people. One reddish fairy flittered around Del. As he became progressively less corporeal, he let go of Lara, saying, "Bless you, Missy," just before he winked out of sight.

Within a few moments, only Raven and the Sidhe remained on the heather-dotted heath along with Lara, Trevor, and the goddesses.

"Thank you," Lara cried, throwing her arms around Brigid and hugging her hard. Pain raced up her arm, but she ignored it. Realizing what she'd just done, Lara backed away, feeling heat flood her face. "I —I'm sorry," she mumbled, embarrassed.

"No need to be, child," Psyche called from her place in the grass. "She's needed something like that for the past few hundred years."

"Your opinion," Brigid retorted, but she didn't sound the least bit angry.

A warm smile lit Psyche's face. "If this is truly the beginning of a revival of goddess worship, then I am delighted. Unless I miss my guess," she sent a meaningful glance Brigid's way, "the fairies told everyone they transported that you are responsible for their rescue."

"Indeed they did," Brigid concurred, looking pleased with herself. She seemed to have forgotten it was Lara's idea. "Furthermore, my fairies shall remain with the people for a time, reminding them to give thanks to the goddess of light, home, and hearth—and all others, of course."

Lara nodded and held Brigid's golden gaze. "I made you a vow," she said simply. "I will do whatever I can to ensure your name becomes a household word again and that people pay homage to you."

Brigid looked hard at Lara. "I will hold you to that, child," she said solemnly.

Realizing it was either sit down or fall down, Lara wove an unsteady path back to Trevor and collapsed by his side.

"How can the two of you know one another?" Trevor sounded mystified as he looked from one goddess to the other. "One of you is Celtic and the other is from Greco-Roman mythology."

"Those differentiations came from humankind," Brigid explained, sounding slightly less formal. "There are only a handful of us, but different groups of humans have chosen to call us by special names." She shrugged. "It matters little, since we know who we are."

"I think I understand." Trevor nodded from where he sat on the ground. "It's like with Diana and Artemis."

"Exactly." Brigid smiled. Lara sensed warmth winging its way toward the man she loved and was glad for him.

Psyche began to laugh. The sound was so infectious, Lara found herself dissolving into giggles. Trevor, Brigid, Raven, and the Sidhe joined in. The air took on a brightly hued glow that pulsed with delight. Lara wasn't sure quite how, but Trevor's arms found their way around her again, and she sank against his familiar body, feeling as if she were a ship returning to port after a long and difficult journey. When she looked toward the waterfall, she saw a shimmery outline of the castle only about a quarter of a mile distant and was relieved Gradoxst's damage was unraveling, so the *Dreaming* could be whole once again.

"Yes." Raven came to sit next to her. "The enchantment is finally broken. Are you ready to go home?"

Lara nodded, not trusting herself to speak. Home had seemed like an impossibility not so long ago, but that was before Trevor had charged in like a knight out of the old tales and slain the dragon.

The joy from the *Dreaming* remained when the familiar walls of the living room rose about Lara. Elizabeth lay in her arms. Gunter barked like a mad thing from the front porch. She thought about letting the dog in and bathing both the baby and herself, but couldn't make her feet take her past the first couch she came to. Too exhausted to do anything but sink down onto it, she dropped immediately into unconsciousness, damp clothes and all. Her last thoughts were whether Psyche might grace her dreams with a second visit that day.

TREVOR FEARED sleep would elude him. After an enthusiastic greeting from a frantic Gunter, he'd settled in next to Lara and his child with the dog lying right next to the couch. As soon as he shut his eyes, though, the stresses from the days since Lara's capture caught up with him and he too, slept.

Wakening brought the same sick sensation he'd carried inside him ever since Raven told him what the price for his tampering was. He'd been able to push it aside while intent on rescuing Lara, but now, with nothing left to do, the specter of his imminent death pecked at him like a crow's beak.

If I'd had a spot more faith, he chided himself, *I would have trusted Raven and the Sidhe.*

But I didn't, another inner voice broke in. *Good thing too. If I'd waited, Lara would likely be dead. Gradoxst was pulling the life out of her when I showed up.*

He shook his head sharply to clear it. *It's not like I'm going to drop dead in the next ten minutes. I need to stop feeling sorry for myself.*

Gunter, apparently sensing his daddy was awake, licked his hand. Trevor ruffled the dog's fur absent-mindedly. Lara was still asleep. Her hair lay in greasy mats, and he wondered just how bad her hand was under its layer of bandages. Elizabeth stirred and Trevor levered himself out from where he was wedged between Lara and the back of the couch, trying not to wake her. He was just reaching down to take the baby, when Lara shifted position slightly, her hands tightening around Elizabeth.

"It's all right, love," he said softly. "I'll just give her a bath and a clean nappy. Then we'll pop back down, you can clean up, and we'll all have a bite to eat."

"Love you," she mumbled and was asleep again before he'd finished straightening with the babe in his arms.

"Sleep, love," he whispered, then turned to take his child into the kitchen so he could heat water on the stove to bathe her. Gunter followed right at his heels, apparently having decided it was dangerous to let his humans out of his sight. Trevor had just started to lay the child in the center of the kitchen table to free his hands when Elidora pushed through the back door.

"Oh, aye. Ye are awake." The witch woman smiled at him. "An' I will be takin' th' bairn. She needs a bit o' a wash and clean garments."

"I was going to do that," Trevor protested, adding, "It's better when I have something to occupy myself."

"In that case, I will be holdin' her for you while ye get her bath together." Elidora walked up next to him, petted the dog, and gathered up the baby. Elizabeth looked up at her, mouth opening in a delighted coo. "All th' bairns love mother Eli," the witch woman told her, a look of maternal indulgence softening her dark beauty.

In spite of his fears for the future, Trevor smiled. Even without him, his child would have Lara and Raven and the Sidhe. They'd see she grew up to be a fine woman. Gunter woofed softly, as if saying he'd help too.

"Aye, that we will," Elidora replied to his unspoken thoughts as he built up the fire and pumped water into the large kettle. "But ye mustna feel so sorry for yersel. All o' us find th' Summerlands. Lara will join you there in due time."

"But it won't be the same," he protested, bending to hunt for a basin he could use to bathe Elizabeth.

"Nay, but it just might be better." A twinkle sparked in Elidora's bottomless, dark eyes. "Besides, lad, ye are far from dead."

He shook his head. "I've had time now to do the math. If I last a year…"

Elidora came to her feet, babe in arms. Striding briskly across the kitchen, she laid a hand on his arm. "No matter," she said fiercely. "It doesna matter if it is a year or two or five. Ye shall live each day as well as ye are able."

That's good advice, he told himself. *Now if I can just do like she says.*

The water in the kettle was warm, so he poured enough out to bathe his daughter. With Elidora helping, he unwound the baby's wet and filthy diaper and the small shirt Lara had sewn for her. After the child was clean and dressed, Trevor handed her back to Elidora and used the rest of the wash water to rinse out the diaper and shirt, hanging the small garments on a clothesline that ran along the back wall of the kitchen.

"I suppose I need to tell Lara," he ventured, looking hard at the woman who had brought him into this world.

She nodded. "'Tis only fair. But ye can wait till she has had a bit o' time to hersel' t' get used t' th' idea she willna be dyin' at Gradoxst's hands. That one poisons the mind. 'Tis as lethal as th' physical pain he passes about."

Trevor shuddered.

"An' I was forgettin' your time with him," Elidora murmured. "Of course, ye would be knowin' that."

Trevor turned to face her. "I killed him."

She favored him with a smile. "Aye, laddie. I know. And I'm glad. He needed killing, that one."

"Thought I heard my name." Lara's sleepy voice came from the front room. "Where's the baby? She must be hungry."

Trevor reached for Elizabeth, but Elidora shook her head. "Th' bairn is just fine. Tell your wife t' go upstairs and clean hersel'. She needs to remove that monster's filth afore she does aught else."

"Trev?" Lara sounded more awake this time.

"Right here, love." He made his way to the living room and sat next to her on the couch. Gunter followed, plopping himself down on the floor next to both of them. "Eli and I just cleaned Elizabeth up, and she's all dressed. You go on up and bathe. By the time you come back down, I'll have breakfast ready and—"

"You look tired," she interrupted, reaching up to trace what he assumed were lines in his face.

"We're all tired," he said, smiling at her. "I fear it'll take more than a few hours of sleep to set things aright. Do you want me to help you upstairs?"

Lara swung her legs over the side of the sofa and made a face. "Ugh, I can smell myself. No wonder you want me to take a bath. Here, let's see if I can stand." Stabilizing herself by holding onto the couch, Lara got her feet under her.

"Okay?" he asked, taking her arm. Worry sluiced through him. Lara had huge dark circles under her eyes and a drawn, translucent look. He reminded himself she hadn't really had a chance to recover from giving birth, since Gradoxst had snatched her within hours of Elizabeth's arrival. For a moment, he worried about things much more prosaic than Gradoxst and his evil. Things like the childbed fever that had killed women in the village where he'd grown up.

"Are you all right?" he asked again.

She met his eyes. "Not really. But maybe with time." She hesitated. "Eli has the baby?" At his nod, she went on, "If Elizabeth is taken care of, I'd love it if you helped me up the stairs. I feel weak as a newborn colt, and it's going to take whatever energy I can gin up to warm a tub of water."

"I could ask one of the Sidhe—" he began, but she shook her head.

"Let's see if we need them, first. While I was shut away in that room where Gradoxst dumped me, I did a lot of thinking. I don't want to talk about it now, but maybe after we're both..." Her voice ran down and he sensed how depleted she was.

"Yes," he agreed. "Later, when we're stronger, we can do all the talking we need to."

CHAPTER 26

Time passed oddly after Lara returned. It might have been a week, since the days—at least at first—merged into a confusing blur. Or it might have been as much as two—or even three. When she took the time to think about it, Lara found herself feeling somewhat better. She thought it had something to do with finally having an opportunity to care for herself properly after having had a baby. Not a small task for someone in their mid-forties. Knowing Gradoxst could never bother them again helped too. Lastly, drawing power always drained her. She'd never asked for quite so much as when she was battling Gradoxst for her life and the life of her child.

Something was wrong, though. While she could see health returning to her gaunt features when she looked in the mirror, Trevor still looked terrible. He had lines in his face she knew hadn't been there before and a perpetually haggard look that was troubling. There'd been a couple times when she walked in on him talking with one of the Sidhe, and he'd clammed up as soon as he realized she was there.

"Time to talk with him," she murmured, plucking Elizabeth from her cradle. The baby was about as good as she supposed infants ever got. She rarely fussed and split her time between sleeping and eating. Her cheeks were plump and she seemed on the edge of smiling, though Lara thought she was probably too young for that. Since she'd never seen children in her practice, everything she'd ever known about developmental psychology had fled years before.

"Twenty-twenty hindsight," she muttered as she carried Elizabeth down the stairs. The ground floor was empty. Though Raven and the Sidhe had taken up more or less full-time residence after her rescue, they were often gone during the long summer days. Lara never asked where they went, since she found she really didn't want to know. Her antipathy toward magic, which had taken root in Gradoxst's tower, hadn't gone away. She'd even considered taking the amulet off, but hadn't gotten around to doing it yet. Since the thought flew right out of her head as soon as it cropped up, she figured the magical moonstone had an opinion regarding its future. And that opinion did *not* include lying at the bottom of a dresser drawer.

The amulet thrummed against her chest, acknowledging her thoughts. "We've gotten to know one another, you and I, haven't we?" she asked. The moonstone trilled a score of notes. Ever since her time in the sacred cave, it had become far more vocal.

Maybe it always was and I have finally developed the sensitivity to hear it.

Her thoughts turned to Trevor once again, as she let herself out the front door. The sun was warm, and the smell of earth and growing things greeted her before she'd crossed half the distance between the house and the barn. Elizabeth squinted against the brightness of the day, and Lara used her hand as a shield in front of the baby's eyes.

Looking at that hand, she winced. Raven had amputated all of her little finger and half her fourth one. The skin looked as if it was healing, but she could still feel those missing fingers, and they hurt at the oddest times. She raised her hand, running her uninjured index finger down the wound that ran from forehead to chin down the left side of her face. It was so deep she figured it would leave a hell of a scar. *None of that matters,* she told herself as she searched for Trevor. *The important thing is we're all alive and together.*

She found him half-buried under the old horse-drawn tractor in the shop. He'd complained about it being persnickety, so something new must be wrong with it. The dog, who hadn't left Trevor's side since his return, lay in a shady spot off to one side, panting in the afternoon heat.

"Trev?"

"Just a minute." His voice was muffled.

She settled in to wait.

When he shoved himself out from under the piece of farm equipment, wiping grease off his hands and out of his eyes, it was all she could do to stifle a gasp. She mostly saw him in the house, since he'd taken to working long hours out-of-doors to make sure their crops would do well. Daylight filtering in through the open shop door wasn't kind.

"Yes, love?" Bright blue eyes—the only thing not changing in his face—zeroed in on her as he got to his feet.

"I think it might be time for that conversation we promised to have the night we came home."

His jaw tightened and her heart sank. Something *was* wrong. She had half-rehearsed what she wanted to say, but it scattered like a fine mist. "What's the matter?" she blurted. "You look like hell. Did killing Gradoxst do something to you?"

He laid the oil-soaked rag to one side and gazed at her. His look was sad and determined all at the same time. Lara wanted to throw her arms around him, but if she did that he might not be able to get through whatever secret he was harboring. She'd wondered if there was something he wasn't telling her. Now she was certain of it.

"Whatever this is," she said as evenly as she could. "We'll face it together. We always have."

His face crumpled. He bit his lower lip. When he started to speak, his voice caught in his throat, and he had to start over.

"You see," he said, looking at the floor of the shop, "I was near devastated when you'd been gone for three days. Raven and Lillian didn't seem to know what to do. Neither did Elidora. They couldn't find you, and they wouldn't tell me why they couldn't figure out where you and Gradoxst were."

Trevor paused searching for words, and she gave him space. A corner of his mouth turned downward. "Oh, they eventually got around to telling me the connection to the source of their power in the *Dreaming* had been severed. But that was after—"

Pain from the hand not holding Elizabeth told her she'd clenched her fingers into a fist. Part of her wanted to scream at him to get on with it. To tell her the important parts, but it didn't work that way. His story had to emerge in its own manner, and he was the author of that, not her. She inhaled raggedly and kept her eyes glued on him, but he still didn't look up.

"I—I was half crazy with grief and worry. I just felt so...so impotent." He did look up then, and she saw tears in his eyes, and fury too. "So one day I went to the library. To see if anything in any of those books would give a mortal like me magical powers."

Oh no. What I saw in that dream really happened.

"I'm guessing you found something." Lara couldn't help herself. She tried to keep her mouth shut, but couldn't.

He nodded and with a small attempt at his characteristic, dry humor, he muttered, "Just my luck I can actually read every language those infernal books are written in."

She waited and after a time, he started talking again.

"I found something—a spell—that looked as if it would work. So," he gave her a crooked smile with all the pain in the world behind it, "I went for it. I knew it was dangerous. But I didn't want to live without you and Lizzie. And I'd never have forgiven myself if that monster had killed you whilst I sat on my thumbs waiting for Raven and the Sidhe to save you."

"Magic has a price," she said in a strangled voice. "It drains me when I use it. What did it do to you?"

"Shortened my life," he said, the words so low she had to strain to hear them.

Hope fluttered in her. *Maybe that's not so bad, then. He's still alive, after all.* Afraid to ask for details, she just looked at him, begging mutely for the news to be bearable.

"Ach, don't look at me like that." The words tore out of him. "It's a month for a day, Lara. The way I figure things I might have a year, not much more."

She tried for control and failed. Eyes welling, she turned away, wanting to offer comfort but battling unbearable guilt that he'd thrown away his life for hers. Forcing herself to face him, she held out a shaking hand. "Oh my beloved," she managed between choked-back sobs. "I am so sorry."

Somehow they ended up in one another's arms, the baby sandwiched between them and Gunter circling, woofing softly. "I'm sorry, Lara," he said over and over again. "I didn't read the bloody part about the time thing, only a bunch of other warnings that were equally intimidating—but not as specific." He pushed away enough to meet her eyes. "But even if I'd read that part, I don't know as how I'd have done anything differently."

Only a year... How can I bear to lose you? Lara buried her face in his chest, inhaling the familiar scent of him. Her throat felt as if it was swelling shut and breathing became a struggle.

"Can the Sidhe do anything?" she ventured after a time. "Or Raven?"

"Uh-uh." He grimaced. "That's the first thing I asked."

"Well, maybe Brigid then, or Psyche…" It was she who moved back from their embrace this time. "I'll ask and I'll look too. Maybe there's something in those books I can to do buy you more time."

"Do what you need to, Lara," was all he said. She could see from his expression that, while he may not have fully accepted his future, he'd given up railing against it.

"Would you like to move back to Seattle?" she asked abruptly, pacing from one side of the shop to the other, because movement helped clear her mind.

"Huh? Why?" Kicking over a round of wood, he sat on it, resting his head on one hand.

"While I was in Gradoxst's tower, I thought about how badly things have gone for us ever since we moved. And about those things Brad snuck back here to tell us. It just seems to me that maybe humans should stay with other humans. That we weren't meant to coexist with magic." She took a deep breath. "You know how I always had a healthy dash of ambivalence about my psychic ability?" When he nodded, she went on. "Well, now I'm thinking I had good reasons for it."

"How about if I come inside and clean up?" he asked. "Then we can talk some more."

"Sure, Trev. That would be fine." Her eyes were still damp and she swiped at them. "I love you," she said. "In spite of how horrible it was to hear, I'm glad you told me the truth."

A corner of his mouth quirked upward in a shadow of his former self. "Glad I told you too. Seems more bearable somehow. And Lara… Thanks for not berating me. No one knows better than me that we wouldn't be in this predicament if I didn't love you more than life itself."

Closing the distance between them in two strides, she sat on his lap and wrapped her free arm around him. "Trev, oh Trev. I've never deserved you." The baby, apparently feeling squished, began to fuss.

"Come on, then, love." He wrapped his hands around her waist and helped her to her feet. "I'll be in presently."

THEY WERE STILL TALKING hours later when the Sidhe returned. As soon as Lara saw Lillian coming through a glowing gateway, she jumped to her feet. "Are you sure there's nothing you can do to undo what Trev's done to himself?" she demanded. Gunter too, ran to the red-haired Sidhe, jumping at her skirts much as he'd done when he was a puppy.

Lillian drew her brows together and squared her shoulders. Hair was coming out from her braids, and it looked as if she'd had a trying day. "So he finally told you?" She answered Lara's question with one of her own. By then, Raven and Elidora had joined them. The three milled about the living room like rudderless ships talking rapidly in Celtic Gaelic.

She figured they must've told Trevor the truth, but decided it wouldn't hurt to ask the same question again, since they hadn't answered her the first time. She broke into their conversation, "Well, is there anything you can do?"

"We might be able to countermand a part of it," Raven began cautiously, but Lillian waved him to silence.

"No." Lara swung to face Raven. "I want to hear what you have to say."

"Because Trevor only *used* the magic he stirred up once, the price might not be quite as severe."

From his place on the couch, Trevor looked up hopefully. Elidora glided over next to him, taking the place Lara had just vacated. "'Tis not that much of a reprieve," she murmured. "Do not get your hopes up."

"Well?" Lara stood, hands on her hips, staring at Raven. "How much can we expect?"

"Not more than five years," Lillian said flatly. "Mayhap not even that."

A whoosh of excitement and disappointment combined in a strange mix that shot through Lara. "That's wonderful news," she blurted. Five years *was* better than what they'd planned on as they'd talked the afternoon away. Much better.

"We have something to tell you," Trevor said, looking meaningfully at Lara.

"You don't have to tell us," Raven growled. "I can read your thoughts clear as the day that's just left us."

"We don't approve," Lillian said firmly, her lips drawn into a thin line.

"Och aye, and ye may live a bit longer if ye remain here," Elidora added, reaching over to pat Trevor's jeans-clad leg.

"Even so," Trevor murmured, laying his hand atop Elidora's, "we're still agreed this isn't the place for us. There's danger back home, but we haven't done so well as all that in the months we've been here."

Mindful of what Brad had told them, Lara walked over to Lillian and took the other woman's arm. "Come sit out on the steps with me," she invited.

Once they were settled on the top riser watching the newly-risen moon, Lara said, "I am grateful to you, Lillian. In many ways, you're like the mother I lost. I don't want to go home—and our Queen Anne house is our home—to get away from you. We're leaving to get our lives back. Especially now that—" Her voice broke and she tried again. "Now that I may not have Trev for all that much longer."

Silence sat between them. Reaching out, Lara took Lillian's hand, holding it gingerly between hers, as she tried not to stir up her injury. "I hope you'll visit us and even stay from time to time. I know you thought it was the right thing for us to settle out here. But even you'd have to admit—"

"What?" Lillian's normally melodious voice had a roughened edge to it. "Admit I was wrong to talk Raven into letting you two come here?" Lillian turned to face her, and the blast of remorse from her green eyes was so intense Lara turned away, understanding for the first time how much Lillian blamed herself for everything that had gone wrong.

"I cannot protect you so well if you move from here." Lillian held up a hand. "No, let me finish. I know things have been difficult. I did not foresee the mischief Gradoxst would stir up. He used to be a pest, nothing more. His level of perseverance shocked all of us."

"Even with him out of the picture," Lara interrupted, "there's no way I'd be able to manage out here all by myself without Trevor. So we think we should move home. At least that way I'll have help with

Elizabeth once…well, after…" Her voice cracked. It was really hard to say *after Trevor's dead.*

"You always were stubborn," Lillian said, but the ends of her mouth twitched into half a smile.

"Me?" Lara croaked incredulously.

"It's your Sidhe blood." Lillian smiled knowingly. "We're all that way. Sure of what we want." She hesitated. "I'd like to propose a bargain."

Lara felt suddenly wary. What could the Sidhe possibly want that would require agreement? "Go ahead." She let go of Lillian's hand and gestured for her to continue.

"You will keep the amulet and continue working with Raven and me on your magic." That half smile lit her face again. "For we will visit. And mayhap more often than you'd like."

Lara opened her mouth, but Lillian waved her to silence. "You'll need to twist the strands of time to keep Trevor with you for as long as you can. For that, you'll require far more skill than you currently possess."

"You knew I was thinking about just shucking the whole thing, huh?" Lara asked sheepishly.

"I know everything that's in your mind, child," Lillian replied. Reaching out a finger, she tipped Lara's chin upward so their eyes met. The love and caring radiating from Lillian's green gaze settled about Lara like a comforting presence, and her ill will toward her magic began to dissipate.

Long moments passed. Lara heard the door open behind them. Gunter stopped to lick her face and brush against Lillian before bounding down the porch steps.

"Ready to come in?" Raven asked gruffly. "Trevor's made us a late supper."

❧

It took them a few weeks to pull together what they'd need,

including the crops Trevor was growing. "Doesn't make sense to leave all this food here to rot," he told Lara, and she agreed.

The canning pot was rarely empty as she, Lillian, and Elidora preserved the garden's bounty. Since they didn't know what they'd find back in Seattle, they'd fill the Ford and BMW with things to eat, rather than with the other things they'd brought to Raven's.

Maybe because he'd shared his burden, Trevor felt more himself as the remainder of summer rolled forward. Some days he forgot about dying altogether. Those days were the best. When he and Lara and Elizabeth and the dog played in the creek and ran about in the grass barefoot after the day's chores were done.

The baby had taught herself to roll over. And she cooed and smiled at them. Trevor was grateful the time she'd spent with Gradoxst apparently wouldn't have any lasting ill effects. When he gazed lovingly at his wife and child, his heart felt full. He remembered Elidora's words about the Summerlands and managed to find spaces of time when he wasn't afraid to die.

Late in the fall, nearly a year after they'd moved, a crisp October day found them loading the cars. Raven surprised them by offering to drive the old Model A, allowing them to fill it with things as well. "Besides, this way if there's some problem I can escort you back here," he informed them.

After a welter of hugs and kisses and goodbyes—Elidora and Lillian weren't going to accompany them back to Seattle immediately—Trevor slid behind the wheel of the Ford. Raven had told them they'd never be able to find his house again without help from him, but Trevor wasn't sure he believed that. After all, the group from the penitentiary had managed to stumble across it. And all Brad had to do was set his odometer. While Trevor had developed a great deal of respect for Raven and the Sidhe, he'd found they weren't quite as omniscient as they thought they were. He chuckled, grateful he was far enough away that Raven couldn't read his mind.

"We'll visit very soon," Lillian called after them as the cars began to move across the bridge and toward the forest road leading to Skykomish and the highway.

"None of this matters," Trevor murmured, patting Gunter's head as he drove. The dog, who topped a hundred pounds, was scrunched into a cramped space on the front seat. But he didn't seem to mind, since he got to be close to his daddy.

"What's important," Trevor went on, "is that what we're doing feels right. I always felt like some sort of barely-tolerated relative—and a not very bright one, at that—living out here. If Raven had gotten angry and withdrawn his permission for us to be there, we'd have been stuck. Better for us to be going home."

The dog whined sagely, as if he couldn't agree more.

It was just getting dark when Trevor turned the Ford into the alleyway running behind their house on Queen Anne Hill. The highways had been so empty, he was sure the government must have started rationing fuel, and he was grateful Brad had filled up the Ford in Skykomish, and that Raven seemed to have his own sources for gasoline. Though they'd stayed together on the road, Lara and Raven had been in the lead, so the gates leading into the back yard were already pulled inward.

So many houses he'd passed lay in ruins that Trevor worried whether theirs would still be there. The breath whooshed out of him when he saw his house—all five stories of it—still standing.

Driving into a space they'd left for him close to the back porch, Trevor killed the engine and sat for a few moments looking at his house. Emotion churned through him. He understood how much he'd missed the place and all their familiar things.

When Trevor finally pushed open the door of the Ford, Brad raced over to him, thumping his shoulder and shaking his hand. "Welcome home," the detective said, a broad smile lighting his austere features. "I was wondering if I'd ever see any of you again."

"You're in uniform," Trevor noted, surprised.

Brad nodded. "Yeah, it's good if people can see I'm the law. Too many of us plainclothes folks were killed, so the rest of us suited up."

Lara ran over, Elizabeth in her arms. Tears streamed down her cheeks. "Yes," she echoed. "Welcome home, Trev. To both of us."

Then Raven was there too. "This is your place," he agreed in his deep, rumbly voice. "Never should've let Lillian talk me out of that."

Trevor felt joy well within him. He got out of the cab of the truck, standing aside to let the dog jump down. "Thanks," he said smiling at everyone. "It's truly good to be back."

"Uncle Brad! Uncle Brad!" Elizabeth's youthful voice rang through the five-story house and her loafers clattered on the stairs. "Come look at what I did in school today."

"He's just coming up the front steps," Lara protested, grabbing her scurrying seven-year-old from behind and marveling at the child's as-always perfect diction. "Let's let him at least get through the door and out of his work clothes first."

"Oh." The child cocked her head to one side in an almost exact replica of one of Trevor's gestures. Her eyes were the same sea-blue as his had been and her hair a mass of coppery ringlets that spilled down her back. While her hair was the same shade as Lara's, the girl had inherited her father's lush curls.

Gunter, who'd long since gotten over his puppy-fear of the staircase, raced down the open risers to greet the detective, who'd just come through the front door.

"How'd it go today?" Lara asked.

Brad petted the dog and motioned for the over-excited canine to sit. He shrugged tiredly. "About the same. The latest riot seems to be burning itself out. Only a few more casualties since yesterday. Oh, yeah." He took his hat off and draped it on one of the hall tree's hooks.

"Chief said to be sure to let you know we could use some more help on that case you were working on."

She nodded. "Of course. Just let me know what more I can do."

Escaping from her mother's clutches, Elizabeth ran to Brad and twined her arms around his waist. "Glad you're home," she said. "Momma says I have to wait to show you my school work, though."

"That would be nice." Brad smiled down at the child, his ice-blue eyes warming at her touch. Lara knew she reminded him of his own daughter and was glad he had another chance to be a parent.

"I'll get some food together," Lara told them, turning toward the kitchen.

My, I've come quite a way from the time when anything I made came out of a can…

As she walked down the short hallway to make an after-school snack for Elizabeth, and get a cold home-brewed beer with cheese and crackers for Brad, Lara sighed. Nearly a year had passed since Trevor's death. The first few months had been excruciatingly difficult. She'd been grateful for Brad because she hadn't had anything in the way of emotional sustenance to give her child, as she grieved for her lost love.

Lillian had been correct that Lara would need a greatly enhanced magical repertoire to wheedle every possible moment out of Trevor's life. The magic had pummeled and drained her, but Lara managed to find reserves somewhere. Even when she was so tired her bones ached, she could always dredge up one more spell. And it would be enough to keep him going for another month—or another few days when the months became too hard to piece together. Brigid had visited periodically, as had Psyche. Both goddesses had helped Lara with her burgeoning magic. Though she couldn't be certain, Lara thought they might have helped Trevor too, since he always seemed stronger for a span of time after their visits.

In the early years after their return, the years when she'd been busy setting up shrines to Brigid and encouraging others to worship at them, Trevor and Brad had taken their house off the grid, using a combination of solar and wind power. For whatever reason, Brad's affair with Elidora never resurrected itself.

Raven had given them the chickens and goats from his farm. The men had built greenhouses and a small barn for the animals in the back yard. And made the fence higher with bands of electrified barbed wire strung along the top. Between riots and food shortages, Seattle's population base had shrunk from six hundred thousand to less than a quarter of that.

Lara sighed, her thoughts returning to Trevor. At times, she'd almost been able to convince herself that his death sentence had somehow been rescinded…until she really looked at him. And then she knew better.

Despite becoming a shrunken old man, Trevor managed to keep busy with household projects and his beloved books until very close to the end of his life. The dog, sensing the imminence of death, rarely left him during those last months. And Elizabeth—always wise beyond her years, with an intuitive magical side—had spent nearly all her time with her daddy from the moment she could walk.

As the girl grew older, she'd somehow known what to do without the elaborate magic lessons that took up Lara's every waking moment when she wasn't by Trevor's side. It had been the child who'd whispered in Lara's ear that Daddy was worn out. That it was time to let him go to the Summerlands. Chagrined her child saw more clearly than she, Lara finally stopped her ministrations, so choked by the taste of her own grief she finally understood why widows threw themselves onto funeral pyres. Had it not been for Elizabeth, she would've been tempted.

As they usually did, tears came when Lara thought about Trevor's death. His last words, as she'd clung to his hand, had been, "I'm a lucky man, love. Don't grieve for me. We'll find one another again."

Everyone had been there, ranged round his bed when he died. Raven and Lillian had sung him to the Summerlands. She supposed Elidora might have helped, but the witch woman had been too broken up to do much more than weep. Lara knew Raven and the Sidhe blamed themselves for not keeping a more watchful eye on Trevor after her abduction.

Guess they're more human than they like to think they are. None of us are immune from guilt.

"Momma?" Elizabeth had come into the kitchen unnoticed, until she'd spoken up.

"Yes, honey?"

"Don't be sad. Daddy isn't."

Wondering how her child could possibly know such things, yet trusting to the magic that ran strong in her, Lara turned and knelt, pulling Elizabeth close. "I'll try."

"Uncle Brad loves you."

Another shock at Elizabeth's wisdom. "Yes, sweetling. I know that."

"He'd like to be my daddy."

"He already is in lots of ways."

"I'm ready to see your school stuff," Brad called from the library, where he always settled after work to unwind.

"Will you be all right?" The child's solemn eyes met Lara's.

"Yes. I think so." Straightening, Lara watched her child race out of the kitchen toward Brad.

School had been a problem. The buildings had mostly been turned into shelters for those who'd lost their homes. Lara, along with wives of other police personnel, had formed a cooperative, hiring teachers and buying books and supplies. Classroom space was purloined from an abandoned building next to a police station where homeless had been squatting. An officer was assigned to watch over the children. Lara knew they'd been fortunate. Most of what was left of the city's children roamed the streets. On his more cynical days, Brad called them the *Future Criminals of America*. School was only for the lucky ones who still had parents with jobs that paid beyond subsistence level.

Working mechanically, Lara loaded up treats—courtesy of the police department's ration coupons and their garden—onto a tray and carried them up half a flight of stairs to the library. Taking a beer, Brad glanced up from Elizabeth's second grade English assignment.

"It's almost the anniversary of Trevor's death," he said. At her nod, he went on. "I know how that is. I feel the same way when it's Adie's death day. I don't think you ever forget. Or that it ever really gets any easier."

Setting the tray on a nearby table and taking the other beer, Lara sat down, surprised that, for once, she wasn't crying at the mention of Trevor's name. "I think I'm about ready to go back to work," she said.

"But you're already using your psychic ability to help the police," he pointed out, keeping his eyes on her face.

"I know. But I want to do more. Elizabeth is in school most of the day now, and I just sort of rattle around here. Brigid's shrines are well established, so there's not much for me to do there, either." She smiled as she thought about all the iterations of groups who'd embraced the goddess banner. "Who would've guessed goddess worship would take off like wildfire?"

"I'd have guessed," Elizabeth piped up. "Goddesses are cool!"

Lara reached over and ruffled the girl's coppery curls. "There is that small group of—well, of others like me. But we don't meet all that often. Mostly we just chat on the Internet. Or we did before the government started rationing net time." She grimaced. "I finally know how Trev felt after the airlines laid him off."

Blowing out a breath, she rested her head on an upraised hand. "There's a domestic violence program that needs a therapist. And I picked up another lead about a shelter looking for someone to work with children who lost their parents in the riots."

"Whatever you want, Lara." Brad smiled at her. "I can flex my schedule around Lizzie and her school when you need to be gone. Hell, I can even sign up for swing or graves if I have to." The child looked up at him from where she was ensconced on his lap and grinned. He smoothed some hair out of her face before going on. "I'll do whatever I need to so one of us is always with her. At least until she gets a whole lot older, that is."

"I know you will." Lara found herself smiling back.

"Whenever you're ready," color stained his fair-featured face, but he didn't drop his gaze, "I'll be here for you too."

"You didn't need to say that." Lara felt flustered. The look on his face that one night she'd fought Goblins, when he'd looked at her as if she was the most beautiful thing in the world, rose unbidden.

"Maybe not, but it seemed as if you needed reminding."

"See, Momma. I told you." Elizabeth skewered Lara with one of her looks. The ones that made her look like a wise and knowing divinity living in a seven-year-old body.

Heat rose in Lara's face. Brad's a good man. Can I give him the love he deserves?

Apparently oblivious to the confusing welter of feelings roiling through her, Brad turned back to Elizabeth. "Read me this," he demanded with mock severity. "You missed one of those words on your spelling list. I want to make sure you know them perfectly."

Lara sat, looking at her hands. The ebb and flow of Brad and Elizabeth's conversation eddied around her. When truth came, it was like a hammer hitting her right between the eyes. Before she could lose her courage, Lara broke into her daughter's recitation of *I have a Little Shadow*. "Lizzie."

"Yes, Momma." The child leveled blue eyes at her.

"How about if you run along and give Uncle Brad and me some privacy."

A broad grin spit the child's face. She hopped out of Brad's lap, whistled for Gunter, and sprinted out of the library.

Brad stared at her, his heart in his eyes. The expression on his face was so unguarded and full of hope, Lara had to look away. "I'm scared," she murmured. "It's selfish, but I don't want to watch someone I love die ever again."

He was on his feet in an instant, pulling her out of her chair and into his arms. "Lara, oh Lara," he whispered against her hair as he moved his hands gently down her back.

She heard the beat of his heart against her ear and wound her arms around him.

"I'm not planning on dying." His deep voice rumbled.

"You're a cop. You put your life on the line every day."

He pushed back far enough to tip her chin so their eyes met. "Well," he cocked his head to one side, "I'm not dead yet. Life doesn't come with any guarantees. You and Trevor tried to beat the odds when things started going to hell and look what happened."

Yes, just look what happened—

He smiled tenderly. "Sometimes you have to take chances. Isn't that what you told your patients for years?"

Lara threw back her head and laughed. "Gee, now who's psychic?"

"Well," he persisted. "Didn't you?"

She nodded, still clinging to him. "That's always one of the things therapists tell patients."

Brad felt good against her. It had been a long time since she'd relaxed into a man's touch. Too long. Lara felt buoyant, almost giddy. She took a breath, then another. There was something mesmerizing about looking into Brad's eyes. In that moment she understood how much she depended on him, counted on him being there for her and Elizabeth. And she knew, if she let down her guard, that she could easily love him.

"Lara? Tell me what you're thinking." He tightened his arms around her, drew her head into the hollow between his shoulders and neck, and gently stroked her hair.

"I'll always love Trevor," she blinked back tears, "but I've mourned long enough."

"I don't want to try to take his place." Brad spoke slowly. "But I'm hoping you'll come to love me too—over time of course." He hesitated. "I'll devote my life to making sure you and Lizzie never want for anything, and that's a promise."

Lara nodded. "I know you will." A lopsided smile warmed from within. "Hell, you already have. You're a good man, Brad, and I'm grateful you stuck by Trevor and Lizzie and me. You've done so much —for all of us. I care about you, more than I've let myself realize."

"Does that mean what I think it does?"

Because she couldn't speak, Lara nodded against his shoulder. He whooped in a very un-Brad-like manner, picked her up, and swung her around. When he set her on her feet, tears to match her own glistened in his eyes. "I do love you, Lara. I have for years. But I loved Trevor too. We're a family."

"Yes." She smiled and swiped at her damp cheeks. "We are. And we always will be."

"I like the sound of that." He cradled the side of her face in his big hand. "You'll marry me, right? Make an honest man of me?"

"What?" She snorted. "No ring? No down on your knees? No—"

"I'll give you all of that—and more. If you'll let me."

His words were so heartfelt, they filled her with hope. "How about this?" She placed her hand over his and threaded her fingers close. "We can set a date, maybe in six months or so. Between now and then, you can court me all you want. We need to consult with Raven and them to come up with a date when everyone can be here."

"You've just made me very happy." He stroked her cheek and brushed his fingers across her mouth.

She laughed. "I sure hope you stay that way. I can be an overbearing bitch."

He laughed along with her. "After all we've been through, we've seen each other at our worst—and our best. I'm not worried."

Lara nodded to herself as the truth in his words sank in. "Neither am I." She tightened her hand over his.

"Let's go tell Lizzie." Brad draped an arm over her shoulders.

As they walked out of the library, Lara twined an arm around his waist. "Life is about taking chances," she murmured.

"Yes, Lara, it is. When we stop tossing the dice, we may as well cash in our chips."

She stopped walking then and, turning to face him, raised her lips for a kiss.

~

IF YOU ENJOYED the Soul Storm books, you might also like the Earth Reclaimed books. They're also urban fantasy, but with a romantic subplot and a happy ever after for Fionn and Aislinn, but it takes all three books to get there. A teaser from *Earth's Requiem*, book one of that series, follows.

ABOUT THE AUTHOR

Ann Gimpel is a USA Today bestselling author. A lifelong aficionado of the unusual, she began writing speculative fiction a few years ago. Since then her short fiction has appeared in a number of webzines and anthologies. Her longer books run the gamut from urban fantasy to paranormal romance. Once upon a time, she nurtured clients, now she nurtures dark, gritty fantasy stories that push hard against reality. When she's not writing, she's in the backcountry getting down and dirty with her camera. She's published over 50 books to date, with several more planned for 2018 and beyond. A husband, grown children, grandchildren and wolf hybrids round out her family.

Keep up with her at <u>www.anngimpel.com</u> or <u>http://anngimpel.blogspot.com</u>

If you enjoyed what you read, get in line for special offers and pre-release special reads. Sign up for Ann's newsletter on her website or her blog.

EARTH'S REQUIEM, FIRST PROLOGUE

SALT LAKE CITY, UTAH

islinn tried to stop it, but the vision that had dogged her for over a year played in her head. She squeezed her eyes shut tight. Mental images crowded behind her closed lids, as vivid as if they'd happened yesterday. She raked her hands through her hair and pulled hard, but the movie chronicling the beginning of her own personal hell didn't even slow down. She whimpered as the humid darkness of a South American night closed about her…

Her mother screamed in Gaelic, "Deifir, Deifir," and then shoved Aislinn again. She tried to hurry like her mother wanted, but it was all too much to take in. Stumbling down the steep Bolivian mountainside in the dark, she ignored tears and snot streaking her face. Her legs shook. Nausea clenched her gut. Her mother was crying too, in between cursing the gods and herself. Aislinn knew enough Gaelic to understand her mother had tried to talk her father out of going to the ancient Inca prayer site, but Jacob hadn't listened.

A vision of her father's twisted body lying dead a thousand feet above them tore at Aislinn. Just a few hours ago, her life had been normal. Now her mother had turned into a grief-crazed harridan. Her beloved father, a gentle giant of a man, was dead. Killed by those horrors that had crawled out of the ground. Perfect, golden-skinned men with long, silky hair and luminous eyes, apparently summoned through the ancient rite linked to the shrine. Thinking about it was like trying to shove her hand into a flame, her pain too unbearable to examine closely.

Aislinn was afraid to turn around. Tara had already slapped her once. Another spate of Gaelic galvanized her tired legs into motion. Her mother was clearly terrified the monsters would come after them, but Aislinn didn't think they'd bother. At least a hundred adoring half-naked worshipers remained at the shrine high on the mountain. Once Tara had herded her into the shadows, her last glimpse of the crowd revealed one of the lethal exotic creatures turning a woman so he could penetrate her. Even in Aislinn's near-paralyzed state, the sexual heat was so compelling, it took all her self-discipline not to race to his side and insist he take her instead. After all, she was younger, prettier. It didn't matter at all that he'd just killed her father.

...Aislinn shook her head so hard, it felt like her brains rattled from side to side in her skull. Despite the time that had passed since her father's murder, she still fell into these damned trance states, where the horror happened all over again. Tears leaked from her eyes. She slammed a fist down on a corner of her desk, glorying in the diversion pain created. Crying was pointless. It wouldn't change anything. Self-pity was an indulgence she couldn't afford.

Pull it together. The weak die.

Even though she wasn't sure why life felt so precious—after all, she'd lost nearly everything—Aislinn wanted to live. Would do anything to hang onto the vital thread that maintained her on Earth.

A bitter laugh bubbled up. What a transition: from Aislinn Lenear, college student, to Aislinn Lenear, fledgling magic wielder. A second race of alien beings, Lemurians, had stormed Earth on the heels of that hideous night in Bolivia, selecting certain humans because they had magical ability and sending everyone else to their deaths.

It was a process. It took time to kill people, but huge sections of Salt Lake City sat empty. Skyscraper towers downtown and rows of vacant buildings mocked a life that was no more. In her travels to nearby places before the gasoline ran out, Aislinn had found them about the same as Salt Lake.

Jacob's death had been a harbinger of impending chaos—the

barest beginning. The world she'd known had imploded shockingly fast. It killed Aislinn to admit it—she kept hoping for a miracle to intercede—but her mother was certifiable. Tara may as well have died right along with her husband. She hadn't left the house once since they'd returned a year before. Her long, red hair was filthy and matted. She barely ate. When she wasn't curled into a fetal position, she drew odd runes on the kitchen floor and muttered in Gaelic about Celtic gods and dragons. It was only a matter of time before the Lemurians culled her. Tara had magic, but she was worthless in her current state.

The sound of the kitchen door rattling against its stops startled Aislinn. On her feet in a flash, she took the stairs two at a time and burst into the kitchen. A Lemurian had one of its preternaturally long-fingered hands curved around Tara's emaciated arm. He crooned to her in his language—an incomprehensible mix of clicks and clacks. Tara's wild, golden eyes glazed over. She stopped trying to pull away and got to her feet, leaning against the seven-foot tall creature with long, shiny blond hair, as if she couldn't stand on her own.

"No!" Aislinn hurled herself at the Lemurian. "Leave her alone."

"Stop!" His odd alien gaze met hers. "It is time," the Lemurian said in flawless English, "for both you and her. You must join the fighting and learn about your magic. Your mother is of no use to anyone."

"But she has magic." Aislinn hated the pleading in her voice. Hated it.

Be strong. I can't show him how scared I am.

Something flickered behind the Lemurian's expression. It might have been disgust—or pity. He turned away and led Tara Lenear out of the house.

Aislinn growled low in her throat and launched herself at the Lemurian's back. Gathering her clumsy magic into a primitive arc, she focused it on her enemy. Her tongue stuttered over an incantation. Before she could finish it, something smacked her in the chest so hard she flew through the air, hit the kitchen wall, and then slumped to the floor. Wind knocked out of her, spots dancing before her eyes, she struggled to her feet. By the time she stumbled to the kitchen door, both the Lemurian and her mother had vanished.

An unholy shriek split the air, followed by another. Aislinn clapped a hand over her mouth to seal the sound inside and clutched the doorsill. Pain clawed at her belly. Her vision became a red haze. The fucking Lemurian had taken her mother. The last human connection she had. And they expected her to fight for them? Ha! It would be a cold day in Hell. She let go of the doorframe and balled her hands into fists so hard her nails drew blood.

Standing still was killing her, so she walked into blindingly bright sunlight. She didn't care what happened next. It didn't matter anymore. A muted explosion rocked the ground. She staggered. When she turned, she wasn't surprised to see her house crack in multiple places and settle. Not totally destroyed, but close enough.

Guess they want to make sure I don't have anywhere to go back to.

Her heart shattered into jagged pieces that poked her from the inside. She bit her lip so hard it ached. When that didn't make a dent in her anguish, she pinched herself, dug her nails into her flesh until she bled from dozens of places. Fingers slick with her own blood, she forced herself into a ragged jog. Maybe if she put some distance between herself and the wreckage of her life, the pain sluicing through her would abate.

As she ran, a phrase filled her mind. The same sentence, over and over in time to her heartbeat. *I will never care for anyone ever again. I will never care for anyone ever again.* After a time, the words etched into her soul.

EARTH'S REQUIEM, SECOND PROLOGUE

*E*ly, Nevada
     Two Years Later

Rune paced from the kitchen to the living room and back again, hackles at half-mast and tail twitching behind him. Marta, his bondmate and the woman who'd rescued him from a trap when he was just a wolf pup, was resting. At least he hoped she was. Something between a whine and a growl slipped past his clenched jaws.

Damn her, anyway.

Didn't she understand she'd been targeted by the dark gods? Ever since she took to spying on the Lemurians in Taltos, their underground city, things turned to rat shit. Something hideous happened on her last trip. He wasn't certain quite what because he wasn't with her, and she refused to tell him. Many moonrises had passed, and she was only just now beginning to talk and think normally.

Rune paused to stare out a large window. The front yard was absolutely silent. So was the road fronting Marta's house, but then it would be since most of the humans were dead, and gasoline to make their cars run had long since run out.

He shook his fur out and came to a decision. Should he tell Marta now or wait until she woke?

She solved the problem for him. The sound of her footsteps made him spin to face the door into the living room. She was dressed to go out and had shoes on. Not a good sign.

"There you are." She favored him with a maternal smile, the one that made him want to bite her. She may have rescued him when he was too young to care for himself, but that was long ago.

"Here I am," he agreed and trained his amber eyes on the woman who meant everything to him.

"I'm leaving for a while—"

Rune's decision roared out of him. "Not without me, you're not. Never again. Look what happened last time."

"Be reasonable." She smiled again, and Rune felt magic prowl beneath her words.

He slapped up power of his own. "Reasonable has nothing to do with it. Last time they nearly killed you. I wasn't certain until yesterday you'd get enough of your memories back to be yourself."

"Neither was I." Her smile developed grim edges. She sank to the thick Oriental carpet and held out her arms.

Rune stayed where he was. "All the more reason to take me with you. You can merge your senses with mine. Together we're stronger. It's why we chose the Hunter bond."

"Aw, Rune." Sadness etched lines around her eyes and into her forehead. "You don't understand. None of us will get out of this alive, but we have to fight until we can't fight anymore. If we don't, it's like turning Earth over to those bastards, and I won't do that." She slapped the floor with the flat of her hand. "I won't."

"Neither will I." He gazed cooly at her. "Where are we going?"

"I can't take you with me. It's too dangerous."

"If you don't take me, you're not going, either." The wolf stood his ground, but it was shaky. She could order him, and he'd have to obey. It was how the Hunter bond worked.

Marta looked away, studying her hands. Her long coppery hair was in its usual tight braid, and she was dressed in loose-fitting black trousers and a black jacket, with stout lace-up boots. She was tall, almost as tall as the Lemurians, and she sat with her legs splayed in front of her.

Rune kept his gaze glued to her, willing her to capitulate. He was fully prepared to take her on in combat to keep her in the house, if she refused his company. "I'm not being stubborn," he said. "I need to be with you for me, not just for you. How do you think I'll feel if you don't return? How can I live with myself if you die in a place where I wasn't there to help you?"

"I could die anyway." She did look at him then, her clear green eyes filled with something he didn't have a name for.

"So could I, but if we're together at least we'll know we did everything we could for each other."

Marta nodded once. "All right. I don't have enough energy to argue with you. We're going to one of the mining camps to the west of us. Some humans are still alive, and they need my medical skill."

"How do you know anyone's alive?" he countered.

She shrugged. "Call it a hunch. I dream things sometimes, and this came to me not long ago. We'll do a travel jump. It's not far. If the place is deserted, I'll bring us right back." The same, sad smile returned. "With luck, we'll be home in time for supper."

"Ready when you are."

She got to her feet. "Are you going to come closer than that? I already said I'd take you, Rune. Bondmates don't lie to each other."

Shame filled him because she'd nailed his reticence. He didn't trust that she wouldn't trick him. He made his way to her side and felt her magic as she opened a portal for them to travel to the place she'd seen in her dream.

They rolled out into high, arid desert, and the remains of a mining camp sprawled about them, buildings falling into disrepair. Bullet holes riddled tin roofs and corrugated siding. Rune sent his senses spinning outward.

Nothing lived anywhere near here.

"Curious," Marta murmured. "I was so sure."

Rune's hackles hit full alert, standing on end the length of his back. "We must leave," he snarled. "It has to be a trap."

Before Marta could reply, another gateway opened a little way away. Bal'ta poured out. Marta flung magic at the disgusting creatures, minions of the dark, but she barely made a dent. They stood between five and six feet tall, with barrel chests, and their bodies were coated in greasy-looking brown hair. Thicker hair hung from their scalps and grew in clumps from armpits and groins. Ropy muscles bulged under their hairy skin. Orange eyes gleamed, and their foreheads sloped backward.

Rune had faced them before. At least they didn't have magic of their own beyond a shared intelligence. The flood had slowed, and he gathered himself for action. He and Marta could take them. They'd faced worse odds. Apparently she agreed, and he felt her merge her consciousness with his.

"I'll take this side," Rune growled and thrust himself into the thick of things, avoiding the cudgels and maces they used in battle. Rune knew to stay out of the line of Marta's magic. He sliced into one neck after another until he was coated in blood. The air was thick with the coppery stench of it. For some reason, Bal'ta avoided him. Something about his animal energy burned them, and he took full advantage of their hesitation.

He glanced at Marta from time to time, grateful beyond thought she was still on her feet. In addition to magic, she held a knife in one hand. A knife dripping blood. Dead bodies piled around both of them.

Rune danced to one side to avoid a cudgel aimed for him skull. He sent out a call for forest wolves, but none came to their aid. Maybe there weren't any living here—or maybe they didn't see the point in taking a stand in someone else's battle.

No matter. He and Marta were winning. Only a few Bal'ta remained. He'd begun to work his way back to his bondmate, when another gateway opened, this one black and edged with flames. A man sashayed through. Rune stopped cold, staring in disbelief. The remaining Bal'ta faded away from that gaping maw; in moments they'd summoned another portal and left.

Rune focused on the newcomer. It had to be one of the dark gods. No one else held that level of deadly beauty. Long dark hair streamed behind him, and he trained his shrewd dark eyes on Marta. She squared her shoulders and stared back.

"Kill him," Rune urged.

"I can't," she ground out. "Much as I'd love to."

The dark god tossed his shapely head back and laughed; the sound was disturbing, discordant. "Your bondmate is wise," he told the wolf. "She's clever not to get too close."

"Which one is he?" Rune demanded.

"You may as well ask me, since I'm right here." Dark eyes crinkled in chilly humor, and he mock bowed. "My name is Tokhots. I'm also known as the trickster." Dark robes fluttered around him, sashed in gray.

While Tokhots had been talking, Marta sidled farther from Rune and severed her connection with him. Worried, he tried to determine just what she was up to. If she planned an attack, he didn't want to be in the way and ruin things. Nor did he plan to leave her to the mercy of the dark god. Maybe if he kept Tokhots chatting…

"What do you mean by trickster? It's not a term I'm familiar with."

Tokhots did a funny little side step. "I play tricks. I'm funny. I'm a hell of a nice guy. If you got to know me, you'd—"

A ball of fire immolated one side of his robes. Tokhots' pleasant expression shattered, and he batted at the flames—and at jolts of power Marta hurled his way. Rune wanted to launch himself at the dark god, but Marta's power kept him rooted in place.

Finally giving up on extinguishing the flames, Tokhots shucked his robe, revealing golden-hued skin beneath. "Bitch!" he spat and raced to Marta so fast he beat Rune, who was also headed that way at breakneck speed.

"Don't bite him," Marta shrieked. "His blood is deadly poison."

Rune aborted a leap in midair and crashed to the rocky ground. He'd been about to close his jaws around Tokhots' neck.

The dark god held a writhing Marta in his grip. "You can't hurt me either," he taunted. "One drop of my blood and you'll be deader than the shades that roam the countryside."

"What do you want with me?" Marta gave a mighty heave.

Rune thought she might free herself, but Tokhots tightened his hold. "You've become an inconvenience. I sent the Bal'ta as a diversion until I could get here."

"What happens next?" Marta's voice was steady, but Rune sensed her fear, and it filled him with fury. He worked his way closer to the pair, not moving very fast.

"That's for me to know." Tokhots laughed again.

Caution departed. Rune judged the distance and leapt. So what if he died? At least Marta would go free. The air around him thickened, holding him suspended above the ground. Darkness dropped over him like a curtain until he couldn't see. He thrashed against the magic holding him and plummeted to earth, landing hard on jagged rocks. Ignoring pain, he vaulted toward where Marta had been, still running blind in unnatural darkness.

She wasn't there. Neither was the dark god.

He still couldn't see, but he could smell and hear. He employed both senses, ears pricked forward and nose snuffling so hard it began to bleed.

Nothing.

Marta's scent was strongest right where he stood.

Rune threw his head back and howled his desolation to the skies. He'd failed. The dark god had his bondmate, and he had no way to go after them.

By the time the darkness receded, his throat was raw with grief. He called for other animals, birds, even insects, to tell him what they'd seen. If they knew anything, but no one answered.

Despondent, guilt-stricken, Rune put one paw ahead of another.

No point in staying with the dead Bal'ta. Tokhots would never bring Marta back here.

The dark god had taken his bondmate on a oneway trip. Rune knew, as clearly as he knew anything, she'd never run by his side again. She was still alive, but her life force ebbed through their Hunter bond.

Soon she'd be no more, and it was his fault. If he'd been quicker, hadn't hesitated…

He shook his head hard and broke into a run.

EARTH'S REQUIEM CHAPTER ONE

*A*islinn pulled her cap down more firmly on her head. Snow stung where it got into her eyes and froze the exposed parts of her face. Thin, cold air seared her lungs when she made the mistake of breathing too deeply. She'd taken refuge in a spindly stand of leafless aspens, but they didn't cut the wind at all. "Where's Travis?" she fumed, scanning the unending white of a high altitude plain that used to be part of Colorado. Or maybe this place had been in eastern Utah. It didn't really matter anymore.

Something unnatural flickered at the corner of her eye and she tensed. Standing still bought trouble with a capitol T. She swiveled her head to maximize her peripheral vision. *Damn! No, double damn.* Half-frozen muscles in her face ached when she tightened her jaw.

Bal'ta—a bunch of them—fanned out a couple hundred yards behind her, closing the distance eerily fast. One of many atrocities serving the dark gods that had crawled out of the ground that night in Bolivia, they appeared as shadowy spots against the fading day. Places where edges shimmered and merged into a menacing blackness. If she looked too hard at the center of those dark places, they drew her like a lodestone. Aislinn tore her gaze away.

Not that Bal'ta—bad as they were—were responsible for the

wholesale destruction of modern life. No, their masters—the ones who'd brought dark magic to Earth in the first place—held that dubious honor. Aislinn shook her head sharply, trying to decide what to do. She was supposed to meet Travis here. Those were her orders. He had something to give her. Typical of the way the Lemurians ran things, no one knew very much about anything. It was safer that way if you got captured.

She hadn't meant to cave and work for them, but in the end, she'd had little choice. It was sign on with the Lemurians—Old Ones—to cultivate her magic and fight the dark, or be marched into the same radioactive vortex that had killed her mother.

Her original plan had been to wait for Travis until an hour past full dark, but the Bal'ta changed all that. Waiting even one more minute was a gamble she wasn't willing to risk. Aislinn took a deep breath. Chanting softly in Gaelic, her mother's language, she called up the light spell that would wrap her in brilliance and allow her to escape—maybe. It was the best strategy she could deploy on short notice. Light was anathema to Bal'ta and their ilk. So many of the loathsome creatures were hot on her heels, she didn't have any other choice.

She squared her shoulders. All spells drained her. This was one of the worst—a purely Lemurian working translated into Gaelic because human tongues couldn't handle the Old Ones' language. She pulled her attention from her spell for the time it took to glance about, and her heart sped up. Even the few seconds it took to determine flight was essential had attracted at least ten more of the bastards. They surrounded her. Well, almost.

She shouted the word to kindle her spell. Even in Gaelic, with its preponderance of harsh consonants, the magic felt awkward on her tongue. Heart thudding double time against her ribs, she hoped she'd gotten the inflection right. Moments passed. Nothing happened. Aislinn tried again. Still nothing. Desperate, she readied her magic for a fight she was certain she'd lose and summoned the light spell one last time. Flickers formed. Stuttering into brilliance, they pushed against the Bal'tas' darkness.

Yesssss. Muting down triumph surging through her—no time for it —she gathered the threads of her working, draped luminescence about herself, and loped toward the west. Bal'ta scattered, closing behind her. She noted with satisfaction that they stayed well away from her light. She'd always assumed it burned them in some way.

Travis was on his own. She couldn't even warn him that he was walking into a trap. Maybe he already had. Which would explain why he hadn't shown up. Worry tugged at her. She ignored it. Anything less than absolute concentration, and she'd fall prey to his fate—

Vile hissing sounded behind her. Long-nailed hands reached for her, followed by shrieks when one of them came into contact with her magic. She snuck a peek over one shoulder to see how close they truly were. One problem with all that light was it illuminated the nasty things. Their backward sloping foreheads leant them a dimwitted look, but they were skilled warriors, worthy adversaries who'd wiped out more than one of her comrades. Their insect-like ability to work as a group using telepathic powers scared her more than anything. Though she threw her Mage senses wide open, she was damned if she could tap into their wavelength to disrupt it.

Chest aching, breath coming in short, raspy pants, she ran like she'd never run before. If she let go of anything—her light shield or her speed—they'd be on her, and it would be all over. Dead just past her twenty-second birthday. *That* thought pushed her legs to pump faster. She gulped air, willing everything to hold together long enough.

Minutes ticked by. Maybe as much as half an hour passed. She was tiring. It was hard to run and maintain magic. Could she risk teleportation? Sort of a *beam me up, Scotty,* trick. Nope, she wasn't close enough to her destination yet. Something cold as an ice cave closed around her upper arm. Her flesh stung before feeling left it. She snapped her head to that side and noted her light cloak had failed in that spot. Frantic to loosen the creature's grip, she pulled a dirk from her belt and stabbed at the thing holding her. Smoke rose when she dug her iron knife into it.

The stench of burning flesh stung her nostrils, and the disgusting ape-man drew back, hurling imprecations in its guttural language. She snaked her gaze through the gloom of the fading day, as she assessed how many of the enemy chased her. Aislinn swallowed hard around a painfully dry throat. There had to be a hundred. Why were they targeting her? Had they intercepted Travis and his orders? Damn the Lemurians anyway. She'd never wanted to fight for them.

I've got to get out of here.

Though it went against the grain—mostly because she was pretty certain it wouldn't work, and you weren't supposed to cast magic willy nilly—she pictured her home, mixed magic from earth and fire, and begged the Old Ones to see her delivered safely. Once she set the spell in motion, there'd be no going back. If she didn't end up where she planned, she'd be taken to task, maybe even stripped of her powers, depending on how pissed off the Lemurians were.

Aislinn didn't have any illusions left. Her world had crumbled three years ago. She'd wasted months railing against God, or the fates, or whoever was responsible for robbing her of her boyfriend and her parents and her life, goddammit, but nothing brought them back.

Then the Old Ones—Lemurians, she corrected herself—had slapped reason into her, forcing her to see the magic that kept her alive as a resource, not a curse. In the intervening time, she'd not only come to terms with that magic, but it had become a part of her. The only part she truly trusted. Without the magic that enhanced her senses, she'd be dead within hours.

Please... She struggled against clasping her hands together in an almost forgotten gesture of supplication. Juggling an image of her home while maintaining enough light to hold the Bal'ta at bay, she waited. Nothing happened. She was supposed to vanish, her molecules transported by proxy to where she wished to go. This was way more than the normal journey—or jump—spell, though. Because she needed to go much farther.

She poured more energy into the teleportation spell. The light around her flickered. Bal'ta dashed forward, jaws open, saliva dripping. She smelled the rotten crypt smell of them and cringed. If they got hold of her, they'd feed off her until she was nothing but an empty husk. Or worse, if one took a shine to her, she'd be raped in the bargain and forced to carry a mixed breed child. They'd kill her as soon as the thing was weaned. Maybe the brat, too, if its magic wasn't strong enough.

The most powerful of the enemy were actually blends of light and dark magic. When the abominations, six dark masters, had slithered out of holes between the worlds during a globally synchronized surge linked to the Harmonic Convergence, the first thing they'd done had been to capture human women and perform unspeakable experiments on progeny resulting from purloined eggs and alien sperm.

Aislinn sucked in a shaky breath. She did *not* want to be captured. Suicide was a far better alternative. She licked at the fake cap in the back of her mouth. It didn't budge. She shoved a filthy finger behind her front teeth and used an equally disgusting fingernail to pop the cap. She gripped the tiny capsule. Should she swallow it? Could she? Sweat beaded and trickled down her forehead, despite the chill afternoon air.

She'd just dropped the pill onto her tongue, trying to gin up enough saliva to make it go down, when the weightlessness associated with teleportation started in her feet like it always did. Gagging, she spat out the capsule and extended a hand to catch it, but it fell into the dirt. Aislinn knew better than to scrabble for the poison pill. If she survived, she could get another from the Old Ones. They didn't care how many humans died, despite pretending to befriend those with magic.

Her spell was shaky enough as it was. It needed more energy—lots more. Forgetting about the light spell, Aislinn put everything she had into escape. By the time she knew she was going to make it— apparently the Bal'ta didn't know they could take advantage of her vulnerability as she shimmered half in and half out of teleport mode— she was almost too tired to care.

She fell through star-spotted darkness for a long time. It could have been several lifetimes. Teleportation jaunts were different than her simple Point A to Point B jumps. When she'd traveled this way before, she'd asked how long it took, but the Old Ones never answered. Everyone she'd ever loved was dead—and the Old Ones lived forever—so she didn't have a reliable way to measure time. For all she knew, Travis might've lived through years of teleportation jumps. No one ever talked about anything personal. It was like an unwritten law. No going back. No one had a past. At least, not one they were willing to talk about.Voices eddied around her, speaking the Lemurian tongue with its clicks and clacks. She tried to talk with them, but they ignored her. On shorter, simpler journeys, her body stayed with her. She'd never known how her body caught up to her when she teletransported and was nothing but spirit. Astral energy suspended between time and space.

A disquieting thump rattled her bones. *Bones. I have bones again... That must mean...* Barely conscious of the walls of her home rising around her, Aislinn felt the fibers of her grandmother's Oriental rug against her face. She smelled cinnamon and lilac. Relief surged through her. Against hope and reason, the Old Ones had seen her home. Maybe they cared more than she thought—at least about her. Aislinn tried to pull herself across the carpet to the corner shrine so she could thank them properly, but her head spun. Darkness took her before she could do anything else.

NOT QUITE SURE what woke her, Aislinn opened her eyes. Pale light filtered in through rough cutouts high in the walls. Daytime. She'd been lucky to find this abandoned silver mine with shafts that ran up to ground level. It would've drained her to keep a mage light burning.

Is it tomorrow? Or one of the days after that?

Aislinn's head pounded. Her mouth tasted like the backside of a sewer. It was the aftereffect of having thoroughly drained her magic, but she was alive, goddammit. Alive. Memory flooded her. She'd been within a hairsbreadth of taking her own life. Her stomach clenched, and she rolled onto her side, racked by dry heaves. Had she swallowed any of the poison by accident?

A bitter laugh made her cracked lips ache. Of course she hadn't. It didn't take much cyanide to kill you. Just biting into the capsule without swallowing would have done it. She struggled to a sitting position. Pain lanced through her head, but she forced herself to keep her eyes open.

The world stabilized. She lurched to her feet, filled a chipped mug with water that ran perpetually down one wall of her cave, doubling as faucet and shower, and warmed it with magic. Rummaging through small metal bins, she dropped mint and anise into the water. Then a dollop of honey, obtained at great personal risk from a nearby hive. When she looked at the mug, it was empty. Her eyes widened in a face so tired any movement was torture, and she wondered if she'd hallucinated making tea. Since she didn't remember drinking the mixture, she made another cup for good measure.

Liquid on board, she started feeling halfway human. Or whatever she was these days. As she moved around her cozy hobbit hole of a home, she glanced at beloved books, a few odds and ends of china, and her grandmother's rug—all that was left of her old life. By the time she'd developed enough magic to transport both herself and things short distances, most of the items from the ruins of her parents' home had been either pilfered by someone else or destroyed by the elements. She'd come by her few other possessions digging through the rubble of what was left of civilization.

Aislinn sucked in a deep breath and blew it back out. It made her chest hurt. Had the Bal'ta injured her before she'd made good on her escape? She shucked her clothes—tight brown leather pants, a plaid flannel shirt, and a torn black leather jacket—and took stock of her body. It looked pretty much the same. The long, white scar from under one breast catty corner to a hipbone was still there. *Yeah, right. What could have happened to it?* There might be a few new bruises, but all in all, her lean, tautly muscled form had survived intact. Before the world had imploded, she'd hated being a shred over six feet tall. Now she blessed her height. Long legs meant she could run fast.

She wrinkled her nose. A putrid stench had intensified as she removed her ratty leather garments. Realizing it was her, she strode to the waterfall in one corner of her cave and stood under its flow until her teeth chattered. Only then did she pull magic to warm herself. It seemed a waste to squander power on something she should be able to tolerate. Besides, despite sleeping, she hadn't totally recharged her reserves. That would only happen if she didn't use any more magic for a while. Aislinn thumbed a sliver of handmade soap and washed her hair, diverting suds falling down her body to clean the rest of her.

Something threw itself against the wards she kept above ground. She felt it as a vibration deep in her chest. It happened again. She leapt from the shower and flung her long, red hair over her shoulders so she could see. Soapy water streamed down her body, but she didn't want to sacrifice one iota of magic drying herself until she knew who —or what—was out there. Mage power would alert whatever was outside to her presence, so she snaked the tiniest tendril of Seeker magic out, winding it in a circuitous route so no one would figure out where it came from. Seekers could pinpoint others with magic. That gift was also useful for sorting out truth, but it wasn't her main talent, so it was weak.

Her magic found a target and she gasped. Travis? How could it possibly be him? He didn't know where she lived. Had her Lemurian magelord told him?

"Aislinn." She heard his voice in her mind. *"Let us in."*

Us no doubt meant his bond creature was with him. When Hunter magic was primary, humans had bond animals. His was a civet with the most beautiful rust, golden, and onyx coat she'd ever seen. *Should I?* Indecision rocked her. Her cave meant safety because no one knew about it. No one who would tell, anyway. She dragged a threadbare wool shift—once it had been green, but there were so many patches, it was mostly black now—over her head and shook water out of her hair.

A high-pitched screech reverberated in her head. Something must've pissed off the civet. Travis shouted her name again. He left the mind speech channel open after that. Locked it open so she couldn't close it off. Edgy, she wondered if he was setting some sort of trap. Aislinn thought she could trust him, but when it came right down to it, she didn't trust anyone. Especially not the Old Ones. The only thing that made working with them tolerable was she understood their motives. Or imagined she did. She still hadn't forgiven them for killing her mother. Poor, sick, muddled Tara.

"Aislinn." A different voice this time. Metae, her Lemurian magelord. The one who'd made it clear two years before that, magic or no, they'd kill her if she didn't come to terms with her power and fight for them. *"Save your comrade. I do not know if I will arrive in time."*

All righty, then.

The civet yowled, hissed, and then yowled again. Travis made heavy, slurping sounds, as if at least one lung had been punctured. Was saving anyone even possible? Dragging a leather vest over totally inadequate clothing, Aislinn slipped her feet into cracked, plastic Crocs and took off at a dead run along a passageway leading upward. The Crocs gave her feet some protections from rocks, but not from cold. She veered off, picking an exit point that would put her behind the fighting. When she came to one of the many illusory rocks that blocked every tunnel leading to her home, she peeked around it. No point in being a sacrifice if she could help it. Travis wasn't that close of an acquaintance. No one was.

She froze, disbelieving. Christ! It couldn't be. But it was. Though she'd only seen him once, that horrible night in Bolivia when her father died, the thing standing in broad daylight had to be Perrikus— one of six dark gods holding what was left of Earth captive. Bright auburn hair flowed to his waist and fluttered in the morning breeze. Eyes clear as fine emeralds one moment, shifting to another alluring shade the next, were set in a classically handsome face with sharp cheekbones and a chiseled jawline. His broad shoulders and chest tapered to narrow hips under a gossamer robe that left nothing to the imagination. The dark gods were sex incarnate, which was interesting, since the Old Ones were anything but. Promises of bottomless passion had been one of the ways the dark ones seduced Druids and witches and all those other New Age practitioners into weakening the gates between the worlds.

Heat flooded Aislinn's nether regions. She wished she'd paid better attention when humans who'd actually run up against the dark gods had told her about it. Something about requiring human warmth to feed themselves, or remain on Earth, or…shit, her usually sharp mind just wasn't there. She couldn't focus on anything except getting laid.

Her groin ached for release. One of her hands snuck under her clothing before she realized what she was doing. *No!* The silent shriek told her body to stand down, damn it. Now was *not* the time, and Perrikus definitely not the partner, but her body wasn't listening. Her nipples pebbled into hard points and pressed against the rough wool fabric of her hastily donned shift.

Wrenching her gaze to Travis—and her mind away from sex—she was unutterably grateful he was still on his feet. Wavering, but standing. The civet, every hair on end, stood next to him, a paw, with claws extended, raised menacingly.

"You know where the woman is," Perrikus said, his voice like liquid silver.

Aislinn heard compulsion behind the words. Hopefully, so did Travis.

"I followed you here," the dark mage went on. "I heard you call out to her. So where is she? Tell me, and I'll let you go."

The civet growled low. Travis spoke a command to silence it.

"I'm right here." Aislinn stepped into view, glad her voice hadn't trembled, because her guts sure were.

"Aislinn," Travis gasped. He lurched in a rough half circle to face her. "I'm so sorry—"

"Can it," she snapped.

The civet hissed at her, probably because she'd had the temerity to raise her voice to its bonded one.

She leveled her gaze at Perrikus. "You said he could go. Release him—and his animal, too."

That lyrical voice laughed. "Oh, did I say that? I'd forgotten."

"Let him go, and I'll, ah, give you what you want." *Should buy me a couple minutes here.* "Just turn off the damned sex fountain. I can't think."

His hypnotic eyes latched onto hers. "Why would I do that, human? You like how it feels. I smell the heat from between your legs."

"Bastard. I liked it a whole lot better when I thought you were just a comic book character." Aislinn wondered how much juice she had. This was one of the gods. Even if she was at her best, she didn't think she'd prevail in anything that looked like direct combat. "What do you want with me?" she asked, still seeking time to strategize. It wasn't easy with what felt like a second heart pounding between her legs. She wanted to lay herself at his feet and just get it over with.

"What do you think?" He smiled. Fine, white teeth gleamed in that perfect jaw. "Children. You have power, human. Real power. And you've only now come to our attention." He walked toward her, nice and slow. Sauntered. His hips swung with his stride. He was ready, huge and hard, under those sheer robes. Unfortunately, so was she, but she clamped down on her craving.

Aislinn ignored the moisture gushing down her thighs and reached for her magic. Travis limped over, joining hands with her. The civet wedged itself between them, warm against her lower leg. She felt the boost immediately, and her sexual hunger receded a tiny bit. Enough to clear her mind. *"On my count of three,"* she sent. *"One, two..."*

"No. Do just the opposite. He won't be expecting it. Pull from air and water. I'll blend fire. Aim for his dick. It's a pretty big target just now."

Power erupted from them. Even the civet seemed to be helping. Since she'd never worked with an animal before, she wasn't certain just how the Hunter magic worked. Aislinn concentrated hard to keep the spell's aim true. Travis was injured, so she took more of the burden.

Perrikus chanted almost lazily. Maybe he was drunk on his own ability, so egotistical he wouldn't guard himself. Her spirits soared as soon as she realized Travis's gambit had worked. Perrikus was using the counter spell for air and water. He hadn't counted on the tenacity fire would give their working. Moments later, a muffled shriek burst from him, and he grappled at his crotch.

"Bitch." No honey or compulsion in *that* epithet. He lunged for her.

Aislinn sidestepped him neatly, letting go of Travis. In a half crouch, she trained all her attention on their adversary. Hands raised, she began a weaving she hoped would unbalance him. Air shimmered at the edges of her vision.

"I am here, child. Take your comrade to safety. He carries an important message from me."

"Me—"

"Do not speak my name aloud. Go."

The shimmery place in the air sidled in front of Perrikus. Fiery motes lapped hungrily at his transparent robes. Not waiting to be told a third time, Aislinn shooed the civet into Travis's arms, draped an arm around him, and pulled invisibility about the three of them. The last thing she heard as she guided them toward the warren of passageways leading to her home was Metae baiting Perrikus.

"I was old before you were hatched. How dare you spread your filth?"

"Wh-Where are we?" Travis's voice gurgled. It had taken time to help him cover the half mile back to her cave. The civet made little mewling noises as they walked, sounding worried about its human partner.

"About two hundred feet below whatever's happening up there." Aislinn flung a hand upward. "Do you have Healing magic?" She pushed him through the thick tapestry that served as a door to her home and caught the civet's tail between fabric and rock. It hissed at her and then ran to Travis, light on its feet.

He nodded.

"Use it on yourself. It's not one of my strengths." Aislinn knew she sounded surly but couldn't help herself. She'd never wanted anyone anywhere near her home. Her body, ignited by Perrikus's execrable magic, screamed for release. Nothing she could do about that so long as she had company. Not much privacy in the one room she called home.

"Make a power circle around me."

Grateful for something to do, Aislinn strode around him three times, chanting. She felt Travis pull earth power from her as he patched the hurt places within himself. Satisfied he had what he needed, she retrieved her mug, got one for him, and made tea. In addition to goldenseal, she added marigolds to the decoction. Both held healing qualities. By the time she finished brewing tea, his color had shifted from gray to decidedly pink. His eyes were back to their normal brown. Moss green was his power color. She wondered if it was sheer coincidence that the civet's eyes were the same odd shade. She understood her Mage and Seeker gifts. The other three human magics—Healer, Hunter, and Seer—remained shrouded in mystery.

Aislinn looked hard at Travis when she handed him the tea. Dirty blond dreadlocks hung halfway down his back. He was well past six feet, but thin to the point of gauntness, his skin stretched over broad shoulders. A leather belt with additional holes punched in it held baggy denim pants in place. Battered leather boots, split along one side, and an equally worn leather vest over a threadbare green cotton shirt made him look about as ragtag as she always did. No one ever had new clothes. She patched what she had until the fabric fell apart. Then she looted amongst the dead, or possessions they'd left behind, for something else she could use.

"Thanks." He took the tea and shifted uncomfortably from foot to foot. "You have books." Surprise burned in his tone. "How did—?"

"You didn't see them," she broke in fiercely. That's what happened when you let people into your house. They saw things they weren't supposed to—like books banned by a Lemurian edict.

"Okay," he agreed. "I didn't see a thing." He hesitated. "Don't worry. I wouldn't get you in trouble. You just saved my life."

"Did you fix your body?" Aislinn grimaced. *That didn't sound very friendly. Pretty obvious I'm trying to change the subject.* "Sorry. I'm not used to entertaining."

He looked away. "Yeah, I'm better. I'm not used to being anyone's guest, either."

"How'd you find me?" she blurted. Not all that polite either, but she really did want to know.

"Metae and Regnol, my Lemurian magelord, told me to give you this yesterday." Scrabbling inside his vest, he drew out an alabaster plaque. About the size of a domino, it contained an encrypted message. "I tried to make our rendezvous on time, but everywhere I turned, something went wrong." He paused long enough to take a breath. "I won't bore you with the details, but it was past dark when I made it to the coordinates. You weren't there, but I knew you had been. Traces of your energy remained." He ground his teeth together. "I also sensed the Bal'ta. Because I feared the worst, I called the Old Ones—"

"What?" she broke in, incredulous. "We're never supposed to—"

"I know that." His voice rose over hers. "I was desperate. They told me not to bother reporting back if I didn't get the message to you. Anyway, they didn't even lecture me for insubordination. Metae told me where to find you. And a whole bunch of other stuff about how she'd wanted to tell you herself, but couldn't break away from something or other."

Aislinn gulped her tea. It was hot and made her mouth hurt, but at least the lust eating at her like acid ever since Perrikus turned those gorgeous eyes on her, receded a bit. Maybe it might, just might, leave her be. She'd even been wondering about a quickie with Travis—after he healed himself. Heat spread up her neck as she blushed.

"What?" He stared at her.

The civet had curled itself into a ball at his feet, but it kept its suspicious gaze trained on her.

"Nothing." She put her mug down and held out a hand for the plaque. "Let's find out what was so important."

Nodding silently, he handed it to her before sinking onto one of several big pillows scattered around the Oriental rug. The cat followed him. "Do you mind?" He pointed at a faded Navaho blanket folded in one corner of the room.

"Help yourself."

"Thanks." He unfolded it and draped it around his shoulders. "Takes a lot of magic to do Healings. I'm cold."

With only half her mind on him, Aislinn held the alabaster between her hands. It warmed immediately and began to glow. She opened herself to it, knowing it would reveal its message, but only to her. The plaques were like that. The Old Ones keyed them to a single recipient. Death came swiftly to anyone else who tampered with their magic. Metae's voice filled her mind.

"Child. Your unique combination of Mage and Seeker blood has come to the attention of the other side. They will stop at nothing to capture and use you. The Council has conferred. You will ready yourself for a journey to Taltos so we may better prepare you for what lies ahead. Take nothing. Tell no one. Travel to the gateway. Do not tarry. Once you are there, we will find you. You must arrive within four days."

"What?" Travis squirmed clearly uncomfortable. He knew he shouldn't ask, but couldn't help himself.

She shook her head. *Alone. Destined to be alone—always.* Sadness filled her. Images of her mother and father tumbled out of the place she kept them locked away. Memories of what it had felt like to be loved brought sudden tears to her eyes.

"Come here." Travis opened his arms. "You don't have to tell me a thing."

The civet growled low. Travis spoke sharply to it, and it stood, arched its back, and walked to a spot a few feet away, where it circled before lying down.

Mortified by how desperately she wanted the comfort of those arms, Aislinn dropped to the floor and crawled to him, taking care to give his bond animal a wide berth. The blanket must have helped, because when she fitted her body to his, it was more than warm. The sexual heat she thought she'd moved beyond flared painfully in her loins. When he cupped her buttocks with his hands and pulled her against him, she wound her arms around him and held on.

"There," he crooned, moving a hand to smooth her hair out of her face. "There, now. Let's take comfort where we can, eh? There's precious little to be had." He laughed, sounding a bit self-conscious, before adding, "Even I could feel Perrikus's spell. Got me going, too."

He closed his lips over hers. She kissed him back, too aroused to be ashamed of her need.